Advance praise for *Greenwich Park*

"A gloriously tangled game of cat and mouse that kept the twists coming until the very last moment."

— Ruth Ware, #1 *New York Times* bestselling author of *One by One*

"Katherine Faulkner is amazingly talented. *Greenwich Park* is gripping and haunting and gorgeously suspenseful. I couldn't put this thriller down and can't recommend it highly enough."

— Zakiya Dalila Harris, author of *The Other Black Girl*

"Wonderfully addictive and electric, *Greenwich Park* gets under your skin from the very first pages and it's impossible to look away from the tangle of friendships, the haunting of a guilty past, and the unease of a growing obsession. While many thrillers are set in early motherhood, Katherine Faulkner brilliantly explores the anxious weeks before the baby is born, when the tension is as high as our hopes. I can't wait to read what Faulkner writes next."

— Ashley Audrain, *New York Times* bestselling author of *The Push*

"A fantastically addictive read. It's so pacy, and there's a real sense of dread on every page. Fabulously unpleasant characters, and a beating feminist heart."

— Abigail Dean, *New York Times* bestselling author of *Girl A*

"I devoured *Greenwich Park* in two greedy sittings. The writing is razor-sharp, the characters deliciously problematic, and the ending utterly gasp-worthy. You'll remember this thriller long after the final page."

— Robin Morgan-Bentley, author of *The Wreckage*

"Deliciously dark and deftly plotted. Faulkner mines the seam of guilt beneath her characters' 'perfect' lives with devastating precision."

— Lesley Kara, *Sunday Times* bestselling author of *The Rumor*

"Brilliantly twisty and full of excellently observed—if chilling—characters, *Greenwich Park* is a clever and knowing delve into the female psyche as well as a classic, pacy mystery. Atmospheric, aspirational, and addictive!"
—Harriet Walker, author of *The New Girl*

"Meticulously crafted and deeply satisfying, *Greenwich Park* has all the hallmarks of a first-class psychological thriller. I read it in two sittings and was left smiling sardonically at the final line."
—Charlotte Philby, author of *Part of the Family*
(Waterstones Thriller of the Month)

"Terrific. Pacy and suspenseful with a nice touch of satire."
—Amanda Craig, author of *The Golden Rule*

"One of the best debuts I've read in a long time. . . . Intelligently plotted, with several completely unexpected gut-punches along the way, *Greenwich Park* is both a psychologically complex and hugely entertaining novel—in short, the perfect thriller."
—Caz Frear, author of *Sweet Little Lies*

"Razor-sharp prose, a properly twisty setup, lots of unlikable characters, and a strong feminist undercurrent—it's got the lot! I raced through it. Absolutely loved it."
—Harriet Tyce, author of *Blood Orange*

"Faulkner offers a clever spin on an expanding subcategory of psychological thrillers set during maternity leave. . . . A twisty, fast-paced read."
—*The Sunday Times* (UK)

"[A] suspenseful thriller . . . with constantly growing levels of menace, this tension-filled novel will keep you guessing through its final revelations."
—*Kirkus Reviews* (starred review)

GREENWICH PARK

Katherine Faulkner

GALLERY BOOKS

New York London Toronto Sydney New Delhi

G

Gallery Books
An Imprint of Simon & Schuster, Inc.
1230 Avenue of the Americas
New York, NY 10020

This Gallery Books Canadian export edition January 2022

GALLERY BOOKS and colophon are registered trademarks of Simon & Schuster, Inc.

For information about special discounts for bulk purchases,
please contact Simon & Schuster Special Sales at 1-866-506-1949
or business@simonandschuster.com.

The Simon & Schuster Speakers Bureau can bring authors to your live event. For more information or to book an event, contact the Simon & Schuster Speakers Bureau at 1-866-248-3049 or visit our website at www.simonspeakers.com.

Interior design by Davina Mock-Maniscalco

Manufactured in the United States of America

10 9 8 7 6 5 4 3 2 1

The Library of Congress has cataloged the hardcover edition as follows:

Names: Faulkner, Katherine, author.
Title: Greenwich Park / Katherine Faulkner.
Description: First Gallery Books hardcover edition. | New York : Gallery Books, 2022. |
   "Originally published in Great Britain in 2021 by Bloomsbury Publishing"
Identifiers: LCCN 2020035821 (print) | LCCN 2020035822 (ebook) |
   ISBN 9781982150310 (hardcover) | ISBN 9781982150327 (trade paperback) |
   ISBN 9781982150334 (ebook)
Subjects: GSAFD: Suspense fiction.
Classification: LCC PR6106.A93 G74 2021 (print) | LCC PR6106.A93 (ebook) |
   DDC 823/.92—dc23
LC record available at https://lccn.loc.gov/2020035821
LC ebook record available at https://lccn.loc.gov/2020035822

ISBN 978-1-9821-8837-5
ISBN 978-1-9821-5033-4 (ebook)

For Pete

AFTERWARD

Her Majesty's Prison Bowood

November 5, 2019

Dear Helen,

I know you asked me not to write to you again. But you need to know the truth, even if after all this time your hands are still clamped over your ears. What did you do that day, after I was convicted? After the knock of the gavel, the soft swish of silk and cotton as everyone else stood up? I looked for you, wanting to find your face. But when my eyes caught on the blue check of your coat, and I saw that you were staring at the floor, I knew then, as sure as the sound of a door slamming shut—there was no way back.

Do you remember, when they took me away, how just for a moment everything was quiet, and my footsteps were the only sound? I have often wondered what you did after that, while I was jolted against the side of that windowless van. Where you went, what you ate. Whom you spoke to. How your life continued after I was taken out of it.

When I think of you, as I often do, I always picture you in your kitchen, holding a mug with both hands, staring out of the window into your garden. I close my eyes sometimes, so I can conjure it exactly. I dress you in your green sweater, your hair twisted up on top of your head. Your parents' paintings on the walls, the crack over the French doors, little pools of light on the counter where your oil and vinegar bottles sit. I make everything the same, just as I remember. Are there birds in your magnolia tree? Are the roses in bloom? In my dream, they are. I hope so.

I think you would find the food here the hardest thing. The forks are plastic. They snap off in the gray lumps of meat, the piles of instant potatoes. Some days the wardens will give you another, if you ask. Other days they won't, and we have to eat with our hands. I know it is a small thing, but when your life has shrunk as much as mine has, small things take up more space than they should.

I find it difficult sometimes to believe I am really here. A danger, someone who is not to be trusted. But then, no one really thinks they are bad, do they? Whoever we are, whatever we've done. We all have our reasons, if anyone can be bothered to listen.

Perhaps you'll never read this letter anyway. Tear it up as soon as you see the postmark, toss it into the fire. I don't think so, though. It's always been too much for you, hasn't it, Helen? The temptation of a sealed envelope. If it weren't, perhaps we wouldn't have ended up where we did.

Don't get me wrong. I'm not saying you are to blame. Whatever you did, you didn't deserve what happened next. I hope you know I never meant for things to end the way they did. I suppose I just lost control. Lately, I've been trying to trace it back, a trail of bread crumbs in my mind. Trying to work out where it all began, where it all started going wrong. And I suppose the real answer is it started years before you could have ever imagined it did.

I wonder if you had any sense then, when you were in it, what that day would come to mean. Don't be cross, but I always had this feeling that your memory of that day had taken on a sort of invented quality. I almost asked you once when you were talking about it. Had it really been like that? The sun so warm, the scent of the grass so sweet? Are you sure, Helen? Are you sure?

I wonder if you knew that those Technicolor memories could ruin you forever by their perfection. That they could cast so many other things in shadow.

I hope you didn't. I hope you didn't know then that nothing would ever be quite the same again, however hard you tried. And I'm glad you didn't know the truth about that day. I suppose I hoped you never would.

But you need to hear it now, Helen. So here it is.

24 WEEKS

Helen

AT THE TOP OF the beer-stained carpet, a taped sign on the door reads National Childbirth Trust. The doorknob feels like it might fall off if I turn it too hard. Inside there is a semicircle of chairs. A flip chart. Trestle tables with juice and biscuits. The sash windows are jammed shut.

Three other couples are here already. I am the only one on my own. We smile politely at each other, then sit in silence, too hot and uncomfortable for small talk. One bearded husband tries to yank a window open, but after a few attempts, sits down with a defeated shrug. I smile back sympathetically, fanning myself with the baby first-aid leaflet I found on a chair. We teeter like bowling pins, our swollen bellies resting on our laps, arching our backs, our knees apart, grimacing.

As the room fills, I glance at the clock on the wall. Past six thirty. Where are they? I keep looking at my phone, waiting for the flash of response to my messages. But nobody replies.

I'd peeled away from the office early, wanting to get here on time. I hadn't been the only one. The air-conditioning has been broken for days. By this afternoon the place had been half empty, just a few desk fans still whirring limply into the flushed faces of middle-aged men.

When I picked up my bag and flicked my screen off, I had glanced at Tom, but he'd been hunched on a call to building services, complaining about the temperature for the third time that day. I'd tried to catch his eye with a sort of awkward half wave, but he'd barely acknowledged me, gesturing me away with a sideways glance at my belly, his other hand still clutching the phone to his ear. I think he'd forgotten today was my last day.

Unable to face the slow suffocation of the Tube, I'd decided to walk instead. The glare had been blinding. Heat bounced off pavements and crosswalks, shimmered between cars and buses. Horns honked in sweaty frustration. It is all anyone is talking about, the heatwave. No one can remember a summer like it. We are constantly reminded to stay in the shade, carry a bottle of water. It hasn't rained for weeks. Shops are selling out of fans, ice packs, garden umbrellas. There is talk of a garden hose ban.

I decided to cut across the park, between the Observatory and the Royal Naval College. The hazy light seemed to soften the edges around everything. Office workers were spread out on the yellowing grass, shoes kicked off, ties loosened, sunglasses on. They were drinking gin and tonics from cans, sharing Kettle chips, speaking slightly too loudly to each other, the way people do after a few drinks. It had felt like walking past a party, one I hadn't been invited to. I had to remember not to stare. It can be hard not to stare at happy people. They are mesmerizing somehow.

It was hot like this the summer we graduated from Cambridge. We used to punt down the river, the four of us. Serena and me sunbathing. Rory punting. Daniel sorting the drinks out, his pale skin reddening in the heat. We'd veer into banks, get tangled in curtains of weeping willow, the sky cloudless, the sunlight catching sequin-bright on the clear waters of the Cam. It felt as if the summer would go on forever. When it ended, I feared we would lose the closeness we felt back then. But we didn't. Rory and Serena came to live in Greenwich, on the other side of the park. Daniel went to work with Rory at the family firm. And now, there's our babies, due just two weeks apart.

The course leader is here now. She jams the door open with a folded beer coaster, then picks up a sticky label and writes her name on it with a thick green marker: SONIA. She presses the label onto her chest, then dumps a faded shopping bag and some Tesco grocery bags next to the flip chart. A whiskery braid runs almost the length of her spine.

"Right," says Sonia. "Shall we start?"

She begins a practiced monologue about labor, pain relief, and Caesareans, one eyelid flickering during the embarrassing parts. Occasionally she is forced to raise her voice over a crash of pots and pans, or a burst of expletives, from the pub kitchen on the floor below.

After she has been speaking for a few minutes, I glance down at my phone screen again, just as a message flashes up from Daniel. I open it. *Meeting only just finished*, he says. *Heading home now. Train gets in at 10.* He is so sorry again about the class, says again that he wishes he could be there with me. He'll make it up to me, he says.

I know he would be here if he could, that he is gutted to have had to let me down. That this last-minute crisis meeting just came at a terrible moment. At the same time, I can't help feeling so disappointed. I'd been excited about these classes, about doing them together, like proper expectant parents.

Sonia starts to pull objects from the grocery bags: a pelvis—through which she squeezes a fully dressed plastic newborn—knit nipples, a pair of forceps, a suction cup. The men look horrified, the women sweaty and anxious. We pass the objects around the circle, trying bravely to smile at each other.

The chairs to my left are still empty. The bearded man has to lean right over them to hand me the objects as they come around. I glance down at the name tags I wrote out for Rory and Serena, sitting on their vacant seats. Those two were supposed to be here at least, to keep me company, make me feel less alone. I feel foolish, like a woman who has invented two imaginary friends. Could Serena really have just forgotten?

Another message comes through. It's from Serena. My heart sinks. Somehow, deep down, even as I tap to open it, I know what it's going to say.

Hey, Helen! I know it's the first prenatal class tonight. Hope you don't mind, but I think Rory and I might skip them after all. I was actually looking online and I found these other ones that look a bit more my thing—beautiful bump classes—they're supposed to be a bit less preachy, and they meet in the organic bakery. I was thinking I might try those instead. So sorry to cancel at the last minute. Have fun!

Sonia is brandishing a red marker at her flip chart now. "So. Can anyone tell me what they know about breastfeeding?"

I try to focus on the breastfeeding discussion. It is not going well. Most of the mothers are staring at the floor. One mutters something about positioning, another offers an anecdote about a friend who kept breast milk in the fridge.

"Anyone else?" Sonia is flagging now, half-moons of perspiration spreading from under the arms of her T-shirt.

Just at this moment, a girl walks in, slamming the door behind her. Sonia winces.

"Fucking hell. Sorry, everyone," she announces loudly. She slips a metallic-gold backpack off one shoulder and drops it down on the floor with a thud. It lands inches from my foot.

"Oops." She grins, one hand on her bump.

Everyone stares. Sonia, still standing in front of the flip chart with her red marker pen held aloft, eyes the girl coldly. The only things written on her flip chart so far are CORRECT POSITION (NIPPLE) and STORE IN FRIDGE.

The girl points a purple-painted fingernail at the seat next to me, the one I had reserved for Serena. "This chair taken?"

I hesitate, then shake my head. I feel the eyes of the other couples on me as I haul my bags over to the other side, scrape my chair out a little to make more room.

Sonia sighs. "Anyone else?"

The flip chart charade continues for a few further minutes. The women begin to shift in their chairs, exchange raised eyebrows, uncomfortable glances. I try to concentrate. The girl next to me, the latecomer, is chewing gum. All I seem to be able to hear is the snap of it between her teeth as her jaw opens and closes. When I glance sideways at her, I glimpse it between her teeth, a neon-pink pellet, an artificial cherry scent. She catches my eye, grinning again, as if the whole thing is hilarious.

Finally, Sonia surrenders, pulling the back of her arm across the moisture on her brow. "OK," she says. "Shall we take a short break?"

A murmur of relief goes up. All the women waddle toward the jugs of juice, and I quickly follow them. Soon they are grouping up, the room filling with the noise of chatter. I am being left behind. I feel a plummeting panic. No Daniel, no Rory, no Serena. How do people make friends? What would Serena do?

I hover on the edge of a group, trying to look casual, waiting to be included. But there never seems to be a good moment to interject. I open my mouth to speak a few times, but on each occasion, someone else speaks first. I end up closing my mouth again, like a fish drowning in air. I feel the trickle of my anxiety begin, the nerve center at the back of my head starting to alarm. I am uncomfortably warm. Can't someone get that window open?

The girl who came in late appears at my side. She is holding two enormous glasses of what appears to be cold white wine, clouds of condensation on the side of the glass.

"Do you want one? I thought you looked like you might need a real drink. One a day can't hurt, surely."

She holds out the glass in front of me. Her painted fingernails are short and chewed. She looks very young—perhaps she just has one of those faces. Round, dimpled, babyish. Yet when she smiles, there is something wolfish in it, her canine teeth protruding slightly, small but sharp.

"What's the deal, then?"

I blink at her. "I beg your pardon?"

The girl places the glasses of wine down on a side table, gestures to the two chairs next to me, the name tags Rory and Serena still lying on them. "Just wondered what the setup was." She shrugs. Then her face snaps back at me, her eyes wide, her fingers pressed to her mouth. "You're not a surrogate, are you?" She laughs. "That would be typical, wouldn't it? Didn't even want it, and now you're left holding the baby!"

The girl hoots. I look over her shoulder, try to catch the eye of one of the other women. But none return my gaze, so I am forced to reply. I clear my throat.

"No, um. No. I'm not." I try to laugh. "It's just that my husband, Daniel, couldn't make it tonight." I shake my head slightly, as if it's just one of those things, doesn't matter.

I pause, before realizing she is waiting for an explanation about the two other empty seats.

"The other couple is my brother and his wife. Rory and Serena. They're expecting in the same month as us. We'd been planning to do the classes together, as a foursome, but . . . I think they . . . obviously decided against it in the end."

The girl smiles sympathetically. "Hopeless. Never mind, you can team up with me, can't you?" She picks the glass up again. "Shall we have this drink, then?"

"Thanks," I say hesitantly. "But I'm not sure . . ."

Why am I incapable of completing my own sentences? I should just say no, thank you, I would rather not drink. I mean, I'm pregnant. We both are. Surely I don't have to spell it out?

"Oh, I know what you're saying," she booms, rolling her eyes and glancing around the room. "Ridiculous, isn't it? All this pressure! The way they change the advice all the time! One minute you can drink, the next minute you can't, then you can 'in moderation,' then it's basically illegal! Bloody doctors."

I clear my throat, unsure how to answer. I am very aware now of the gaze of the other women in the room, looking from me to the girl and the wine, and back.

"Well, fuck doctors," she continues. "Our mums all got smashed when they were pregnant. We all bloody survived!" She is speaking far too loudly. The room is silent, and people are starting to openly stare.

The girl looks over at the other mothers, registers their disapproving glances, then raises her eyebrows at me and giggles. She holds the wine-glass aloft to toast her own sentiment. She brings the glass to her lips. "Fuck the NHS," she spits. "That's what I say." She tips the glass to her lips and drinks. As she does so, I notice one or two of the other mothers actually wince.

The girl picks up the drink she has brought for me. She holds it out, like a threat, or a dare.

"Come on," she hisses. Her eyes flick down to my name badge. "You know you want to . . . Helen."

Later, after everything, I will come to wonder why I act as I do in this moment. For even now, there is something about this girl. Something that makes me want to edge away, to look for a place of safety. Like the feeling of being on a cliff-top path, when the wind is just a little too strong at your back.

But I don't step away. I take the wine. And as I do, the other women turn their heads, as if by taking it I have answered all their questions. I want to tell them I'm just being polite, that I have no intention of actually drinking it. But they are already looking the other way.

"Thanks," I say weakly.

"Nice to meet you, Helen. I'm Rachel."

And then Rachel clinks her glass against mine, knocks back another deep glug, and winks at me, as if we share a secret.

Helen

THE HEAT IS MORE bearable today. A breeze from the river flows into Greenwich market hall, and the cloths over the stall tables billow like boat sails. Sunlight shines through glass panels in the roof, casting warm islands on the floor. In the green-painted metal rafters, pigeons coo and clamor. They sail down to the feet of the cafe tables, jabbing at abandoned croissants.

I have always loved the streets around the market: little crooked lanes, handsome Georgian windows, the musty scent of books and antiques. The dusty lamplit gloom of the pubs, with their worn leather and low ceilings. The brackish smell, carried on the breeze from the river. The mysterious names, left over from an age where Greenwich was the center of the world: Straightsmouth, Gipsy Moth, Turnpin, Cutty Sark.

Daniel and I often come here on a Saturday, even though the whole experience is usually a letdown. You can never get a table at the coffee place, and the takeout line stretches around the block. The aisles between the stalls are so packed that I am left constantly apologizing, my bump pushed up against people's backs as I squeeze past. We end up wandering aimlessly, looking again and again at the same handmade children's clothes, quirky hats, worn-out furniture. Squabbling with tourists over tiny samples of expensive cheeses, then feeling obliged to buy it.

I had to get out of the house, though. I'd made my way downstairs this morning—still in my pajamas, clinging to the filthy banister, attempting to dodge the gauntlet of tools, insulation, dustcovers—to be greeted by a host of embarrassed-looking builders. I mumbled a good morning, but the only one I really know is Vilmos, the boss, and he wasn't there. I don't think any of these ones spoke English. They just nodded and smiled, clutching their cans of Red Bull, cigarettes perched behind their ears. I could already see what the day would have in store. Drilling, dust, smashing plaster. Strange men urinating in my bathroom, dirt being tracked to and from the kettle. Anything had to be better than staying at home.

I still haven't completely forgiven Daniel for missing the prenatal class. When I woke the next morning he was already up and showered, perched on the sofa with his laptop on his knee.

He looked up when he saw me. "Hey, how was it?"

I shrugged, fiddling with my robe cord. "Embarrassing."

"I'm so sorry, Helen."

"I know. It's just, you know I hate stuff like that. On my own."

He closed his laptop, rubbed his eyes behind his glasses. Tried to explain. The new development he's working on had gotten another dreadful write-up in the *Evening Standard*. It had come out late afternoon, and the client had gone mad, demanded to know why they hadn't been warned, why the press seemed to have it in for the project. It had been up to Daniel to race to Edinburgh to meet with the client, try and calm everything down.

"Couldn't Rory have dealt with it?"

Even as I said it, though, I knew what the answer would be. Daniel rolled his eyes. "Nowhere to be found," he said. "As usual."

Daniel had joined my brother, Rory, at his architecture firm a few years ago. It was my suggestion, so I can't help but feel responsible for the fact that my brother has proven a less than ideal business partner. It always seems to be left to Daniel to keep everything going.

Daniel hauled himself up, wrapped his arms around me.

"I'm sorry," he murmured into my hair. "I promise I'll make it up to you. Let's go into town this weekend, have a proper look at things for the nursery."

I pulled away to look at his face. It felt like a significant concession: he finds things like that hard, I know, after what has happened before. He still can't bear to hope, to put his trust in the idea that this time things really are going to be different.

"Really? And you won't spend the whole day complaining?"

He laughed. "Promise. We can look at as many tiny pairs of socks as you like. I won't say a word."

Today the market is wonderfully sleepy. Most of the sellers are sitting back, eating lunch from brown takeout boxes, chatting. There are no lines, so I take my time choosing serrano ham, hard cheeses, a glistening apricot tart. In the bakery, I pick up a flour-dusted loaf of sourdough. In the stalls outside I gather handfuls of red and yellow tomatoes in crinkling brown paper, smooth and round as gemstones.

Maybe it won't be so bad after all, having nothing to do. I was advised to start my maternity leave early. This isn't my first pregnancy—the others didn't end well. I am a high-risk case, scanned every two weeks, my baby checked and checked again. I have been told I need to take it easy. Spend time at home. Do nothing.

I decide to take my time, do a full loop around the market, gulping in the smells of fresh bread and newly cut flowers, the faded melody of the busker on the steps outside. I linger over the stalls I never buy anything from—the ones that sell silver jewelery, old-fashioned children's toys, homemade candles, rustling skirts, silk dresses, tie-dyed tunics. Things that Mummy liked to look at when we came here together. I pretend to be interested so I can touch things. Feel the silver, the velour, the crushed silk. Things that remind me of her.

The lady in the clothes stall—an aging hippie with a nose piercing and a leathery face—doesn't seem to mind me lingering. She is eating what smells like a lentil curry from one of the hot-food places, stabbing at chunks of paneer and butternut squash with a fork, a bluebottle batting at the canvas behind her. I sift through her tunics and skirts, moving the hangers one by one with my fingertips. I imagine which ones Mummy might have chosen.

Once she bought a blue velvet dress here. She held it up against herself, her head cocked to one side, looking in the chipped mirror in the lady's makeshift changing room. That mirror is still here, with its rainbow rim. I have the dress at home, although I don't like to look at it much. I keep it in a drawer, hidden away. I can't understand sometimes how things like that are still the same. Things that she touched, things that she wore, that were once warm against her skin, mirrors that held her reflection. They are all still here, in the world, with me. But she is gone, and never coming back.

I head back into the main square, where the coffee place and the metal tables are. I think about getting an orange juice and sitting here for a bit. I could look at Serena's Instagram for a while, see what she's up to. She does her yoga class on a Wednesday and usually posts something afterward, a picture of herself upside down, flexed like an acrobat on a pale pink mat, her trailing hair completing the perfect circle of her body. Or an inspiring quote from a book, which is usually easy enough to find and order online. I think about having a look at these other prenatal classes she's found, the ones that meet in the bakery. But I've already paid hundreds of pounds for the NCT ones. Daniel would go mad.

And that's when I see her. The girl from the prenatal class. Rachel. She is sitting at one of the metal tables, reading a newspaper, the free one they hand out at the Tube station. That rape case is on the front page again. There's a hardness in her expression as she reads, her mouth clamped in a tight line.

I could say hello, obviously, but I don't really have anything to say, and can't think why I would want to initiate another round of awkward small talk. I'd been desperate to get away by the end of the class, but she had tried to strike up another conversation. I got the impression she was hoping to hang around, have another drink. I'd muttered an excuse and left as quickly as I could, marching home to scold Daniel over his nonappearance.

I can't resist studying her a bit, though, seeing as I am here unobserved. She looks young to be having a baby, I think—much younger than most of the others in the group. She is quite pretty really, though she has made the mistake of overplucking her eyebrows, and her long hair is dyed too dark, so it makes her face look shockingly pale.

Rachel seems completely absorbed in her newspaper. The coffee on the table in front of her looks untouched, a speckle of chocolate powder sitting perfectly on the foam. She has left her phone and wallet on the edge of the table, rather recklessly. Anyone could snatch her things from a table like that. I notice the wallet is stuffed with bills—so many that she has only been able to zip it up halfway.

Rachel places the newspaper down, picks up her phone, and starts tapping away. That chipped purple polish is still clinging to her fingernails. The garish gold backpack is at her feet again, plus a clutch of shopping bags. Her cell is clad in a gold plastic case, the sort you see on teenagers' phones, an outline of a Playboy bunny studded on the reverse in diamanté.

I have stared too long. She glances up, spots me immediately. I try to look away, fiddle with my bags, but it is too late.

"Helen!"

When I glance back up, the serious expression has been replaced by a wide grin, her pointed teeth on show again. She tilts her head to the side and motions me to come over. As she does so, she shoves the bulging wallet into her bag, away from view.

"So great to see you!" she cries. I start a tentative wave, but instead she stands up and pulls me into a bear hug, as if we're old friends who haven't met in ages, rather than near strangers who met just a few days before. The hand I'd raised in greeting is squashed awkwardly between our two chests.

"They've signed me off work early, too! High blood pressure, same as you. What are the chances?"

What *are* the chances? I think. I suppose blood pressure issues are hardly uncommon. Although I'd sort of assumed it was linked to my being a bit overweight. Whereas she is so skinny and slight, her small round bump incongruous against her matchstick-thin arms and legs.

"Oh no, I'm sorry to hear that. Poor you," I say tentatively. "Are you on the labetalol, then?"

She looks blank for a moment. "Yeah," she says vaguely, glancing off to the left. "Something like that." Her hands flap my question away, as if it's not important. "Come on, let's have a coffee. We can catch up properly."

Catch up? On what? I open my mouth to object, then close it again, my brain having failed to supply me with an excuse. Rachel is looking over my shoulder, beckoning a waiter with a purple-painted fingernail.

"Excuse me? Hello?" The frown is back. "Fuck me," she mutters. "Service is slow around here."

I place my bag and my basket of groceries on the floor between us. As I do, I start to form excuses in my mind. Friends around for dinner, I'll say. Can't stay long. I sit down, the silence between us already feeling uncomfortable. I take a stab at small talk.

"Have you been shopping?" I ask, gesturing rather stupidly down at her bags.

"Yes!" She beams. "Baby stuff, obviously. I've literally gone mad. I know they say not to buy too much. Can't help it, though. It's all so fucking cute!"

I laugh awkwardly. I know what she means. The little velour jackets, the tiny towels with bear ears on the hoods. It's like an addiction, once you get started. I'll have to pretend to Daniel that I've waited, as he said we should—that baby shopping this weekend is a big treat. In reality, I've been hiding bags from him for weeks.

Rachel presses her lips to the coffee mug and sips, leaving a crescent of coral pink on the rim. "So," she says, replacing it. "Tell me about this husband. Did he have a good excuse?"

"Sorry?"

"For not showing up!"

"Oh." I laugh nervously, glancing at the tables on either side of us. I wonder if other people are finding her voice a little too loud, or if I'm just imagining it. "He just had a nightmare at work. It was one of those things."

Daniel used to love his job. When he first went into practice with Rory—at the architecture firm Daddy founded, and that Rory took on when he died—I thought it would be perfect. Even if Rory didn't always pull his weight, surely it would be easier for Daniel, being his own boss. The firm is based here in Greenwich. He can walk across the park to work, choose his own hours. At least, that's what Rory appears to do.

But I seem to see Daniel less and less. He comes in with these bags under his eyes, a slant in his shoulders, like he's carrying rocks in his backpack. He tells me everything's fine, that it's just this demanding client, this difficult new project. But between that and the remodeling work at home, it's as if he has started to hate it. Maybe it's the pressure of the baby coming, too—I don't know. I should talk to him about it, ask him properly. But sometimes when I see his face when he walks in, I'm worried to ask how his day was.

"Work! A likely fucking story." Rachel laughs, slapping a hand down on the table. Her rings clang against the metal. I jump. A gaggle of pigeons that had gathered at our feet flutters away.

Rachel glances at me, then places her coffee down. She resets her expression, puts a hand on my arm.

"Sorry, Helen. That was a joke. I'm sure he was gutted."

"It's fine." I try to get the conversation back onto a comfortable footing. "I was cross with him, to tell you the truth. My brother and his wife were supposed to be there as well, but they couldn't make it either, so—"

"Oh yeah, you said. That's a shame." She pauses. "Must be exciting, though—to be having babies at the same time. Especially when you live nearby."

I nod. "It's lovely." I couldn't believe it when Serena told me her and Rory's baby was due just a few weeks after mine. After all the times before, it felt like a good omen, at last. I'd somehow felt sure, then, that things would be different this time.

"Do you get on with her? Your brother's wife?"

"Serena? Oh God, yes. She's amazing. She really is like a sister," I gush, then feel a hot curtain of blood rising through my face. Do I sound childish? "We were at university together, the four of us," I add quickly. I'm careful not to say Cambridge—Daniel told me once that it sounded boastful, talking about it all the time, especially to people who might not have even been to university. "Rory was in the year above me. And Rory and Daniel are in business together now, so we see them both a lot."

"Your husband and your brother? In business together? Doing what?"

"They're architects. My father was an architect, too. He was . . . well, he was sort of a bit famous, I suppose. He died a few years back."

I pause automatically, waiting for the usual condolences, the usual curiosity about Daddy. But Rachel doesn't react. She is using her index finger to spoon the dusting of chocolate powder from the froth of her coffee directly into her mouth. When she is finished, she starts to work the moistened finger around the rim of the cup, where a little tideline of chocolate is stuck to the lip.

"When Daddy died, Rory took over the firm. Haverstock and Company," I continue, even though I'm not entirely sure she is listening. "By then Daniel was doing pretty well at another place—he'd won awards, that sort of thing. So it was an easy decision, really. Rory asked Daniel to come on board as his partner, and now it's a real family firm. They are brilliant. Daniel is in the process of remodeling our house. We're getting rid of the ground-floor bathroom and putting a new one in upstairs—it's going to have one of those lovely Victorian roll-top baths, and a big walk-in shower, with these gorgeous tiles I found. And we're putting in a new staircase and landing where that was, and eventually there will be a big basement addition, a whole new floor, with a sunken living space and glass roof, and—" I stop, wondering if I sound boastful. "Anyway. A few other bits. Daniel's designed it all. We're quite excited about it."

I sense my talk of the architectural work is boring Rachel. She finishes her coffee: a little M of froth left behind on her top lip, a smudge of chocolate in either corner of her mouth. I motion to my own lip; she giggles, wipes the marks off. She stretches her hands above her head, lets out an exhale, glances around the market.

"Shall we have another coffee?" she suggests, even though I haven't actually had a coffee yet, just watched her drink the one she had already. "You could even risk one with actual caffeine!" Rachel smiles, taps her leopard-spotted bump. I can't work out whether she is making fun of me or not. She seems to believe the babies only exist in abstract, that adhering to the health guidelines is entirely a matter of personal taste.

"Actually, could I just have an orange juice?"

She looks amused. "OK. Sure! I'll go up and order—quicker than waiting for these jokers."

She says this loudly, causing a passing waiter to look up, dumb-founded. Rachel ignores him, strides into the cafe.

When I see she is safely inside, I can't resist peering into her shop-ping bags. Furtively, I lower my hand, separate the top of the bag with my thumb and forefinger and root around to feel the fabrics. Disap-pointingly, though, I find there are no baby clothes in the first bag at all. All I can see is a scruffy old sweater, dirty around the cuffs, and what looks like a pair of old leggings. A few clothes tags, an empty sun-glasses case.

"Oh shit!"

I look up sharply. For a second, I'm sure Rachel has spotted me look-ing into her bags: she's staring straight at me.

"He's given me a coffee instead of orange juice. What an idiot, Helen. Will you be OK drinking it or shall I go back?"

"Of course," I tell her, trying to disguise my relief. "One won't hurt."

Maybe I can get away with abandoning it, I think as she sits back down. Like I did the glass of wine.

Then without warning, Rachel has reached over, and her hands are on my belly.

"So weird, isn't it?" she muses. "Being pregnant. Where do you reckon the baby's head is?"

The contact is made before I can voice any objection. I can't help but flinch. The suddenness of pale hands, cool against my stomach, the tips of her chewed purple nails brushing over my thin cotton top.

"I—I don't know," I stutter. Rachel doesn't seem to notice my stunned reaction to her touch. She continues to stroke, back and forth, setting off nerve endings in my stretched skin.

"It's easy to tell," she continues, staring at my belly. "You just feel for the neck. I'll show you."

Rachel spreads her knees to face me head-on, and starts to probe with a finger and thumb, down at the bottom of my pelvis, as if trying to pinch the sides of the baby's head.

"Rachel, you're pressing quite hard," I gasp. "Are you sure it's safe?"

"Of course!" She presses harder still. "There it is," she says trium-phantly. "There's his head."

I gasp again and recoil, my spine pushing against the back of the chair. In my mind's eye I see my baby floating in utero, Rachel's alien hand pressing through the red, glowing walls of his universe.

26 WEEKS

Helen

DANIEL AND I ARE at the prenatal clinic, the lights down low. I have stripped from the waist down, cold jelly smeared on my belly over the red scratches of my stretch marks. I wince at the temperature. The sonographer tells me the probe is coming, that it is going to be cold. Daniel looks at me. "I love you," he mouths. He squeezes my hand, and I squeeze back.

I try to be soothed by the feel of Daniel's slim fingers in mine, try not to clench as it slides into me, this hard, alien object. We sit in silence, the low hum of the machines filling the room. There is a smell of bleach. My heart feels full of blood.

Even though I am big enough now to feel the baby move—a daily confirmation that he is still there, still alive—I can't help but remember how so many of these scans have ended for us. The ripped blue squares of National Health Service tissue pressed into my hands to dry my sobbing face, a sonographer wiping ultrasound gel from between my legs as I beg them in vain to check, just one more time.

But soon the room is filled with the watery thump of a heartbeat noise and a wiggly blue line darts across the screen. Daniel doesn't say anything, but I see his chest deflate in a way that tells me he had been holding his breath. When the sonographer turns to us, I can see from the wrinkles around her eyes that she is smiling, even though a mask covers her nose and mouth.

"Heartbeat sounds good. Baby is strong."

It feels as if someone has opened a window. All the muscles in my body relax.

She starts to move the probe around, telling us what the pictures mean. She tells me not to lift my hips and I try not to. When she is happy, she pulls out the probe and starts to move the external ultrasound over my bump.

"As you know, in the past we have had some . . . complications," she says. Her words are devoid of emotion, consonants sharp as scalpels. I close my eyes, but the pictures flash up anyway, of the babies that came before. The flat pods of their eyelids. The shapes of their heads. My chest heaves; the thump of my heart feels too fast, my face too hot. I feel Daniel's grip on my hand tighten. I know how hard this is for him, too.

"We are just being extra careful this time, OK? I'm checking for everything."

I nod, and we both wait while she alternates between moving the probe across my belly and typing up notes.

"Oh-kay, baby is in good position. Here, look."

We are both entranced by the flickering screen—there he is, a real baby, with arms and legs and a tiny nose.

"Oh my God, Helen," Daniel says. I can hear the smile in his voice, but I can't tear my eyes away from the image of our son, his large, outsized head, his wriggling body that is yet to catch up. Fourteen weeks to go.

"This is the umbilical cord, see here? And this is the placenta." Patches of blue and red pulsate on the screen to show the blood flow.

"OK. Heart is good, lungs are good. Spinal cord OK. Now I'm just measuring the fluid at the back of the neck, but it's looking very normal."

Sometimes we catch a nose, or a hand—something human—and Daniel and I look from the screen to each other and back to the screen again, both making the same noises at once, noises somewhere between a nervous laugh and an expression of wonder. Then the probe will move, and it will flicker, darkly, into something else. Something that could be human or reptile.

"All fine. Baby is perfect," the sonographer says. Her voice is still muffled by the mask. I close my eyes, saving her words for later, like coins in a purse. There is nothing wrong with him. Nothing. He is perfect.

She takes the probe again, gently moves it down toward my hip. The screen is filled with a hand.

"Ah, see? Baby is waving."

I look at Daniel, smiling at his mesmerized expression. He squeezes my hand again but doesn't take his eyes off the screen. The image of the baby is reflected in his glasses, two lit squares of black and blue.

She flicks the lights on and hands me some tissues. "All done for today. I'll make a picture for you to take home."

As I turn to look at Daniel again, I see that he is still staring at the screen. His entire face is wet with tears.

"Oh, Daniel," I say, half laughing. "You're worse than me."

He does not seem to hear me, though. His eyes are locked on the freeze-frame of the baby's waving hand. When the sonographer switches the screen off, and the image is gone, he continues to stare at the gray square of the monitor.

"Daniel? Is something wrong?"

Daniel drops his head into his hands, his shoulders shaking. I put my arm around him. The sonographer is back, standing in front of us, apparently unsure what to do. She snaps her blue plastic gloves off, first one, then the other. I see her glance at the clock. She has other couples to see.

"Daniel? Come on, we need to go."

I stroke his back, try to drop my head, meet his eye. But no matter what I do, he can't seem to stop.

Greenwich Park

IN GREENWICH PARK, THERE are old doorways. He noticed them the first time he came here. Even in the moonlight, they stay in shadow. He walks through the park at night, past the line of bent trees, twisted over to one side by the wind on the hill. His shadow is long, looping over the asphalt paths that crisscross the lawns. She makes him hunt her, her hot blood smell.

She likes doorways. Alleyways. Walls wet with ivy wet with rain. The backs of churches. Once even a graveyard, the stones lined up against the path. Dark, cold, secret places where she is the only warm thing. She grips him, tightly. They move quickly, on all fours, or against walls. They bite, scratch, claw at each other's wrists. When she finishes, she gasps, like she is drowning, and in that moment, he feels that he is not old, or young, or rich or poor or even himself, really. He is just here, awake in the dark, an animal, and alive.

Does he want to get caught? Does she? He is not sure. God knows what she wants. Mainly he just wants this feeling, this feeling like he is falling, like he might die if he lands, but in the falling he is alive, to his fingertips.

He wonders sometimes what he would do without it. How he would exist. He doesn't know. He doesn't know how he would breathe without this, without knowing it is coming.

27 WEEKS

Helen

IT HADN'T MATTERED SO much when we were both at work. But now that I've had to give up, and I'm stuck at home, I'm finding my patience with the remodel is slowly unraveling, like a fraying hem. With every new misery, another thread comes loose.

The work was Daniel's big idea. I wasn't convinced we needed it at first—to me, the house is beautiful as it is. It has a huge garden, which Mummy loved and filled with flowers—foxgloves, delphiniums, rambling roses. Upstairs there are five big, light-filled bedrooms, perfect for us and the three children I hope we'll one day have. Admittedly, having the bathroom on the ground floor is a bit old-fashioned, as is having the kitchen, pantry, dining room, and living rooms all separate and comparatively small—but they are always like that in homes as old as this one. It had never bothered me before, and anyway, you can't just knock through walls—not in a house listed on the English Heritage register.

Eventually, though, Daniel convinced me that once we had a family, we would want a big, modern living area: open plan, for the children to run around, with light flooding in from above. Daniel knew that the English Heritage people wouldn't let us change the old house, or stick a modern addition on the back. But they loved the idea of his "underground courtyard"—a huge, free-flowing living and dining space built around an ultramodern kitchen with island—especially since it will be almost invisible from the ground, save for the old patio becoming a huge skylight window. To one side of the main "courtyard" will be a wine cellar and laundry room; to the other, a study for Daniel. A new staircase will lead up our old cellar steps, with a landing where the bathroom used to be.

The whole project is a dream for Daniel, and I don't want to keep punishing him for it. I have seen the way he cringes when he sees me bending to wipe dust off the expensive new bassinet in the hallway, or haul kettles of hot water upstairs for a bath because they've had to turn the water off. But as I get bigger and heavier, the pile of small miseries gets harder and harder to bear. The hideous layer of filth over everything. The constant unsettling presence of strangers in our home. The head-splitting sound of drills. Sometimes I even hear it in my dreams. Then I wake up to find the noise was real, that it has started again.

When I told Daniel I was worried about being stuck at home alone for weeks on end because of my early maternity leave, he'd rolled his eyes at first. "Oh come on, Helen," he said through a mouthful of toast. "It'll be great! Watch daytime TV and eat biscuits."

Then, when he looked up and saw my face, he stopped eating. Reached out, put his hand on top of mine. "Oh, love, I'm sorry. I'll have a word with the builders, OK? Make sure they keep the noise and mess under control."

But there is little evidence of that happening. On the day of the next prenatal class, I arrive with yet another headache from the drilling. It is so intense that it feels as if it is pressing against the sides of my brain, the insides of my eyes. I arrive at the pub early, slump down at a table by the door to catch my breath.

"Helen! You're here!"

It's Rachel, standing at the bar. She is wearing a short denim dress that is clearly not designed as maternity wear, the buttons straining a little over her bump. Her feet are clad in lime-green flip-flops. She walks over to the table and sits down next to me without asking first. She is holding two glasses of orange juice in her hands. Up close, I can see she has misapplied the blusher on her cheeks. It gives her face a lopsided appearance, like a badly hung painting.

"Finally got you that juice you asked for, ha! Only a week late. Look, I'm having one, too. Being good. Don't worry, I promise I haven't spiked it!"

I smile awkwardly, and take the drink. "Thanks, that's really kind," I say. The glass feels sticky, as if she has been holding it for a while.

"How's things, anyway, hon? How's it all going with the megabasement?" Rachel leans in toward me, resting on her elbows, sincerity etched on her face. It is almost as if she has been genuinely looking forward to receiving an update on the progress of our addition. When I don't reply, her smile wilts a little.

"What's up?" she asks, cocking her head to one side. "Why is Daniel not here again?"

I look down at the juice, then at Rachel, and to my horror I feel my throat tightening in the face of her kindness, the sting of tears in my eyes.

"Helen?" She frowns. "What's wrong?"

"I'm sorry . . . It's just . . . it's just . . ."

There is no stopping it. I'm a trembling mess of sobs, my face hot and wet in my hands. I'm causing a scene, but I can't seem to calm down.

I don't think I'd realized until now how upset I was about Daniel. At first he tried to blame work. He'd been left holding the fort with a project that was at risk of falling apart—Rory having announced that he and Serena were going on an impromptu vacation, a "babymoon," they called it. He was struggling to get out at eight at the moment, let alone in time for the classes at six.

"I'll read the books," Daniel had said. He was avoiding eye contact. "I promise, I'll learn it all. Do we really need the classes?"

That's when it had dawned on me. He didn't want to come to the classes at all.

"Is this really about work?"

I'd looked at Daniel, still not meeting my eye, fiddling with his watch. And I'd thought then about what the counselor had told us, about us grieving at different rates. How she had made me understand that his grief was not less, but different. I couldn't understand this, for a long time. My grief is raw and bloody, tearful, and surfacing often. It is kinetic, feverish, greedy. It makes me impatient, makes me clutch at hope, at progress, at the anticipation of the new baby, the expectation of healing. Daniel's is the opposite. A sort of paralysis of the heart. It makes him withdraw. Makes him terrified to hope, to plan, to believe in the future.

And then I'd thought about how he'd spent all weekend putting nursery furniture together, crawling around the house on his hands and knees covering all the plug sockets, getting the baby monitor we'd bought working. How he'd gone, without complaint, to the post office to collect the huge breastfeeding pillow I'd ordered, and arrived home with a packet of prawn cocktail chips after I told him I'd been craving them.

But for me, this is all part of it. Sitting in a circle and talking about the opening of the pelvis, like all first-time parents do. I want to be able to tell funny stories about it, like other mums. And Daniel just doesn't seem to understand the impact it has, having to do everything connected with the baby on my own, because he can't face it.

Rachel has been an enthusiastic listener, her eyes wide open, her head nodding like a toy dog.

"I'm sorry," I say, shaking my head, searching for a tissue in my bag. "I feel ridiculous getting so upset."

"Not at all," Rachel says. "I'd be annoyed, too." She passes me a napkin from underneath the glass of juice. It's rough and papery, and sticky from the juice, but I take it gratefully.

As I blow my nose, two of the other mothers arrive with their partners, heading for the stairs. When they see my tear-stained face, they avert their gaze, quicken their step. I feel the color rising to my cheeks. Rachel places a hand on my arm. "You sure you don't want me to spike that drink?" I laugh, wiping my eyes. It's been a while since I really laughed.

Rachel smiles. "Come on," she says, gesturing to the stairs at the back of the pub. "We'll miss all the fun."

The class starts. Sonia tells us to prepare for a "breathing exercise" with our partner, and I am surprised to find myself intensely relieved that Rachel is here. The exercise involves me kneeling on all fours on the wooden floor, one of Sonia's grubby tie-dye cushions under my knees. Meanwhile Rachel has to rub my back and encourage me to inhale and exhale through the "surges"—the word Sonia uses when she is talking about the agonizing pains for which we all know we are destined.

Sonia is weaving between us, hands splayed, wrists rotating, spinning some tale about waves on a shore, something about a ribbon around our uterus unraveling. The other women on all fours crane their necks to hear. Her voice is mostly drowned out by Rachel's commentary.

"You are smashing it, Helen!" Rachel cries. She slaps her hands down on her thighs. "You've got this. You're all over it. Push, Helen! Push! Oh God, I can see the head!" She roars with laughter. One of the other women actually tuts.

By the time the class concludes—with a surreal Playmobil demonstration of a Caesarean section—it occurs to me how grateful I have been for Rachel's companionship. I find myself admiring her. She is so upbeat about it all. Would I be so cheerful in her situation? Although she hasn't said so explicitly, it's clear there is no father in the picture. And she is so young. I wouldn't have the strength to do all this on my own. I mean, he might have been a bit useless lately, but I don't know what I'd do if I didn't have Daniel.

Rachel is standing up, pulling a jacket on over her bump. "Pub?" she says brightly. "I mean, I know we're already at the pub so . . . drink, downstairs?" She giggles. "We can go crazy and have another juice. Our vitamin levels will be through the roof!"

I glance at the clock. It's 8 p.m. Daniel will be home soon. But I look at Rachel's face, and somehow it seems a bit unfriendly to say so. Especially for someone who, presumably, has no one waiting for her at home.

I shrug, return her smile. "Why not?"

Greenwich Park

UNDER THE SHADE OF the plane tree, the girl pulls the envelope from her bag, inspects the contents.

He keeps watching, through the glass. He wants to keep watching until he is sure she is gone, until she is nothing more than a speck, a tiny pixel, drowned in the canvas of his view. Only then will his fists unclench, his pulse slow down.

He feels better when he is outside, on the Thames path. There is a breeze from the river. A briny smell, the gray-green swell, the black eyes of seabirds, floating lumps of foam and rubbish. The railings on the Thames wall are hot to the touch.

He turns away from the water, heads toward the park. He hears the gulls scream behind him as they fight over scraps.

That had better be it, he thinks. That had better be the end of it. Somehow, though, he knows it is not. That it is just the beginning.

28 WEEKS

Katie

THE GRAY FLOORS OF the entrance hall at Cambridge Crown Court are streaked with rain. There are three in front of me in the line for security checks. As I stand waiting, I feel the water soaking through my cheap flat shoes.

The metal detectors sound when I walk through them.

"I think that's my watch, sorry," I say. "Here, look. Could I just—"

A full-chested woman in a Courts Service sweater ignores me and steps forward. "Arms out, please."

She takes a handheld black metal detector, waves it over my outstretched arms, my chest, my legs. Then she comes closer. We avert our eyes from one another while she searches my body with her hands, feeling along my collar, my waist, around the pockets of my trousers.

I see reporters I recognize from other papers overtaking me, piling into the elevator, the doors behind them closing. I should be in there with them. The press gallery will be full. I shift my weight from one foot to another. Another security guard has unzipped my backpack and plucked out my makeup bag.

"Can you open this purse for me, please?"

He does not look up as he says it. I smile, unzip the bag, try to look helpful. As he starts rooting around inside it with his two meaty fingers, I glance at my watch. A mascara topples to the floor, followed by a blister pack of headache tablets.

When I finally reach courtroom three, the press benches are packed. I'm lucky to get a seat. The barristers, in their black gowns and white collars, are already in place, and the defendants are in the dock. I examine them carefully. Both are wearing somber, expensive-looking suits. Dark ties, combed hair, and straight spines. They are flanked by bored-looking security guards. One looks like he is about to fall asleep.

In the public gallery, one of the mothers is already clutching a squashed tissue, her eyes bloodshot. The fingers curled around the tissue are trembling. The father next to her is grim-faced, his hand clamped on to her knee. I think he must be the earl, rather than the former agriculture minister. He stares at the press benches with barely concealed fury.

"All rise."

The judge enters in a long red gown, thick white fur at the sleeves, her wig yellowed, her spectacles black-rimmed. The clerk speaks. The walls all around us are paneled with fake wood, the light artificial. There are no windows.

"The case before Her Ladyship is the Queen against Mr. Toby Letwin and Mr. Roland Bartholomew."

Simon, from the Press Association, is in the seat in front of me. I tap him on the shoulder. "Have we got opening statements?" I hiss at him. He rolls his eyes, pulls a folded piece of paper from his notebook, and hands it back to me, like a schoolboy passing notes.

"Toby Letwin, you are charged with rape contrary to section 1 of the Sexual Offenses Act 1956, in that you, Toby Letwin, together with Roland Bartholomew, did on the fourteenth of October 2017 rape Emily Oliver at 22 Green Street in Cambridge. Do you plead guilty or not guilty?"

"Not guilty."

As the clerk reads out the charges, I pretend to take notes. But instead, I am searching the public gallery, looking for the detective. I am sure he will be here somewhere.

Eventually I spot him, sitting in the back row, away from the families. He is off duty, no uniform, but he has worn a suit anyway. His face does not change as the clerk speaks. But when the first defendant states his not-guilty plea, his expression hardens.

The prosecution barrister stands for his opening statement. The court falls silent. We hear of a drunken night out, of words exchanged over social media, about girls, about sex, about bravado. And then we hear the stuff of female nightmares—of DNA scraped from sheets and from the internal reaches of a woman's body, of bruising, of vomit, of a neighboring door battered late into the night. Of a barefoot stranger, a tearful appeal for help.

When the court rises, I watch the detective carefully. I slip out as quickly as I can, and try to head in his direction. For a moment, I can't find him, and I worry he has left already. But then I see him retreating down the corridor, his footfalls echoing against the high ceilings.

"DCI Carter?"

He stops, turns around slowly, looks me up and down.

"Katie Wheeler, I presume," he says.

"That's me." I smile, pleased.

"I had a feeling it was you, eyeballing me from the press bench." His tone is stern, but he looks as if he might be suppressing a smile. "You do realize stalking is actually a crime, don't you?"

"Sorry. Like I said in my message—"

"Messages."

"Oh, right. Yes. Messages . . . um, I was hoping we could have a chat. About the background."

He opens his mouth to speak, but stops when another reporter brushes past, shooting me a suspicious glance.

"Look," he says, lowering his voice. "You have to go through the press office like everyone else, Katie. You know that."

I do know that. In theory. But I have done my homework—well, I've asked Chris, the crime correspondent—and I know that Detective Chief Inspector Mark Carter is a bit old school, and therefore not averse to chatting to reporters sometimes. And that he's done his thirty years with the Cambridgeshire Constabulary, and is expected to retire not long after this case.

"Please?" I say, in a way I desperately hope is charming. "Just a couple of tiny questions? All embargoed until the end of the trial, obviously. And definitely, definitely off the record."

He says nothing, but he doesn't say no. He glances over my shoulder, at the door that says Rest Area.

"The coffee in there is horrible," I add.

He laughs, rolls his eyes. "Fine, you win," he mutters. "The coffee shop, round the back. Downstairs table. Fifteen minutes. Max."

In the end, he doesn't give away much, but it is enough to fill in some gaps. As I suspected, the police and prosecutors are incredibly nervous about this trial. The victim has already been vilified on social media, something DCI Carter believes has been led by friends of the defendants. He also thinks the boys and their wealthy families have been tacitly supporting this vile campaign against her—though it sounds like he doesn't have proof. There are even rumors of the boys' fathers offering substantial sums in return for any evidence against the victim.

Meanwhile, the girl has already had to have two new identities as a result of being named on the Internet. She has been moved away, for her own protection, to an area where she has no family support. Something he says makes me wonder if she has made an attempt on her own life.

"I'm trusting you to tread carefully here," he says firmly, jabbing a stirring stick into the remains of his coffee and swirling it around. "This is all for the end, and nothing came from me." He glances down at my notebook. "No quotes."

"I could just put 'a source close to the—'"

"No."

He is staring down into his coffee cup. I pause, wondering if I should push my luck. After a few moments, I slide him a sealed envelope, a letter I wrote last night.

"Is there any chance you could pass this to the victim?"

DCI Carter looks up, sees the envelope. He almost laughs.

"Katie, don't hold your breath."

"I know. But if there is any possibility. We would love to talk to her. You know. So she can tell us her side."

He sighs. I can imagine he's heard it before. All the same, he takes my letter, puts it into his jacket pocket. Then he wipes his mouth.

"Anyway. I need to get off." DCI Carter is getting to his feet.

I stand up. "Thanks so much. Can I have your card? Your . . . cell number maybe? Just in case there's, um, anything else?"

He rolls his eyes, reaches inside his jacket, and flicks out a card between two fingers. "Just for you." He fixes two pale blue eyes on me, taps the card against the table. "Not everyone in the bloody office. Got that?"

"Absolutely." I grin. "Thanks."

"And don't talk to me at court. I don't want the whole world on my case."

"Got it."

I feel the thickness of his card in my hands. He pulls his coat off the back of his chair, swings it over his broad shoulders.

"Thanks for talking to me," I hear myself babbling. "Really. I'm so grateful. And, you know. Good luck."

He stares at me. I wonder if I've said the wrong thing.

"I just mean—I know they aren't easy, these cases," I add quickly. "You don't always get the right result."

DCI Carter grimaces and rubs his palm against the back of his head, his hair flecked with gray.

"No, Katie," he says. "You don't."

Helen

IT IS STILL WARM for September, the leaves on the trees green and shimmering as I make my way across the park and through the quiet streets around Royal Hill. Rachel is sitting in the pub's outside area at a painted wooden table, the sort that are permanently damp with beer. Strings of white festoon lights trail in a canopy overhead.

When Rachel had asked if I want to meet again today, I'd decided it wouldn't be all that bad. I've nothing else planned. I wonder if I can persuade her against the pub this time, though. Perhaps we could have a glass of lemonade and then go for a walk up to the observatory, or shop for nursery things near the market. Something I can upcycle into an anecdote to drop into conversation with Serena and Rory, when we see them for dinner this weekend.

The pub is busy. When she sees me approach, she grins and motions that she is going to the bar for us, leaving her bag to save our place. I ease myself onto the wooden bench, extract a tissue from my bag to wipe down the surface.

As I wait for Rachel to return, my eyes drift over to the antiques shop opposite. It is selling huge, old-fashioned ship lights, mounted on teak and metal tripods. Some are set out on the pavement, hand-drawn price tags on brown cord hanging around their necks. Greenwich is full of strange objects like this, from a time when ships mattered in a way that is difficult to fathom. They are old collectors' items these days, their tarnished bronze, copper, and chrome just a fashionable design quirk. Serena has a light like this in her study, which I have admired before. I don't think I really like them, now that I look at them. They look a bit like spacecraft, their single alien eyes cocked at us from the other side of the road.

Rachel returns from the bar with an orange juice and lemonade for me and a pint of Guinness for herself.

"Full of minerals," she says. Then, after seeing my expression, she adds quickly: "I'll only have a few sips." She sets it down carelessly on the table. Foam spills out onto the already beer-soaked wood.

Clouds chase each other across the sky, the sun disappearing behind them, then appearing again. I close my eyes, feel the sunlight on my face. The warmth is dwindling now. We've missed the best part of the day. Still, I find myself happy to be out.

"So, what have you been up to, hon? Apart from practicing your breathing exercises." She sets her phone down on the table next to her pint. She sticks her little finger into the top of her Guinness and slops the finger full of froth into her mouth.

"Oh, this and that."

The truth is, I've been doing almost nothing. I've rattled pointlessly around the house, trying to think of jobs to do. I have sorted out all my bedroom drawers, made and frozen meals. I have read my baby books, tested the breast pump. I am painfully bored already. I've still got nearly three months.

I've tried to arrange things, but somehow it never seems to quite fit with people. None of my friends from the advertising firm I work for replied to my message asking if they fancied a coffee—despite saying how much they'd love to keep in touch. I know their lives are full of meetings, work drinks, conferences—things I stopped being invited to almost as soon as my bump started to show. Then there's Katie, who is always busy at the newspaper. Serena is away. And I'd even considered contacting my little brother, Charlie. It would be good to use this time to try to reconnect. But then I thought about how much of a hassle it would be, getting the train all the way over to Hackney. Also, Charlie is basically nocturnal—he works as a DJ, which he insists is actually a real job—and tends to be asleep until three in the afternoon, when he goes to collect his daughter, Ruby, from school. The only person who always seems to be free is Rachel.

She is patting at her denim jacket now—first the breast pockets, then the hips, as if giving herself an airport security check. It takes me a moment to realize she is looking for a packet of cigarettes. She pulls out the packet, plus a plastic lighter. The lighter is adorned with a green cannabis leaf design on one side and a cartoon portrait of Bob Marley on the other. As she flicks the yellow-blue flame to life between her thumb and knuckle, she gives me a sideways glance. I try and arrange my features into a fixed expression, but even so I feel my eyes dart left and right, hoping no one from the office walks past.

"Oh God, I know I shouldn't," she says, seeing my face, waving the unlit cigarette between us. "Honestly, I've cut down loads. I'll be off them soon, definitely. So fucking hard when you're in a pub, though, you know?"

She lights it, cupping her small fingers around the flame, then takes a deep drag, before blowing a trail of smoke sideways away from me, contorting her face to one side as she does so. Even so, I lean away a little.

"You ever smoked?"

"No."

She closes her eyes, nods. "Clever girl." She takes another deep inhale.

The man from the antiques shop is packing up the ship lights from the pavement outside, their chrome eyelids closing. They clank against each other as he heaves them through his door. In the distance I can hear the church chimes of St. Alfege's, the rustle of the trees along the faraway edge of the park. The sun has disappeared behind a thick cloak of cloud. I pull my cardigan tighter around myself.

I watch Rachel as she smokes, eyelids down. Suddenly, she snaps her eyes open, like a doll. "So," she says. "Tell me more about Rory and Serena." She says the names Rory and Serena as if they are a single word, or the name of a TV show.

"Well, Rory works with Daniel, like I told you," I begin. "You might have seen their new development—it's the big glass building right on the river, past the Trafalgar Arms?" I gesture down the hill, past the market, toward the river—pointlessly, since you can't see it from here.

This is the development that the papers hate. A massive redevelopment scheme, the demolition of loads of old social housing to make way for luxury flats. As well as the sniping about it in the *Evening Standard*, there have even been pieces in the *Guardian* and the local papers— mutterings about social cleansing, foreign money. The "keep London shit brigade," as Rory calls them.

There was even talk of a protest at one stage—Lisa, the secretary, apparently saw something on Twitter or Facebook. She printed it out, placed it on Daniel's desk, without comment. A march against gentrification, they called it. "Anarchists and weirdos," Rory had muttered. Still, they'd had to tell the client. Now there's more security around the site; big bull-necked blokes in black polo shirts patrol the perimeter like nightclub bouncers, walkie-talkies crackling at their hips.

"And what about her? Serena? She's a photographer, right?" Rachel exhales, releasing another plume of smoke. The sun slips behind the clouds.

I frown. Did I tell Rachel that Serena was a photographer? I must have, though I don't remember it. "Yes," I say slowly. "She is. It has been a lifelong passion for her." I blush, realize I'm directly quoting the line from Serena's website. Rachel won't know that, I tell myself. "She has her own studio, on the other side of the park."

Rachel nods, as if considering this. "And Rory. Is he excited about their baby and everything?"

The question catches me off guard—I had been concentrating on staying out of the way of her smoke. I put my glass down, unsure how to answer. Of course he's excited about their baby. What does she mean?

"I mean, you know"—Rachel twirls the cigarette around in the air— "you were saying the other day that Daniel was being super supportive with making all the furniture, and getting really emotional at the scans and everything." She starts turning her lighter sideways and upright, then sideways again, like a Tetris piece that won't fit. "Is he the same? Rory?"

"I think they are both delighted."

Rachel is gazing downward now, into the creamy surface of her Guinness glass, tapping her cigarette rhythmically against the edge of the silver ashtray. She looks lost in thought. I wonder if she is thinking about the father of her own baby. But before I work out how to frame the question, she takes her sunglasses off and speaks as if she has read my mind.

"It wasn't just a casual fuck or anything, you know." She tilts her chin up, squinting into the sun, so she can look me in the eye.

"Oh, I didn't . . . I hadn't assumed . . ."

"Yeah, well," she says gruffly, casting her gaze down again. "I did love the guy. The dad. It just, you know. Didn't work out."

She brings her cigarette to her lips and takes another long inhale, spreads her fingers with her bitten fingernails out on the table. She starts again with the lighter, tapping it onto its base, then its side, then its base again. Her eyes seem to pinken a little, her pale fingers tense.

"Are you all right?"

"Yeah, fine," she mutters. "Sorry."

Unsure what to do, I place one of my hands over hers. She stares at my hand, and for a moment I wonder if the gesture was too intimate. It is the sort of thing I can misjudge. But then she looks up and smiles, her eyes looking slightly wet.

"Cheers, Helen."

I smile awkwardly, though I'm not sure what she is thanking me for. She doesn't say anything more. I feel my curiosity growing like an itch, a buzzing in my ear that won't be batted away.

"Do you mind if I . . . ask what happened?"

Rachel pulls her hand out from under mine and starts fiddling with her phone.

"Oh, you know. We met at work. I was working at a music venue. Behind the bar." She shrugs. "Anyway. We liked each other. I didn't mean to get pregnant. Obviously. Who does, right?" She laughs. I try to force my face to smile, even as I feel my jaw tighten, my leg start to tremble slightly under the pub table.

"I did want it to be something more. But after I got pregnant, I found out . . ." She rubs her thumb against her index finger, as if sifting for the right words. "Well. He already belonged to someone else."

I nod, hoping my face is sympathetic. I mean it to be. I know she's not the first to have an affair with someone who is taken. I try to affect a casual voice.

"How did he react? When you told him about the baby?"

Rachel smiles sadly. "He doesn't know." She sighs, tapping her nearly finished cigarette and pushing her pint of Guinness away. "I haven't seen him in a while. I just . . . thought maybe it was better to leave it."

I hesitate. "Don't you think you should tell him?"

She looks at me, seriously. Then nods, slowly.

"I probably should." Abruptly, her expression lightens. "Thanks, Helen," she says. "You know. For not judging." She takes a final drag of her cigarette, her lips pursed tightly. "Means a lot." She breathes smokily, closing her eyes again, stubbing it out. "A lot."

I force a smile. "Don't be silly." I try not to think about the fact that actually, I was judging her a bit.

When I get home that night, I see Daniel's sneakers on the dust-covers in the hallway, where the builders have been traipsing in and out with drills and spades, preparing for the basement dig. Normally it would annoy me—how many times have I asked him to put them away?—but tonight, instead of being cross about it, I think again how lucky I am not to be Rachel. How grateful I should be to have a loving husband. Imagine being pregnant and going home to an empty house. The thought makes me shudder.

I put Daniel's shoes in the cupboard under the stairs and head into the kitchen, rolling up my sleeves. I prepare some fish and roast vegetables for dinner. While they are cooking, the landline rings. I wipe my hands and snatch up the phone, wedging it between my ear and shoulder.

"Hello?"

There's silence for a few seconds, the click of the connection. Then a voice, sounding far away.

"Mrs. Thorpe, hello. I'm just calling with regards to your refinance. Are you OK to go through a few things now, or should I call back?"

"I'm sorry?"

"The refinance on your property. We're just putting the final details together for the application."

I frown. Refinance? Then the line crackles lightly. There is a delay. It's obviously some dodgy call center somewhere. I know these calls all too well.

"I'm sorry," I tell her coldly. "You must have the wrong number. There's no refinance application."

"Mrs. Thorpe . . . "

I hang up, shaking my head, putting the handset back. Ever since Mummy and Daddy died, we've had loads like this. Scammers, trying to trick us into giving away details. I think poor old Mummy had gotten herself onto some database—suckers' lists, they call them. She was forever answering the phone to people. Daniel thinks we should just get the landline disconnected.

I wash up and put away all the dishes, clean the counters until they are gleaming, and set the table. I mop the floor, the water in the bucket turning black with building dust. But when it's done, I feel better. I tip the dirty water away on the patio outside, put some music on, and open the windows to air out the house.

But the light drains from the sky, the windows darken, and Daniel is still not home. I check my messages. He is working late again. I think about calling Katie, asking if she feels like coming over. But the food is ready now, and she lives miles away. And anyway, she is probably busy with Charlie. I take a fork from the table and eat my dinner alone, picking the flakes of white fish from the bones.

29 WEEKS

Serena

"I CAN'T REMEMBER A summer like it," Helen is saying. "I can't believe how warm it was today!"

We are sitting outside, the four of us. The air is cooler now, but it is still warm enough for outdoors, just about. Only a slight breeze blows, though it's usually windy on this side of the park. The baby in my belly is snug and still, lulled by the rock of my hammock.

Rory is piling logs in the outside fireplace. He is kneeling as if in prayer, his hair flopping into his face. Daniel and Helen are sitting together in the swing seat. I have put candles in glass storm lanterns, twisted strings of fairy lights through the branches of the cherry tree. The wooden decking glows silvery in the light. I must remember to take a picture for Instagram.

"Well, I'm loving the heat. Can't get enough of it," Rory tells her.

"Yes, well, you're not pregnant." Helen shifts in the swing seat. She is wearing an ankle-length dress with a flower pattern: it covers her enormous belly like a tent. She is so much bigger than me already. Her hands rest on top of her bump, fingers spread, pale and fat as starfish. "I'm fed up with it," Helen is saying. "We need a bit of rain. Have you seen Greenwich Park? The grass is all dead and yellow."

"It will grow back, Helen," Rory mutters. "You're being dramatic."

I place a cool hand on his shoulder to silence him.

"We've got a few more warm days at least, I heard," I say. "Chilly in the evenings now, though, isn't it? Do you want a blanket or anything, Helen?"

Rory tuts and rolls his eyes. "Of course she doesn't need a blanket! For God's sake. When is it ever warm enough to sit outside in the evenings in this bloody country? Let's enjoy it!" He says it as if the rest of us are stopping him from doing so.

Crossly, he picks up the kindling for the fire, turns to face me. "Do we really need this on?"

"Yes," I tell him. "It's atmospheric. Besides, your sister is cold."

At this, Daniel looks up, blinks at me through his glasses, as if he had been asleep, and I have just woken him. Next to Helen's outsized form, Daniel looks insubstantial somehow, his trousers and shirt crumpling where he fails to fill them out. He turns to his wife.

"Are you cold, Helen?"

Helen says she is fine, but pulls her gray cardigan closer, like a life jacket. Daniel starts to take his jacket off, and I motion to him to leave it on.

"Don't worry, I'll fetch you a blanket," I tell her. I pull myself up out of the hammock and head to the kitchen. There, after a backward glance at Rory, I slide the laptop out from under the papers on the table where I put it when he came in earlier. Positioning myself so I can't be seen, I delete the search history. It only takes a second.

I look back at the three of them, through the French doors. From inside the house, the veranda looks like a little raft on a calm, dark sea. Behind the swing seat, the scattered lights of the city blink and flicker, like a civilization on a faraway shore. Sometimes Greenwich can feel a long way from anywhere.

It was Rory who wanted to live on Maze Hill. Our house is the one with the huge sycamore tree. Rory loves to point out the blue plaque on the house next door, tell people about the famous architect who once lived there. From the way he tells the story, you can tell he wants a plaque like that on our house, too, one day, talking about him.

I don't care about the plaque, but I love the view from the balcony in our top bedroom. You can see the whole city stretched out like a silver platter, the cranes against the metal sky, dotted with red lights. The shot-silk sunsets, the leaden shimmer of the Thames. I was up there earlier, trying to take a photograph for Instagram. But I can never get it quite right—the low light makes the sky seem duller, the little lights bleed into one another.

I pick up the cashmere blanket and step outside, closing the doors behind me carefully. I step over Daniel's legs to reach Helen. He hardly seems to notice. He is eating a handful of pistachios, without much apparent pleasure. He holds them in his lap in one cupped hand, using the other to rub off the shells before transferring them mechanically, one by one, into his mouth, staring expressionless into the distance.

"At least it's due to get cooler now," Helen is saying. "It was so hot in the park the other day, when I was going to meet Rachel, that I had to stop and sit down in the memorial garden. I thought I was going to faint!"

I'm almost as far gone as Helen is, but I just don't seem to be experiencing the same thing at all—this heaviness she talks about, this loss of energy. I feel charged, fortified by the baby. I love to feel her, sitting firm under my clothes, snug as a weapon. She feels powerful to me, her kicking feet, her racing heart. I feel stronger and stronger, suffused with her energy. She floods me with blood. I can feel myself growing new tissues. I walk and walk, my headphones in. My libido is high. I can feel my small breasts are swelling, my hair thickening. The muscles in my legs growing hard and firm.

Helen and Daniel live at the bottom of the park, in the house she and Rory grew up in. That was the deal, when their parents died: the company went to Rory, Helen got the house, and Charlie retains a small slice of each, and got the rest of his inheritance in cash—cash that, word has it, he has mostly squandered.

When people admire Helen's house, as they often do, Helen always tells them that Daniel only married her so he could get his grubby architect's hands on it. She is joking, of course. She always squeezes his hand as she says it, I have noticed, and he always smiles fondly back at her. And yet I have sometimes wondered whether there is a scratchy little grain of truth in there somewhere. Not much, but enough to make Helen's little joke not very funny.

"It was packed in the park when I was there the other day with Rachel," Helen is saying now. Rachel has been mentioned twice now. I haven't heard her mention a Rachel before, and the statement feels designed to entice me to ask who she is, but somehow I can't bring myself to bite. Helen tries another line of attack.

"It always gets me thinking of summers in Cambridge, when the park is full like that," she says. "You know, all the picnics everywhere. Everyone sitting on the grass."

"I thought the grass was all dead," Rory mutters.

"Not all of it," Helen mumbles, stung by the sharpness in his tone.

We left Cambridge ten years ago. Yet Helen seems to lean on the memory of those summer days like a crutch. I don't know why she must talk about it so endlessly, why it seems to matter so much more to her than it does to us.

"God, it doesn't feel like ten years ago, does it?" Helen sighs wistfully. She prods at her brother. "Do you remember the time you stole that punt?"

Rory throws a final log into the fire pit, then hauls himself up, brushing his hands on his jeans.

"Borrowed," he corrects. "And I think you'll find Daniel here was my accomplice." Rory slaps Daniel on the shoulder as he passes to sit back in his seat. Daniel's blank expression is unchanged.

"I don't remember," Daniel says after a pause, throwing the last of his shells into the bowl. "We went punting loads of times." The fire crackles in the silence.

I study Daniel's face. This is an odd thing to say. It's not unusual for Helen to remember things that some of us don't. All kinds of flotsam seem to live in her memory. She embroiders things a bit sometimes, too, adding all sorts of pretty details that weren't there before. But Daniel remembers that day, I'm sure of it. It had been like one of those perfect summer days—so perfect that you can't be sure whether you trust your own memory, or whether you've mixed it up with a photo, or a film, and made the colors more brilliant than they really were.

The boys had snuck the college punt out of the boathouse—we

weren't supposed to use it, for some reason I can't remember. A surprise, they said. After weeks in the silence and stale air of libraries and examination halls, it had been intoxicating to be drifting underneath a luminous blue sky. The smell of the grass on the banks, the *sock sock sock* of the punt hitting the riverbed, the reflections in the water. The boys had taken turns punting while Helen and I swigged from a bottle of cheap fizz they'd bought at the college bar. For Helen and me, finals were over, and Rory and Daniel had a long summer ahead before their MA year began. Life after university felt like a distant speck on the horizon, with all the time in between just a vast, delicious expanse of summertime.

Sun soaked and tipsy, we'd laughed at Daniel's skinny legs, at Rory getting so distracted posing with his shirt off that he forgot to duck at the bridge and nearly fell in. Then he did fall in, and got back on the punt, and pushed Daniel in, and then Rory had taken his clothes off—he was always taking his clothes off. Finally, we all got in, clothes abandoned. Even Helen. Giddy and drunk, we'd raced each other down the river. Rory had swum underneath Helen, picked her up on his shoulders, her mouth a little wet O of surprise. *Rory! Put me down! I thought you were Daniel,* she had screamed. We'd watched her from the other side. The water had been dark and cool. You couldn't always tell.

When we got back to the halls that day, it had been later than we'd realized. My skin was still clammy and cold from the river water. My hair had been bleached by the sun; even Helen had colored. We hadn't bothered changing. Little constellations of freckles had appeared on Helen's cheeks and I remember seeing Daniel kissing them, in the line for the club. It had seemed intimate, so much so that it made me look away, gave me a strange feeling. I remember how I couldn't wait a minute longer for Rory that night, that we'd collapsed into his single bed, a hot tangle of limbs. His sweat had tasted sharp and sweet, his body different then, hardened by hockey and squash. I still remember the feel of his arms, the weight of him. When we finally fell asleep, his arm underneath my neck, light had been leaking in through the sides of the curtains, the beginnings of birdsong stirring.

"You must remember, Daniel." Helen seems upset. She searches Daniel's face for signs of recognition. But he looks at her for a moment as if she is someone he has never met before. He shrugs, looks down. The flames from the fire pit dance on his face, sharpening the shadows under his eyes, the ridge of his brow.

"I'm sorry we bailed on the prenatal classes, Helen," I say. "I hope you don't mind me switching to those other ones. They're a bit nearer to here."

Helen smiles weakly. "Oh no, don't worry about it."

I suspect a better explanation is demanded. Not having one to hand, I decide to change the subject. "Shall we eat?"

Rory sits down at the table, starts filling glasses. It is our practiced routine: he does drinks, I do food. Helen reaches out two hands for Daniel to haul her out of the swing seat. Daniel does it effortlessly with the wiry strength he has, a strength that his slim body hides. Daniel won medals for gymnastics when he was at school. He showed us once how he can support his entire body aloft with just his wrists, the sinews in his forearms straining. He held himself like that for over a minute on the pommel horse in the university gym, his torso as flat as a pencil, his face a blank oval of control. When he takes his glasses off, Daniel looks like a completely different person.

"So," I say. "How have they been anyway? The classes? Are you finding them useful?"

It's true that I had agreed to do this course with her, that I'd let her book it and get all excited, when in all honesty, I couldn't imagine anything worse. Sitting in a hot room with her, Daniel, and Rory. All that talk of stretching, bleeding, pushing, cutting. I had also completely forgotten about it until the day itself. Helen seemed to think we'd had a letter or something, but I don't remember it. By the time I saw the reminder on my calendar, I'd made other plans.

"They haven't been that great, really." Helen is watching me carefully. She has registered my lack of enthusiasm and tempered her own accordingly. "Actually, they're pretty boring. And it's been boiling hot in the room where they hold them. Awful! So stuffy. You haven't missed any-thing." She takes a sip of her water. "Daniel hasn't managed to make it to any of them yet, either." She looks accusingly at Rory. "But I suppose someone has to hold the fort at work, with all this uncertainty over the project."

Neither Daniel nor Rory reacts to Helen's remark. Sometimes I think they simply don't listen when she talks. I sense danger, reach over to pour more wine. I watch it wash around the sides of the fishbowl wineglasses. I can almost taste it, feel it whizzing into my bloodstream, sending the baby somersaulting dizzily in utero. But I glance at Helen and decide to refrain.

I often find myself wishing Helen wouldn't be such a stickler for the rules. At least, I wish she wouldn't make such a song and dance about it, leaning over in restaurants to make sure the waiter can hear her tell him she's pregnant, as if the poor bloke doesn't have eyes in his head. It's not her fault, of course. She has reason not to trust her own body. It has let her down before. This time, she is taking no chances. I think she believes that if she follows the rules, she can make a bargain that way. With God, the universe. Whoever. If she follows the rules, the rules will keep her baby safe.

I had been planning to make a toast to the babies. But as soon as I fill his glass, Daniel brings it straight to his mouth, draining nearly half the wine in one go. For a few moments there is quiet, just the scrape of silver-ware against dinner plates, the snap of the fire, the faint sound of music from a party in one of the other gardens on the hill. The candles flicker darkly in the smoked-glass lanterns.

I glance at Rory. He is sipping his wine, cheerfully piling mouthfuls of tart and salad onto his fork. I kick him under the table. He looks at me blankly. I glare at him.

"This is lovely, darling," he says loudly.

There is a murmur of assent.

"It's super easy. Loads more if you want it."

It is cooler now—perhaps eating outdoors was a mistake. But no one mentions the temperature. No one is saying anything at all. The evening feels like it has blown off course. I wonder how to steer it back. I glare at Rory again until he catches my eye.

Rory looks up, flicking his head straight and pressing his hands on the table, as if the conversation is only just beginning, now that he has started to pay attention to it.

"So. I hope you guys are coming to my little birthday dinner?"

I sigh. The birthday dinner is going to be anything but little. He just keeps inviting people. I think Rory thinks that things like dinners just happen on their own. But then, I suppose, why wouldn't he?

"Oh, definitely," says Helen, looking up and beaming. "We're looking forward to it."

"Good." Rory beams back. "I saw our baby brother the other day, Helen. Asked him to come along, too."

Helen pauses for a moment, her cutlery midair.

"You saw Charlie?"

"Yeah, we thought we'd try going to one of these DJ nights he's always inviting us to. It was rather fun, wasn't it, darling?"

Helen raises her eyebrows and looks at me.

"Yes, they dragged me along, too." I smile. Roll my eyes in exaggerated forbearance. Hopefully Helen won't be too cross that none of us mentioned it to her. She'd have hated it, but she also hates to be left out.

"Yeah, we took the client," Rory is saying. "It was great, actually. Wasn't it, Daniel?"

Daniel shrugs. Helen is frowning—she obviously wasn't told about this outing, much less invited. In any case, she always seems uncomfortable when anyone mentions Charlie. I don't think she can understand why, when he is nearly thirty, her little brother is still living in some sort of run-down apartment in Hackney, working as a DJ in a club the authorities have repeatedly threatened to shut down.

He's a bit of a hopeless case, really, Charlie. A few years ago, he casually fathered a daughter with some Swedish girl whose name I can't remember. Then, last year, there was some trouble with the police—

drugs, I think it was. I seem to remember Helen had to bail him out. I'm not sure of the details.

Now apparently he and Katie are back together. I wonder how Helen feels about that. She hasn't mentioned Katie in a while.

"Oh well. It'll be nice to see Charlie." Helen laughs hesitantly.

I fix my face in an expression of equanimity. "How's Katie doing these days?"

Helen frowns. "Actually, I haven't seen her much lately," she says. I glance at Helen's pained expression. It sounds like she and Katie have had some sort of falling-out.

"I imagine she must be busy with her work," I say. Katie is a journalist on a national newspaper—not a particularly upmarket one. She never tires of telling us all how busy she is.

"Yes. She has been busy, I think." Helen nods. "She's up in Cambridge, covering that awful court case with the—" Helen stops, blushes. "Well. I'm sure we've all read about it."

There is an exchange of grimaces. I drop my fork, pick up my napkin, and press it to my mouth. Trust Katie to introduce inedible thoughts into a pleasant evening, even when she's not actually invited.

All of us know the case Helen means—there has been little else in the papers this week. The two accused of rape are both former public schoolboys, and—to add extra tabloid appeal—one is the son of a former Cabinet minister, and the other the son of some earl or other. The victim was young, a drunken eighteen-year-old student, in her first week at the university. There has been blanket coverage, with the boys' families and their privileged upbringings referenced endlessly. Their parents have been photographed daily on the steps of the court, their mothers' eyes haunted, their fathers' faces a picture of blank devastation. I'm sure I'm not the only person at the table who is already sick of hearing about it.

"Weird, isn't it?" Helen says carefully. "How . . . similar it all sounds."

For a moment, no one speaks. I glance at Daniel. He is staring at Rory.

Rory clears his throat. "More drinks, anyone? Another soft drink, Helen?"

"Let me get them," Helen says. "I need to go to the bathroom anyway." She hauls herself up with an effort. Daniel is gazing into space, barely seeming to notice. Rory reaches to help her.

"Thanks," Helen mutters.

I smile at Rory, pleased he has changed the subject, that he is looking after Helen. He stands, winks at me, takes my glass, and follows Helen into the kitchen.

"Have you fed Cleo, darling?" Rory calls back at me from the kitchen.

"Oh no," I say. "Sorry."

Moments later, I hear the clatter of kibble as Rory feeds the cat. The baby in my belly starts to stir, landing a single hard kick under my rib cage. I shift in my chair and gaze at the twitching bump, feel the living wonder of it. I put my hands to the necklace around my neck and feel the cool silver charm between my fingertips, sliding it slowly up and down the chain.

Helen

I AM IN RORY and Serena's bathroom. I've been here longer than I should. Everyone is outside, waiting. I can't take as long as I'd like. I settle for a condensed version of the usual routine.

First, I dust a little of Serena's face powder—middle drawer—on my cheeks. Then I spread on a thick layer of her hand cream from the silver tube—top left drawer. I coat it on until my hands are slippery, right up to my wrists. It doesn't take long to sink in. Then I start opening cupboards. I breathe in the scent of her shampoo, read the prescription labels on her medications, smell her towels, pull the brushes out of her nail polishes to admire the colors in the light.

The lights in the bathroom are turned down, and Serena has set two candles flickering by the sink. I make a mental note to find the same ones for when our new bathroom is finished. On a driftwood shelf, I notice something I haven't seen here before: a collection of bath oils in old apothecary bottles. Twigs of lavender in one, an unfurling hibiscus flower in another.

I decide to try only the tallest bottle. It has a sprig of rosemary inside, the length of a cat's tail. I pull out the glass stopper, close my eyes, and drink in the smell.

As I do, the bottle stopper slips from my grasp. It falls with a clang against the bathroom tiles, the noise echoing around the walls. I look down just in time to see it roll under the legs of the bathroom cabinet.

"Are you all right in there, Helen?"

It's Serena's voice. "Just a second," I call back, glancing toward the frosted glass of the door. I bend down on all fours, my huge belly skimming the cold tiled floor. I feel the dust on my fingers as they close around the bottle top. I replace it, wash the dust off my hands, and open the drawers to make sure everything is back where it was. As I replace the powder case, my hand brushes against something—a piece of paper, tucked right at the back of the drawer.

I pull it out to examine it. It is one of those tiny envelopes—the ones you might find pinned in a bouquet of flowers, or with a receipt inside from an expensive shop. The envelope is a dark red, and it bears three letters: RRH. Rory's initials: Rory Richard Haverstock.

It looks like some sort of love note. Something from Serena? Even as I hesitate, I know I'm going to open it. I'm already anticipating the heady thrill of discovering a detail of Serena's intimate life. I hear Serena's laughter outside, and it makes me hurry, pushing a fingernail inside. A note on thick, cream card.

> *Darling RRH*
> *Wear to show me*
> *Evermore*
> *W*

I frown. The handwriting doesn't look anything like Serena's. And when I read the last initial, my stomach lurches. W?

I have a sickening sense that I have found something I wasn't supposed to see, something bad. Is it is a love note to Rory? What does it mean—*to show me*? Show me what? And who is W?

My stomach tightens. I stuff the note back into the envelope, hide it in my bra. Decide to think about it later.

When I go back out onto the terrace, the plates have been cleared away, and Serena and Rory are in the swing seat, snuggled up under the blanket. Serena's little bump is as neat and round as a melon under her silk top. Silver twinkles in her ears, on her wrists, around her neck. I watch the two of them, as she smiles at me and buries her face in Rory's sweater. Rory's hand plays with the golden strands of her hair. Daniel is sitting on another chair. There is no room for me.

I perch on the stool next to Serena.

"We can scoot up." She unfolds her legs.

"No, don't, I'm fine."

Serena sits up anyway, lifting Rory's arm from around her neck. As she does so her necklace swings forward, a tiny figurine dangling on the end.

"Lovely necklace," I tell her. "What's that charm—a little dog?"

"Think so," she says absentmindedly. She leans in toward me, puts a cool hand on my arm. "Is everything all right with Katie? You haven't fallen out, have you?"

"What? With Katie? No, nothing like that," I say. "I think she's just been busy with work." Something about the way Serena asks the question does make me wonder, though. Has Katie been a bit off with me lately? Is it odd that we haven't seen each other in so long? "I'm seeing her soon," I add. "She's got a day off, so we're having lunch."

Serena smiles. "Good."

"You'll have to take a day off from your new best friend."

I turn, realizing Daniel is talking to me. Everyone stares at him. It occurs to me he has barely spoken all evening.

"Who's that?" Serena says.

I wish I hadn't told Daniel about Rachel now, in the beginning, before I got to know her better. I wish I hadn't gone on quite so much about her drinking, her smoking, her phone case, her clothes, her loud voice. Now that we are here, it feels important to me to make it clear that I was fine at the prenatal course, on my own—that I coped perfectly well, without them all, and made a nice, normal friend.

"He's being silly," I tell Serena, feeling my face redden. "It's just someone I met at the NCT class."

"Oh, is that the girl you mentioned? Rachel? What's she like?"

Daniel snorts. I stare at him.

"What, Daniel?"

"I didn't say anything!"

"You haven't even met her."

Daniel touches his glasses, as if adjusting them so he can see me properly. "Hang on," he says. "I'm only going by what you told me. I thought you said she was a bit extreme."

"I didn't say that," I say shortly, though it's entirely possible I did. "I didn't say that at all, Daniel. I like her." I turn to Serena. "Daniel is just annoyed because the other day she came over and—"

"Turned all our sofas upside down," Daniel finishes. Rory laughs. Serena shoots me a quizzical look.

I pause, grasping for an explanation that Serena would understand, that would make Rachel sound like her sort of person.

"We were making space for . . . yoga," I say, improvising.

It was the first time I'd invited Rachel back to the house.

"This is us," I'd said.

"What— All of it?"

She'd let out a low whistle as she'd shrugged off her denim jacket, walking around with her head tilted back, gawping at the chandeliers. "Bloody hell, it's amazing." I couldn't help enjoying it just a little. I led her into the kitchen, started to fill the kettle.

"Have you ever checked to see if there's any gold under the floorboards?"

I turned the tap off, thinking I'd misheard over the sound of the water. "Have I what, sorry?"

"Checked for gold, under the floorboards. Loads have got it, the houses this side of the park."

I set the kettle back. I couldn't tell if she was pulling my leg. I've been told I'm terribly gullible about things like this.

"You really haven't heard this story?"

I shook my head.

She hopped onto a stool, gestured up to the ceiling rose, squinting. "Back when these houses were built, it was all these wealthy merchants living in them." She spun a pointed finger around at the windows. "People were always traveling back and forth over the park with gold, jewels, money, cloth, all that sort of stuff."

She paused. Narrowed her eyes a little.

"But on the other side of the park, Blackheath—that's where the robbers were. The road to Woolwich was safe—it had these big, high walls—no highwaymen. But sometimes you couldn't avoid Blackheath. And the robbers were merciless."

She glanced out of the window, as if making sure none of them were watching us from the rosebushes.

"There's all these stories about it—how they'd tear the jewels from the throats of women, take an axe to a carriage if they thought there were gold coins inside. They'd slash at the harnesses so they could steal your horses and ride away. No one could hear you there. If you screamed."

I tried to laugh, to show Rachel that I wasn't taking it seriously, but I found I wanted to hear the rest, even if I didn't believe her.

"What the royal household didn't know," she went on, spooning sugar into her tea, "was that the wealthy merchants of Greenwich were in league with the robbers on Blackheath. That's why they got away with it all. The merchants protected them—and in return, they always took a share of the gold. Of course, they'd be hanged if the king found out, so they hid it in these houses. Usually under the floorboards. Honestly! I read all about it somewhere." She stared at me. "I seriously can't believe you haven't heard these stories. So many people round here have found stuff in their houses—jewelery, antiques, all sorts of stuff. A fortune, sometimes."

I thought for a moment. Did it ring a bell somewhere? Mummy saying something once, about some people down the road, finding a hoard of old coins?

"Maybe," I said uncertainly.

Rachel shrugged, threw me a wolfish grin. "You don't want to look now?"

I find myself blushing at the memory of it. How I'd pointed Rachel to places upstairs—away from the building work—where the floorboards might be loose. How I'd pulled up Mummy's rug, turned the sofa over, both of us giddily intoxicated with the idea of finding hidden treasure. Rachel was so convinced—she'd insisted on looking for loose floorboards in the bedrooms, in the bathroom, all over the house. But of course, we didn't find any that would come up on their own, and we couldn't work out how we'd get them up without making a huge mess, so we didn't bother in the end. Rachel seemed to lose interest in us having coffee after that. By the time Daniel got home, she was gone, and I hadn't had the energy to put the furniture back.

"She sounds perfectly normal to me, Helen," Serena says loyally, casting a wry look at Daniel. "I'm glad you met someone nice." She is so good at this: smoothing things out, like wrinkles in a tablecloth. Daniel smiles at her, then turns to me, speaks more gently.

"I wasn't annoyed. I was just a bit surprised about the furniture." He is slurring his words slightly, which makes me even more cross.

"The sofa thing was one time," I hiss at him. "I don't know why you keep going on about it."

"Oh, relax, Helen," he says quietly. "I'm teasing." But the anger is gathering in my throat, and somehow I can't let it drop.

"It's not as if our living room is a very pleasant place to be. Moving the sofa was hardly going to make much of a difference."

"Oh, here we go," says Daniel. He is cross now, too. "The remodeling work. All my fault."

"I didn't say that."

"It's all you ever say."

Our words jab back and forth at each other, and Rory and Serena start to avert their eyes from us, sitting in a tactful silence. I realize, to my mortification, that I have seen them do this before, when forced to witness one of our marital spats.

I hold my tongue, determined not to let it escalate. Only when the heat dissipates do I risk a glance over the table. Daniel has filled his glass again, then pretends to study the label on the wine bottle. When I catch Serena's eye, I grimace, mouth "sorry" at her. She furrows her brow in a "don't be silly" gesture, shakes her head, telling me not to worry. Fills up our water glasses, and Rory's.

Later that night, Daniel passes out drunkenly on the bed, his eyes closed over flitting eyeballs. Soon he is making the little whistling breathing noise that means he is sleeping deeply. His glasses sit on his bedside table on top of his pile of books, as if keeping watch. Without his glasses on, Daniel's sleeping face looks untethered, incomplete, sort of like a child's drawing.

I unfold the note I found in the bathroom. I press out the creases with my thumbnail, and stare at it for a long time. RRH. I wonder if W could be a nickname for Serena? But somehow, I know that's not it. I have found something bad, something I shouldn't have ever seen. Oh, Rory, I think. What are you up to?

I stare and stare until the letters start to swim in front of my eyes, until they are not like letters anymore, just shapes, symbols. Eventually I give up. I slide the note into the back of the book I'm reading, turn the bedside light out.

I listen to Daniel's breathing, deep, rhythmic. I listen to the little bursts of laughter in the night, the hum of the washing machine on downstairs, the wind blowing on the hill, how it whistles past our window glass. It takes me a long time to fall asleep.

30 WEEKS

Helen

I SEEM TO BE bumping into Rachel all the time—in the market, or at the bandstand cafe, or walking across the scorched grass of the park. I suppose it's no great surprise. She lives locally, and we're both off work. But I never bump into Serena that much. Or Rory. Or even Daniel. But then, I suppose I have never been off work before. I'm constantly surprised by how many people are around in the day. What are they all doing?

This time is odd in itself, this strange no-man's-land between pregnancy and birth. I find myself constructing my entire day around a medical appointment, a trip into town to buy a baby monitor or a TENS machine. On the Tube, everyone else is glued to their smartphone, emailing and messaging, organizing fuller lives than mine. Quite often no one looks up to see whether there is a pregnant woman needing a seat. I always feel too embarrassed to ask. Everyone keeps telling me to make the most of the time, to enjoy myself. I'm not sure what they mean. It feels like a dead time to me. A time defined by absence, by waiting.

When I finally manage to set a date for lunch with Katie, I find myself looking forward to it much more than I normally would, a little bright flag in my otherwise blank calendar. Even so, I find myself a bit jangly on the morning of it for some reason.

As I walk to the station, I wonder whether to tell Katie about the note I found in Rory and Serena's bathroom. Katie is good at digging around, finding information. She'd be able to work out what Rory was up to.

I see Katie coming out of the station in her leather jacket, her headphones in, a coffee cup clutched in one hand and a faraway expression on her face. Katie is only eighteen months younger than me—the same age as Charlie. She was his little friend from down the road when we were growing up, and then she became mine, as the gap grew to feel less and less important in our teenage years, then university and beyond.

But looking at her now I have the sudden sense that she is much younger than me again. After all, there is so much more than a year and a half separating our ages—a marriage, a house, the babies, the pregnancy. Looking at her now, I feel old.

I wave and her face breaks into an astonished smile. She bounds over and hugs me.

"Jesus, Helen. You're huge!"

"Oh, thanks!"

"Sorry, I didn't mean it like that. You look great. It's just . . . I suppose it's been a while, hasn't it?"

The observation feels heavier than it should. I try to meet her eye and smile, to tell her it's all right. She smiles back, a look of relief on her face.

"Come on, let's go," she says. "I'm starving."

We walk through the park, where the giant horse chestnut trees are just starting to shed. An early smattering of golden leaves have sailed out of the iron gates and onto the pavements, collecting in rusty pools in drains and doorways. Some people are sitting on the outside tables at the pavilion, bathing in the disappearing warmth. They sit in coats, but with their faces to the sun, eyelids closed, enjoying every last drop. A waitress weaves around them, clearing the tables, balancing coffee cups and crumb-strewn plates on her tray, her pale gray apron tied in a little bow at her waist.

The inside looks full. I ask, but the waiter shakes his head. No tables free. Do we want to wait? Katie says she doesn't mind. My feet are hurting, my stomach starting to groan. I cast my eye over the inside tables, try to work out if anyone will be leaving soon.

When I see her, my first instinct is to quickly avert my eyes, pretend I haven't. But it is already too late: our eyes have met, and Rachel is grinning at us. She is sitting by the window, a newspaper spread out in front of her. She starts waving frantically.

"You again!" Rachel folds the newspaper and rushes over, still carrying it, bumping into the backs of people's chairs. She is wearing a gold sequined skirt, oversized black T-shirt, and green sneakers. "How funny!" She launches herself at me with a hug. I feel myself slightly limp in her grip. Katie looks at me expectantly.

"This is Rachel," I say when she releases me. "Rachel, this is my friend Katie." They smile at each other. I pause. "Rachel and I met at our prenatal class."

"And now we just seem to keep *bumping* into each other!" Rachel laughs loudly at her own joke. In the cafe, heads turn to see what all the fuss is about. "What are you doing here?"

"We were planning to have lunch," Katie says. "But it looks like they're full."

"Come and sit here, with me!"

I glance at Rachel's table. She has bagged the best spot in the cafe, right by the window, exactly where I had hoped we could sit. But the thought of her joining us makes my heart sink.

Rachel looks at me and her face clouds over, as if she has read my thoughts. "Oh, I'm sorry—I'm barging in." She forces a fake laugh, looks down at the floor, starts to fold the newspaper up in her hands. "Here," she says, gesturing jerkily at the table. "You two take it. I was going anyway. I can pay at the counter."

Rachel keeps folding the newspaper until it is too thick and won't fold anymore. There is something about her movements that makes the hairs stand up on the back of my neck.

Katie takes a step toward her, places her hand lightly on her arm. "Don't be silly, Rachel," she says warmly. "It would be lovely to have lunch together. If you are sure you don't mind us joining you?" She looks at me. "What do you think, Helen?"

Rachel looks at Katie, and then at me.

"Will I be in the way? Say if I will."

Soon inquiries are being made about spare seats, tables being shifted, a chair being found and carried over the heads of other diners. Rachel and I sit in the comfortable seats, facing one another; Katie takes the rickety chair, another diner squashed up against her back.

"How far along are you, Rachel?" Katie asks.

"Everyone in the prenatal class is due in the same month," I answer for her. I can't stop my voice from sounding defensive.

"Oh, right."

"Don't worry, some people just carry a lot bigger than others," Rachel tells Katie in a hushed voice, glancing at me. "So anyway—you must be the journalist! Look—I've just been reading your article! It's such a weird coincidence!" Rachel retrieves her newspaper and waves it at Katie. "Helen told me all about you, about your court case. I literally just bought the paper to check it out!"

She opens the paper to an inside spread, with Katie's name at the top. There are pictures of the two accused arriving at court, both holding the hands of their pretty girlfriends, flanked by their parents and lawyers. There is no picture of the victim—I suppose they're not allowed.

Rachel taps on the paper with her chipped fingernail. "It's unbelievable, this stuff. Tell me everything about it, Katie. Seriously, everything. I like to know all the details."

Hesitantly, Katie starts to talk about the case. I shift in my seat as she recounts the facts of the case, trying not to think too hard about how much it reminds me of what happened before. Rachel is rapt, her eyes wide, mouth slightly open. As I watch her, I try to think whether I told her I was meeting Katie here today. I can't have. Can I?

When the waiter arrives, Rachel orders a smoked salmon, cream cheese, and dill baguette with a large hot chocolate, followed by a chocolate brownie. She goes out to smoke cigarettes twice during our lunch, situating herself directly outside the window and grinning and waving as she does so, as if she wants to keep an eye on us. We smile back uncomfortably.

When she returns from her second cigarette break, Katie and I order another coffee and chamomile tea. Rachel abruptly announces that she is leaving. "I've got so much stuff to do, it's literally crazy," she says, as if we have been the ones keeping her. There is a little dusting of chocolate powder on her cheek.

Rachel reaches for her wallet, throws a fifty-pound note down on the table. Katie stares at her.

"That's too much."

"Oh, don't worry." Rachel grins magnanimously, waving Katie's objection away. "I've had such a nice time." It feels oddly as if she is tipping us.

Before she leaves, Rachel sucks me into a huge bear hug. The embrace lasts longer than I expect it to, as if she won't be seeing me for a while. Chance would be a fine thing, I find myself thinking.

"Thanks so much for letting me crash your lunch," she says. "You're both so sweet. Can't wait to read your next article, Katie." She makes an odd gesture at Katie with her thumb and forefinger, the finger pointed, the thumb bent slightly—somewhere between a thumbs-up and a gun gesture. Then she turns and pushes the door open, a little too hard, so that it bangs against the outside wall, shuddering on its hinges. And then she is gone, the little bell jangling behind her.

I watch her cross the park, keeping my eyes on her slim outline as she walks past the playground, where schoolchildren in brand-new uniforms are dropping reading folders as they race toward the swings.

"She seems nice," Katie says.

I cringe. "She's a bit intense. I'm sorry. I didn't know she would be here. Obviously."

"It's fine. It was nice to meet her."

Both Katie and I are still staring after her as her figure disappears into the park. For some reason, I feel I want to be sure she is really gone.

Helen

IN THE END, I stop trying to arrange to meet my work friends. After one lunch is canceled at the last minute, then another, I get the message. People are busy, too busy for me, anyway. I've already been forgotten.

My appointments are more frequent now, my blood pressure causing concern. Midwives bend to check my ankles for signs of swelling, ask frowning questions about dizziness, shortness of breath. On the way home, I feel the anxiety ebb away a little. Then, day by day, it edges up, and up, until the next time.

I find myself stretching out mundane activities into hours, sometimes whole afternoons, in order to fill my time, try to take my mind off the baby, off the endless nag of doubt. If the sky is clear, the sun shining, I might go out into the garden and pin sheets to the clothesline, radio on, trying to ignore the drilling, the builders traipsing through the kitchen. Some days, if the noise is bad, I walk across the park just so I can sit in a cafe, read my book, have a cup of tea in peace, and walk back again. I take time preparing elaborate evening meals, chopping vegetables into neat multicolored piles.

Today rain is hammering at the rooftops, staining the slate tiles a dark, slippery gray. I decide to spend the morning tidying the upstairs of the house, the parts the builders aren't attacking—an attempt, I suppose, to reestablish some vague sense of order, of control. I tackle the closets first, bagging up old clothes in trash bags to take to the charity shop to make space for the baby. Then I start to sort through drawers and cupboards. I am starting to quite enjoy tasks like this, the hypnotic nature of them. I sit on the bedroom rug, a mug of chamomile tea at my side, listening to *Woman's Hour* on the radio, an old box from the top of Daniel's closet wedged between my knees, the sound of the rain lashing at the window glass.

At first I think it's just a box of Daniel's old university stuff—course notes, essays, architecture textbooks—most of which can go in the trash, I think. I linger over the pages, trace my finger over his notes in the handwriting I know as well as my own. The rows and rows of words in blue fountain pen, the only thing his father ever gave him. I smile as I remember how, when we were at university, he always had a smudgy tide line of blue fountain pen ink from his little finger to the heel of his palm.

I remember the first time I climbed the winding staircase up to Daniel's room, a tiny attic overlooking King's Parade. Knocked shyly, tried to sound casual as I asked if he wanted to come to the bar. How he looked up from his textbook, the evening light from the window on his face, and pushed his glasses up his nose and smiled, as if it was the first time he had ever seen me. As if he knew what I was really asking. And he said, "Sure," and I remember how it made me catch my breath, how easy it had been, after all that time.

I try to think back to those days, two students in an attic room. How I used to watch him sleep, just to drink him in, like a drug. His chest going up and down with his breath. His curled hand resting on the pillow. Are we really the same two people? Is it possible to be? I think of how we used to laugh at everything. How we used to talk until the early hours. How we used to touch each other, even when there was no need to, just because of the way it felt. It used to make me gasp to look at him, the lines of his eyebrows, the hardness of his body, the smile that came only when he really meant it. I mean, I still love him. We love each other. But sometimes, I struggle to remember when we last touched, just for the sake of touching. When I last looked at him, when we last really looked at each other. Is that normal? I wonder. Or is it not?

Under the essays, I find a load of documents to do with the inquest. There's even a copy of Mummy and Daddy's will. I wonder how all that got into his university stuff? I sort the papers into piles quickly, trying not to look too closely at anything, to think about the nightmare of all that—the will, the probate, the life insurance, the endless paperwork that felt like it was going to consume us all forever.

Shoved down one side, though, I find something else. An old photograph of me, Serena, Rory, and Daniel at Cambridge. Serena is in the center. She is wearing a scarlet-hooded cape, hair tumbling down one side. I recognize it immediately—it is the outfit she wore in our college play, in which Serena had the leading role. The play had been odd—a surrealist retelling of some old fairy tales. Serena had gone in for all this amateur dramatics stuff at university. I'd never really understood it. She'd even talked the boys into taking part. Both of them are in costume, too—costumes I helped to make: Daniel in his tall, pointed wolf ears, Rory with a tinfoil axe swinging from his hip. He'd been the woodcutter—the hero. And then there's me, leaning in from the sidelines, the only one without a speaking part.

I pick up the photograph carefully. It is lined with deep creases, as if it's been screwed up into a ball, and then flattened out again. In fact, when I turn it over, I see that it has actually been torn up, then stuck painstakingly back together. On the back, there are four oily pale blue marks, one in each corner. And it's this that makes me realize where it is from. It must be the photo I ripped from the wall at Serena's bachelorette weekend. How on earth did it get here?

I think back to that awful weekend in Cornwall, years ago now. I had never been to a "bachelorette party" before that. I'd never thought to have a party like that for myself. It would never occur to me to ask people to pay all that money to celebrate my life, my marriage. I remember I'd been pleased to have been invited, even if the emails about it had been rather bossy. I hadn't really known what to expect. Perhaps there would be five or six of us, I had thought—just her very closest friends, a private chef, perhaps a few after-dinner games?

I'd brought along a special bottle of wine to give to Serena, her favorite, the same vintage we'd drunk on her twenty-first birthday. It had taken me weeks to track it down. I'd surprise her with it. I had imagined the moment while I was sitting on the train, as I held the bottle, the neck of it smooth in my hands. How touched she'd be. How her eyes would glisten with appreciation.

Of course, as soon as I'd gotten there, I had known straightaway that I had made a mistake, that I hadn't understood things properly, that my elaborately planned gift had been a terrible waste of time. I had stood for what felt like ages on the doorstep, my incessant ringing drowned by the stream of whoops and catcalls from within. I waited and waited, my hands getting cold, the wine bottle heavy in my bag. Eventually, the door was answered.

"Amber. I don't think we've met." The girl had a long, equine face, a nylon sash with the words Maid of Honor emblazoned across it.

"Sorry," I'd said, although I wasn't sure what for. "I'm Helen." I held out the wine. "This is for—"

I was silenced by a burst of laughter from inside. Before I could say more, she had taken the wine from my hand and we were headed for the kitchen.

"Thanks," she'd said distractedly. "We were out of red."

Everyone had been in the sitting room, talking noisily in groups. There wasn't any space on the sofas for me to sit, so I sat on the floor. When I'd first caught Serena's eye, she'd made a charming expression of delight and surprise, smiled, and waved, but then returned immediately to the conversation she'd been having. She had barely known I was there.

I spent that first night perched on sofa arms and kitchen sideboards, trying not to take up too much room or stand in front of cutlery drawers. I clutched my lukewarm cava, trying to be helpful, pretending to have a good time. Later, I found my wine bottle lying empty in the recycling bin. I don't think Serena even had any.

For the rest of the weekend, I mostly remember being left on my own, while everyone else was either out drinking, or in bed, curtains drawn, nursing hangovers. All the activities that had been organized seemed to involve a lot of drinking. I was trying desperately to get pregnant. I could see my very presence was a downer. Most of the time I decided it would be better to simply take myself elsewhere. No one really seemed to mind.

On the Saturday night, they'd all gone out, and it was raining, so I just wandered around the house. It was huge, with long hallways that were inexplicably covered with clocks that ticked out of sync with each other. The walls had been covered with old pictures of Serena, from her glossy blond pigtails childhood to the present day, which one of her bridesmaids had taken the trouble to print out and stick up.

The pictures, someone told me, were supposed to be "embarrassing old photographs," which Serena would find "hilarious." As far as I could see, though, she looked beautiful in all of them. It must have taken hours to stick them all up with Blu-Tack. I had secretly hoped they would leave marks on the walls, and that Amber would lose her deposit. Her horsey face had featured prominently, leading me to suspect the gallery had been her idea. Rory was in a lot of the pictures, of course. I even spotted Daniel in a few. But my face was nowhere.

Eventually, of the dozens and dozens of photographs, I had found this one. The single photograph that featured me, stuck outside the downstairs toilet. I presume it counted as an "embarrassing" photo because Serena was in a costume, even though she looked, as usual, extraordinarily beautiful. But it wasn't that that made the tears prick at my eyes. It was the sight of myself, before Mummy and Daddy died. I was pretty. I never knew it, but I was. And my face. So young and soft and full of hope. Grinning into the camera, into my future. Before I knew what it would bring. I couldn't even look at photographs like that. I hated them.

My cheeks sting as I remember how I'd ripped it off the wall in a rage, how I'd torn it in half, right down the middle. Then I'd taken the Blu-Tack off the wall and shoved it on top of one of the other photographs, over Amber's stupid head. After that, she was just a floating body. A pale blue blob where her face should have been.

Now I hold the photograph in my hands and look at it for a long time, until the rain stops and my tea goes cold. I hated this picture. I never wanted to see it again. So why has it been smoothed out, stuck back together? Why did I do that? Did I do that? I feel a strange prickle down both arms. I must have. There must have been a reason. Why can't I remember?

31 WEEKS

Helen

HOW DO YOU UNMAKE a friendship? It turns out it is strangely difficult—especially with someone as persistent as Rachel. I never seem to have enough excuses not to see her. She knows I'm free, all the time. She knows I'm not working, that everyone else is. She knows that Daniel and Serena and Katie are usually too busy to see me, and that I don't see much of Charlie. She knows my parents are dead. She knows my work friends don't want to meet up with me. She knows all these secrets now—I have revealed them to her, one by one. She knows I've got no excuse.

Lately I've started trying to fill my calendar, so I can have a reason not to see her, if I want one. I have started feigning even more medical appointments than I really have—claiming more blood pressure and baby movement scares than have actually occurred. I find myself arranging to get my nails done, my hair cut, just so I can tell her I have things in my schedule. But the truth is I'm finding it harder and harder to construct my days around clearing cupboards or alphabetizing bookshelves. I am starting to get lonely.

The remodeling work seems to get worse and worse, the foundation dig endless, spewing mountains of rock and soil into the front and back gardens, crushing all Mummy's flowers and plants. Now that it's getting cold, dark, and wet, it feels increasingly like there is no escape. I trudge through Greenwich like a homeless person, paying £2.75 for a cup of tea so I can shelter in a pub, or a coffee shop, or a museum cafe. But after a while it's uncomfortable, and the chairs feel hard under my sit bones, and I can't concentrate on my book. My heartburn flares, my lower back starts to ache, the edge of the table digs into my belly. And meanwhile, my phone sits on the table next to me, and texts from Rachel keep flashing up. Am I all right? Do I feel like "hanging out"? Am I busy? It does get to the point where you wonder if you can keep saying no.

One day, when the rain finally clears and an autumn sun emerges, I decide to go for a walk in the park. I'm in the hallway pulling my shoes on when I hear the knock on the door. Even through the cloudy glass, I can see it is her again. Her wobbly outline shrinks and balloons in the panels in the front door as I turn the key in the lock. I have come to recognize her form, her height. Her way of knocking. Three blows, evenly spaced. Deliberate.

Rachel is standing on the doorstep, grasping one of the gray paper bags from the Italian deli on the hill. It is overflowing with meats, cheeses, olives, a loaf of ciabatta, some shiny green and red apples. She holds it out in front of me, like bait.

"I should have called first, I know." Rachel is grinning. "Have you got plans already? I just thought . . . you said Daniel was away."

I hesitate. She knows, because I told her when I last saw her two days ago, that Daniel is away for a few nights. She knew I'd be alone. The thought makes me uncomfortable.

"To be honest, I'm sort of exhausted, Rachel," I say, improvising. "I was planning on having a nap this afternoon." It's a pathetic excuse, and we both know it. Rachel's face falls.

"Oh," she says. "Oh, OK, then."

Rachel is shifting the handles of the bag between her fingers. As I watch her, I notice her smile seems a bit off today, as if she is straining to keep the corners of her mouth upturned. She starts to transfer the bag from one hand to another, and as she does so, it falls from her hand. Peaches and apples tumble out, followed by a round of cheese, bouncing down the steps at the front of the house like a toy cart wheel.

I sigh, bend down slowly. "Here, let me help."

"No," she says sharply. "Don't, Helen."

She sounds close to tears. She drops the rest of the bag, starts chasing down the road after the cheese. When she returns, she is sniffing.

"Sorry," she says. "Ignore me. I'm just, you know. Having a really bad day. I thought you might . . . I thought maybe." She rubs her eyes with a vigor that is slightly alarming, using the heel of her palm, so her elbow jabs toward me at an odd angle. When she has finished, a half-moon smudge of dark makeup is left under one eye. Oh God, I think.

"Rachel, I'm sorry," I say. "Why don't you come in? I'll put the kettle on."

Once inside, Rachel seems much happier. In the kitchen, she switches the radio on and hikes up the volume, pulling knives from the knife block seemingly at random, hauling out the heavy marble boards we save for best and clattering them against each other. She slams down the bread and starts sawing off great hunks of it, so the knife scrapes against the marble. My fingers twitch. Those knives were a wedding present. They'll be blunt by the time she's finished.

"I've got enough food here for an army! You don't mind if I change the station, do you?"

Before I can answer, she has retuned the radio from Daniel's sports coverage to some pop station I don't listen to. She bops around the kitchen, her bump bouncing with her. I am out of touch with music and can't place the song. It is the sort of music they play in bars, hairdressers, coffee shops. It always gives me a headache.

"Got any chutneys or anything?"

Rachel is rooting around on the top shelf of the fridge. Jars of mustard and mayonnaise clunk loudly against each other. She pulls a few out, piles them up between her arm and her chest, sets them on the counter. Before she closes the fridge door, she plunges her hand into an open basket of raspberries, helps herself to a handful, and tips them into her mouth.

"This will be great," she announces through a mouthful of smashed red fruit. "A proper feast."

Rachel turns to rummage in one of her bags, leaving a knife wobbling on the edge of the board. I'll just move it out of her way, I think. Before it falls, hurts someone. But just as I'm about to close my fingers around the knife, Rachel snatches it up and spins around, the metal glinting.

"Oh no you don't."

The knife flashes in her hand. I feel hot and cold at once.

"I'm doing all this, silly!" she cries, chuckling and waving me away. "I told you. My treat. You sit down, relax." She turns back to the board, starts hacking at the cheeses. *Clack, clack.*

I lower myself down on a stool. I realize I have been holding my breath; I let the air out of my lungs slowly, so she doesn't notice.

"Is Daniel into football, then?"

The comment throws me. What is she talking about now?

"What do you mean?"

"The radio," she says. "It was on 5 Live."

"Oh, right. Yes, he is."

"Which team?"

"Newcastle United."

"He from up there, is he?"

"Um. No. His parents are. Do you want a cheese knife for that?"

"No, this is fine."

Clack. Clack.

"Rachel—are you all right?" I say eventually. "You seem a bit . . . you said you'd had a bad day?"

"It's fine," she says with a manic shake of the head. She turns back to the board and begins to pile up sticky slices of ham and pastrami, which she pulls from cellophane packs. Doesn't she know we can't eat that?

"Just, you know. Men," she mutters.

My curiosity returns, like an itch I can't scratch.

"Did you decide to tell him, in the end? The father?"

Rachel doesn't seem to hear. Having carved up an entire wheel of Brie, she now appears to be moving on to another.

"Rachel," I tell her. "That'll be loads. I'm actually not all that hungry."

"Oh really?" She drops the knife. It clatters down onto the marble block. She turns to me, rubbing her eye. "You know what? Let's forget it. Let's forget the whole thing," she says. She shoves the block away from her, so it slams into the wall with a bang. "It was a stupid idea."

"Oh no, no," I say, alarmed by her rapid mood change. "Not at all. It was a lovely idea. Let's take it out to the end of the garden, shall we? Away from where the builders are. We can, um . . . graze."

Rachel eyes me suspiciously.

"Really, Rachel. It's fine." I glance at the knife, hear the sound of my own breathing in my ears.

"OK." She smiles. "Great! I'll make you a tea, though. You always like a cup of tea."

"Oh. Yes," I say. "Lovely. Thanks."

Rachel flicks the kettle on, flings open the cupboard above it, and pulls out two mugs. Dives into another cupboard for tea bags, sugar. She knows where everything is. She hands me a mug, then shovels three heaped teaspoons of sugar into her own.

"I'm just going to use your other bathroom," she says, heading for the stairs. "Then we can tuck in." She has left the tea bags in hot wet puddles on the counter. A pale circle of spilled milk. A dusting of sugar.

I perch on a stool and listen to Rachel's footfalls on the stairs, the flush, the sound of the tap. She doesn't return. Then I hear a scraping noise, the creak of floorboards far at the top of the house. What is she doing? Surely she's not trying the floorboards again? For a mad moment, I think about the note, tucked in the back of the book on my bedside. Why would you suspect she would go and poke around up there? I ask myself. *Because it's exactly the sort of thing you would do*, a voice in my head answers.

The thought of Rory's note has been turning over and over in my mind all week, like a leaf in the wind. Each night, when Daniel is asleep, I flick my bedside light on and slip it out of the drawer. I hold it between my fingers, examine it again.

Darling RRH
Wear to show me
Evermore
W

I can't make sense of it. To show me what?

Darling RRH

I suppose it is wrong of me to feel so involved. But if Rory is up to something, if he is having some sort of affair with this W, whoever she is, then I can't help but feel he is violating something that involves me, too—the four of us, Daniel and me, Rory and Serena. The only family I've got left, unless you count Charlie, but he's hopeless. My mind leaps ahead, imagines it all coming out, the horror of our family falling apart. Of separation, even divorce. That would spoil everything between Serena and me—all the things I've planned. The maternity leave coffees, walks with our babies, yoga classes. All gone. She won't want to see me now, will she? Not after my brother betrayed her. The thought makes me feel sick, as if there's a guillotine hanging over us all, and only I can see it.

"Been looking at your photos. You look banging in this one. Was this at your wedding?"

Rachel is back, standing by the kitchen dresser, holding a photograph in a silver frame.

"That's right," I say carefully. "It's me and my two bridesmaids. That's Katie on the left, who you met." I hesitate. "And the other one is Serena."

It's not the greatest picture of me, really. I'd insisted on wearing Mummy's wedding dress, on doing it in Marylebone Town Hall, like Mummy and Daddy had all those years ago. I thought it would be nice, a sense of tradition. In truth, the whole thing had been so drab. I don't know what I'd been thinking.

The reception had been in the Chelsea Physic Garden. I'd imagined buzzing bees, the smell of grass, candelabras of magnolia in bloom. But we ended up taking most of the pictures inside, because of the rain. People kept saying the rain didn't matter, but it did, of course it did. All the aunties had their husbands' jackets over their dresses, their shoulders hunched forward, their fascinators wilting in the wet. Not many people had stayed until the end.

I gave Serena and Katie both silver-framed copies of this picture. I'm not sure where Serena keeps hers. I've looked in all her rooms, but I've never seen it on display anywhere. On her mantelpiece, she has a picture of her own wedding, her own bridesmaids. It is an informal photograph—professionally taken, elegantly framed—flooded with the sunlight of her and Rory's beautiful July wedding day. Serena is grinning, and the bridesmaids are laughing uproariously at some joke. Some joke from which I have been forever excluded.

I had just assumed Serena would choose me as a bridesmaid in return for her being mine. But she didn't. At the wedding, I had made sure to smile delightedly as the bridesmaids passed, two by two, in their floor-length, made-to-measure gowns, clutching elegant wildflower bouquets. Their dresses were duck-egg blue, a color that has never suited me. *She'd have loved to have had you,* Rory told me afterward. *She's just got so many close friends.* Unlike you, he might as well have added.

Rachel hands the picture back, and I set it on the table. "Shall we go outside now?" I say. "I could do with some fresh air."

So we sit at the end of the garden. It is sunny, but too cold, really, for sitting outdoors. The lawn is dusted with fallen leaves, the wisteria turning from green to yellow, rustling in an autumn breeze. But it is dry, and the sky is clear, and at least we are away from the building noise. It takes us several trips to take out all the food. Then I lay out one of Mummy's old tartan blankets, put some cushions on top of it. I find I'm hungrier than I thought.

After I have eaten, I bend to check on our four roses, gather the white petals from their beds. I'll need to prune them soon, but not quite yet. Their blooms are wilting, browning at the edges, but they are still soft, still beautiful.

Rachel is sunbathing, taking up more than half of Mummy's blanket, her legs stretched out on the grass, my cushion under her head and shoulders, stuffing her mouth with raspberries and peach slices. She looks perfectly relaxed. Whatever crisis brought her to my door—if there even was one in the first place—appears to have passed. She has a new pair of sunglasses on today, the lenses heart shaped, cartoonish against her baby face. She is wearing denim cutoff shorts and a baggy T-shirt. Her bump sits underneath, a little bigger, but still tiny compared to mine. She must not feel the cold.

"When was that other picture taken?" Rachel asks.

"Which picture?"

"The one you've got on your hallway wall, by the mirror. The one with the four of you. In a boat."

"Oh," I say. "That was just one day in Cambridge. We were punting."

"Yeah, I thought it looked like a punt."

I look at her, surprised. "Do you know Cambridge?"

She frowns, shakes her head. "No. Never been. I just heard it's nice." She cradles her bump with both hands, her lips berry stained. "Did you say Serena took photographs?"

"Yes. Her studio is in the mews, just behind that street over there." I point, but Rachel isn't looking.

"What does she take pictures of?"

"Portraits, mostly, I think. Or that's what she sells most of. She's got a big exhibition coming up. She's doing really well."

The truth is, I don't really understand Serena's photographs. She has them hanging all over the house, some in color, some black and white. A wrinkled old man she saw in India, glowing-faced children with fishing nets she saw in Bali, a panoramic shot of the floating markets in the Mekong Delta, which she and Rory visited on their honeymoon. I always admire them, obviously. But I'm never sure exactly what makes a photograph good or bad. I suppose they don't make me feel anything much.

"You don't like them." Rachel has turned her head and is looking at my face, grinning, a hand flattened over her eyes.

My head snaps up. "Sorry?"

"Her pictures!" Rachel giggles. "Come on, Helen. I can tell by your face."

"I don't know anything about art," I stutter, but I find myself laughing a little bit. I'm surprised to find how dizzyingly pleasurable it is, this minor act of disloyalty, rebellion. To laugh at Serena. To belittle her passions, her so-called talent.

"To be honest," I hear myself saying, "I think most of it is a load of nonsense."

Rachel throws her head back and hoots.

"I mean, not just her," I say, already feeling guilty. "Most art, I mean. I'm sure hers is good. I just . . . I probably just don't get it."

But Rachel is shaking with laughter. She pulls a packet of cigarettes out of her pocket, and places one between her smiling lips, so it sticks up straight from her mouth, like a pencil.

"You crack me up, girl," she says, flicking at her lighter with one thumb. She lights the cigarette, inhales, then takes it between her fingers and blows a plume of smoke straight up in the air. She yawns extravagantly, her arms stretching out overhead, revealing gritty stubble in each armpit.

"Maybe I'll get one of her portraits," she says through the yawn.

"What?"

"A portrait. By Serena. Be nice to have some proper photos of the bump. All the celebrities do it now, don't they?"

She winks at me, then places her hands on either side of her belly, her cigarette still perched between the fingers of her right hand, and starts drumming gently, as if she is playing the piano.

I look at her, try to gauge whether or not she is being serious about going to see Serena. The thought fills me with an irrational sense of dread.

"I'm so comfy," Rachel says, yawning loudly again. "I might have a little nap here. You don't mind, do you?"

Without opening her eyes, she gropes around for the raspberry box, takes another handful, and tips them into her mouth.

It's only later, when I notice the wedding photograph Rachel brought down, that I realize I keep that picture on my bedside table. What was she doing in our bedroom?

32 WEEKS

Serena

IF IT WASN'T FOR the rain, I'd probably have gone home. There didn't seem much point in staying. But it started again about five thirty, lashing down, hammering at the skylight over my desk. I hadn't remembered my umbrella.

I like being in my studio when it rains: I put the heater on under my desk, listen to the hum of it while I boil the kettle for tea. The studio is in a tiny mews off the high street. Hardly anyone comes down here. It is deliciously quiet. When it rains, that's all you hear, like a rush of pebbles, a gorgeous white noise. The cobbles in the mews shine when it's wet, like polished wood. I photographed the rain on the cobbles once, the stones rising out of puddles like tiny islands. It looked like an alien landscape, or the hide of a huge crocodile.

At the back of the studio are the darkroom on one side and my desk on the other. Next to my desk is a corkboard of photographs, art postcards, things I've ripped out of newspapers and magazines. Places I'd like to go one day. A window looks out to the little paved courtyard, where there is just enough space outside for a tiny table and chairs, a few plants in some old milk pails I got from the antiques place in the covered market.

I grow herbs on the windowsill in white ceramic pots: parsley, rosemary, fresh mint. I use the mint leaves for tea, which I make in my bright green mugs, with spoonfuls of dark brown sugar. I bought the mugs from the woman opposite, who rents the pottery studio. I feel a bit sorry for her. I don't think she sells much.

I sip my tea. The sugar makes my baby dart inside me, like a fish. After university, Rory and I went backpacking in Morocco and drank fresh mint tea with sugar while we were camping out in the Atlas Mountains. Cold nights under scratchy wool blankets. The air was so clear you could almost drink it. In the nearest town, the houses were painted blue to match the huge desert sky.

There's a photograph of us there on my corkboard. We are on the ridge of a mountain, him in his gray alpaca sweater, grinning widely, his hair messy, sun bleached, the snowy peaks reflected in his mirrored sunglasses. He has his arm around me, my hair is blowing over my face, and I'm squinting in the sunlight. We are happy. It radiates from the surface of the picture, like heat.

We'd argued last night. He is still so upset about the interview. He can't stop talking about it. The journalist had seemed nice, he said, genuinely interested in the development, in the company. In wanting to hear his side of the story. I couldn't believe he'd been so naive. What did you think would happen? I asked him. You know what people are saying about the development. Why didn't you just keep your head down? Why did you say yes? I knew the real answer even before I typed the name of the journalist into a search engine, brought up her smiling professional picture. But of course, it wasn't just about the interview. Not really. He thinks he's losing his grip.

He'd stormed upstairs. I knew he was going to have a cigarette on our balcony. He likes to think I don't know about the cigarettes. Or the coke. He likes to think I don't know a lot of things. I'd picked up the magazine, thrown it into the recycling. On the cover, his face looked like somebody I didn't recognize.

Later that night, when he was asleep, I'd finally committed it to words. The question I typed stared back at me accusingly from the bright white search box on the screen.

How do I know if my husband is having an affair?

I stared at them for a while, and after a few minutes my eyes strained under the white light of the computer. Then I took a swig of Chablis and hit return.

Of course, there were thousands of results: articles, quizzes, checkbox guides. How modern, I thought, to turn to a search engine for answers. How many millions of women, I wondered, have sat, as I do now, in a beautiful home, wineglass in hand, or a baby in their belly, or both, tears pricking at their eyes as they typed these very same words?

I selected an article at random—one of the checklist-style ones. More Chablis. Then I clicked on it. But I heard Rory's voice. He'd woken, noticed I was up. I deleted the search history, again. Snapped the laptop cover down. It is one of those paper-light ones: it had closed noiselessly, like an eyelid.

I watch the rain outside, how it washes the green leaves of the plants in my courtyard, how it pools on my chair, my metal table. I'll finish my tea and stay another half hour, wait and see if the storm dies down. But when I reach the last dregs, it seems to be getting worse, the sky darkening into an angry bruise. I flick the kettle on again, decide to get on with some developing. That's when I hear the knock.

The first thing I notice about her are her feet. She is wearing lime-green flip-flops; her feet are bare, other than a chipped purple manicure. Her legs are bare, too, even though it's freezing outside. The rest of her body is shrouded in a huge winter coat, the enormous fur-lined hood pulled down over her eyes, dripping onto the cobbles like the mane of a soggy lion.

"Can I help you?"

I see the chin lift, but I still can't see her face under the flap of the hood.

"Sorry I'm late. Can I come in? It's really cold."

I stare at her, puzzled.

"I'm sorry—are you my three o'clock?" I pause. "It's past six."

"The traffic was really terrible. Is that fresh mint tea? Lovely. Do you mind if I take this off? It's wet."

She turns away from me to hang the coat on the radiator by the front door, like a dead animal. Underneath she is wearing a blue velvet dress. The back of it is very beautiful, though a little old-fashioned. Both of us hear the growl of thunder.

"So close!" Her voice is excited, like a child's. "We must be right under it."

She looks up, as if she is expecting the roof to have blown off. The flash of lightning follows, flickering on and off like a faulty lightbulb. I still can't see her face.

I clear my throat. I'm not exactly sure what to do about this bedraggled visitor. On the one hand, she is ludicrously late, and I've every right to tell her to get lost. On the other, the weather is foul, and apart from her now drenched coat, she is completely underdressed.

"Look, feel free to stay here for a bit," I say briskly. "But I can't photograph you today, I'm afraid. I was actually just finishing off a few emails and then leaving. Sorry."

The girl is still facing the wall. "The thing is, it needs to be today." She says it like it's as much my problem as hers.

"Like I said, I'm sorry."

The girl bends down, reaches inside her bag, and pulls out a bulging brown envelope. The flap is not sealed. It is full of fifty-pound notes.

"I've got the cash with me. And I brought extra for the prints."

She places the envelope next to the radiator, under her coat. The rain is still rattling the roof, but the thunder has faded to a low rumble. I clear my throat.

"Sorry, what did you say your name was?"

Finally, the girl turns around. It takes me a moment to place it. Her strange, childlike face, her dimpled cheeks, her pointed teeth. She smiles.

"You remember me, Serena, don't you?"

33 WEEKS

Helen

DANIEL HAS BEEN MAKING an effort lately, I've noticed. Work seems to have eased up a bit. Tonight he is home on time, bouncing in his shiny work shoes, a bulging bag of shopping dumped onto the kitchen counter.

"I got that hot chocolate you like. I saw we were out," he is calling from the hallway, hanging up his coat. When I open the bag, I see there are other things I need, too: antacids, vitamin supplements, bath oil, the expensive granola I've been devouring bowls of in the middle of the night.

"I thought I could cook, and the new series of *Luther* is on. Fancy it?" He pulls off one shoe, then the other, and puts them neatly in the shoe rack, as I've asked him to.

I smile to myself. This is what I wanted it to be like. Nights in, on the sofa. No more eating alone. "Thanks, sweetheart," I say. "*Luther* sounds good. I'll help you cook."

The rain has stopped, for now. Yellow evening light is seeping through the kitchen window, casting little rainbows over the wooden counter where it reflects through the oil and vinegar. Outside, birds in the garden are calling over the traffic. Soon there is a hum of football commentary on the radio; Daniel's team is playing. The roar of the crowd is far away, just a white noise, like the sizzle of the onions I am frying on the stove. I brush chopped garlic from the board into the pan.

"How was your day?" I ask Daniel, turning the radio down. But he is not listening to me anymore, or the football. He is pushing piles of paper this way and that on the kitchen table, opening and closing cupboards.

"Where's my laptop, Helen?"

His tone makes me stop what I'm doing.

"I don't know. Have you tried the study? By your bed?"

"I'm sure it was here. On the table."

He turns on his heel, marches upstairs, and I hear him stomping from room to room, the floorboards straining. Then he is back down again.

"I've looked everywhere, Helen. It's gone." The use of my name tells me that he suspects it is my fault.

"Well, maybe you left it at the office."

"I didn't."

I toss the celery and risotto rice in with the onions, starting to turn the grains over with a wooden spoon.

"I'll help you look," I tell him. "After dinner, though. Did you grate that Parmesan?"

Daniel starts to hack at the cheese, inexpertly, grating it as if it were cheddar for a child's packed lunch, not in the nice flakes I prefer. "Bloody hell. How much did this cost, Helen?" he asks, examining the wrapping.

I stare at him. "I can't remember. It's proper stuff, from Modena. Why?"

He rubs his eyes behind his glasses. "We spend so much money, Helen," he mutters. He takes his glasses off and polishes the lenses.

I look at him. "What do you mean?"

He puts his glasses back on. "Nothing," he says. "Forget it."

The truth is, he is right. Shopping has become my therapy, my guilty secret. Sometimes, after my hospital appointment—briefly reassured that everything is, at least for that moment, all right—I will step off the Tube feeling lighter than usual. I will go to the gift shops on Turnpin Lane, telling myself I deserve it. That I have the right to celebrate. I will thumb through the tiny sweaters with knit animals, the little boxed bonnets and booties, the baby blankets in pale ice cream colors, closing my eyes as I finger the softness of the cashmere. Then I watch them being wrapped up for me in tissue and ribbon, turning my credit card over in my hand. Wondering what else I am going to do for the rest of the day.

He finishes grating the cheese, leaves the dirty grater in the sink. He huffs, rubs the sides of his face with his hands.

"What, Daniel?"

"Do you think you might have taken it out somewhere, left it in a cafe, maybe?"

I turn away from the stove and stare at him. It takes me a moment to work out that he is talking about the laptop again. I turn the heat down.

"No, Daniel, I haven't. I haven't taken it out of the house. I've been with Rachel all day today, I told you. And anyway, why would I take the laptop to a cafe?"

He exhales loudly. "It'd be a lot easier to find things in this house if there wasn't so much crap everywhere." I survey the kitchen table. He has a point. The table is covered with newspapers and magazines I said I'd read but haven't gotten around to, a stack of pregnancy books, a TENS machine, an empty bottle of antacid, a yet-to-be-inflated birth ball and pump. He starts lifting the piles of newspapers and magazines from the table with unnecessary aggression, shoving them into the recycling. Leaflets drift out from between the newspaper pages and float onto the floor.

"Hey, don't throw away the mags. I haven't read that Rory thing yet."

I press my lips together. Too late. I shouldn't have mentioned the Rory interview. It does nothing for Daniel's mood. His hand freezes over the bin. He extracts the magazine and chucks it onto the table.

"Don't be so cross, Daniel. It'll turn up."

"Sorry. I'm just a bit stressed."

While Daniel takes out the recycling, I glance over at the magazine. Rory's face stares up from the front cover in monochrome. He looks unlike himself—menacing, somehow. Something about it reminds me of Daddy, in his bad moments. When he used to get cross, when he was someone else. I haven't read the interview yet, but the headline is bad enough.

I stare outside at Daniel. I can see from his movements that he is frustrated with the overflowing bins. He is stuffing the bags in, one after another, even though it's clear the lid won't close.

He and Rory have argued about the article, I know. After all the controversy, Daniel thinks Rory should have known it would end in tears—a big interview, just as they are poised to unveil the next phase of the development. When it came out, Daniel went mad.

Apparently he hadn't even known Rory had done an interview—Rory hadn't warned the client or anything. Daniel told Rory he was an idiot, asked why the hell he hadn't talked to him before he agreed to it. Rory had snapped that that was rich coming from Daniel, and why hadn't Daniel mentioned the fact he was moving the company's money offshore, and how had he imagined that was going to look. Daniel said it wasn't dodgy, everyone did it, it was just good accounting, and what would Rory know about that since he had never taken the slightest interest in keeping the company's finances on track. I didn't like the sound of it. I hate it when they fall out.

Daniel is back in the kitchen, washing his hands. "I'm out again on Monday night, I'm afraid," he says, raising his voice over the water. "With the client. To try and repair some of the damage." He dries his hands on the tea towel, then throws it back on the side in a heap.

"All right. You haven't forgotten about Rory's birthday dinner, though, have you?"

Daniel blinks. He obviously had.

"Do we have to . . . go to that?"

"Daniel, he's my brother and your business partner! Of course we have to. Come on, the article can't have been that bad."

"Yeah, well, like you said, you haven't read the article. It was bad."

I sigh, wondering how we have ended up arguing again when the evening started so well. I pour a glass of sauvignon blanc into the risotto. It bubbles up quickly, soaks into the rice. I turn the heat up, make sure the alcohol is evaporated. I smell it over the pan, heady, disorienting for a moment, then gone.

"Want a glass?" I pour some of the wine, pass it to him. I've been discouraging his drinking lately, since his performance at Rory and Serena's, but this feels like an easy peace offering. Daniel seems mollified by the gesture. He looks at the glass, stops rummaging for his laptop. "Thanks," he says. "Think I'll have a beer, though." He reaches into the fridge. "How was your day?"

"Fine," I say. "Except I'm still getting these cold calls all the time."

Daniel frowns. "Sorry, I keep meaning to get that landline disconnected."

I shake my head. "These are weird, though. It seems to be the same company calling, saying something about a new mortgage, or a remortgage. They're saying I've applied for one."

"Well, you haven't, have you?"

"No, of course not."

"So just put the phone down, Helen. That's the whole thing—they want to keep you on the line, get you talking about your finances. You just have to hang up."

I bite my lip. I'm sure Daniel is right. But the woman was really persistent earlier. She knew my full name, our address, our current mortgage provider. She had insisted I was the one who had requested the application. I'd hung up, but it had nagged at me. It hadn't felt like the people calling about payment protection insurance claims, or asking whether I'd been in an accident.

"I honestly wouldn't worry," Daniel says. "They're clever, some of them. They can buy data on you, find out stuff that makes them sound genuine."

"I guess."

I stir the risotto, adding the stock slowly, ladle by ladle, moving it around the pan before it bubbles.

"Oh, also, I bumped into Rachel in the deer park earlier," I say, changing the subject.

"Again?"

"Yeah. It started raining so we went to the Maritime Museum. Had a coffee."

"That sounds nice."

I frown. "Yes," I say distractedly.

Daniel closes the fridge door and leans back against it, fiddling with the bottle opener on his key ring. He is smiling at me.

"Why are you making that face, if it was nice?"

I glance up at him as I stir, wondering if I should share my thoughts with him.

"I don't know," I say eventually. "I mean, do you think it's weird, how I keep bumping into her all the time?"

He shrugs. "What do you mean?"

"Like when I was having lunch with Katie. That she just happened to be there, sitting at the best table, reading Katie's newspaper article."

He considers this.

"And how she turned up here unannounced that time, when you were away?"

Daniel looks at me blankly. It's obvious he's forgotten what I am talking about.

"I told you about this," I say, rolling my eyes. "She knew I was alone, that you were away. And she just turned up uninvited. With a picnic. She pretty much let herself in."

Daniel pauses. Then he bursts out laughing.

"What?"

"Sorry," he says. "Just doesn't exactly sound like the crime of the century to me. Your pregnant friend, turning up with a picnic, hoping for a cuppa and a chat."

I force myself to laugh along. "OK, fine," I say. "It just felt a bit much, that's all." I pour some more stock into the rice.

Daniel takes a swig of his beer, rotates his shoulders back and forward. "If you didn't want to see her, why didn't you just say you were busy? Why did you agree to hang out with her again today?"

"I don't know—she is fine really. It's not a big deal. She's just a bit unpredictable. That's all. She does random things like that. Grabbing my bump. Turning up unannounced." *Going into our bedroom and moving photographs around,* I add in my mind. *Looking for treasure under our floorboards.*

Daniel laughs again. He puts his beer down on the sideboard, comes up behind me, places both his hands on the bump.

"I don't know—I haven't met her. But I just think maybe you're overthinking it. She sounds all right to me." His hands are warm on my belly. "Am I allowed to grab the bump still?" he asks, murmuring into my neck. "Or will you think I'm a weirdo, too?"

I smile, feel my shoulders loosen. His touch is so comforting; I sink into it. "Don't be silly," I say. "That's different." I stroke his knuckles. "The baby's kicking loads today, feel. Just . . . here." I move Daniel's hand to the top of my bump, just under my ribs, where I'd felt the pressure a moment earlier, like a fingertip poking me from the inside. But as soon as I do it, the baby stops.

"Oh. Sorry, he's gone. I'll tell you next time."

"Mm." Daniel's hands drift downward. I try to relax, try not to think about how long it has been since he touched me like this without my clothes on. How enormous I feel. His hands move up to my breasts, and he starts to kiss the back of my neck. I am surprised to feel a shiver of anticipation. Maybe that's the answer.

Daniel stops, his hand on my necklace.

"What's this?"

I feel the sinews in my shoulders clench. I try to keep my voice even, casual, but I am sure he can hear the wobble in it.

"Just a necklace." I wriggle free of Daniel's grip, my cheeks still hot. "I saw it in town. Don't you like it?" I return to the stove, start ladling more stock into the rice.

"It's the one Serena was wearing, isn't it? Helen . . ."

"What?"

"I thought we'd talked about this."

I'd seen it in the jewelery shop on Turnpin Lane, when Daniel and I were walking back from the market last weekend. It was hanging in a glass cabinet, the little charm moving from side to side ever so slowly, beckoning me. I recognized it straightaway, remembered it glinting against the silk of Serena's top.

I'd gone back the next day. With no Daniel to stop me, I'd asked the curly haired sales assistant if I could have a look. It had been more expensive than I'd expected. But it was so beautifully made, the markings on the dog so intricate, even though it was no bigger than my thumbnail. Before I knew it I was nodding yes, I'll take it, watching as she slipped it into a blue leather box, wrapped it in tissue.

"It's a lovely necklace," the girl had said, cutting a length of ribbon. She had a diamond piercing in her nose, jade rings on her fingers.

"Yes," I'd agreed. "The dog is sweet."

"Oh, do you think it's a dog?" she'd said vaguely. Then she'd glanced at me and backtracked, worried she'd put me off. "You're right," she'd gabbled, snatching my credit card before I could change my mind. "It does look like a dog."

Daniel is watching me as I move around the kitchen. I switch off the gas, start piling the risotto into bowls. The match is breaking for halftime. I turn down the radio, tuck the necklace inside my sweater. I top the bowls with chopped parsley. As I set them down on the table, I feel the heat of Daniel's gaze at the back of my neck.

While we eat, I try to talk about my day, ask Daniel about work. But we don't seem to be able to get much of a conversation started. After a few mouthfuls, he finishes abruptly, places his fork back into the bowl. He always eats in this manner, as if it is a chore, a waste of time. He gathers up the bowls, even though I'm not really finished, and leaves them stacked by the sink. I stare at the empty table. Is this it now? Is this how it is going to be? Even after the baby is here?

I finish the washing up and walk into the living room. Daniel is down on his hands and knees, reaching under sofas, going through the drawers in the coffee table.

"What are you doing?"

He glances up at me guiltily, as if I've caught him doing something wrong.

"Just thought it might be under here. The laptop."

"I'll have a proper look tomorrow. Can we not worry about it now?"

"Hmm."

"I thought you said you wanted to watch *Luther*."

"Oh yeah. OK."

So we sit down to watch TV, sheltering together in the one corner of the living room that we've managed to preserve from the building work. The nicer chairs and tables are draped in white sheets like ghosts. I watch the blue light of the TV flicker on Daniel's face, and wonder what my husband is hiding from me.

Greenwich Park

IN THE HIGH STREET, car headlights and streetlamps flicker on. Shop shutters start to come down, like eyes closing. She watches, and waits.

The man is behind the glass, a window that stretches from the floor to the ceiling. All the other lights in the building are off. His is the only one remaining.

She shifts on her feet. The sky is darkening, the light draining out of it in streaks of pink and orange over the houses. He would normally be home by now. But something is keeping him here this evening. Something stopping him going home to his beautiful wife.

The man stands up, slings a bag over his shoulder, gathers his things. Picks up a magazine on his desk, tries to tear it in half, but it's too thick. Now, feeling foolish, he glances up, as if he senses he is being watched. Her neck prickles—has he seen her?

But no, the man has not seen her. Of course not, she scolds herself. She is safe here, in the shadows. The man tosses the magazine into the wastepaper basket instead. Then, finally, he picks up the envelope on his desk. Here we are, she thinks. Here we are. The man takes the envelope, rips it open, and pulls out the contents onto his desk. She watches gleefully, this silent film. She feels her fingers twitch, the saliva pool in her mouth, as the bag slips off the man's shoulder, as he grabs for the side of his desk, as if he has been tossed, untethered, into space. Into a place without air, a place without gravity.

Katie

AS I SIT IN court, I try hard to focus on the evidence. I take down the defendant's answers in shorthand; my pen makes a scratching sound against my notebook.

"Her eyes were open." The defendant is tall, blond, with bright blue eyes. His palms are turned up and outward in the body language of honesty. "She pulled me toward her."

"And then what happened?"

"We kissed."

"You kissed her?"

"Yes, and she kissed me back."

"And you were in no doubt whatsoever that she consented to this contact?"

He smiles, looks straight at the jury. "None whatsoever."

Scratch, scratch, scratch.

"And what happened after that?"

The weather is getting cold now; the clerks wear cardigans and scarves inside the courtroom, portable heaters plugged into the walls. Everything about the room is starting to grate on me; the awful, cheap patterned carpet, the filthy plug sockets, the musty smell, the dust along the windowsills. DCI Carter is here again. He is wearing a diamond-patterned sweater under his suit jacket. I nod at him and he gently nods back.

After we went for coffee that time, I'd kept thinking about the way he'd reacted when I said that thing about rape cases. It made me wonder whether something had happened in the past. Back at the office, I'd pulled up the digital archive, searched for his name. There were murder cases, kidnapping cases. Not many for rape.

Eventually, I'd found it. The papers had called it the Boathouse Rape. The echoes with the current case had been obvious. The privileged backgrounds of the accused. The obvious vulnerability of the victim. The beauty of the backdrop. The ugliness of the detail.

It had been even worse for the victims back then. They couldn't report this girl's name, of course—she'd have anonymity for life under the law. But everything else about her life had been laid out in lurid Technicolor. The underwear she'd had on, the number of drinks she'd had at the party. The way she'd been dressed, the way she'd behaved, how much sexual experience she'd had before. It was all in the stories, every last bit. She had been just fifteen years old.

I guessed the conclusion, even before I came to the end of the cuttings. There was a picture of the two smirking defendants on the Cambridge courtroom steps. Quotes from their lawyers complaining that they should have had anonymity, too, that their young lives had been shattered. And at the very bottom, a few words from the senior investigating officer, about the bravery of the victim in coming forward, his hope that the verdict would not deter others from doing so. His name was DCI Mark Carter.

I saved the cuttings in a folder on my laptop, clicking and dragging each article one by one. As I did so, I noticed the date of the offense. It had all happened in the summer of 2008. I counted on my fingers. Hadn't Helen still been at Cambridge University that summer?

The next time I spoke to Helen on the phone, I asked her if she remembered it.

"There was loads in the national papers," I told her. "The Boathouse Rape, they called it. A young girl who turned up at one of those May week parties at Cambridge, the summer you left. She said two male students had got her drunk and raped her."

Helen didn't respond straightaway.

"Helen, are you still there?"

"Yes. Sorry. Can't remember it," she said vaguely. "Why do you ask?"

"No reason really. Just researching the detective on this current case. Thought you might remember it, what it was like being at the university when something like that was happening."

"Oh, right, I see." Her voice was odd. She sounded relieved. "Well, I think we'd left by the time all that was really in the news." I frowned. I thought she'd said she didn't remember it being in the news.

"All rise."

The case is breaking for a bit. Everyone stands. When I look up, DCI Carter is gone. He must have slipped out the back. I had been hoping to lure him to the pub at lunchtime, try and get a bit more out of him. Ask if he ever passed the victim my letter.

I head to the toilets. It occurs to me how tired I am. I think about seeing Charlie tonight. He has promised to cook me pasta, and I can stop thinking about the case for a while. Maybe after dinner we can watch *The Apprentice* and laugh at the contestants. If I can get back in time—the last time I drove from Cambridge to Charlie's flat in east London, it had taken me two hours. My heart had sunk when I'd seen the long snake of red brake lights cramped together on the motorway. It occurred to me how much I wanted to get back to Charlie, how homesick I felt for him, how much I longed to see the light on at the window of his little top-floor flat.

I step out of the cubicle to wash my hands. I close my eyes as the warm water runs over them, inhale the lemon smell of the soap. I haven't had a day off for weeks now. I long to lie in a bath, soak the exhaustion from my body. Curl up under a duvet without first setting an alarm for 6 a.m.

When I open my eyes, she is standing straight in front of me, on the cheap linoleum of the courtroom toilets, next to the hand dryers. Her cuffs are pulled over her fingers, her fists balled up inside the sleeves of her cardigan as if for protection. Her hair looks unwashed, her eyes puffy. It's Emily Oliver. The victim.

Our eyes meet. I take a deep breath. The situation feels surreal. Surely a victim in a criminal case has access to their own toilet? It seems hideous that she is here, that she should have to bump into me like this.

"I got your letter," she says flatly. She rubs one eye with a balled-up hand. "But they told me not to talk to you." I notice the skin around her thumbnail is bitten to bleeding.

"I'm sure they did," I say. I shake my hands dry gently, wipe them on my trousers. I don't want to come closer, to risk setting off the hand dryers, breaking the spell. I don't want any noise.

"I can't talk to anyone. Even my therapist," she says. She looks up at me, angry now. "Did you know that? Even what I say to my therapist could be used against me. That's what they said." Her voice is brittle, catching in her throat. "I can't talk to anyone."

I pause, weigh my words carefully. "The police are right," I tell her, my voice so soft it is almost a murmur. "They're trying to protect you. They're right that you shouldn't talk to anyone—not at the moment. Not before the end of the trial. So if anyone asks you to—any of the other journalists—I would say no."

"What about after?"

I take a deep breath. She is a bird, inching toward my outstretched hand. One false move and she will fly away.

"That's up to you," I say slowly. "But if you would like to tell your story, I could help you, if that was what you wanted."

In the mirror I can see the door, its tarnished handle, the sign that says Please Wash Your Hands. I stare at the door and will it not to open. If anyone else comes in, this conversation will be over.

"Do you believe me?"

I take a tiny step forward. Look her in the eye.

"Yes," I tell her. "I do."

"Does the jury?" Her voice is slow, controlled, but her teeth are gritted. "Or do they believe them?" This last word is pronounced with quiet venom.

I hesitate. I think about saying yes. But I need to tell the truth. And the truth is that it is complicated. She is not the perfect victim. She drank. She flirted. She prevaricated over the decision to report.

"I don't know," I say eventually. "But you have done everything you possibly could."

The girl's hair falls in front of her face. She pushes it straight back behind her ear crossly, with a small, pale hand. When she hasn't said anything for a few moments, I reach inside my bag, feel for the sharp edges of my business cards. I take one and slowly reach toward her, holding it between my thumb and forefinger.

"I'm Katie," I say.

She stares at the card, the black-and-white logo. She doesn't take it.

"My dad doesn't like your newspaper." She sniffs. "He says it's a rag. That it twists things."

I nod, shoot her a rueful smile. "It does sometimes," I admit. "But I don't."

"He reads the *Guardian*." She eyes me carefully, goading me, wanting to see if I'll react.

"My dad reads the *Guardian*, too," I say truthfully. "I'm a bit of a disappointment."

She considers this. Looks down at my card.

"You're here every day." She sighs. "And all the others are blokes."

I nod. Finally she takes the card. Holds it between her fingers, as if she isn't sure how it works.

"Listen," I say. I take another tiny step toward her. "You need to concentrate on the trial. But afterward, if you did want to . . . tell your story, I could help you do it in a way you were happy with. We could write it together."

She looks up, a skeptical expression on her face. "What do you mean?"

"I could send you the whole thing. Before we published. You could read it, and if you didn't like it, we could change it." I look at her. "I swear. No twisting."

I hold her gaze, try to ignore the roar of blood in my ears. Copy approval, that's what I'm promising. Something we never promise, we never agree to. I hear the screams of my boss, Hugh, in my ears. But surely this is different. Surely Hugh will understand.

"If I did it . . . you would pay me?" She looks at the ground as if she is ashamed for asking. "It's not about that," she mutters. "I just . . . we're not rich."

We are in dangerous territory now. I should not be having this conversation. Not while the trial is still going on. But she has sought me out. And I might not get another chance.

I take a deep breath. "We could pay you. But we shouldn't really discuss that now."

As I finish my sentence, the speakers in the corner of the toilets blast into life. The clerk's voice is calling us back into court. The girl takes a deep breath.

"Listen," I say. "You've got my card. If you want to, when it's all finished, call me. It's my cell on there—you can call me anytime, day or night. I won't mind. And we can discuss the idea of an article and I can answer any questions you have. No obligations. OK?" I pause. "If you don't want to go through with it, that's absolutely fine. Even if you decide to go with another paper, I can try and help, give you advice on all that, if you want."

Hugh's voice is still screaming. What the fuck are you saying, Wheeler? You might as well give her the number of the fucking *Guardian*! I silence him. Concentrate on the girl. She is still holding my card.

"But if you did want to go ahead, that's how it would work with me. We'd do it together. You'd be in charge. And if it would make you feel better, you could bring someone. A friend. Or the detective could be there with you. DCI Carter. I'm sure he wouldn't mind."

She looks up at me. I have guessed correctly; he has been kind to her, won her trust. At the mention of his name, she has softened. I take a deep breath, try to ignore DCI Carter's voice in my ear now, asking me what the hell I'm doing, getting him involved in a media interview.

"OK," she says. "I might."

34 WEEKS

Helen

THE BUILDERS HAVE GONE for the weekend. Daniel, home early again, is in a good mood, humming as he mixes a Seedlip and tonic for me. I'm determined that this time we will have a nice evening.

I had been looking forward to celebrating our anniversary this year, before the baby comes. In truth, I think we need it. We've been snapping at each other more than normal—about the building work, about the prenatal classes, about money. We need time, I have decided. Proper time, just the two of us.

I told him I had booked us a fancy restaurant in town, one I knew he would like. But he insisted we should stay at home. Secretly, my heart sank. I wanted us to get out of the house, have a change of scene, make it feel special. But I didn't want to fall out over it, so I agreed.

Daniel has insisted he will cook dinner himself. He is not a natural cook, but he is methodical, rules based. He follows recipes exactly, and his dishes usually turn out well. I saw him earlier searching for how long you should cook lamb shoulder. He will want to ensure mine is well done enough. He is protective of me and the baby with things like that, which is sweet. And there are signs he is making an effort. He has cleaned the grime from the table, laid out place mats, and lit candles. Rolled the dustcovers off the floor, so the room looks more normal.

"Let me do it," he says when I try to help. He pulls me away from the table, takes the cutlery from my hands, plants a kiss in my hair. "The meat will be a while. Why don't you try out your new bath?"

The new bathroom is the first thing that has made the remodel work seem at all worthwhile. It smells of cool tiles and fresh paint. I can hardly wait to fill the deep roll-top bath, slip under the warm water, and soak, looking out over the garden. Earlier, I arranged all my new things on the driftwood shelves. I made them put some in at the last minute, after I saw Serena's. Surely Daniel won't notice a few little shelves that are the same as hers.

I run the water and go to fetch my book from where I left it, on the chair in the bay window. And that's when I see her.

The first thing that occurs to me is why on earth is she tapping at the window? She looks even more waiflike than usual, her eyes red rimmed. Her belly sticks out like there is something wrong with it. As if she is a starvation victim instead of a pregnant woman. I wonder how long she has been standing there, looking into our front room at us.

"Who's that?" Daniel shouts from the kitchen.

"I think it's Rachel." This is a stupid thing to say. I can see perfectly well that it is Rachel.

"Rachel? What, your new friend Rachel? What's she doing here at this hour?"

"I don't know."

It's only then I notice her neck. Three red welts in straight lines, like huge burns, the size and shape of fingers. Her eyes are bloodshot. She is biting at the skin around her thumbnail, twitchy and fearful.

"Get rid of her, will you? It's our anniversary." He is craning his neck now, trying to see through from the kitchen, one hand on a saucepan.

"I know," I say, waving at Rachel through the glass. "I'll just see what she wants."

When I open the door, it looks worse. For once, she doesn't say anything. Just stares at me.

"Rachel? Oh my goodness! What happened to your neck?"

Rachel opens her mouth to answer, then closes it again. Then she bolts into the house, pushing past me quickly, as if she is afraid of who might be following her.

Her anxiety is infectious. I glance right and left up and down the road, wondering if she has been followed by her assailant—whoever he is. But there is no one, just a couple of people with drinks outside the pub on the corner.

Rachel is pacing around in the front room. Her heavy footfalls on the floorboards cause the whisky glasses to jangle in the drinks cupboard and send our cat, Monty, scampering up the stairs. She pulls out a cigarette, pats down the breast pockets of her denim jacket for a light. I open my mouth to ask that she smoke it outside. But something stops me. As I watch her struggling with the lighter, I notice her hands are trembling. Her right hand is swollen, pink and fat as a cat's paw, with cuts all over the knuckles. As she walks up and down, I see there is a single red mark on the other side of her neck, too. The bruising is deep, angry, more like a burn. It makes me wince to look at it.

Rachel finally succeeds in lighting the cigarette. The smoke twists up toward Mummy's chandeliers. She appears to have forgotten I am actually here. She is swearing, over and over, in short, foggy exhales.

"Fuck," she is saying. "Fuck."

In the kitchen, I hear that Daniel has switched off the radio and is turning down the gas on the stove. He strides into the front room, flipping a tea towel over his shoulder. I feel as if I am watching a traffic collision, one I am powerless to stop.

Rachel gives Daniel a pained smile. "Hi. You must be Daniel. Heard loads about you." She grimaces. "Sorry. Sorry. Sorry I'm such a mess. I just, um . . . Just need a minute."

Rachel places her palm over her face, the cigarette still balanced between her index and middle finger. She lowers herself down to the ground until she is crouching, balanced on the chunky heels of her boots, and stares at the wall. Over her head, Daniel blinks at me. I shrug hopelessly. The smell of cigarette smoke starts to overwhelm the aroma of the steaks browning on the stove. Behind Daniel, the candles on the table drip wax down the sides.

"Can I get you a drink?" Daniel asks eventually, peering down at Rachel. He is staring at her neck. "A cup of tea, maybe, or a glass of—"

"Yeah, a glass of water would be amazing. With ice and lemon, please. If you've got it."

Silenced, Daniel returns to the kitchen.

"Rachel?"

I feel awkward addressing Rachel when she is crouched on the floor. There's nothing for it but to crouch down, too. She won't meet my eye, so I find myself addressing the bottom bookshelves next to where she is crouching.

"Rachel," I plead. "What happened?"

Rachel winces, as if I've touched an open wound.

"I had an argument with somebody," she croaks.

I hesitate. "Was it . . . the father? Is this because you told him?"

Rachel shakes her head. I don't know if she means no, or that she just doesn't want to talk about it. I look again at her neck and find myself involuntarily touching my own. Someone did that to her. I can barely comprehend it. A young, pregnant girl. In my world, such a thing feels unthinkable. But elsewhere, apparently, things are different.

I open my mouth, but before I can think of another question, Daniel reappears, holding a glass of water. He hands it over awkwardly, glancing down at Rachel's bump.

Rachel stands, somewhat shakily, and takes the glass in her left hand, allowing the swollen hand to fall to her side. She mutters her thanks, then looks past Daniel at the laid table, the dimmed light.

"Am I interrupting?" she asks. "Say if I am."

"No, no," I say hurriedly. "Of course you're not." Daniel glares at me.

Rachel buries her head in both hands and seems to sob, her shoulders convulsing, her breathing coming out in heaves. She rocks back and forth on her heels, ash dropping onto the floorboards.

I shuffle closer, place an arm tentatively around her shoulder. Without looking up, she grips my hand.

"Helen," she says, "can I stay here tonight? A couple of nights, maybe?"

I find myself answering even before I have computed what the words will be.

"Of course. Of course you can."

Her face is so full of gratitude that I am forced to turn away. I dare not look at Daniel.

"Rachel, why don't you sit here for a second? We can all have something to eat." I glance at Daniel. "Maybe Daniel could find you a bag of peas or something for your . . . the swelling."

Wordlessly, Daniel returns to the kitchen. I persuade Rachel onto the sofa. She lights another cigarette, her hands shaking less this time. I fetch a side plate from the laid table, and slide it under the ash falling from her cigarette.

When I return to the kitchen, Daniel spins around, hands outstretched, the sinews in his neck visible, as if he is struggling to keep his head fastened to his body.

"What is going on, Helen?"

I shush him. "She'll hear you."

"I don't care! What is she doing here? Can't you just tell her it's our anniversary? Asking for fucking ice and lemon!"

I stare at him, stunned. "Are you serious? She's upset! Someone has assaulted her. Can't you see what's happened to her neck?"

"That doesn't mean you had to say she could stay here! For fuck's sake, Helen!"

"Daniel! Stop swearing! Can you just try and find something cold in the freezer, please? I can't bend down that far."

Daniel kneels, pulls a freezer drawer out too forcefully. It falls onto the kitchen floor in a smash of ice and plastic. I can't understand why he is quite so angry.

"Jesus, Helen. Are there even any peas in here? Do we even buy peas? Why are these drawers so full? What is all this stuff?"

He holds up a handful of freezer bags, shakes them like pompoms.

"It's chicken casserole," I say weakly. "The book says to batch-cook a selection of healthy meals. You know, for when the baby comes."

Daniel just stares at me, at the bags, and then at me again. I might as well have just told him they contain human body parts. I kneel down next to him, holding on to the kitchen sideboard to lower myself.

"Come on. There are definitely some peas in here somewhere. Let me look."

"For fuck's sake, Helen. I don't care about peas or fucking . . . casseroles!" He slams the freezer door shut.

"Daniel, she's a friend of mine. She's young and pregnant and alone and . . . vulnerable."

"Yes, but—"

"Just calm down for a moment. She needs a bit of help. I can't just turn her away, can I?"

"Why not? You said yourself you thought she was a nutcase."

Suddenly, both our heads jerk to the side. Rachel is in the doorway.

"I didn't say that, Rachel," I say quietly. "I promise I didn't say that." I glance at Daniel. He is scowling, but I can see he has been shamed into silence.

"I'm the one who should apologize," Rachel says, looking at Daniel. "I'm sorry. I'll go. I was just after those peas. Or whatever. Anything. Anything cold." She presses a palm to her forehead, one eyelid flickering slightly. She looks like she might be about to faint.

I open the freezer drawer and dig out the peas. Daniel snatches them up, gets to his feet, closes the freezer door, and hands her the bag. On the stove, the onions that Daniel had been frying lie still in the pan, oily and gray. Pools of ice are melting on the floor. I'm worried the casseroles will start defrosting if I don't replace them, but it feels inappropriate somehow to start putting them back.

The smoke alarm beeps and there is a smell of burning. Daniel rushes to the oven door, whips the tea towel off his shoulder, and opens it, but it is too late. A cloud of black smoke fills the kitchen. Rachel screws up her eyes and coughs loudly.

"I was doing sweet potato chips," Daniel mutters, slamming the door shut.

"It doesn't matter about the dinner." I mean it kindly, but when I hear how it sounds, I instantly regret it. Daniel glares at me.

Rachel exhales, a serious expression on her face. She picks up an apron that is hanging off the back of a chair, ties it around her waist. "Let me help," she says in a resolute voice, as if we are first responders at a terror attack.

"There is no need, really," Daniel tells her. His teeth are clamped together, his jaw tense. He touches his glasses where they sit on the bridge of his nose.

"I insist."

Rachel bends down deftly, mops up the pools of water, slides the freezer doors shut. It is clear that Daniel and I are equally stumped as to what we should say.

When the mess is cleared up, Rachel turns to me.

"Do you want me to go?" she whispers, glancing at Daniel, who now has his back to us.

I look at Rachel, then to Daniel, then at Rachel again, at the marks on her neck. I look out of the window. It has started to rain. Drops flick at the window like glass shards.

"You should report him, Rachel," I say. "Whoever did this to you." I turn to Daniel. "Daniel, don't you think she should go to the police?"

Daniel stares at me, then at Rachel.

"Of course," he says.

Rachel meets his gaze, then looks back at me.

"I'll . . . I'll think about it," she says. "But, Helen, please can I stay?" She bites her lip, looks down at the floor. "Just one night. Please? I'll be gone after that. I swear."

Later, Rachel is comfortably installed on a fold-out bed in the spare room—the room that is soon to be our nursery. I wish we didn't have to put her in there, but all the others are crammed full of furniture that has been moved from downstairs because of the remodeling work. I lie awake, listening to the rain against the window. Daniel falls asleep, but I can't seem to settle.

Unable to drop off, I turn the bedside light back on and look for my book, where I have been keeping the note I found in Rory and Serena's bathroom, and the torn-up photograph I found in Daniel's old box. But my book is not on the table, or in the drawer, or down the side of my bed.

A day or two later, I find the book on our kitchen table. I can't work out how it would have gotten there. I'm sure I hadn't taken it downstairs. And when I open it, I find that both the note and the photograph have gone.

35 WEEKS

Helen

A WEEK SINCE HER arrival, there has been no mention of what Rachel plans to do next. We come home to find her damp towels coating the bathroom floor, circles on the woodwork from her coffee mugs. At breakfast, she saws wonky chunks of sourdough and squeezes them into the toaster, then forgets about them until the kitchen is filling with smoke.

With Rachel around, Daniel is here less and less. When he is here, his every movement betrays his irritation. He slams doors, makes loud banging noises while he empties the trash. Daniel keeps telling me I need to talk to her, ask her how much longer it's going to be. I have told him that it won't be more than a few days. That she is vulnerable, that I can't just tell her to get out, when someone has so obviously tried to hurt her. But I'm now starting to wonder myself whether she is actually planning to leave.

For a woman fleeing a violent attacker, Rachel seems remarkably cheerful. I've tried to ask her gently once or twice about what happened. About who has been hurting her. But she just changes the subject, refuses to meet my eye, starts chewing on her cuffs, or her fingernails. She promises she will go, just as soon as she has found somewhere new to live—somewhere safe, she says, with a look that forces Daniel and me into guilty silence.

She claims she is flat hunting. But as far as I can see she spends most of the day on the sofa, playing pop music on her phone. She has a habit of skipping each track before it's finished, which sets my teeth on edge. When we are trying to get to sleep at night, I hear the squeaking sound of her opening the old sash window in the spare bedroom to smoke. She doesn't seem to feel the cold. With the window open, I can hear every footfall on the street below, shouts from the park, sirens on the Trafalgar Road. In the morning, you can feel the draft from under her bedroom door.

I've been at the hospital all afternoon for a prenatal blood screening. They make you fast for it, to see if the baby has given you diabetes. Now I'm exhausted and ravenous, the baby low in my belly, pressing painfully down on my bladder as I trudge home. The air is getting colder now, pinching at my cheeks as I step off the Tube. The whole way home, I think about the last bagel from the bakery that I saw this morning in the bread box. I am going to smother it with butter, cheddar cheese, and chutney, and grill it, then devour it with a huge cup of hot, sweet tea and the remains of the *Sunday Times*. Please let Rachel be out, I think. Please.

At first it seems my prayers have been answered. No Rachel, and no builders, either. For once, the house is blissfully silent. When I lift the lid off the bread box, though, there is nothing but crumbs, a crumpled paper bag. Daniel never eats breakfast. It must have been Rachel. I flick the kettle on so forcefully I nearly knock it off the base.

As the kettle boils, the phone rings. I snatch it up.

"Mrs. Thorpe, this is Monique calling regarding your remortgage. We have been trying to—"

"Listen," I say. "There's no remortgage on this property."

"OK, can I just ask you a couple of security questions and then we can discuss—"

I sigh, slam the phone down. Isn't there some kind of law against this sort of spam calling nowadays? I think about searching online for what you can do, how you can stop them. But the thought evaporates as the kettle flicks off and my stomach groans. I pull the fridge open, reach for the milk. But the carton is empty. Rachel. I toss the carton into the recycling. Where is she, anyway?

I find the door to the spare room slightly ajar. Through the crack, I can see plates piled up against each other on her bedside table, still bearing crumbs and smears of food. I push the door open to get a better look. It's even worse than I suspected. Mugs of unfinished black coffee congregate on the chest of drawers, the one that is meant to double as a changing table for the baby. There is a pile of unfinished takeout boxes there, too—slimy noodles, rice stained orange by the strange Chinese food she buys at places near the station. I glance left and right, though I know there is no one else here, then I step inside.

I wrinkle my nose. A stale duvet, unwashed clothes all over the floor. I step over a gold sequined skirt, some black tights all twisted up with a pair of dirty red underwear. I unscrew the sash window, throw it up, breathe in the cold fresh air. The sky is white and overcast, flat as a bed-sheet. I can see Monty skulking along the garden fence like a tightrope walker, stalking a wood pigeon.

I collect the mugs from the chest of drawers, pinching one between each of my fingers, and balance the plates on my arm. As I lean over for the final mug, my bump almost throwing me off balance, I see her battered suitcase. I had only noticed that later, the fact she'd brought a suitcase. After I'd said she could stay, I spotted it, sitting there in the hallway. She'd had it the whole time.

I consider the suitcase, clothes trailing out of it from all directions, as if a bomb has gone off inside. Underneath a crumple of leopard-print fabric, a smooth silver rectangle poking out of the top catches in my eye, a white plug and wire wrapped around it. It looks exactly like Daniel's laptop. The one that's gone missing.

I try to remember when it disappeared. A sick feeling gathers in my stomach. Surely not.

I set the mugs carefully back down on the chest of drawers, the plates beside them. With an effort, I lower myself down to the floor, first one knee, then the other. I extract the laptop from the suitcase, unwrap the wire from around it, and switch it on. It blinks into life, a generic loading screen. A scratch on the keypad that I'm sure I recognize.

The little blue bar is inching across the screen. It's taking ages. She's probably only gone out for cigarettes. She could be home any moment. I look around the room, in an effort not to focus on it, as if that might make it go faster.

But then I hear a key in the door.

"Helen? It's me!"

Rachel. I slam the laptop down, wrap the wire around again, shove it back into her suitcase. It'll have to wait. But as I stuff it back in, something else falls out. Something red.

"Helen, are you upstairs?"

I can hear Rachel's footfall on the stairs—she never, ever takes her shoes off. I grab the thing that fell out, snatch it up quickly. As I turn it over, my breath catches in my chest.

A small crimson envelope, with nothing inside it. Just like the one I found at Rory and Serena's. But this cannot be the one that went missing from my book. Because this one doesn't have Rory's initials on the envelope. This one bears just a single initial on the front.

W.

Helen

"JUST TIDYING," I SAY as she reaches the landing. My arms are full of mugs. We eye each other for a moment. I try to disguise my breathlessness.

"Oh yeah," she says. "Sorry. There's some plates in there, too." She pauses. "I'll get them."

I step to the side to let her pass, our eyes still locked. She walks past me slowly into her room, looking back at me as she closes the door in my face.

In the kitchen afterward, I put the mugs in the sink, run the tap, my heart still pounding. I try to explain it another way in my mind. But I can't. The envelope was exactly the same size and color as the one I found in Rory and Serena's bathroom. But if she is the other person—if she is W—then she knows Rory. She knows my brother. But how? What is she up to?

I pray that Daniel will be home early, that I'll be able to talk to him about it. But he messages to say he will be late, again. I am stuck with her. Should I confront Rachel? Something tells me I shouldn't. Not while I am on my own with her.

I hope she will stay upstairs, but as soon as she hears me cooking, she appears in the kitchen, wearing her pink velour jogging bottoms and a pair of Daniel's old socks.

"Are you doing carbonara? My favorite! Thanks! Shall I put that film on?"

We end up watching the whole of *Sliding Doors* together, even though it is on ITV so there are ads to sit through and it doesn't finish until late. I watch her, her black hair all wet from another bath, as she coils long, sticky threads of my spaghetti around her fork and shoves them into her mouth, eyes glued to the television. As soon as she sets her bowl aside—onto the sofa, nearly tipping grease all over the cushions— Monty leaps into her lap. She tickles him and he bats at her hand occasionally, but he doesn't let his claws come out. For some reason, he seems to love her.

"Cats." She yawns, turning to look at me. "They don't give a fuck, do they?" There are little smudges of pasta sauce at the corners of her mouth. She reaches for my hand, squeezes it.

"This is so nice, Helen," she says. "Thanks so much. You're a good friend."

For a moment, I feel genuinely touched. I think how nice it is, not to be alone. To be watching something I would actually choose, instead of another of Daniel's police dramas. But then I remember. The note. And the laptop. I've just caught her stealing from us, for God's sake! Passing love notes to my married brother! Any normal person would have thrown her out. Yet here I am, playing best friends with her.

The envelope—the W—it can't just be a coincidence. But why would she be exchanging notes with Rory, unless . . . unless something was going on between them? I glance down at the bump in her lap. I feel my stomach churn, like when I was first pregnant. The feeling of seasickness, except you're on dry land, and nothing will make it stop. Who is she, this girl, curled up on the sofa with my cat? What has she done?

I decide to check her suitcase again as soon as she goes out. The film drags on; the baby shifts in my belly. I change position, then again. I wait for her to fall asleep on the sofa, or go out to the twenty-four-hour shop for cigarettes, like she would usually do. But she doesn't do either. When the credits start rolling, she stretches extravagantly, arching her back, her arms in the air. Monty leaps off her lap.

"I think I'll call it a night."

She trails up to her room, leaving her dirty bowl abandoned. She closes the door. As I wash up, little blasts of pop music start to blare intermittently through the ceiling.

Helen

AFTER I FOUND THE laptop and the envelope, I wasn't able to sleep. I lay on my side, the baby kicking softly, until Daniel finally got home. When he came into the bedroom, I told him I'd been thinking about what he said, and that he was right. We needed to talk to Rachel. Ask her what her plans are.

I decided not to tell him about the things I'd found. He'd have gone mad about the laptop, blamed me for letting a thief into our house. This way was just easier. As I predicted, he didn't ask why I'd changed my mind. He just seemed pleased and kissed me good night. He fell asleep far more quickly than I did.

When I wake the next morning, I can hear that Rachel is in the bath downstairs. I pull on my robe, head to the kitchen, make myself a cup of herbal tea. When she eventually emerges, Rachel is wearing a towel of mine around her body and another on her head.

I tell her I will make us all some breakfast.

"Lovely," she says. "Anything I can do?"

I glance down at her. "Don't you want to get dressed?"

She shakes her head, grinning. A flash of pointed teeth. "I'm fine like this," she says. "I'll make the eggs."

When Daniel arrives in the kitchen, I have finished the bacon and toast, set plates on the table for all three of us, with glasses of orange juice. Rachel is still leaning absentmindedly against the sideboard, cracking eggs into a bowl without looking properly, so the whites are dripping down the sides, tiny pieces of shell flecked in the mixture. She has started reading a magazine, which she has placed next to the bowl.

Daniel walks straight past her without saying good morning. "I'll just have bacon," he mutters.

"Me, too." I sigh.

We both sit down at the table. Daniel starts to butter pieces of toast rhythmically, in horizontal lines. He looks at me, then at Rachel, and then back again.

"Rachel, why don't you come and sit down?" I suggest when she doesn't join us.

Rachel looks up, closes her magazine. "Oh, sorry. I was miles away." She sits down and takes the piece of toast that Daniel has just buttered, spears a piece of bacon onto her fork. "Thanks," she says. She takes the ketchup and empties it onto her plate, a huge red pool. The smell makes my stomach churn.

"Rachel, we were wondering." My voice is reedy, my mouth slightly dry. "How are you getting on with finding somewhere else to live?"

"Oh, really good actually!" Rachel looks up, smiles at us. Daniel and I are silenced.

"Really?"

"Yeah! I found a flat. It's great. And they said I can move in really soon."

I glance at Daniel. I don't remember her going to any flat viewings.

"That's great, Rachel." I pause. "When . . . When exactly did they say you could move in?"

Rachel opens her mouth wide, presses her bacon sandwich inside, tomato ketchup seeping from the bread. "Oh," she says through a mouthful of bacon. "Um, like mid-November?"

I try to gauge Daniel's reaction. He is frowning slightly. I suspect that like me, he is unsure quite how to react. On the one hand, the fact that she is moving out—that we don't have the anticipated battle on our hands—is unexpectedly good news. On the other, that means two and a half more weeks with her in our house. It feels like a lifetime.

"Listen," Rachel says, wiping her face, looking from me to Daniel, then back to me again. "You've both been so nice to let me stay. Thanks so much." She glances at Daniel, her eyes narrowing slightly. "I'll keep out of your hair for the next couple of weeks." She waves her hand in the air. "You won't even notice me. I swear."

Daniel looks away. Nods. "All right," he says eventually.

Rachel beams. Then, before I can say anything, there is a knock on the door.

Serena

HELEN IS LEANING ON the kitchen counter, fiddling with the pile of napkins, avoiding my gaze. "I suppose I just wish you hadn't invited her tonight, that's all," she mutters.

"I'm sorry, Helen. I didn't know I wasn't supposed to. Could you pass that bowl, please?"

I am not really listening to Helen. I am thinking about the canapés, and whether we've ordered enough lamb racks, and whether I should have bought that second case of champagne, and how many people might want elderflower cordial instead. I am keeping an eye on the pale sky, checking whether it looks like rain. Counting napkins, squeezing ice cubes into the water jugs.

I hadn't intended to come over this morning. God knows I had enough to do. But Helen had been asking for ages to borrow a book I'd been reading about hypnobirthing, and as I was passing her house I realized I had it in my bag.

When I'd knocked on the door, it wasn't Helen who answered. Or Daniel. It was her. That pale face, black hair, that strange smile showing off little pointed teeth, that sticky-out bump. For a mad moment, I wondered whether it was my body wash she had been using—the entire hallway smelled of rosemary.

"Hello, Serena."

She had one of Helen's fluffy white towels twisted on her head like a turban. Another was tied around her like an indecently short dress. I'd glanced over her shoulder, hoping Helen or Daniel might arrive with an introduction, an explanation. Rachel had tilted her head to one side, shaken her wet hair free of the towel.

"Are you here to see Helen?"

She asked it as if this was her house, too—as if it were equally possible I'd come over wanting to see her. She twisted her hair up with her finger, piling it onto the top of her head, revealing a pattern of angry purple marks around her pale throat. I winced. They looked painful. As I followed her into the kitchen, I saw that they spread all the way around the back of her neck.

Once we reached the kitchen, Rachel turned to look at me, as if she'd caught me staring, even though she couldn't possibly have seen. The room smelled of bacon. Helen and Daniel were sitting at the table. When they saw me, they looked up as if they were being held hostage.

"We're all having breakfast," Rachel said. "Can I get you a coffee? I was just about to make one." I noticed the skin around her eyebrows was red, as if she'd been plucking them. They were pencil thin.

Rachel flicked the coffee machine on and reached up into a cupboard for mugs. I sat down next to Helen. "Hi, darling." I had to raise my voice above the sound of Rachel grinding and banging at the coffee machine, the hiss of steam. "I just came to drop that book off."

"Thanks," Helen said. "That's so nice of you." She paused, glanced sideways toward the coffee machine. "This is Rachel."

"We've met," Rachel trilled. She started placing coffees in front of us all. "Just now, I mean," she added quickly. "Sorry, there wasn't much milk. Let me see if I can find some sugar." Helen took her cup and peered into it warily before placing it back down on the table. While Helen was distracted, Rachel shot me a theatrical wink.

I took the book out of my bag, slid it across the table. "This is the one you wanted, isn't it?" Helen didn't reply. She was staring at Rachel's wet hair, which had fallen out of the twist and was now hanging lank over her shoulders, dripping puddles onto the kitchen tiles. I saw Helen's eyes trace the line of watery footprints that had followed Rachel from the stairs, down the hallway and back into the kitchen. I tried a different subject.

"I didn't know your bathroom was finished, Helen."

Helen opened her mouth to answer, but Rachel had got there first.

"Oh my God, it's a-ma-zing." She grinned at us both. "Best bath ever. It's so comfy!"

This was odd. I tried to catch Helen's eye again, but couldn't. Daniel had picked up the sports pages, and was holding them out in front of him so I couldn't see his face, like a child attempting to hide.

"Well." I eased myself off a stool, deciding that whatever was going on here, I'd be best off out of it. I smiled at Helen, as if this had all been lovely, rather than hideous. "I'll see you at Rory's birthday dinner tonight—right?"

"Yes," she said, glancing nervously at Rachel. "Of course."

Rachel's head had popped up.

"Oh, are you doing something tonight? Helen didn't say."

We both stared at Rachel. I tried not to react.

"Just a dinner, for my husband's—Helen's brother's—birthday."

"Oh," Rachel said. "I see. Quiet night in for me then, I suppose."

I glanced at Helen. Her cheeks and neck had colored, and she was staring down at her breakfast plate. The silence was too much to bear. It had felt unavoidable.

"You'd be very welcome, Rachel. If you're not doing anything."

"Great," Rachel said, grinning. "That sounds lovely. Thanks, Serena. Can't wait." Helen looked up at me in horror. But by then, it was too late.

Now Helen has arrived, hours early, alone. She is lingering in the kitchen with me, nibbling at her thumbnail. I decide to give her a job. "Please could you set out some more champagne glasses?"

This is not really necessary, but it is the only thing I can think of for her to do. Helen likes to come early and help when we are having a dinner. I always tell her there is no need, but she invariably insists. I am not entirely sure why she does this. Perhaps she believes it confers on her a special status, like a cohost.

"Is Rachel coming later, then?" I ask her.

Helen doesn't reply. She seems to be unable to set out the glasses without clinking them together. Sooner or later, she is going to smash something.

"Helen? What is it?"

I look at her in her maternity party dress, teetering on her uncomfortable heels. Her ankles are swollen, her belly enormous. She looks rather unhappy. In fact, she looks like she might be about to cry.

"I'm sorry," she mutters. A single fat tear rolls down one cheek, and she paws at it miserably. There is the sound of a knock on the door.

I go to Helen's side, hold her hand.

"Rory will get it, don't worry," I tell her. "Do you want to sit down?"

"I'm OK."

I sigh. "What are you upset about?"

Helen shrugs hopelessly. "It's Rachel," she says, burying her head in her hands. "I think maybe I made a mistake, saying she could stay with us."

"I did wonder what all that was about this morning. She's your new friend from the prenatal class, right? Why is she staying with you all of a sudden? How long for?"

"I don't know."

"Well, how long has she been there?"

"Only about a week or so," Helen murmurs. "She just turned up one night." She rubs her eyes. "It was the night of our anniversary. I thought she was in some kind of trouble. Did you see those marks on her neck?"

"You can hardly miss them. What happened to her?"

"Well, she wouldn't say exactly but . . . she was so upset. I felt so bad for her. I felt I couldn't say no."

"I can see that," I say carefully. "But now—what? She's driving you both bonkers?"

Helen laughs halfheartedly. "No— I mean, well, yes . . . she is—but it's more than that." Her face clouds over. She brings a cardigan cuff to her mouth, starts chewing on a thread. "The thing is, I think—I know this sounds mad, but—I feel like she might have another reason for being here."

"What do you mean, another reason?"

Helen looks away, color rising to her cheeks. She places her hands together, as if in prayer, drops her head. A confession is coming.

"I know I shouldn't have, OK," she mumbles into her sleeve. "But I went into the room where she's staying and looked in her suitcase." She flicks me a guilty glance.

I shrug. "And what?"

"And—" She stops, covers her mouth, as if she doesn't want to let the words out.

I try to sound firm. "Helen, what was in her suitcase? What are you worried about?"

Helen winces.

"Serena, I think Rachel might . . . I think . . ."

Just then, I hear Rory. "Only a delivery," he calls. "You know, darling, I think I will pop out and get more champagne." I can tell without looking that Rory is studying himself in the hallway mirror, smoothing his hair down at the sides. When he steps into the kitchen, he sees Helen.

"Ah, sis!" He grins widely, plants a kiss on Helen's cheek. Helen closes her eyes. "Where's my present?" Rory jokingly pokes her in the ribs. She makes a stab at a laugh but manages only a sort of cough. She brushes at her eyes with her cuff. Rory looks at my face, then back to Helen. His smile wilts slightly. "What are you two looking so serious for?"

Helen straightens her spine, shakes her head.

"Forget it," she says, giving Rory a strange look. "It doesn't matter."

Helen

SERENA AND RORY'S LIVING room is empty, as I had hoped it would be. It looks even lovelier than usual—the high ceilings, the huge bay windows looking to the front and the back. There is a grand piano at the garden end, and a courtyard of sofas at the front, arranged around a mango-wood coffee table holding architecture books with gold-embossed spines, the bowls they bought in Morocco.

Serena has made up a log fire; the kindling crackles and spits softly, a plume of smoke rising. It doesn't seem possible that it is the time of year for fires already. The thought of winter fills me with gloom. I think of the early darkness, the layers of scratchy clothing, of collars pulled up against the wind.

I hear snatches of laughter from the dining room. I should go in, but I just need a minute. A minute to sit. And be away from Rachel.

After our awkward breakfast this morning—and Serena's visit—Daniel stood up as if he could take no more. He grabbed a bag and strode out of the house saying he was off to play squash, even though he hadn't mentioned anything about it before. Rachel said she was going out, too. Something about getting her nails done, for the party, as she kept calling it.

As soon as I heard the door close after them both, I was in Rachel's room, throwing open her suitcase. No more messing around. I had to know what she was up to, why that note had been in her bag. I couldn't bear to think about what I might find. A whole load of those red envelopes, a whole string of her and Rory's letters to each other? A diary, photographs even?

I searched through her case, carefully at first. Then—deciding it was such a mess she'd never know either way—I turned the whole thing upside down, slid my hands inside all the pockets.

But there was nothing. The laptop had gone. The note addressed to W was nowhere to be found. Nor were the things missing from my book—the note I found at Rory's, and the taped-together photograph—even though I'm sure now that it must be her who has taken them.

I looked everywhere then. The chest of drawers, the bedside table. Behind the books on the shelves. Under all her clothes on the floor. No sign. By the time I got to the end, my hands were shaking.

I stare into the crackling fire. There is a scrape of chairs. People must be sitting down to eat. I know I should go and join Daniel and the rest of them next door, but the thought of eating turns my stomach. I hear a muffled chorus of happy birthday. Charlie must have arrived—as usual, he is singing the loudest, completely out of tune. Then I hear Rory laughing, telling them all to shut up. Starting a speech. He is so good at speeches. He always makes everyone laugh.

I feel a prickle of anxiety, the dull ache of dread. Is it possible I imagined it? Finding the note, the laptop? Impossible. I can't have. But if I didn't, then where have they gone?

"Helen? Are you in there?"

That sounds like Serena. I haul myself up, straighten my spine. Rub at my eyes so no one can see I've been crying.

Katie

RACHEL HAS FOUND A coffee mug from somewhere and is pouring what looks like an expensive bottle of red wine directly into it. Everybody's conversations sort of trail away and quiet until the *glug glug glug* of her pouring is the only thing any of us can hear.

"Don't worry, I'll just drink out of this," she says. She says it as if it's the answer to a question.

She is standing right in the middle of the room, by the kitchen island. She is wearing a red dress, cut low over her breasts. I can't seem to not look at her, her dark, catlike flicks of eyeliner, her glossy-painted mouth. I see other eyes darting at her, too. It takes a few moments before I realize it isn't just the crimson dress, the pale, exposed décolletage that is attracting these glances. It is the ugly necklace of marks, like huge purple welts, all around her throat. What on earth has happened to her?

With dinner over, the kitchen is filling up. People are gathering in groups, eager to finally be in company of their own choosing. Me included.

I search the kitchen for Charlie or Helen. I'd hoped Serena would seat me next to Helen for the dinner. I'd been feeling guilty that I hadn't seen her since that lunch—she keeps asking if we can go for a coffee, and I keep having to tell her I can't, that work is just too busy because of the trial. But I looked at the plan as I came in, and both of them had been on the other side of the room. I knew from experience that no one would dare defy Serena's seating plan, the little name cards propped up on the plates. The dining room had been full of candles and roses, the cutlery on each plate tied together with little scraps of lace and a sprig of rosemary. Anyone would have thought they were hosting a wedding reception.

When I glanced over to see who Charlie was seated with, I could see he was next to Rachel.

"Katie! So good to see you again!"

Rachel has noticed me. I smile, trying to stop my gaze from drifting down to her throat. She smiles back, her mouth wide, glassy and cherry red. Her lip liner is slightly off, making her smile appear lopsided. Most of her body is sparrow thin, but her breasts are swollen full, her tummy starting to curve. She still doesn't really look pregnant as much as someone whose torso has been inflated like a blow-up doll.

"Hi, Rachel," I say. "How are you?"

Apparently, Rachel is living at Helen's house now. Over dinner, I tried to ask Daniel about it, but he was sitting diagonally across, a few seats away, and we couldn't hear each other properly. He just rolled his eyes and shook his head.

I glance at the doors out to the veranda, wondering if Charlie might have gone out to smoke. The doors are open, and Serena has set out lanterns on the decking, fairy lights in her cherry tree. It rained a little earlier, but now it is cool and fresh, the plants wet, the air from outside thick with the smell of earth.

"How's the rape case?"

Rachel asks this loudly. A few people turn around to stare at me, silenced by the mention of the word "rape."

"Hard work at the moment, actually. I'm glad to have a night off."

It had been past midnight when I'd finally gotten back last night. The drive home from Cambridge was a nightmare. The motorway had been closed because of an accident, and I'd had to take a detour down a rabbit hole of dark country roads, the rain pelting, my windshield wipers on full whack.

Hugh had told me to get a hotel. "You're shattered, Wheeler. Don't drive in this weather." He was being kind, but I couldn't stay—I just wanted to be home, to be away from it for a bit. I only had one CD in my car, and I listened to it on repeat, the volume turned right up. I had hoped it would help me forget about the evidence that afternoon, about the splinters they said they had found under her fingernails. The way she'd looked down at the floor of the witness box, her hair falling in her face, as they'd said it. As if she was the one who should be ashamed. And how the defendants, in their expensive suits, just sat there looking bored, or passing notes, or smirking when the jury wasn't looking. Even when she had told the court how she felt, after it had happened. How she thought she might be better off dead.

When they'd gone through the medical evidence, I couldn't stop thinking about what it must have been like for her when they collected it, the fibers, the fluids. A white examination table, the cold touch of the metal instruments. I wondered whether I'd have had it in me to go through all of that, after what had come before. As I was leaving court, I saw her across the street, belting her coat. Her lawyer was saying something to her, but she didn't seem to be listening. She saw me and our eyes met, just for a moment. I nodded, and she looked away.

Afterward, as I'd typed it all up in the pub down the road from the court, my jaw had clenched at having to be balanced about it, to report their side, too. *Both of the defendants deny all of the charges against them.* When I'd pressed send I'd taken a long, deep breath.

I'd been so grateful to see the signs for London, the lights on the motorway, the drunk faces of the stumbling revelers in Camden Town. The scruffy terraces of the end of my road. The sound of my key in the lock, the purr of Socks, rubbing his cheek against my legs. My flat was a mess, the doormat piled with unread letters, the fridge empty. I'd turned the water on full, peeled my clothes off, and shoved them all in the washing machine on the hot water setting. I'd stood under the shower for what felt like a long time.

"I read your piece today," Rachel is saying now. "About those scumbag rapists." I startle at her language.

"You know, I reckon they should just hang blokes who do stuff like that to women." She takes a swig from her mug. "Or, you know, firing squad, electric chair." She pops an olive into her mouth. "Whatever. Just as long as they're fucking dead."

To my relief, Helen appears in the kitchen. She heads to one of the cupboards, then starts filling bowls of nuts and chips, as if this is her house, and not Rory and Serena's. When she sees me, she smiles, then eyes Rachel warily, her smile slipping. Her nose and eyes look pink, as if she has been crying. Her bump looks so heavy under her dress.

I hug her. "Are you all right?"

"Hmm? I'm fine."

"Your eyes look a bit red."

She shakes her head. "I'm fine," she says again.

Charlie appears through the open veranda doors. "Hey, you." He leans in to kiss me on the cheek and misses. Instead he catches the bottom of my ear, the side of my neck. He smells of tobacco and shampoo and something else, something that is uniquely him. I glance out at the garden behind him. I wish we weren't standing in this hot kitchen. I long to be outside, in the cool. Charlie shoots me a curious look. Helen looks cross. Rachel is staring at me. No one is saying anything. Drinks, I think. I will get us all a drink.

"Right," I say. "Does everyone want a drink? Are you, um, all right, Rachel?"

It turns out that everyone has a drink, and Helen doesn't want one. All I've done is draw attention to Rachel's coffee mug of wine. The four of us all look at the mug, the dark red liquid inside half drunk. The silence is deafening.

"I'll have a refill," she chirps.

It feels odd, filling up a mug of red wine for a pregnant woman.

"Cheers," she says, lifting her mug. Everyone smiles politely, tilts their glasses to the middle. Rachel extends hers, insisting on a loud clunk with everyone before taking another gulp. It is all deeply uncomfortable. Charlie seems to be staring at Rachel, an odd expression on his face. Helen is looking nervously at me, as if hoping I will resolve the situation. I grasp at the only other passing person I recognize—Lisa, who works with Daniel and Rory.

"Rachel, have you met Lisa?"

Lisa spins around when I say her name, as if I've caught her doing something wrong. As usual, her dress is elegant, expensive for a PA— though perhaps she just has a good eye. High at the front, bare on the shoulders. The kind of dress not many people can get away with. I suspect she spends a lot of time in the gym.

"Hi, Rachel," Lisa says. She puts out a hand to shake Rachel's. It feels a bit odd, overly formal, as if she is still in work mode, welcoming a client to the Haverstock offices.

Rachel looks at Lisa's hand like it might be a trick. Then she takes it, but doesn't shake it. Then she lets it go again.

"Have we met before, Rachel?" Lisa's face is somewhere between a smile and a frown. "At the office, maybe?"

Rachel shakes her head, bemused. "Rory's office? I don't think so."

Helen is staring at Lisa. Lisa looks at her, then back to Rachel.

"Oh," she says. "Right. My mistake."

"I've been reading about Haverstock. About your latest project," Rachel is saying loudly. Lisa's expression shifts almost imperceptibly, like an animal scenting danger. I can't decide whether to cringe or stifle a laugh. No one else would dream of broaching the subject of Rory and Daniel's latest project—not with the coverage it's been getting lately.

"Sounds like a lot of people are pretty unhappy about that estate being knocked down, doesn't it?" she blunders on.

"Yes, well, housing in London is quite a complicated issue," Lisa breathes. Her tone is a warning, but not one that Rachel can hear.

"Complicated? Hardly." She snorts. "Do you know how long the list is for a council house in Greenwich?" She looks around. "Anyone know?"

Everyone else in the room has studiously turned away now. Even Charlie looks awkward. The atmosphere feels heavy, as if a storm is coming. I realize I'm holding my breath.

"Eighteen thousand people ahead of you," Rachel announces triumphantly. "And you're knocking down a load of council houses for a few fancy apartments with a gym." She rolls her eyes, grinning, as if this is all hilariously funny, instead of hideously uncomfortable. "I bet most of it is foreigners, isn't it? Buying from abroad? I bet half of them won't even live there."

Lisa's expression hardens from lukewarm to glacial.

"Lovely to meet you, Rachel," she says. "Excuse me."

She turns to join another group that has gathered around the kitchen island. Charlie excuses himself, too, says he is going for a smoke. Rachel's eyes follow him out of the room.

The space around Helen, Rachel, and me seems to be getting smaller, filling with noise and elbows. Arms reach into cupboards for spirits, extra glasses. There is a pop of more champagne corks. I glance again at the doors to the garden.

"So, Helen," I say. "Have you decided on whether to do the fireworks this year?"

A fireworks party at Helen's house is an old tradition. When we were little, the Haverstocks used to have one every year, with the most amazing bonfire. When Helen and Daniel moved back into the house, she told everyone they were going to bring her parents' tradition back. But then, with everything that's happened over the past few years, I don't think she's felt up to it. I was hoping this year might be different.

"Ooh, you didn't tell me we were having a bonfire party, Helen," Rachel says abruptly, taking a fistful of nuts from a bowl. She fixes Helen with her gaze. "Sounds brilliant!"

Helen looks blankly at Rachel, as if she is speaking another language. Then she turns to me, gives me a hard stare.

"We're not having a bonfire party," she says. "I never said we were having the bonfire this year. Katie, what are you talking about?" Her tone is unusually firm.

Before I can answer, there's a huge crash. Everything happens at once. Rory has arrived, holding a bottle of champagne, but he seems to have slipped and dropped it somehow, and in the process, smashed a load of glasses that were set out on the side.

There are gasps, cries of "Careful, Serena!" Serena is standing with her back to Rachel, her hands on her bump, a deep line etched across her brow, as if she is clamping her face shut. There are glinting shards of glass everywhere. Rory is staring at his hand. It is red with blood, coursing from his thumb to his elbow. Hands reach for napkins, paper towels, wet cloths. I crouch down to help. Serena and Rachel are urged to avoid the glass. Hands are held out as they are lifted over the jagged puddles of red.

36 WEEKS

Serena

IT IS NEARLY TEN. I have been up for hours, sitting on the veranda, wrapped in my cashmere blanket, with my mint tea on the table. I hadn't posted on Instagram for a while, and I wanted to get the light just right.

It is so gorgeous in the garden at this time of year. Shafts of pale sunlight illuminate a lawn dusted with yellow leaves. A wet mist blurs the edges of everything. The wall climbers behind our hammock have started flaming orange and red, a last hurrah before they are claimed by the cold of winter.

It was a day like this the first time I came to Greenwich, the day I first met Rory's parents. The first time I really met Helen, and Daniel, too, or at the least the first time I spoke to either of them properly.

Rory and I had been in bed in his college room all afternoon. Now he was at the window, blowing smoke out over the quad. From his window, all you could see was a rippling mass of golden leaves from the sycamore tree outside. I was reading a dusty book I'd picked up off his nightstand, the duvet pulled up over my bare breasts. All of a sudden, he had stubbed his cigarette out on the sill. Started getting dressed, fishing at the back of his wardrobe for a shirt.

"Are we going somewhere?"

Rory hadn't even turned round. It was his little brother Charlie's birthday, he said. He was going home for a dinner. Did I fancy joining him, meeting the parents? I closed the book, looked up from the bed, surprised.

"They're dying to meet you," he said. "If you're up for it." Helen would be coming home, too, he added, sensing my hesitation. She was bringing a new boyfriend. "They haven't met him, either, so, you wouldn't be the only one getting a grilling."

I knew his younger sister, Helen, only a little then. She was at the same college, but we didn't exactly hang around in the same crowd. Since Rory and I had been seeing each other, she'd started waving to me sometimes, shyly, in the line for the dining hall, or in the bar, where she and her friends never seemed to be able to get a table. She waved to me on Kings Parade while she was cycling past me once, and nearly wobbled off her bike.

Anyway, I agreed to go, and when Rory and I got to the station, Helen was there, grinning and waving. She was bundled tightly in a winter coat, a thick scarf wound like a neck brace at her throat. "Hi, Serena," she gushed. Helen had already bought the tickets, and she doled them out to us from her mittened hands, like a teacher shepherding a school expedition. "This is Daniel. Have you met Daniel? He's studying architecture with Rory." She motioned to the tall, quiet boy standing next to her, dark overcoat buttoned up like a pallbearer. Daniel locked his dark eyes on mine, held out a wiry hand, hair flopping over his glasses.

It seemed like a long time before we finally reached Greenwich. Rory and I walked silently, hand in gloved hand, under the soft glimmer of Victorian gas lamps dotted along the edge of the park. The trees rustled, their brown leaves falling like crinkling paper bags. When we passed the pub at the end of their road, a blast of warm air escaped from the door, the cackle of laughter, the snap of a roaring fire. I noticed the walls enclosing Greenwich Park were studded with tiny doors. It felt so mysterious to me. Their street seemed hidden away, as if lost in time, perfectly preserved, untouched.

And then their home, with its perfect symmetry, the box hedges, the matchstick-straight black railings. The yellow glow of log fires and lamplight shining from its tall Georgian windows—windows that gazed straight out over the park. It looked like a painting.

"Here we are." Helen was beaming. She couldn't disguise the catch in her voice; of pride, of nervousness, of wanting us to love it. She kept glancing at me, as if my approval mattered to her almost as much as her boyfriend's. Neither Daniel nor I said anything. I couldn't believe this was really their home.

Helen rang the bell, and moments later, they were upon us: the mother kissing me on both cheeks, pulling an awkward Daniel into a bony hug with her long slender arms, then steering us all into the kitchen.

The father, Richard—apparently some sort of famous architect, though I'd never heard of him—was in there, on his hands and knees. He was attempting to relight the ancient-looking gas oven with a pipe hanging out of one side of his mouth while still holding a glass of port. I came to suspect it was not his first of the evening. He rose to his feet to hug Rory and Helen. Then he pumped Daniel's arm before beamingly thrusting a gin and tonic into my hand and planting a hot kiss on my cheek.

All evening, Daniel and I were treated as if we were their long-lost children. We were fed profusely, and solicitous questions were fired in our direction. Daniel kept having to bring his hand to cover his mouth to answer without displaying a mouthful of food. Every detail of Daniel's dull upbringing was deemed utterly fascinating, my every half-formed insight into law—my subject of study—met with enthusiastic assent. And how were we finding life in Cambridge? Was I keeping Rory under control? Had Daniel witnessed him actually turning up to any of his architecture lectures?

Even Charlie was nice to us. On the train there, Helen had warned us darkly about this "difficult" younger brother, who refused to apply to university and who lived in a twilight world of *Call of Duty* and marijuana in the uppermost bedroom. To me, though, he seemed pleasant enough, telling me about his plans for a music course at the local college, passing me the bread, asking Daniel thoughtfully about the football team he supported—although it was painfully obvious that this was a rugby family.

As the night went on, I realized Daniel was being treated with particularly lavish attention. Everyone was in raptures over the middling bottle of wine he had brought with him, over his shyly stated thoughts on architecture. Even Rory was at it, I noticed. Slapping this shy, diffident boy on the back, making out his jokes were funnier than they were. Over the course of the evening, he was enthusiastically invited to an entire calendar of family occasions—the country for Christmas, Courchevel at Easter, sailing in the summer.

I tried to work out if he was finding it at all strange, how eager they all seemed for the evening to be wonderful, for him to be pleased with everything we ate, drank, and saw. Looking at his face, I think he just didn't know what to make of it, of their exuberance, the decadence of it all, the platter of riches he was being offered. A few times, I noticed him glancing over, as if pleading for help.

When Daniel had quietly asked Helen about the time of the last train, Richard had waved his question away, insisted we all delay our return to Cambridge until the next day. Daniel protested stutteringly about a meeting with his faculty adviser first thing that he wouldn't have time to rearrange, but the look on Richard's face had silenced him.

Months later, when Helen and I had formed our obligatory friendship, she blushingly told me the story of what had happened later that night. How she had crawled down Daniel's body in her childhood bedroom and taken him into her mouth. I imagined poor Daniel, staring at the teddy bears on Helen's shelves, the branches of the horse chestnut tree tapping against the tall windows. Helen had giggled at the memory of how he had voiced concern about the noise, about her parents hearing them. She had silenced him. I imagined her flushed cheeks, her fox-colored hair spread out over the pillow. A pool of rusty red.

Perhaps Daniel hadn't detected it then, what lay behind the grinning faces, the elaborate overtures. The extravagantly prepared food, the carefully laid table, the noisy, parentally sanctioned fuck. I think he probably would have, if he'd known to look for it. They did their best, of course. But it is, in the end, not an easy thing to hide. The unmistakable stench of desperation. The cringing eagerness of the salesmen of damaged goods, for whom they'd finally found an interested buyer.

Helen

DANIEL AND I HAVE stopped talking about Rachel's presence. In fact, with her being around all the time, listening to our every conversation, we seem to have fallen out of the habit of talking altogether. In the morning, we wander from drawers to toaster to kettle, politely moving out of each other's way, like lodgers in a shared kitchen, while she sits at the table, slathering cream cheese onto bagels and slurping coffee. At night, we brush our teeth in silence. Daniel has started putting in earplugs before he is even in bed. He doesn't say good night.

I can't face the thought of telling him about my suspicions, about the note I found, and what it might mean. He is cross enough with me about Rachel being here without me making it worse by telling him she is a thief, not to mention a potential homewrecker. I still can't make up my mind on the latter. Sometimes I decide it's just too ridiculous to imagine anything could be going on between Rory and Rachel. But other times, the more I think about it, the more the pieces seem to fit. After all, hadn't Rachel more or less admitted to an affair with a married man, who wasn't interested in the baby? It would explain her determination to be friends with me. Her strange interest in Serena, asking whether Rory was happy about Serena's pregnancy. Why else would she ask something so odd about someone she'd never even met?

Then there was Rachel's excitement at being asked to Rory's birthday meal. And Rory's reaction. As soon as he'd seen her, he'd dropped all that glass. The look on his face, as if he'd seen a ghost. Could it have been the sudden apparition of his lover, standing right next to his wife, at his own birthday dinner, that threw him off balance?

And then, to add to all that, there was Lisa. She'd seemed so sure she had seen Rachel before. It's not as if she'd any reason to lie. And why else would Lisa have seen Rachel if not at Rory's office? That could, I thought queasily, have been where they had their secret assignations.

The thought of them together, at Haverstock—conducting some secret affair in the offices of the company Daddy built from nothing, while Serena sits clueless and pregnant at home and Daniel slaves away trying to save the company—makes my stomach sick with fury. How could Rory do something like that? He'd never have done this if Mummy were still here. It's like he's forgotten about her now. It's like he doesn't think he needs to be good anymore.

With the thought of the two of them at Haverstock comes another, awful prospect. Maybe Daniel isn't in the dark after all. Maybe he knows about it, too. Could that be why he is so weird around Rachel, so unhappy that she is here? Has he been covering for Rory? Are Serena and me the only ones in the dark? Then, of course, there's the most horrifying thought of all. Rachel's baby. If they have been having an affair, could the baby be Rory's? A child of my own flesh and blood?

Since Rory's birthday dinner, I've been back in Rachel's room time after time, looking for the things I found there. The laptop, the photograph of the four of us at Cambridge, the note I found at Serena's. I know she has taken those things. I know they are there, somewhere. But I can't find them. Last night—while she was splashing around in our new bathtub, yet again—I took another look, but there was nothing but clothes in her suitcase. In desperation, I looked in her handbag, found her wallet. No love notes, no photograph. Just the usual stack of fifties—where on earth is she getting all this cash?—and a battered old provisional driver's license that expired years ago: Rachel Wells.

What I still can't figure out is what Rachel wants. If she wants Rory, wants to force him to choose, why doesn't she just come out with it? Or perhaps he has ended it already—but she refuses to accept it? Perhaps this is her twisted way of getting close to him. But why? Is she tormenting him, punishing him for choosing Serena? Or is there more to it?

And then there are the marks on her neck. They are almost gone now, faded to little clouds of yellowish gray. Barely noticeable. How did she get them? Who wants to hurt her? And above all, why is she still living in our house, sitting and eating breakfast with us, coming out with her weird, jarring small talk? What does she want from us?

I am desperate to talk to Daniel about it properly. Daniel always knows the right thing to do. We used to talk about things like this, solve problems together. We used to feel like a team. I can't bear this distance that seems to be opening up between us since she's been staying.

But I know what he'll say. He's always so logical. He'll say I'm reading too much into things. That I'm imagining it, making things up. He will want proof, or he won't believe me. And a part of me doesn't even want to know what is really going on. I just want it gone. I want *her* gone.

When I traced it back, I couldn't quite work out how I'd even gotten to this point. Had I ever even liked this girl, really? Had I encouraged her friendship? I didn't think I had. Yet somehow she had become my problem. A problem I wasn't sure how I was going to solve.

Greenwich Park

SHE HAS ALWAYS HATED meeting in the tunnel. She prefers to smell the grass, the earth, the moss. But the rain is coming too hard tonight. Besides, they don't have much time.

The skies are heavy now, the tumbling clouds epic, the growl of thunder chasing people into their homes. The rain comes, scattering them like mice. She walks past the warm glow of other people's houses.

She makes her way through the tunnel, through its concentric circles of light and shadow. She passes signs on the tunnel walls: S9, S11, S12. She doesn't know what the numbers mean. The ceiling drips, and her footfalls echo north and south.

S19, S20, S24. She feels the pressure of the water overhead, the weight of it, the dampness, seeping through into the air. They usually meet by the bulb that flickers, insectlike, beside a sign that says No Cycling. As she nears it, the sudden bump of a bicycle over a storm drain makes her jump. It passes, its light flashing into the darkness. She continues.

When she arrives, he is pacing, breathing heavily, eyes wild. He is angry, she can tell. He lifts her, roughly, pushes her against the wall. The white subway tiles are cold on her back, his breath hot on her neck. She feels weightless.

They said they wouldn't do it again. But now the landscape has changed, the horizon shifted. Their doors are closing, sooner than expected. The thunder comes again. They need to start making plans. He feels frightened. Of her, of them, the thunder, both. Frightened to go. Frightened to stay. Frightened of what they might do.

On her way home, the thunder has stopped, and something in the atmosphere has shifted. She walks quickly, past the doors in the park walls. She wonders who uses those doors. She has never seen them open or close. Autumn leaves are gathered at their feet, like rusty hands spread wide. The bricks darken in the rain.

The next day the birds are circling over the park, sweeping across the sky like iron filings. They are gathering their numbers, flying south for the winter. It was he who pointed it out to her, this melancholy wheeling. Now she can't not see it. She can't not think about it. Wishes they could go with them. She wishes they had gone already. She fears it might be too late.

And now it is, and now they are here. Left behind in a world without birds, to face the cold.

37 WEEKS

Helen

I AM LOCKING MONTY in our bedroom at the top of the house. He stares up at me miserably as I set his food and water bowls out beside the closet, a litter tray next to the door. He hates being shut up here. But the last time Charlie brought friends along to one of our parties, one of them thought it would be funny to singe his whiskers with a cigarette lighter. I'm not taking any chances.

Even though I can't imagine anything I feel less like doing at the moment, I somehow ended up agreeing to throw this bonfire party. Katie kept going on about it, saying how it was her first weekend off in ages, and how nice it would be to have fireworks at the house again, to do something to celebrate the baby coming, even something low-key. To fill the house with lovely memories again. I told her I wasn't sure. The remodel work is nowhere near finished. The house looks a mess.

"No one minds that," she said. "Anyway, that's the perfect time to have a party, because it doesn't matter if things get ruined."

"I thought you said it would be low-key."

"It will. But you want it to be a *party*, don't you?"

And then before I knew it, Charlie was talking about bringing his DJ turntables and some friends from the club. I made him promise not to invite too many. I told Daniel I didn't want the house any more ruined than it already was. But weirdly, Daniel seemed keen on the idea of a party.

"I think Katie just thought it would be nice," Daniel said. "An old-fashioned bonfire night party. Like your mum and dad used to do."

"Mummy and Daddy used to do toffee apples and sparklers and sausages, Daniel," I groaned. "Not Charlie and his idiotic druggie friends, smashing up the house."

"It won't be that bad. Give your brother a break."

"You know what he's like, Daniel! Say the word 'party' to Charlie and he starts inviting everyone he's ever met."

I thought back to our engagement party, when we'd first moved into the house. I'd hoped for a small, intimate gathering, a few jugs of Pimm's on the lawn. I was secretly pregnant anyway, so I wasn't drinking. Then Charlie had turned up, a whole gang of friends in tow, and insisted on starting a game of something called beer pong in the garden. By the end of the night the house was littered with drunken bodies. We'd had to have a whole section of carpet replaced.

Daniel smiled and shrugged, gesturing out of the window. "We could do with having a bonfire anyway, don't you think? We've got all those cuttings in the garden. And fireworks are always fun."

I cradled my mug of tea in my hands, letting the warmth seep into my fingers, and gazed out at the wasteland of our garden. I couldn't make out why Daniel was so keen to do it. I couldn't understand why he thought all the cuttings needed to be burned, instead of just put in the garden waste bin. I hated the thought of people in our garden, trampling on the roses. And Monty can't bear parties, or fireworks. He'd be traumatized for weeks.

"I don't know, Daniel."

"Think of it as a last hurrah before the baby."

He seemed to be actually excited by the idea. I couldn't remember the last time he'd seemed excited about something. Him, Charlie, and Katie. That was three against one. I opened my mouth to protest, then closed it again.

"How about I speak to Charlie?" he said, pulling me into a hug. "Keep the guest list under control?"

"You can try," I muttered. Suddenly I felt too tired, too pregnant to argue.

"And after the party, if she hasn't gone by then, we'll talk to Rachel again." He pulled away then, looked me in the eye, a serious expression on his face. "We'll be nice about it, but she does need to go now. I mean, for God's sake, Helen, our baby's coming in three weeks. I know you're worried about her. But she can't just live here forever, can she?"

I sighed. "OK. We'll talk to her again. After the party." And just like that, I'd agreed to have the party after all.

I rub Monty's ears and he purrs softly. Just for a moment, I wonder whether I could simply lie down here on the bed by his side, a pillow between my aching knees. Stay here all night with my fingers in my ears, safe from the explosions. Pretend that none of it is happening.

Helen

WHEN I TRY TO recall the night of the party, my most vivid memories will be of sticky floors, the smoke in my clothes, the hot air from the flames, the cold wet of the earth. And most of all, the hum of the dehumidifier.

Wherever I go in the house, I can't seem to escape it. It seems to be gathering, rising in pitch, building to a crescendo that never quite comes. As the night goes on, I feel a dull headache spreading, growing like a tumor. Like storm clouds gathering.

The dehumidifier has to stay on all night. And no one, under any circumstances, can go into the cellar. The man who came to lay the cement was very clear on that point. I have written NO ENTRY on a piece of paper in large red capital letters and stuck it on the cellar door.

Charlie and Daniel started the bonfire in the garden together, but it's begun to rage out of control. Flames keep leaping toward the fences in the direction of the wind. The flames seem so high, so bright. I'm worried it might set the neighbors' gardens on fire.

I'd invited some of the neighbors, just to try and soften the blow of what I feared would end up being a noisy and unpleasant evening for them. To my great relief, the family on our left said they were going to be away skiing that weekend. But Arthur and Mathilde, the elderly, childless couple to our right, had seemed pleased to be invited.

They arrived early, wearing charming smiles, eager to socialize. Arthur—who knows about old churches and had been friendly with my father—thrust what I suspected was a very good bottle of Muscadet into my hands, while Mathilde, a retired music teacher, brought along a plate of her homemade gravlax, with sprigs of dill and chunks of fresh lemon.

As she laid it down and started to fiddle with the cling film, I realized to my horror that her nails had been painted, her silvery hair blow-dried especially for the occasion.

I tried my best to make conversation with them both, but my efforts floundered somewhat. I didn't really know anything about music, or curing fish, or the architecture of British churches, and Mathilde looked blank whenever I said anything about my pregnancy. I kept glancing around for someone I could safely introduce them to, but was unable to identify a single suitable candidate. Daniel and Charlie were busy with the fireworks, and there was no sign of Katie yet. Instead, the house was filling up with strange, edgy people I didn't recognize, none of whom seemed remotely interested in speaking to us, or in trying Mathilde's homemade gravlax, which lay barely touched on the sideboard.

Within an hour of their arrival, I could tell by their faces that Arthur and Mathilde were mentally plotting their escape. I cringed as guest after guest barged past us, forcing Arthur to wheel around out of the way and Mathilde to pin herself up against the pantry door. By now, the noise from the garden was making it increasingly difficult to hold a conversation. Arthur's eyes darted nervously over my shoulder every time there was a smash of glass, a snap from the bonfire, a burst of explicit rap music. When Mathilde was knocked against the kitchen sideboard by a bloke in a purple dress and sneakers carrying a huge speaker—"She's only just had her hip done," a stunned Arthur muttered—I could see that all was lost.

Soon after that, the two of them were politely making their excuses. They were terribly tired—too old for parties these days, they said, with rueful smiles, hurriedly pulling on their scarves and gloves. They kept repeating what a lovely time they'd had, thanking me so profusely for inviting them that it made me want to cry. I helped them with their coats, apologizing over and over about the sideboard incident, telling them how lovely it would be to catch up with them both again, though in what context after this I couldn't really imagine. As I closed the door after them, Arthur carrying the barely touched gravlax plate, Mathilde wobbling as she reached for the railing, I dreaded the thought of what they'd be saying on the way home.

It is not long after their departure that I start to feel odd. I head out to the garden, hoping some fresh air might help. The lawn is already littered with decaying pears, cigarette butts, spent fireworks in fairground colors, cans bent double. I close my eyes. There is a smell of gunpowder and rot. I can't understand why the fire is producing quite so much black smoke.

My eyelids feel heavy, like I'm using all my strength to keep them open. After a while, I can't even seem to see things properly—it's as if I'm looking at everything through tinted glass. I wonder if it is the smoke from the fire affecting me—I keep rubbing my eyes on my sweater sleeve.

I go back inside, thinking my eyes might feel better. But it seems to be almost as foggy in here. Perhaps people are smoking indoors. Despite my begging, Charlie has brought two towering black speakers, plugged them in where Mummy's floor lamp was. As I pass, bending to dab at a wine-splattered wall with damp paper towel, a shaven-headed guy at the turntables looks up at me, one headphone on and one off, like I've seen Charlie doing. He just nods, then closes his eyes again.

Bass vibrates through the house, shaking the glasses in the cabinet. In the gaps between, the dehumidifier clicks and hums. Charlie dances into the room, eyes half closed, nodding to the music.

"Who on earth are all these people?" I hiss at Charlie.

He shrugs. "Mates."

"You could have come and spoken to Mathilde and Arthur."

"Who?"

I roll my eyes. "Our neighbors," I snap. "The ones who have lived here forever, who were friends with Daddy, who used to always throw your football back for you."

He stares at me blankly.

"They asked after you. It felt rude."

Charlie still looks puzzled. "Sorry, I didn't even know they were here."

I rub my forehead. My head is throbbing. Charlie smiles, tries to catch my eye. "Honestly, don't look so worried, Helen. Everything's fine." I squint at him suspiciously. He'd better not be up to his old tricks again. I note that as usual, he is looking faintly unwashed, and in need of a haircut. I turn away. Sometimes it hurts even to look at Charlie. His face is all Mummy—her wide smile, her light brown eyes.

"How's Ruby?"

"She's fine. At her mum's."

"Is Katie here yet?"

Charlie shrugs again, as if I've mentioned some passing acquaintance rather than his girlfriend. "Haven't seen her," he says. "What about your new mate? Rachel? Is she here?"

"I don't know where she is," I say. "She went out for cigarettes this afternoon. She's been ages." I narrow my eyes. "Why? What do you want with her?"

"Nothing," Charlie says distractedly. He plucks a joint from behind his ear. "I just wondered. How about Rory, is he coming? And Serena?" He taps his pockets for a lighter.

"Charlie, you can't smoke in here!" I snap. "Tell your friends they can't smoke in here."

"Relax, Helen!" He laughs, putting the joint back. "I was just getting it ready!"

"I don't know if Rory and Serena are coming," I say crossly. "Rory has better taste in parties than you. Whatever his other faults might be."

"What does that mean? I didn't think Rory and Serena had any faults, according to you."

I shake my head, pawing at my eyes again. "Nothing. It doesn't mean anything. Go and annoy someone else. I need to clean this wall. The one your friends have ruined."

Charlie is barely listening. He puts his arm around me, kisses me drunkenly on the temple. His stubble is scratchy.

"Look at you, sis! A thousand months pregnant and you're hosting a cool party! People are having a good time!"

I wriggle free, push him away. Tell him to buzz off.

Later, as I bend to collect more beer cans from my herb garden, I feel a gathering sense of heaviness in my limbs, so much so that I doubt for a moment whether I'll be able to haul myself up again. I'm tired. So tired. Too tired to protest. Too tired to make my stand. I decide I will just go with it. Let Charlie and Daniel have this one silly night before the baby comes. Things will be different after that.

At least tonight I won't have to think too much about Rachel. I haven't seen her since this afternoon, actually. Maybe she's done one of her disappearing acts.

I put my hand to my temple; it feels as if my head might be about to explode. Even if she does turn up, I tell myself, it'll hardly make a difference. She'll find someone else to talk to, one of Charlie's strange friends, probably. I'll just stay out of her way. For once, she'll be the least of my worries.

I am wrong about that, as it turns out.

Katie

I TAKE ANOTHER SIP of Helen's mulled wine, exhale deeply. Charlie and Rachel are talking by the bookcase, away from everyone else. She seems all right now, I think, slightly bitterly. Her neck seems to have cleared up. Just a few little blotches of yellowy green, almost nothing.

Rachel is holding a glass in one hand and a straw in the other, swirling the ice cubes around coquettishly. She is wearing a blue velvet dress, sort of old-fashioned, and shoes that tie in bows at the backs of her ankles. As she and Charlie talk, she tilts her head to one side. The music is loud, and she says something into his ear, leaning close so that her lips graze the edges of his skin. I hear him laugh his real laugh. And then as he brings his hand to his mouth, I swear he just brushes against the side of her body, his fingers against her waist. Maybe. Maybe it's the wine. Maybe not.

He does this, Charlie. He does something to women. He could be talking to you about anything—the weather, the wine, the carpet. It's the way he looks at you when he does it. Makes you feel as if the rest of the world is spinning, and he is the only fixed point. I should know. He has been doing it to me since we were both at school. But he shouldn't do it. Not to this strange, pregnant girl, I think. He shouldn't.

The more I hear about Rachel, the odder it all sounds. Apparently she is still living here, with Helen and Daniel. When I asked Helen about it, she seemed defensive. She said something about her being vulnerable. Someone hurting her, or something like that. That she needed a safe place to stay. "Anyway, it's not for long. She's promised she's leaving in the next couple of weeks." I wanted to ask more about the marks on her neck, but Helen's expression stopped me delving further.

My wine is disappearing faster than it should be. It's sweet and spicy; the taste of Christmas. I think Helen is pleased someone is drinking it. I wonder if she realizes that some of the other people here are indulging in less wholesome substances. I am not sure Charlie has kept his promise about not inviting too many people.

As I look at Charlie and Rachel, I think about years ago, when Charlie and I broke up the first time, and he introduced us all to Maja. I'd been the one to end things between us, so I'd no right to be hurt. But he'd moved on so quickly. And then there was Maja, and everyone loved her—her wide, mischievous smile, her Swedish drinking games, her mad midsummer parties. I had to smile, pretend to go along with it. And then, after what seemed like hardly any time at all, she was pregnant—a happy accident, they'd said—and I realized too late that I'd made a mistake.

It feels like a long time ago now, all that stuff. I take another deep drink of the wine. Maybe I'm stupid, thinking we can try again now, after all this time, that things can go back to the way they were, before all that. Maybe I need to grow up, find an ordinary man, like Daniel. A house, a baby. Somehow, though, the thought makes me feel slightly depressed.

I don't notice the two drunk girls dancing behind me until it's too late, and they are careering into me. My remaining mulled wine is splattered across the rug on the floor. Fuck. They apologize and disappear. I blush, hoping Charlie and Rachel haven't seen me. I'm too drunk already, I think. I decide to leave them to it. They are only talking, for God's sake. I need to go somewhere else. I need to pull myself together.

The bathroom upstairs is locked. I can hear someone inside. I wait, and finally the door opens. It's Serena. So they are here. I take in her manicured nails, long, buttery, Hollywood hair, her perfect half-moon stomach. She is clutching one of those jeweled bags that looks too small to put anything in.

"Hello, Katie."

"Hi," I slur. "How's it all going?" I motion clumsily to her belly, and she gives me a tight smile.

"Fine, thanks," she says. She swishes past, her long silk dress trailing behind. "See you later."

I shut the door behind me. The bass is still reverberating through the floor. I can see Rachel's gold sequined skirt peeping out of the laundry basket, her green sneakers in a pile in the corner, along with a pair of dirty checked pajamas. On the sink is a crumbling black eyeshadow, a tube of lipstick, postbox red, a color Helen would never wear. Three toothbrushes lean uneasily against each other in a glass.

I decide to head out to the garden, have a cigarette. Calm my nerves. I'll watch the fireworks, I think. And keep away from Rachel.

Helen

THE RUG WAS ONE of Mummy's, which she'd brought back from her travels in Greece, rolled up on her backpack. And now it is probably ruined. The stain is red wine, something from Daddy's collection, no doubt. As I scrub at the stain, bits of the scourer are coming off in a dark green rash, fibers from the rug itself starting to disintegrate. I am making it worse.

Then suddenly there are other particles swimming in front of my eyes, too—little black-and-white twists in my vision, a scattering of red and yellow spots. I remember these. I have had these before, when I was taking the medication. When I wasn't well, after the babies.

I feel hot tears at the back of my eyes. I want the rug to be like it was. I want the rug to be clean. I think of Mummy, when she was young, her hair cut short, tanned shoulders, before she met Daddy, heaving this rug onto ferries and buses, people telling her she was mad. She'd loved it. Wanted to put it in her home. There were pictures of me on it when I was a baby. And now I've let someone spoil it.

When I stand, the dots and twists come again, swimming in front of my eyes like a hallucinogenic screen saver. And then they fade away, and then I see her. Rachel, standing with Charlie, whispering something in his ear. And she is wearing Mummy's blue velvet dress. The one she had looked so beautiful in. The one she'd bought from the hippie stall in the market with me, all those years ago.

I feel like I've been punched in the stomach. I stagger upstairs to the bathroom, slump down on the floor. My arms feel like dead weights. What is happening to me? I think I'm going to either cry or be sick. What is Rachel doing? Why is she wearing Mummy's dress? What else has she stolen? A laptop? A photograph? A dress? My brother? Who is this person I've invited into our house?

When the nausea passes, I lie down on my side, one cheek against the cool tiled floor of the bathroom. I lie for a while, until my heart slows down. The smell of bonfire smoke, the thump of music, the noise of chatter floats in through the open window. My stomach settles into a hard knot of anger. I have stood this long enough. I am going to ask her what the hell is going on.

The spare room is on the other side of the landing. I push the door open, my eyes still swimming slightly. And then I notice something. Something that wasn't there before, or it was, and I didn't see it. A slight unevenness in the tilt of her bed. Is it just the mess of the sheets, making it look that way? I climb down onto all fours, check the legs of the bed. And that's when I see it, under one of the legs. One of the floorboards is sticking up, as if there is something pushing up from underneath.

I shut the door behind me against the noise of the party. But I can still hear the bass, like the thump of a heartbeat. The room is hot. I get back down on my hands and knees. I wasn't imagining it. There is a floorboard out of place. It looks as if it has been cut out, pushed up, like a jigsaw piece.

It takes all the strength I have to push the bed to the side. I try pulling up the board, and sure enough, it comes away in my hands. A swirl of sawdust flies upward, and I see what lies underneath.

The objects are set out neatly between two dusty joists. The laptop is there, with its cable wrapped around it. And the envelope, the one I'd seen in her suitcase, the W neatly printed on the front. There are fifty-pound notes—loads of them, flat, perfect, and as neat and unreal as Monopoly money, stuffed into a plastic sandwich bag that looks as if it came from the roll in my kitchen.

I push the notes to one side. There is more underneath. A pile of newspaper cuttings, some new, some yellowed and curled with age, held together with a hair grip. I pull them out and lay them in front of me. The old ones are on the top. They are from a decade ago—when we were at university. When I look closer, I see they are dated 2008, the year we left

Cambridge. And then I realize they are *about* Cambridge. About the case Katie was talking about. About what happened to that girl, the summer we left.

Then I see more things. The photograph I found, of us after the college play. The one that had been stuck back together. And underneath that, more paper. What looks like a printout of some flight documents and boarding passes, stapled together, folded in half so I can't quite see the details. As I reach for them, I see a passport. But as I do, I become aware of footsteps on the stairs, of someone getting closer.

My hands trembling, I abandon the flight details and pick up the passport, open to the back page.

The name is Helen Mary Thorpe. The date of birth is May 9, 1986. The place of birth is London. The passport number is mine. It's my passport. It must be.

But on the left-hand side, where my face should be, there is only a blank space. My face has been cut away.

The hinge of the door creaks. I spin around, my entire body shaking now.

It is her.

Katie

OUTSIDE SOMEONE OFFERS ME a cigarette. I take it. I don't really smoke. The fact I want one is a sure sign I've drunk too much. I thank them, and stumble down to the bottom of the garden. I feel like being on my own for a bit.

As I sit and smoke, I look back at the bonfire, the big, beautiful lit-up house. I have always loved Helen's house, its red brickwork, its tall, wooden-shuttered windows, the pretty gables in the gently sloping roof. It is at its most beautiful now, in the autumn when the wisteria turns yellow and the brambles at the end of the garden are heavy with unpicked fruit. It's silly, but I suppose I like to think of it as my childhood home, too.

I close my eyes, inhale the smell of wet leaves, bonfire smoke. I remember how the Guy Fawkes Night parties here used to be, when Helen's parents, Richard and Anna, were alive. Rory, Helen, Charlie, and I would be sent to Greenwich Park to find kindling, looking for the driest sticks, stuffing them into our backpacks. When we returned, we'd present our collections for Richard to inspect. He would decide who was the winner. He'd usually say it was me. I think he and Anna felt a bit sorry for me, after my mum and dad split up. I think they knew I preferred to be at their house instead of my cramped apartment, at the cheaper end of the street.

Before the parties, Richard would let us put nails in fence posts for the pinwheels, dig holes in the cold, wet earth for the rockets. He let us do everything. We would make lanterns out of washed-out jam jars and brown string, put tea lights in them, light them ourselves with matches, and climb the ladder to hang them in the pear tree. Helen and I would write our names with lit sparklers, trying to get from the first letter to the last before the ribbon of white light was swallowed up in darkness. Rory would throw firecrackers at us from up in his tree house. Charlie told him to stop it, but Rory just laughed. He only did it because Helen shrieked so much. We told her that, but she didn't listen.

Remember, remember. I remember it all, the scratch of hats and gloves and socks, the hiss of spent sparklers in buckets of cold water. All their friends arriving. The feeling it was a grown-up party, and we were staying up late. One time we came down the next morning in our pajamas to a frost, and the buckets had turned to ice, with the sparklers stuck inside. Anna made us eggs on toast, the steam from the boiler pipe blowing clouds over the kitchen window. The kitchen tiles were cold; she brought me green socks to borrow. It's funny, the things you remember.

Now they are dead, their house in ruins. The garden a wasteland of bricks, a cement mixer, tarpaulins. The massive bonfire heaves and breathes and paints the bricks a luminous orange. The heat over the bonfire makes the tall windows seem to wobble, like a circus mirror. It feels like an apocalypse. I look at the discarded cans and cigarette butts that litter the beautiful garden, the rotting fruit from Anna's beloved pear tree. I wonder what Helen's parents would think of their children now.

Helen

"WHERE DID YOU GET that dress?"

My words snap like teeth. For once, Rachel has the grace to look embarrassed.

"Sorry," she says. "I didn't think you'd mind. It was in your bottom drawer. I hadn't seen you wear it before—I thought maybe you didn't like it."

"What were you doing in my bottom drawer, Rachel?"

"You did say I could borrow something," she says. She looks puzzled, as if she doesn't understand. "Remember?"

For God's sake. I had said vaguely, once, that she could borrow something. It hadn't been an open invitation to rifle through my cupboards.

"And you left that red dress out for me, the other time, when we went to Rory's thing," she adds, frowning. "I thought you'd be cool with me taking something else for tonight."

I stare at her. I have no idea what she means about the red dress. I'd never seen that thing before, and even if I had, I would never have dreamed of suggesting she wear it to a dinner at Serena's house. What is she talking about? But as she fiddles with the hemline of the blue velvet dress, I remember the real source of my fury.

"I know you've taken other things," I say, a tremor in my voice. "I know you took that note from inside my book. That photograph—it was you who stuck it back together, wasn't it? Why did you do that, Rachel? Where did you even find it?"

"What note? I didn't take anything from your book. I didn't stick any photograph back together. Seriously. I don't know what you're talking about, Helen."

I ignore her. I am shouting. "What is this all about? Look, I found your hiding place!" I point at the hole in the floor. "What have you done to my passport, Rachel? Was that some kind of sick joke, cutting my face out?"

Rachel shakes her head. "No, hang on," she is saying, looking upset. "You've got this all wrong. It wasn't me who did this."

"For God's sake, stop lying! I found your hiding place." I throw the passport down in front of her. "I let you stay here. And this is how you repay me—snooping around? Stealing things? Cutting up my passport? Lying?"

Rachel holds up the palms of her hands, looks me in the eye. "I didn't take a note from your book, Helen," she says slowly. "Or a photograph. Honestly. That must have been someone else. Whatever it was about, someone else is on to you—not me."

I hear the blood pounding in my ears, still not drowning out the incessant noise of the dehumidifier. On to me? She's insane. Completely insane.

"Rachel," I say. "You stole our laptop. You stole my passport—cut up my bloody passport! You stole my mother's dress . . ." I pick up the note from her suitcase, the one addressed to W. "So what's this, then? Is this yours? Or did you steal this as well?"

She steps closer to me. I remember the touch of her cool hands on my bump that time in the market. The feeling it had given me, like I was teetering over the edge of something. Instinctively, my hands fly to my belly.

"I don't know what happened to whatever note was in your book," she says again. "But I can explain everything else. All of this." She gestures to the laptop, the passport, the cuttings. "Look, Helen. You've been good to me. I know you didn't have to let me stay here. But you need to listen to me now, OK? Because I know other things. Things you really should know. Before this baby comes." Then she reaches out, closes her hand over my stomach. "I had to wait before I told you—I just had to make sure I understood it all."

I flinch, horrified by the feel of her fingers on my stomach, and catch the shelf with the back of my head. A glass vase falls, but I manage to turn, pin it clumsily to the wall before it hits the ground. I feel the weight of it in my hands as they close around it. The thick rim, the heavy glass bottom. I think about it, just for a moment. I just want her to be quiet, I think. I just want her to go away. Leave me alone.

"I'm on your side, Helen," she says. "Trust me, OK?"

"Trust you? After this?"

"I'm serious. You need to listen to me—or we could both be in danger. I mean it."

I look at her and, at last, I see her for what she is. A fraud, a meddler. A source of trouble. A thief, in a dress she stole from my dead mother, overplucked eyebrows and a face of cheap makeup. She is a joke. I don't trust her. I don't believe her. I don't want to hear another word she says. I just want her gone. For good.

"Rachel," I tell her, "we're not friends. We never were."

Rachel's mouth drops open, her eyes wide. For once she is speechless, gawping at me like a child.

"I'm sorry. I want you to leave, tonight, and not come back."

Katie

AS I WALK THROUGH the hallway, my hand finds the wall. I've had too much, far too much. I turn toward the kitchen. That's when the velvet dress catches my eye again. I only see it for a moment. It must be Rachel, heading down to the cellar, following somebody. I can't see who, and in a split second they are both gone.

I stare after them. Who was that? Was it a guy? Was it Charlie? The two of them have been together most of the night. What the hell are they planning on doing in the cellar? I feel my body stiffening. I can imagine what Charlie might want to do in a cellar. He likes enclosed spaces. Places that are cool and dark. Come on, Katie. Too stupid. Don't think about it. Don't.

In the kitchen, I find a dirty glass on the sideboard and rinse it to pour myself a glass of water. A large one. Then when I've finished it, I pour myself more wine, stumble back to my spot at the end of the garden. It's nice out here. I light another of my cigarettes—where did they come from? No matter, no matter. I sit on the grass and watch the fire. After a while it starts to swim in front of me, as if it is burning underwater.

A figure emerges from the smoke and darkness. Charlie. He is grinning. I frown, take another drag, determined not to let a smile show on my face, hating the way my heart lifts up in my chest at the thought that he has come to find me.

"All right?" he says cheerfully. He passes me a beer.

"I brought wine. Thanks."

He shrugs, puts the beer on the grass, twisting it into the earth so that it stands up.

I glance over at Charlie's clothes. He is covered in dust. My stomach twists. So that *was* him, going down into the cellar with Rachel.

"You're a mess," I tell him. I brush the dust off his leg. I can hear the slur in my speech, feel the clumsiness of my movements.

He looks down at his clothes, then back up at me. "You're wearing a dress." He grins again.

I smile without meaning to, look away. "I do that occasionally."

"Yeah, well," he says. "I've been down to the cellar. Wanted to see the big refurb."

He doesn't mention Rachel. I feel a tightening in my heart. I want to ask but stop myself.

"How's it looking down there?"

"Like a load of wet concrete. They only laid the foundation today. Too wet for me to even write my name in. Can I have a drag?"

I roll my eyes, but pass him the cigarette. He takes it, his fingers brushing against mine. I close my eyes. I long to put my face against his chest.

"I can't understand why they're doing it," he says.

I turn to look at him. His voice is different now. Does he sound upset?

He takes a drag. "Dad always said the house was perfect. That it didn't need a thing. I always thought Helen thought that, too."

"Helen didn't talk to you? Before they went ahead with the work?"

He shakes his head, takes another drag of the cigarette.

"No," he says. "She didn't."

The fire crackles in front of us. I study his face in the flames, but I can't make out his expression. I have never asked him how he feels about the terms of the will. I got the impression it was pretty simple in the end—that Rory would get the family firm, that Helen would get the family home, and that Charlie would get everything else, a sort of cash equivalent. I have sometimes wondered whether he got the raw end of the deal. But for all his faults, Charlie has never been bothered about money.

"Rachel seems nice," I say carefully.

He frowns, looks at me, head tilted to one side.

"What do you mean?"

"I mean she seems nice." I pull my jacket around myself. "I saw you talking to her, that's all."

Charlie stubs the cigarette out on the tree at the back of the garden.

"I see."

"Oh, do you?"

"Yes."

We sit in silence for a moment. Charlie cranes his neck, trying to catch my eye.

"Oi." He is laughing at me. "Come here, will you? I'm cold."

"No, you're not," I say, shrugging his hand off my shoulder. "There's a great big fire right in front of us."

"I am. I'm freezing." He slips his fingers in between mine. Pulls me toward him, forces me to meet his eye. Then he kisses me on the mouth. Despite myself, I smile in the darkness.

Serena

WHEN I WALK INTO the kitchen, Helen is leaning over the sink, gripping its porcelain edge, her face dropped down between her arms.

"Helen?"

She turns around. A stripe of sweat glistens across her forehead; her eyes sit in deep blue-gray hollows. She looks hot and cold at once; flustered, haunted. When her eyes focus on mine, I realize her pupils are dilated. It is as if she takes a moment to register that it is me.

"Serena." She sounds relieved. "I didn't see you."

She pulls a shaking wrist up to her face, wipes her nose with her cardigan cuff.

"Are you all right? You've got a bit of tree in your hair."

I reach out to twist the twig out of the stray hairs on the top of her head. It is extraordinary, Helen's hair. Such a vivid red. Russet, I think you would call it. Helen looks up gratefully.

"I was in the garden. I thought I saw Monty near the fire. I was trying to bring him inside but. . ." A look of confusion crosses her face briefly, like a cloud passing in front of the sun. "I think I disturbed someone. Or rather, two people. Down at the bottom, in the . . . at the back."

I cringe, smile sympathetically. I wouldn't be at all surprised. Between the fire and the emptying of Helen's parents' old spirits cabinet, the party has taken on something of a bacchanalian air. The garden is foggy with bonfire smoke and the smell of weed, the dining and front rooms have become dance floors. Ironically, as parties go, Helen's has been something of a triumph. People are starting to trail away now, though. Just a few strange characters are still wandering around, slumped in her armchairs, smoking in the bushes.

I comb Helen's hair with my fingers, tuck a loose strand behind her ear, like one might do to a child. She seems to hardly notice. She is still staring out at her garden.

"My dead babies are down there, Serena," she murmurs. "Did I ever tell you that?"

She didn't. But Daniel did. The little funerals they held, alone in the rain, clinging to one another. The four tiny packets of ashes they had scattered with their trembling hands among the flower beds. And the four climbing roses they had planted there. One for every missing heartbeat.

I don't say anything. Instead, I run my hand up and down her back, from her shoulder blades to the base of her spine.

"I had the most terrible argument earlier," she blurts. "With Rachel. I told her to leave."

I glance up at the kitchen clock. It is past one.

"Don't worry about it now, Helen," I tell her. "It's late. Let's have a drink."

She sniffs. "Not for me," she mumbles automatically.

Poor Helen. She has been through so much. I turn so I am standing square on to face her, take her hand.

"Helen," I whisper. "You are very strong, stronger than you think. Your baby is strong, too. And he is going to be fine. You are not going to hurt him now. Even if you have this glass of wine with me."

Helen smiles at me weakly. But she is surprisingly firm.

"Really," she says, looking me in the eye. "I'd rather just have a tea. I think I'll just have a cup of tea and take it up to bed."

So, the tea it is.

Katie

WHEN I HEAD BACK inside the house, it is later than I thought. The music seems to have stopped. The gauntlet of builders' waste, still-hot embers, and broken glass sobers me up. Poor Helen. She was right. It does look like things got a bit out of hand. Perhaps it was thoughtless of me to encourage her to have a party when she is so pregnant. And Charlie should never have invited so many people.

Serena is the only one in the kitchen. To my surprise, she appears to be cleaning. She has washed up all the glasses, and is wiping the kitchen surfaces down, scrubbing out purple rings of wine. She has piled her long hair onto the top of her head in a scruffy bun and stuck on a pair of Helen's rubber gloves. They look comically large on the ends of her long, skinny arms. She has collected cans and bottles into a green recycling sack. Maybe I've misjudged her.

"Do you want a cup of tea?" she says, seeing me. "I've just made Helen one."

"Thanks, I'm fine."

I notice a bottle of what look like headache tablets next to the kettle. I could do with one of those, I think.

"Where's Helen?"

"Gone to bed." Serena smiles, motions at the chaos. "Just thought I'd make a start."

I nod. "Let me help."

Greenwich Park

HE TELLS HER HE will keep watch awhile, just to make sure. They don't want any more surprises. When she leaves him, he hears her moving around in the house, like a ghost. The floorboards creak underfoot. The house straining to keep its secrets.

When he can't sit there anymore, he switches off the light and goes and sits outside. He takes the bottle of Scotch. He drinks and waits and drinks until his throat is raw. He is waiting for the morning, as if the morning might bring with it an answer. But the morning does not come when it is supposed to. And it is dark, so dark.

In the embers of the bonfire, something moves. At first, he thinks it is a fox, or a rat. But then he sees the smooth sheen of feather, black that shines blue in the light, like a velvet dress. Not velvet. Feathers. A raven, come to bury the dead.

The raven perches on the hedgerow, folds its wings, and cocks its head at him against the moon. There is silence. Its eyes are ink black, its feet red raw. A hunchback. Its head moves all the way around. In the background, four roses stare at him, their faces blank and pure.

He looks at the raven and lifts his glass in salute.

Nevermore, he says to the Raven.

And the Raven speaks back.

Nevermore, the Raven says.

Nevermore. Nevermore. Cellar Door.

TEN YEARS EARLIER

I WONDER WHEN THE music stopped, and where I can get some water. I need to get up, but I can't get up. That's when bits of my body start to come back. Arms first. My wrists are heavy. I imagine them weighed down by bracelets. Gold and diamonds.

No, not bracelets. Something warm. Something that is squeezing tight.

I force my eyes to focus. The sky has gone, too. It is different now, wood and a rippled metal, the underside of corrugated iron. And on either side of me are boats, but we're not on the water. The boats are piled on top of each other, their edges long and shiny, painted numbers on the side. I wonder if the person who paints the names is the same. What names? I can't remember. Can't remember.

Then on the walls. Long spoons, giant ones. Not spoons. Paddles? Oars. They are oars.

It's so quiet, so cold in here. Yet there is a hot feeling pressing into me. And only now do I notice the pain, like a red flag in the distance. But as soon as I notice, I can't not notice. And then it is everywhere, spilling out like ink in water. Starting down, moving all over. It hurts, it hurts. And now I see his face.

The face I saw before. The dark bangs, the hooded eyes, watching me. What happened to me? The quiet one is on top of me. The pain is him. The wrists is him. The noise is him. It's all him. The blanket scratches on my neck.

Huh. Huh. Huh.

And behind him, another. A laughing face.

Huh, huh, huh.

The panic comes now, replaces the pain. I pull my head up off the ground, but my shoulders won't follow. My wrists are pinned. I open my mouth. I have to speak.

Hey, I hear myself say. I mean it as a shout but my voice sounds far away. Like a whisper. It's all I can say. Hey. Hey.

37 WEEKS

Helen

THE MORNING AFTER THE party I wake with my head heavy and spinning, almost as if I had been drinking last night. I am aching all over, my chest clammy against my clothes. I wonder whether I might be getting the flu.

I walk downstairs to survey the damage. The kitchen floor is cold, and when I run the hot tap, ghosts of hot steam drift out of the boiler pipe, escaping into the frosty garden air. I take a deep breath, rub my eyes, flick the kettle on. My shoulders ache. I don't feel right. Maybe I should take some ibuprofen. I put my hands to my throat. It feels red raw, as if I have spent the whole night screaming.

I pull my blue check coat over my pajamas, stepping into my wellingtons with one hand on the wall in case I topple over. The coat will no longer fasten over my bump.

Outside, the bonfire has burned out, leaving a huge black wound in the center of the garden. There are crows in the trees and on the fence, diving down to pick over the charred remains. I shoo them away, make a path through the wet grass to check on my roses. I pluck a cigarette butt out of their beds, retrieve an upturned wineglass. When I stand up again, the earth swims. I grasp at the trellis. I can see those twists at the sides of my vision again. Little spirals of black and white, like ticker tape.

I make my way back to the kitchen to make tea. It is spotlessly clean, the surfaces wiped, with that artificial forest smell everywhere. The mugs and glasses are all washed up, sparkling and stacked neatly on the drain board. Did I do all that? I don't think so. Katie must have stayed after I'd gone to bed, helped to clear up the house. I suppose it might have been Daniel, though he doesn't normally leave anything this neat. It won't have been Charlie. Charlie always disappears whenever there's work to be done.

I lift the lid of the bread box, reach inside. Empty. I sigh crossly. Rachel must have finished the bread again. With the thought comes a memory. We argued last night, Rachel and I. The laptop! That's right. I found the laptop in her room. I told her to leave. Did she leave?

When I knock on the spare-bedroom door, there is no answer. I push it open and stare. Rachel is gone. All her stuff is gone, too. No suitcase, no mess. The bed has been stripped, the bedside table cleared. The sheets and the towels she's been using have been piled into the laundry basket.

I go to wake Daniel. I push his books and glasses to one side on his bedside table to make space for the tea. Then I sit down on the bed, lay my hand on his chest. He is still sleeping, but fitfully. His T-shirt is drenched in sweat. When I move my hand to his arm, his eyes snap open.

"Daniel?"

He sits up, wincing, as if his body aches all over, too. Oh God. I hope it isn't flu.

"What?"

He rubs his eyes with his fingers. He sits up, takes the coffee, and drinks deeply from it. Pats around for his glasses, then fumblingly pushes them onto his face with a flattened palm.

"What's up? Why are you looking like that?"

"Rachel's gone."

Daniel stares at me. He doesn't look at all well. His skin is almost green, as if he is about to throw up.

"What do you mean?"

"Rachel. She's gone. All her stuff is gone. She stripped the bed and everything."

Daniel throws his legs over the side of the bed and marches down the stairs in his T-shirt and pants, as if he doesn't believe me, wants to see it for himself. After a few minutes he returns. He looks agitated.

"Didn't she say where she was going?"

I shake my head. "No. I feel terrible now—we had an argument last night . . ."

"What about?"

"You're not going to believe this. I found your laptop in her room."

"Seriously? She stole it?"

I shrug. "I suppose so."

"Jesus. And then what?"

"That's the thing," I say slowly. "I know I told her to leave. But—it's so weird—I can't seem to properly remember what happened afterward. Going to bed, and stuff like that—I only remember it really vaguely. It's almost like I'd been drinking."

Daniel sits down on the bed next to me, pushes his glasses up his nose. "Could you have drunk something by mistake?"

"Of course not." I pause, start to pick at the skin around my thumbnail.

"Oh, Helen." Daniel pulls me toward him, holds me tightly. "You've just been so tired." He starts to rock me gently.

I squirm away from him. "Something's not right. Did you see her, before she left? Was she upset? Did she tell you she was leaving?"

"She didn't say anything to me."

"Did you actually see her leave the party last night?"

"No. I must have already gone to bed."

He stretches his head one way, then the other, his neck clicking slightly. Then he takes my hand.

"Do you think we should do anything?" I ask.

"Like what?"

"I don't know." I rub my eyes with my hands.

"Come on, Helen," Daniel says. "Rachel is an adult. She can look after herself. And I'm sorry if this sounds harsh, but I'm glad she's gone. I don't think it was good for us. Her being here."

I look at him. "What do you mean?"

"Nothing. It's just—I don't think we need any extra stress. Look, I'm sorry, you were right about the party. I should have been firmer with Charlie. I had no idea he would invite all those people into our house."

"What's that got to do with Rachel?"

"Nothing. I know you didn't want to have the party, that's all. I'm sorry I said yes to it. I'll clear everything up."

I pull at a loose thread from my sweater sleeve. The seam inside is unraveling.

"Do you think we should report her missing or something?"

Daniel looks at me. "What? Why?"

"I don't know . . . I mean, it's weird, her just disappearing. Isn't it?"

Daniel shrugs. "Although you did ask her to leave, didn't you?" He puts his hand over mine again. "I just think we need to get back to normal. Focus on us, and the baby." He pauses. "I can repaint that room now, can't I, if it's empty? If you still want me to."

"Really?"

"Of course."

Daniel pulls his tee over his head, throws it onto the floor, and heads to the bathroom for a shower. As I listen to the sound of the water, I lie down on the bed. The room is spinning. I close my eyes, try to remember exactly how I left things with Rachel. But my mind isn't working. It's like when you wake up and you can't quite remember a dream. Every time you try to snatch at it, it edges further out of reach.

Daniel emerges, rubbing his hair dry. When he sees my expression, he stops, throws the towel into the laundry basket, and comes to sit beside me.

"All right," he says. "I can see you're worried. But first things first. Why don't you just send her a text, asking if she's OK? She's probably fine. You might be worrying about nothing."

I nod. "Good idea."

Daniel rotates his neck. He still looks pale. "You know what? I think I'm going to head out for a run. Will you be all right?"

I blink at him. "What?"

"I won't be long."

"But you just showered. And you don't look all that well, Daniel."

"I'm fine."

My vision wobbles again. "OK," I mutter. "I'm going to lie down here for a bit."

I hear the front door close behind him, the soft pat of his footfall on the path. I take off my coat, curl back under the covers. I tap out a message to Rachel, hit send. To my relief, ten minutes later, she replies—an unusually long reply for her. She is fine, she says. She is sorry about the argument, and she has decided to go and stay with her mum for a while. She hopes we are still friends. She wishes me luck with the baby.

I try to feel relief. She is fine, I tell myself. She is fine, and she is gone. She is really gone. But for some reason, deep down, I know that this is not the end of it.

Helen

MUMMY'S ILLNESS STARTED WHEN we were little, and kept coming back to her all her life, like the circling birds we watched together in the park. It never went away for good. And gradually she slipped under the water of it, like a bath filling up that she couldn't control. She got cold in it, from the inside out. So when she turned the wheel that day, into the concrete median at ninety miles per hour, the most surprising thing to all of us was that she hadn't done it years before. That, and the fact she did it with Daddy in the car. That was the hardest part to understand.

The water that came for Mummy nearly came for me, too. A few times, when I was younger. I came pretty close. That's why Mummy and Daddy wanted me to study where my brother was, so I would have someone watching over me. And why they were so happy when I met Daniel. I suppose I became less of a burden to them once he was in the picture.

I was all right for a while. But the water came again when, just a few months after we lost Mummy and Daddy, I lost the first baby as well. I'll never forget how they took him away, a ripped piece of blue NHS towel over a silver kidney dish. Like he was nothing. Like he was rubbish. They told me that I wouldn't want to see. But I did, I did. I told them I didn't care what he looked like. That he was mine. That to me, he would be perfect.

But they shook their heads and gave me a liquid that tasted sickly sweet, and I drifted away on a papery pillow, and when I came back again it was all still the same, the square white lights, the beeping machines, the hard bed, the empty feeling in my body. Except there was a tube in my arm this time, and somehow I didn't have the strength to feel as bad about it all anymore.

When we got back from the hospital, I lay in our bath for hours, the door locked behind me. Daniel stopped knocking, and gradually I chipped away all the flakes of peeling white paint on the windowsill with my fingernail. They fell into my bathwater, floated on the top like snow-flakes. Through the window I saw London, the dark cloak of night over the river. I looked away from my reflection. I let the water go cold and I willed it to go over my head.

Later, Daniel had to collect the baby's ashes from the crematorium. He asked me what I wanted to do with them. I didn't know. I didn't want to do anything with them then. I felt so dark, so broken. I wanted to be asleep, in the earth. To be with my baby. I didn't want ashes. I wanted to take him to the park, push him on the swings. I wanted the warmth of his body against mine. I wanted to lie down with him, to close my eyes.

Daniel swore he'd never leave. But I didn't believe him, especially not after it happened to us again, and again. Why would he stay, when all I gave him was this? Hospitals, nightmares, bleeding, misery, dead ba-bies. He was chained to it, to my useless body: bloated, bleeding, bearing the ugly scars of pregnancy and birth, but with no life, no child to show for it. I started to feel I was dead already.

After it was bad for a while, we started seeing someone. Daniel thought it would help. I didn't. I knew that Daniel would go eventually. I could see how it all was for him.

When I was on the drugs, things were easier, mostly because I didn't feel very much at all. But sometimes that would frighten me, the feeling nothing. And I didn't want to feel nothing about my babies. I wanted to grieve for them. It was all I had left of being a mother.

So then I would tell him that was it, that I didn't want to take the pills anymore. And then I'd be all right for a few days. And then it would happen again. We'd go to a cafe, order eggs and coffees. Do the sort of thing that Katie and Charlie do on the weekend, tell ourselves we were having a nice time. All the time Daniel would be glancing at me, to the door and back, would be fiddling with the keys in his pocket, waiting for it to happen. And then it would. A tiny, perfect baby, asleep in a pram, its little curled-up hands thrown over its head, a pastel-colored blanket over its chest. And I would be hunched over, sobbing, like I'd been punched. People passing by, asking if I was all right, if there was anyone they could call.

I'd been barely aware of Charlie and Katie's breakup, of him finding someone else, Maja. Then suddenly, they were having a baby. The sight of her growing belly made me feel sick. I felt like the whole world was taunting me. I started looking for excuses not to see them. When Ruby was born, I tried to go a few times. The therapist encouraged me to try. I knew I had to. I even bought presents. I got as far as the car. But I couldn't do it. I just couldn't. I would call and Charlie would say they understood, that it didn't matter. But I couldn't bear the ugliness of my thoughts. This accidental baby. My useless brother. Undeserved. It still sits between Charlie and me now, those missed months. I missed so much of her.

It took me such a long time to get better. To not feel like that anymore. To go and meet Ruby, close my fingers around her chubby palm. To take the ashes Daniel had saved and scatter them in our garden. Daniel helped me plant the roses. One for each of our little babies. He did so much, put up with so much. He was the one who kept me alive.

The last time I saw the therapist, she said that I had come a long way, that both Daniel and I had. I believed her. I didn't want to see her ever again. I didn't want to go back.

But now, when I think about the night of the party, I get that same sense of low-level dread, of darkness behind the windows about to close in on us. It frightens me so much to feel that again.

I wish I hadn't shouted at Rachel. And now that I think about it, I don't even completely remember why I was so angry. Was it just the laptop? Was there something else, something I hadn't seen before? I am almost sure there was. But all I can remember are fragments, pieces of a whole that don't make sense on their own. The muffled thump of bass vibrating through the four white walls. Snatches of laughter drifting up from the garden. Footsteps on the stairs, steady as a heartbeat. The turn of the doorknob. The low hum of the dehumidifier, getting louder and louder and louder.

38 WEEKS

Helen

SINCE THE PARTY, I keep finding myself consumed by an urge to wash things, to clean everything in the house. It's normal—I've read about it. Instinctive. A sign that your body is readying for labor.

I have scrubbed every surface in the house, bleached every floor. Scoured the baseboards, some of them twice, my huge belly pressing against my thighs as I bend. Daniel suggested we call off the building work for a few weeks, until after the baby's born, and I agreed. He's right—we need some time to be just us. We need the house still, quiet.

And clean. There is no limit to my hunger for the chemical smell of lemon, the scalding bliss of hot soapy water. At night I dream of cleaning. In the morning I haul myself bolt upright in bed, flip my legs over the side, pull my maternity tracksuit bottoms on.

"It's the weekend, Helen," Daniel complains. "Can't we just relax?" But I want to keep going. I clean the windows with water and newspaper until they gleam. I polish the banisters on the stairs, dust the ceiling rosettes. I wash all the baby clothes, load after load. I lay them out to dry on the rack, then take them to iron in front of the TV. I stack the short-sleeved onesies in little piles for the drawer, arranged by size. The newborn ones are so little I am not sure I know how to fold them. They feel so small, so strange to my hands. The idea that soon I will have a newborn baby, that I will be placing him in these clothes, is still not real to me, even now.

I have tried to put Rachel out of my mind, to focus on us, on the baby. I always thought I'd be delighted if she just disappeared. But whenever I think about the night she left—the night I can't remember—I'm filled with that sick feeling. My thoughts keep looping back to her, to the spare room and our last encounter.

The more I try to remember the end of the party, the further away it seems to drift. I try to think if there is any chance I could have drunk something accidentally, like Daniel said. I haven't touched alcohol for nine months—I'm sure it wouldn't take much. But enough to make me forget how I got to bed?

Over the past few days, I keep finding myself on the stripped bed in the spare room, looking around as if the room might hold the answers somewhere. I sit there for a long time sometimes, staring up at the cornices on the ceiling, the blind cord, the shelves on the far wall, the baby stuff piled up in the corner. Anything that might jog my memory into life. The air in the room feels cold, quiet, thick. She is gone. I got what I wanted. But if everything is all right now, like Daniel says, why does it feel like it isn't?

The other night, Daniel found me in there. I'm not sure how long I had been sitting on the bed. It had gotten dark, but all the lights were off. I hadn't noticed I was sitting in the dark. When he asked what I was doing, I wasn't sure what to say.

The laundry is probably a displacement activity. But it seems to work better than most things. The soft hiss of the iron, the clouds of steam that come and go in front of my eyes, the smoothing of creases— all of it is hypnotic somehow.

Daniel says he is going out for a run. Running seems to be a new obsession, like mine is cleaning.

"Don't you want to watch this?"

I have been encouraging Daniel to watch episodes of *One Born Every Minute* with me. I think it will be useful for him. Every time one of the babies is born, I find I have tears all down my face. Daniel doesn't seem to enjoy it as much as I do, however.

"You carry on. I think I've seen this one."

"No, you haven't, it's one of the new—"

"I won't be long."

He is still out when the knock on the door comes. I place the iron upright on the board, brush my hands on my jeans. Steam clouds the windows, little drops of condensation gather in the corners.

Two blurry shapes in the glass of the door.

Only when I open the door do I see the police badges. The man speaks first. He is tall, red-haired, gangly, young looking, his jacket sleeves just slightly too short.

"Good evening. I'm DS Mitre and this is DC Robbin."

Detective Constable Robbin nods, her eyes traveling from my face to my bump, and then up again. She is thick limbed, powerful looking. Her skin the color of coffee, her eyebrows plucked into two elegant arches.

"We're from Greenwich CID," DS Mitre continues. "We're looking for Rachel Wells. We understand she was staying here."

Katie

YOU GET TO KNOW every detail of a court building when the jury is deliberating. The grubby windowsills, the scuffed green plastic chairs. The elevator buttons, the smeared mirrors in the toilets. You learn the graffiti on the backs of the cubicle doors by heart.

Hours stretch into days. You stare out of the windows, watch the traffic crawl by. You sip hot drinks from the machine in the lobby, get to know which combination of buttons to press for the closest thing to a coffee. You field phone calls from the desk, always asking when. You come to dread these calls, save up fragments of information for them, pretend insights. Which lawyer seemed upbeat or downcast. Whether the jury had come back with questions and what these might signify, whether there has yet been a majority direction. What the jury mix is— how many young, how many old, how many women, men, white, black. And what it all might mean. We reporters exaggerate these small insights, try to encourage the impression that our being here, while we type up background pieces, is worth it. But the truth is, no one knows. No one knows anything at all.

In the end, it takes over a week. The boys are guilty. In the public gallery, the families in their printed T-shirts gasp. A girlfriend's head sinks into her hands. A pretty sister screams no, no. The judge cautions. The boys look stunned. One drops his head into his lap, the other holds his hands up in front of him, stares at his barrister, as if demanding an answer. One set of lawyers turn in their chairs with smiling handshakes for their juniors, nods for their client. The others sigh, put on spectacles, straighten their spines, brace themselves for questions about appeals and challenges that could stretch into years.

Either side of me, the other reporters who have stood for the verdict fumble with phones under the cover of the press bench, eager to be the first to alert their news desks. At the back of the court, DCI Carter raises his gaze to the ceiling, closes his eyes, and lets out a long, deep exhale. And behind the curtain, the victim bends at the waist and sobs.

The force's leader, Chief Constable Bannon, is waiting outside already, his statement all prepared, the cameras trained on him, resplendent in his smartly pressed uniform. Hair cut short at the sides, he is holding his police hat under his arm, in what seems to me a somewhat theatrical touch. A high-profile rape conviction—after a string of controversies about such cases being abandoned—is a much-needed triumph for the force and the Crown Prosecution Service, and I can see that the media glory is to be reserved for the top brass.

"I would like to pay tribute to the courage of the victim in this case," Chief Constable Bannon is saying to the circle of outstretched hands holding booms and microphones. "That young woman has shown a great deal of resilience and strength in very difficult circumstances. I sincerely hope that the guilty verdict will provide some closure on her horrendous ordeal, and that she will be able to rebuild her life, which was shattered by these events."

I'd already had the printed handout of what he was going to say, the press release with IN THE EVENT OF CONVICTION emblazoned on the top. I don't need to hear the live version. Instead I slip away from the pack, get into my car, and tap in the postcode of the hotel where I've arranged to meet both DCI Carter and Emily, the girl at the center of what has turned into the biggest court case of the year.

Emily has brought her sister along for support. They sit together on a sofa in the hotel room I have booked, overlooking Parker's Piece. The cake and drinks I nervously laid out sit untouched on the coffee table between us.

While I talk to her, DCI Carter sits at the back of the room, nursing a takeout coffee. He throws me stern glances as I fiddle with the recorder, pour glasses of water. In the end, he needn't have worried. Emily is clear and brave. She ignores the photographer, and he gets on with his job.

She looks me in the eye, answers all my questions. She does not shed a tear. I notice that her spine is now straighter, her gaze unafraid to meet mine. And I learn, for the first time, what power there is in justice, in being believed.

By the time we have finished it is dark outside. There is a drizzle of rain. The paving stones are dark and wet, the headlights of cars bright in the distance. DCI Carter holds an umbrella over Emily and her sister while I hail them a cab, pay the driver in cash.

"Thank you," I tell her.

She nods. "Don't forget to send me that copy, like you said."

"I won't."

Then, for the first time since I've met her, she smiles. "Thank you, too."

I watch as the brake lights on the taxi recede into darkness, the puddles on the pavement bright with the lights of cars. The wind picks up. I pull my scarf up over my chin, turn to my left. DCI Carter is still there, still holding the umbrella, staring after the taxi.

"I have you to thank for that, I suspect," I say. I have to raise my voice over the rain.

"Not at all," he mutters. "Entirely her choice."

I smile. I don't believe him.

"Well, thank you anyway."

He turns away, embarrassed. Then he pushes the umbrella into my hand. "Here you go," he says. "Don't get wet." His fingers are warm against mine. He looks at me for a moment, and I can't make out his expression. Then he shoves his hands into his pockets, turns on his heel, and disappears into the darkness.

As soon as DCI Carter has gone, I race back to the hotel room, slam the door shut behind me. I flip out my laptop, fire off an email to the desk, tell them the interview is in the bag, but that they will have to wait for copy. I hadn't told them it was definitely happening until now—I've found it's best to manage expectations. They call me straightaway, but I ignore my vibrating phone. They just need to let me write. I skip back to the start of the sound file and hit play. I work fast, have a sense of writing well. The noise of the rain outside somehow seems to help my mind to focus. There is a lot here, I think, relieved. More than enough.

When my phone vibrates for the third time, I hit pause, pull out my single headphone, and snatch it up.

"Hugh, I'm going as fast as I can," I snap.

"Katie? It's Sally."

At first I can't place the name. Then I remember. Sally in the flat below. Sally who is feeding Socks, my cat, while I'm in Cambridge.

"Sally? Hi. Is everything all right? Socks OK?" My stomach twists. Immediately I think of the screech of tires, the joyriders who speed down Dartmouth Park Road at night. A splatter of blood across the road.

"Socks is fine." She hesitates. There is a silence on the line for a moment, a slight fizzing noise. "It's just, um, there's a couple of police officers here."

"Police? For me?"

"Yes." She coughs. "They said something about a missing girl— Rachel something?"

I frown. "Rachel?"

"They um . . ." I can hear someone in the background, a man's voice, his tone sharp, impatient. I hear Sally murmur something back, then clear her throat. "They were wondering when you might be back."

Helen

AS THEY SIT DOWN at our kitchen table, the tall officer pulling his tie loose from his shirt, reaching his long fingers into his breast pocket for a pen, I feel a gathering sickness, a heaviness in the pit of my abdomen.

I clear my throat. "Can I get either of you a hot drink? I'm making a latte for myself anyway."

Neither of them answer. I decide to start making coffees anyway. I feel it is important somehow that I make them. Establish myself in the role of helpful witness, respectable local property owner. Someone who is on their side.

"Rachel has been reported missing," DS Mitre is saying. "A family member contacted us, concerned for her welfare. We're keen to try and establish where she might be."

"Oh. I see."

I can hear a waver in my voice. For God's sake, I think.

I concentrate on steaming the milk, holding the jug at an angle, my hands trembling. I bet they'll be grateful for a nice coffee. They're probably used to machine coffees, fluorescent-lit waiting rooms, scaly communal kettles. Or the houses of criminals, I suppose, where no one thinks to offer them a drink. When I try to imagine what those places might look like, my mind draws a bit of a blank. Public housing flats with brick balconies, lines of dumpsters, walls with anticlimb paint. Signs that say No Ball Games. Places I only ever see from the outside.

"You said that Rachel had been living with you?"

I sense their gaze on my face. I have a strange, anchorless feeling, as if I am not in my kitchen at all, but adrift on a vast sea, being carried farther and farther from the shore.

"Yes, she had been staying here," I say eventually. My hand is trembling on the jug. The metal of it makes a slight vibration against the coffee machine. "Just for a couple of weeks," I add. I place the jug down, wipe my hands on my jeans. They feel clammy.

"And how did you know her?"

I take a breath.

"We met recently," I say. "At a prenatal class."

"A prenatal class?"

"Yes."

"I see." DS Mitre's expression suggests this was not within the range of answers he had expected.

I place the coffees down. DS Mitre thanks me. The female officer doesn't.

"So, how can I help?" I ask, easing myself into a chair slowly, trying to look casual. "Is Rachel OK? When you say missing—she's not in any trouble or anything, is she?" I try to make my voice sound normal.

"We're just keen to establish where she is," DS Mitre says. "I'm sorry, Mrs. Thorpe, did you say you met Miss Wells at a prenatal class?"

"Yes, that's right."

"Why was Miss Wells at a prenatal class?"

I stare at her. "Because she was pregnant," I say, looking from one detective to the other. They glance at each other, then DS Mitre speaks.

"Are you sure about that, Mrs. Thorpe?"

"Of course I'm sure. We did an NCT course together."

The detectives look at each other, write down notes. They seem to be writing quite a lot. They ask more questions then—how many weeks she was, which hospital she was giving birth at. I try to remember any details she might have told me. Can't they just access her medical records or something?

"When did you last see Rachel, Mrs. Thorpe?"

"It was the night of our bonfire party." I pause. "The fifth. Of November, obviously."

"I see."

DS Mitre drops his gaze to his notebook and starts writing, his long, pale fingers curled around a black ballpoint pen.

DC Robbin takes over now. She is speaking just a little bit more loudly than she needs to. Her tone makes me sit up straighter.

"Before she left, did Rachel say where she was going?"

I shake my head. "No—she left without saying anything. I mean, she had told us she was moving out, around the middle of November. That she had found a place." The detectives write this down. "But no, we didn't know she was leaving that night. We woke up the next morning, and she'd gone."

"Any idea where this new place was?"

"She didn't really say," I murmur. "Sorry."

"You don't know why she might have left so suddenly?" DS Robbin's head is cocked to one side, her thin eyebrows arched like punctuation. Her eyes are fixed on mine. The room feels airless, my tongue dry and thick, as if it is stuck to the top of my mouth.

"No, not really."

"So there hadn't been an argument at this party, nothing like that?"

My pulse is climbing. My face feels red hot. Before I've even really thought about it, I find I am shaking my head and saying: "No."

"So you weren't concerned? At her leaving like that, without telling you why, or where she was going?"

"No, I was concerned, of course I was," I say, feeling the heat in my cheeks again. "I texted her. I wanted to make sure she was OK. And she replied, pretty much straightaway." I reach for my phone. "She said she was going to her mother's. Here, let me find the message."

I pull my phone out, find the message she sent me the day after the party, show it to DS Mitre. I think for a moment that he will be pleased, will thank me for my time, tell me he'll give her mum a ring now and he's sorry to have wasted my time. Instead, the atmosphere changes. The officers both examine the phone. They exchange glances again.

"Is that not where she is, then?" I ask. "At her mum's?"

DC Robbin closes her notebook, leans forward slightly.

"Mrs. Thorpe, what did she mean when she said she was sorry about last night?"

I blink.

"I . . . I don't know."

"You don't know?"

"Well, I suppose we'd fallen out a bit. Not badly."

She looks at me intently. "I thought you said you hadn't had an argument."

I'm tapping my leg under the table, the bench underneath me shaking slightly. "We h-hadn't," I stutter. "Not an argument. That's not what I meant." I force myself to stop, place my feet flat on the floor. I wish Daniel were here. He said he was just going out for a run. He's been ages.

"I mean, look . . . it had been a bit awkward, the three of us. We'd been a bit—a bit snappy with each other, perhaps. I did tell her that night that I thought. . . perhaps the time had come for her to leave."

"You wouldn't class that as an argument?"

DS Mitre looks at DC Robbin. His radio crackles, and he glances down. None of this seems real, I think. None of it belongs in our kitchen, on our quiet Sunday evening, with the sounds of the washing machine, a car outside, the next-door neighbor's girl doing her clunky piano practice.

DS Mitre leans toward me.

"Mrs. Thorpe, would it be all right if we took that phone away with us today?"

I stare at him. "My phone? Why?"

"It might help our inquiries to do some analysis. Help us locate Miss Wells. Make sure that she is safe."

The way they say it, I feel like I can't say no. But can they really do that? Take my phone?

"The thing is," I say, "I'm about to have a baby. And I'm having our landline disconnected. Too many cold callers, you know? So . . ." I look from one officer to the other. "I really need my phone. Anything else is fine, but—I really need it."

DS Mitre glances down uncomfortably at my bump. Then he looks at DC Robbin. She gives an infinitesimal nod.

"Very well. Just a few more questions, Mrs. Thorpe."

There are a lot more questions, it turns out. They want a list of who was at the party. I write down the ones I know. I tell them they will have to talk to Charlie about the rest. They want to know other things, too. Like whether I have the details of anyone who might know her. Associates, is the phrase they use. Friends, colleagues, anyone she knew locally. And do I know much about the father of her baby?

I seem to be unable to give them any of the answers they want. The more they ask, the more I realize how little I knew about Rachel. "I'm so sorry," I say for what feels like the twentieth time. "Like I said, I only really know her through that prenatal class."

"And yet she moved into your house."

"Not moved in—it wasn't like that."

I need to reset my tone of voice. I sound shrill, defensive. I sound like someone who has done something wrong. DC Robbin has stopped writing things down. She is leaving that to DS Mitre. Instead she is looking at me, her lips closed, her eyes unblinking.

"It was meant to be just a couple of nights at most," I say, more slowly. "It turned into a bit longer. That's why there had been a bit of tension, I suppose. She said she'd found a new place. That she was moving out in mid-November. But it was all a bit vague."

"I see. And where had she been living before she came to—stay, with you?"

I shake my head. "I know she lived around here, but I never went to her home and I . . . I never met any of her friends."

The detectives glance at each other. I have the feeling I am getting everything wrong somehow.

"And the father?"

"She never actually mentioned a name. Just that it was someone she met through work."

"And they were together?"

"I don't think so. They had a relationship—I got the feeling it was quite casual—and the pregnancy wasn't planned. She said she would have liked to be with him but—but she'd found out that he . . . he was taken." He belonged to someone else. Those had been the words she used, hadn't they, that time at the pub? I remember the damp smell of the tables, the staring eyes of the ship lights.

"You say she'd met the father through work," DS Mitre is asking now. "Where exactly was that?"

"I, um . . . I don't know. I think she once said something about working for a music venue or something. But she was on maternity leave early, like me, you see—for health reasons."

"Health reasons?"

"Yes. She had the same as me, I think—very high blood pressure. Risk of preeclampsia. So you're advised not to work too much, certainly not in the third trimester. We just never really talked about work, because neither of us was working. It was mainly babies and stuff." I glance at DC Robbin, wondering if she has children. I guess she doesn't. She doesn't look much older than me, if at all. She must be clever to be a detective. I wince, thinking how dull I must sound to her. "Sorry," I mutter.

DC Robbin doesn't say anything. She keeps looking at me.

"Not at all." DS Mitre flips his notebook shut and stands up. "You've been very helpful, Mrs. Thorpe. Thanks for your time."

I lead them both into the hallway and open the door.

"Look," I say, my hand resting on the latch. "Can I just ask? Sorry if it's obvious, but—is she not at her mother's, then? Like she told me she would be?"

DS Mitre glances at DC Robbin. He pulls his jacket on, the sweater cuffs sticking out of the too-short sleeves.

"We'll be in touch," he says. "In the meantime, if you do hear from Rachel, please do give us a call."

"Of course."

They step outside and I close the door behind them. I lean back against the weight of it, slide down to the floor until I am crouched in the hallway, my bump pushed up against my knees. I am shaking, actually shaking, all over, as if I'm outside in the cold. When I close my eyes, all I can see is Rachel's face, her slightly parted lips, her childlike horror, like a burst balloon, as I utter those awful words, the last ones I said to her. *We're not friends. We never were. I want you to leave, tonight, and not come back.*

I open my eyes again. You are a liar, I tell myself. You are a liar, Helen Thorpe.

39 WEEKS

Katie

HE IS LATE, AS usual. The venue was his choice, an Indian restaurant on Church Street in Stoke Newington. There are thick white tablecloths, a tea light at each place setting, paintings of Kerala on the walls; fishing nets against an orange sunset in Fort Kochi, houseboats in the lush backwaters. There is a smell of cardamom and fennel. The Virgin Mary watches over us from a candlelit shrine in the corner. Outside, raindrops dribble down the windows. A passing woman abandons her umbrella after it is blown inside out by the wind, leans over a puddle to shove it into a trash can.

I am the only person here, and my presence seems to be a source of relief to the waiters. They are smartly dressed and startlingly young, like teenagers on their way to a dance. They treat me with exaggerated politeness, pulling out a chair for me, bringing me a glass of the house red, as requested. They tip the bottle gently, enclosed in a folded white napkin. I drink the wine quickly, nibbling on a dry papadum. It is crisp, still hot from the oil.

When Charlie finally arrives, he looks flushed, the ends of his hair wet against his neck.

"Sorry, Katie."

He leans to kiss me, but I pull away.

"Ugh, Charlie, you're wet."

"Sorry." He pulls away grinning, leaving my cheek clammy. "You look nice." He snatches a papadum, shoves it into his mouth as he sits down. "Starving," he says.

Soon Charlie has ordered a bottle of wine, another round of papadums, and a whole load of starters I have no interest in eating. When the waiter has finally disappeared, Charlie looks at me.

"What?" he says. "What's wrong?"

"The police came to see me," I tell him. "They said Rachel has gone missing. That she hasn't been seen since the night of Helen and Daniel's party."

Charlie frowns. "Yeah," he says. "I know. They came to see me, too."

"Did they?"

"They wanted a list of everyone at the party."

The speakers blare into life—some mournful Hindi song. I twist my napkin in my hands.

"They kept asking me about when I saw her last."

"Yeah, they asked me the same thing." Charlie pauses, frowns. "And? Why are you looking at me like that?"

It was a stupid idea, coming here. Why didn't we go somewhere private?

The food Charlie has ordered arrives, worryingly quickly, in a series of little metal bowls. My stomach turns over in protest. I can't look at the creamy sauces, the lurid colors of the chutneys.

"Come on," Charlie says when the waiter is a safe distance away. "What is it?"

I lower my voice. "The last time I saw her, at the party, she was going down into the cellar. With you."

"Wait, hang on. I didn't go down to the cellar with her."

I examine him closely.

"I didn't!" He is looking me straight in the eye. "Honestly, Katie. I went down to the cellar, yes. But I was on my own."

"Charlie, I saw her go down there. I remember the blue dress she was wearing—I saw the back of it. She was following someone down there. Then ten minutes later, I saw you and you told me you'd just been down in the cellar. You were covered in dust."

Charlie is shaking his head. "Yeah, I had been down to the cellar. But I was there on my own. I wanted to see the renovation work, that was all. There was nothing to see! Just a load of wet concrete. I came straight back up. Got a beer. Came out to find you. Rachel wasn't down there with me." Charlie is searching my face. "It's the truth, Katie. Why would I lie?"

I know Charlie, I tell myself. He is not perfect, but I know him, I'm sure of it. I know his face. I would know it if I was blind, if I had to feel it in the dark. I know his heart. I have always believed that fundamentally he is good. Now, as I look into his eyes, I believe he is telling the truth. But could I be wrong?

"Hang on. Did you tell the police you saw me go down to the cellar with her? Is that what you're trying to tell me?"

I stare at him, then look away. "Not exactly," I mutter.

"What do you mean?"

"I was sure it was you," I tell him. "I thought you'd be in trouble."

"So what?"

"So I didn't tell them, all right? I didn't tell them that I saw her going down to the cellar with anyone. And now I don't know what the fuck to do."

I still don't quite understand why I didn't tell them. But the way it happened just didn't feel like lying. It just felt like it didn't come up.

So you saw her talking to Mr. Charlie Haverstock, the detective had said. *And you think that was around eight fifteen?*

Yes, I think so.

All right. And that was the last time you saw or spoke to Miss Wells, was it?

It didn't feel like a lie, you see. It just felt like agreeing. It felt like being polite. Not making things difficult, for anyone. In the moment, it was the *truth* that felt like a lie. This vague idea that I'd seen her again later, when I was coming back from the bathroom . . . After all, it was only the back of a blue dress that I saw, and what looked like the shadow of someone else. It felt weird to bring up. I told myself it was something that might mislead them, confuse matters, obstruct the investigation. And then before I knew it, they were shutting their notebooks anyway. Nodding their goodbyes. And that was it. It was too late.

I'd convinced myself it wasn't a lie. But it feels like a lie now. The more I think about it, the worse it feels.

"This cellar thing—it might be important, Charlie." I twist the napkin again. "Don't you think? Whoever went down there with her—it might have something to do with her going missing."

Charlie frowns, his mouth full of food.

"The detective left her card," I say quickly. "She was nice. I'll call her. I'll tell them I just . . . remembered it." All of a sudden I can't wait to call them. I'm flooded already with the relief of it, with the release from guilt.

"Katie, I wouldn't if I were you."

Charlie's voice is quiet, but firm. I look at him, confused.

"What do you mean?"

Charlie takes a deep breath. "Look," he says. "Ultimately, it won't really matter what you told them. They're interviewing loads of people about what they saw at the party."

"So?"

"So—why would you want to draw attention to yourself—get yourself more involved? Admit that you lied when they spoke to you the first time?" He raises his eyebrows. "Think how it'll look, Katie."

I feel a rising panic in my chest. "No, hang on," I say. "I didn't lie, Charlie, it wasn't like that. I just . . . I just didn't tell them that one thing. They even said if I remembered anything else, that I could—"

Charlie snorts. "Yeah, right." He shakes his head, smiling sadly. "They want you to think that. That it won't matter if you change your story, that you can tell them anything. Trust me, it doesn't work like that. The worst thing you can be is inconsistent. They'll make something of it, if they want to."

"Oh, Charlie, you're being paranoid. The police aren't going to go after me!"

He shrugs. "If you say so." He snaps off a piece of papadum and dips it in a sauce. "I'm just saying, they twist things. Think what they were like with me."

I sigh. I know how much he hates talking about what happened last year. He was an idiot to take coke into the club, of course. But he isn't some kind of dealer. The irony was he had taken it in for Rory and his mates.

Though he would never admit it, Charlie still looks up to Rory, just like he did when they were little. He still tries to please him, does what he asks. When he was caught by an undercover cop, it didn't take me long to work out why Charlie refused to say who the "friend" he'd bought the coke for was. And because he wouldn't name names—and maybe, a bit, because of his dad, and his money, and his smart mouth, which doesn't do him any favors—the police threw the book at him. Charged him for possession with intent to supply. Wanted to make an example.

Fortunately, the lawyer Rory paid for did a good job, and the judge was more sympathetic than the cops. She accepted his plea that it was just for him and his friends. Still, he was lucky to get a suspended sentence. To be able to keep working.

The waiter reappears with the main courses. He sets down a wooden board with naan, then the curries. He says the bowls are hot, that we should be careful. The table is crowded, the wineglasses clinking against the metal bowls. The smell of ginger and garlic is almost too much. For a moment I think I'm going to be sick.

"Look," Charlie says eventually, putting his hand over mine. "For a start, I'm sure Rachel is fine."

I look at him, feel my throat tightening again. I want to believe it is true. "Do you think?"

"Of course." He squeezes my hand. "She'll have just gone back to her boyfriend or something. Or her mum. Or a friend. Christ, I don't know, Katie—it could be any number of random things. As far as I can tell, there's no reason to think that anything bad has happened to her."

I pull my hand away, twist my napkin. "The police wouldn't be involved if they didn't think something bad had happened to her."

"OK, but even if something *has* happened—I don't know. This . . . this cellar thing? It might not even matter." He pulls his hand back, dips his naan into one of the chutneys, staining it red. "I just think if you change your story now, they might think it's weird. And it might distract them from something that really is important." He takes a bite. "Don't you think?"

I look at him. I think back to that night, when I saw him and Rachel together, how his hand brushed against her side.

"Charlie, what were you talking to Rachel about? When I saw you that night?"

His face darkens. "What do you mean?"

"Oh, come on. You were together, by the bookcase. Just the two of you, for ages. You were standing really close to her. Why did you have so much to talk about when you'd only just met her?"

He looks away, out into the blur of rain.

"What, Charlie?"

"Nothing!"

"What do you mean, nothing?"

"I don't know . . . nothing! We were just chatting. Normal stuff."

He is staring into his lap now, then back to the rain-splattered window. I was sure he wasn't hiding anything before. Now I don't know. I want to believe he is telling the truth. I want to, so much. But then I think again about the way he and Rachel looked when I saw them talking at the party, the intensity of it.

And then later, when he came out to find me in the garden. Why was he covered in dust, if he'd only gone down there for a moment?

When he speaks again, Charlie's tone is different. Harder.

"I don't get it, Katie," he says. "You met this girl what—once, twice? Why are you interrogating me about it?" He leans closer. "What are you asking? Are you saying you think I've got something to do with her going missing?"

"Of course not. Don't be stupid!"

"Well, what then?"

"I just . . . I need to know what happened."

"Well, maybe we'll never know. People go missing all the time, usually because they want to. We don't know what was going on with her. It could be any number of things. It could be nothing at all." He pauses. "Don't you think?"

I stare out of the window, watching the rain thrash against the glass, the bent backs of people walking through it. I watch the buses and taxis throw waves of water over the pavement, the brown rivers running into drains. I think about what happened to the girl in my court case, about how she ran for help, her bare feet cold on the cobbled street. Anything could have happened to Rachel, I think. She could be out there, in this. Hitchhiking by a roadside. In a ditch somewhere. Under a bridge. She could have been hit by a car. She could have run away, somewhere north, Scotland, abroad. She could be facedown in water, her bloated body lolling against a harbor wall. I close my eyes.

"I don't know," I say. "I don't know what to think."

Helen

WHEN WE FINALLY GO out shopping for a stroller, it isn't as enjoyable as I'd hoped. Daniel suggests one of those out-of-town discount shopping places. It is a long train ride away, and we sit for what seems like an hour as the gaps between the stations lengthen.

He hardly says anything when we are there, or on the way home, the new stroller wedged next to us in the wheelchair bay. Stupid not to have driven.

"Is it the expense?" I ask after Daniel has been quiet for most of the journey. "I know the joint account is getting a bit low, but we have all those savings, remember. Why don't you transfer a chunk over, for the baby things? This is what they are for, isn't it?"

He insists it isn't that. That everything is fine. "I'm just feeling a bit run-down," he says, smiling tightly. "Need an early night."

So we sit in silence. I watch the ramshackle suburban gardens backing onto the train line, a moving gallery of broken bicycles, Fisher-Price slides, trampolines full of rainwater. The backs of the houses are pockmarked with broken satellite dishes. My eyelids start to feel heavy. I didn't get much sleep last night.

Since the police came about Rachel, I can't seem to rest. I thought that text message had meant she was all right. But she can't have just gone to her mother's, or the police wouldn't be asking questions, would they?

Daniel keeps telling me not to worry. He says she was obviously fine the day after the party, when she sent that message. If she changed her mind about going to her mother's, so what? She'll be off with the father of the baby, or with another new best friend.

Sometimes, for a few hours, he convinces me. I allow myself to decide it's not my fault, not my problem. I mean, we're not responsible for her, are we? We were just gullible enough to take her in for a few weeks.

And yet, when I close my eyes at night, it all looks different, my thoughts harder to dismiss. And for all his attempts to reassure me, I think the worry of it is eating away at Daniel, too. The police went to his office the day after they spoke to me. He didn't say much about it. But it upset him, I can tell. I want to tell him not to feel guilty. That we weren't to know. But every time I try to talk about it, he shuts me down, changes the subject. Stands up, takes his plate up to the study to eat alone, mutters about needing to get on with work.

Daniel has always had periods of insomnia. Sometimes, if he really can't sleep, he will get up in the night and disappear downstairs for a while. But since Rachel left, he is worse than ever. Whenever I wake in the small hours, his side of the bed is empty. Sometimes I hear him rattling around, like a restless ghost. There is the sound of the kettle boiling. The TV noise fading from laughter to music to explosions, as he thumbs from channel to channel. When I ask him why he can't sleep, he never gives the same answer. Or any answer at all.

I asked him the other night, when he got back into bed. Is it Rachel? Are you worried about her? I worry about her, too, I told him. He just said I should get some sleep.

I've called the detective a couple of times, just checking in, seeing if there's any progress. No one seems to know. If I could just be sure that she is somewhere else, that it wasn't me, that I didn't do anything. Of course, it can't have been. I would remember. Wouldn't I?

I wondered if I should tell the police about the notes, my suspicions about her and Rory. But the more I thought about all that, the less certain I was. I mean, I never really found any proof, did I? And Rory is my brother. I couldn't say anything. Not unless I was sure.

On the walk back from the station, the cold bites at my hands and cheeks. Daniel pushes the empty stroller, his fingers gripping the bar tightly. It has started to sleet. The stroller's pebble-colored sunshade is already starting to darken and stain.

When we get home I turn the key in the front door and flip the light switch, but nothing happens. A fuse must have blown.

"I'll have a look," Daniel says.

I find a flashlight, hold it for Daniel at the top of the cellar steps while he climbs down to get to the fuse box. When he pushes the lever up, there is a slight fizzing sound, and the bare bulb hanging in the cellar flickers on.

"Well done," I tell him. I switch the flashlight off.

"I'll get some dinner on," Daniel says, hauling himself back up the steps.

Just as I'm about to turn the light off, I notice it. "Daniel," I say, "have you seen that?"

"What?"

"Look. In the floor."

The crack is as fine as a pencil line. It cuts through the middle of our newly laid foundation, from the top to the bottom, like a jagged tree root. For some reason, a verse comes into my head. Something remembered from school, from the Bible, I think.

And behold, the curtain of the temple was torn in two, from top to bottom. And the earth shook, and the rocks were split.

Katie

I WAS BRACING MYSELF for it to be difficult. The name was common enough. But by the time I have worked through all the listings, I find there is only one Rachel Wells of the right age listed as currently living in London. I frown. That can't be her, can it? The address isn't anywhere near Greenwich.

I email the desk, tell them I am checking out a tip, that I'll be on my cell if they need me. I slip out before anyone can ask questions. I look at my watch as I hurry through the glass doors: 5:55. The roads will be jammed. I'll have to catch the Tube.

It takes a while to get from west to east. I hurtle through darkness, pressed against strangers, staring up at the long white lights in the ceiling of the Tube cars, like dashes from here to there. None of us speak. There is only the shudder of the train, the anonymous whistle of air and metal. My eyes flit between the ads. A sign says we should report any suspicious activity. A new lot of people crowds on at Oxford Circus, their hair soaking wet. Puddles start to form on the floor, umbrellas dripping, coats and backpacks splattered with water.

The address turns out to be a high-rise flat, one of the few left on this side of town. After Grenfell, we'd done a big investigation into these buildings, tried to find out how many more were death traps, coated in dangerous cladding, at risk of infernos. I'd been haunted by thoughts of fire for a long time after covering Grenfell. I couldn't stop thinking about all those people, trapped like animals on the upper floors.

This must have been one of the death trap high-rises, because it looks like they are starting to strip it. The outside is covered in scaffolding, billowing tarpaulins hitched to it like ragged sails. It looks as grim as ever.

These blocks are all the same inside. The same piss smell in the elevator, the same blokes eyeballing you on the staircases, the same bloodred scrawls of graffiti on the peeling gray walls, the same stagnant, overflowing dumpsters. As the elevator creeps up to the fourteenth floor, I think how it must have felt for people living in these buildings, when Grenfell happened. To read about how, on the upper floors, the windows only opened an inch. All the families trapped there had to huddle around them, take turns to breathe. Everything else was choking, suffocating blackness. The windows in these flats are like that, too. Not for the first time, I think how lucky I am to own my tiny one-bedroom in Dartmouth Park, to have dodged the rental trap so many graduates like me have fallen into. Paying hundreds of pounds a month just to live somewhere like this. Somewhere where the windows only open an inch.

When I knock on the door of the flat, it sounds hollow. I hear the pad of slippered feet approach the door, then, finally, it opens.

"Hi," I say. "I'm Katie. I'm a friend of Rachel's." I'm not sure this is quite true, but it feels necessary.

The girl looks at me. She is wearing fluffy pink slippers over a pair of black tights, a cheap polyester work dress. She has a large forehead, her hair scraped back.

"Jane." She sighs. "You'd better come in."

Helen

THE NEW DETECTIVES TURN up a few days later. It's a freezing night. Daniel and I have been to the cinema. When we get back, they are waiting in a car parked right outside our doorstep.

The female one is tall, boyish-looking, a thick scarf right up to her chin, tucked into a long puffer jacket. "I'm DCI Betsky and this is DI Hughes," she says. Her words turn into clouds of steam in front of her face. Bits of sleet are settling in DI Hughes's trendy beard.

Daniel opens the front door, gestures for them to come in, pushes the stroller out of their way. The detectives wipe their shoes carefully. Blackened slush melts into puddles on the floor. We lead them into the kitchen. I offer to take their coats. They both decline. I decide not to bother with coffees this time.

"I assume this is about Rachel," I say. "Is there any news?"

DCI Betsky looks at me. "I'm afraid not, Mrs. Thorpe," she says. "Rachel is still missing."

"I'm sorry to hear that," I say. "I have been trying to call your colleagues—the ones I spoke to before."

The two detectives glance at one another.

"Just to see if they'd found her or anything."

"The detectives you met before were from Greenwich CID," DCI Betsky says slowly. "The investigation has been passed over to specialist crime. We'll be leading things from now on."

There is a pause.

DI Hughes clears his throat. "Is it all right if we take a look around her room?"

"Her room?"

"The room where Rachel was staying prior to her disappearance. Just to see if there's anything there which might help us."

Daniel and I glance at each other.

"We've actually just repainted it," Daniel says.

The detectives stare at us.

"You have repainted the room she was staying in," DCI Betsky repeats.

I feel suddenly sick. "It's going to be the nursery, for our new baby," I explain. "No one said . . . no one said . . ."

"I see," says DI Hughes. "All the same. If you don't mind."

Daniel leads them up the stairs. I prepare to follow, but DCI Betsky raises a palm in protest. "Please," she says, looking down at my belly. "There's no need, Mrs. Thorpe. I'm sure your husband knows the way." She doesn't smile.

I perch on a stool, a blast of heartburn flaring in my chest. I lean forward a little, listen to the floorboards creaking, the muffled sound of them asking Daniel questions. They are up there for what seems like a long time. I try to flick through a magazine on the sideboard, but I can't seem to focus on anything in it.

When they come back down the stairs, DI Hughes speaks first.

"We need you to come to the station. Now, please. We'll need a recorded statement. From both of you."

I look at him, then to Daniel, then back again.

"But we already spoke to your colleagues," I say. "The, um, the ones from Greenwich—"

"The detectives from Greenwich CID, yes," DCI Betsky interrupts. She looks impatient now, clicking the lid onto her pen, pushing it into the breast pocket of her long jacket. She is speaking to us differently, this detective. Why does she not smile? Why doesn't it feel like she is on our side?

"I'm sure you can appreciate it's been a couple of weeks now, Mrs. Thorpe. We are very keen to exclude the possibility that Miss Wells could have come to any harm."

Daniel picks up our car keys.

"Don't worry," DCI Betsky tells him, "you can come with us."

"I'll drive," Daniel says. "I'm sure this won't take long, and my wife is tired. We will need to get home." He sounds furious. The detective gives him a look, but doesn't disagree.

When we get to the station, we are led into separate rooms, opposite sides of a narrow corridor with laminate floors peeling at the edges. The interrogation goes on for what feels like hours. None of the questions seem to have satisfactory answers, or at least not ones I am able to provide. There are a lot of silences.

Most weirdly of all, they don't appear to have known that Rachel was pregnant.

"You're absolutely sure about that, Mrs. Thorpe?"

"Look, I didn't see her without her clothes on, if that's what you mean." I'm almost laughing, but the detectives are deadly serious. "I mean, if she wasn't pregnant, then she was going to prenatal classes and wandering around Greenwich with a fake baby bump. Are you seriously suggesting that's what's happened?"

When they finally let me go, my head is spinning.

"Thank you, Mrs. Thorpe." DCI Betsky presses a card into my hand as I pull on my coat. "You haven't got any long trips planned, I presume?"

I stare at her. "I'm about to have a baby," I say.

She looks at me for a moment longer. It is late. I ache for my own bed, for pillows, sheets, oblivion.

"We'll be in touch," she says. Then she walks away.

Unsure what to do, I ask at reception. They say Daniel was let out ages ago. He is waiting for me in the car.

"Helen," I see him say, although I can't hear through the glass. He opens the passenger door, holds his arm out to ease me in. His eyes are wide. "For God's sake. What on earth were they doing, keeping you so late?"

"I don't know," I say, my voice wavering. He takes my hand.

"What did they ask you?"

I try to answer him, but it already feels like a blur. I have the sense of having failed, having botched an important test. I think about the look on DCI Betsky's face and the way she played with her blue ballpoint pen, twisting it between her fingers as she leaned forward.

"Mrs. Thorpe, forgive me for asking again. But we're still not entirely clear. What exactly happened between yourself and Rachel Wells on the night she disappeared?"

Katie

JANE WAVES ME THROUGH to the kitchen. Her slippers stick slightly to the laminate floor as she walks. There are dirty pans and dishes in the sink, and the whole apartment smells faintly of unwiped surfaces and cheap tomato sauce. The view from the window is blank and featureless, London's landmarks too distant to make out, the city a scribbled line on the horizon.

"The police came already," she says, opening the fridge. "I told them. I've got no idea where she is. She left here a few weeks ago and she hasn't come back."

Jane starts reheating sloppy leftover pasta from a plastic-wrapped bowl in the fridge. A grubby extractor fan whirrs in the wall above her head; little cobwebs of clotted grime quiver in its wake, like streamers.

"Do you know much about the father of her baby?"

The microwave beeps and Jane yanks the door open, tips her steaming pasta onto a chipped plate.

"I've been through this with the police. If Rachel was pregnant, that is news to me," she says, slumping into a chair diagonally opposite me.

"I'm sorry?"

"I saw her a few weeks ago. Just before she moved into your friend's. And OK, it was cold, she was wearing a big coat, but she didn't look pregnant to me. She was no different. Strange as ever." She rolls her eyes. "I'm sorry," she says through a mouthful of pasta. "I know she was your friend. But she was driving us mad, to be honest. We had quite a few problems with her, and basically, she needed to move out."

I smile as warmly as I can. I don't want her clamming up.

"Sorry, it's just—I don't know if police told you this, but she had actually been attending prenatal classes, in Greenwich."

Jane considers this. "Well, that's weird," she agrees. "And she looked pregnant, did she?"

I nod. "That's how she met my friend Helen, how we got to know her. I mean—she looked pregnant to us."

"Well, I don't know what to tell you. Maybe she was, maybe she wasn't."

I walk over to the window, try to think logically. Could Rachel really have faked being pregnant? And if she wasn't pregnant, and she didn't live in Greenwich, what reason could she possibly have had to be at that prenatal class? There must have been something. Some reason she would want to get close to Helen. To us. I change tack.

"Before she moved out—had Rachel been seeing anyone?"

"No. I mean, she had blokes back here, I'm pretty sure of that. They didn't exactly stay around for breakfast, though, if you know what I mean."

"Do you know who?"

She shakes her head. "I assumed it was just guys she picked up at the club."

"The club?"

"Yeah. The club. Where she worked. What's it called—the X?" Her eyes narrow. "Hang on, I thought you said you were her friend. Didn't you even know where she worked?"

"She wasn't working anywhere when we got to know her," I say. "Are you sure it's that club? The X?"

"Sure," Jane says. "I went there once. Didn't care for it. Full of smack-heads."

I take a deep breath, try to smile. "OK," I say. "I guess I'm just a bit surprised that . . . she would work there. That she would pick up guys at a club. I didn't think she was like that."

Jane snorts with laughter. "Well, think again. Sorry, but she was a nutcase."

I try to smile again, though I'm definitely not warming to Jane. "I'm sorry, I'm sure the police have already asked. But, well, we're all so worried. Do you have any idea where she might have gone?"

"Nope." Jane shakes her head, wipes a smudge of pasta sauce from the side of her mouth with her hand. "We had a fight when she left. About the rent. She was late with it. And then I saw she had all these fifty-pound notes in her purse. Must have been at least a grand in there. I was livid. But she refused to hand it over. It was six hundred pounds she owed us. Still does."

Jane picks her fork up again.

"I told her if she wasn't going to pay rent, she needed to go. My dad's a solicitor. I told her we'd take her to court. I know it sounds harsh, but me and my roommates—we'd had enough. It wasn't just the drinking, the smoking, the blokes, the mess. She was just so weird, and rude. And—ugh, she was just mental." She shivers at the memory. "Sorry. Maybe she was going through a bad time, I don't know. Anyway, she left then. Didn't say a word. She packed up her things, took her suitcase, and left. She said we could keep her desk." Jane motions to Rachel's old room with her dirty fork, gives a hollow laugh. "As if an old desk makes up for the six hundred pounds. It's a piece of shit from Ikea! I don't know what she even used it for. It's not as if she was studying or anything. But she would sit there for hours, playing her annoying music. She used to say she was doing some project. She had all these newspaper cuttings up on that wall at one point. She left about a thousand Blu-Tack marks. We'll probably lose our deposit."

"Newspaper cuttings? Of what? What was the project about?"

"Oh, God knows. I didn't look, I didn't care."

"Do you mind if I take a look? At her cuttings?"

"She took them all with her." Jane gestures to the hallway. "It's just mess in there. Just a pile of old rubbish."

"Still, can I see? Was it the room at the end?"

Jane finishes her plate of pasta, takes it to the sink. Then she turns around and glares at me.

"Do you know what, actually, yes. I do mind. You shouldn't even be here. I don't know what you're doing, digging around, but I don't want to get involved. I don't want anything to do with it."

Jane moves back to the sink and turns the tap on full, as if to indicate our conversation is over. "I think you should probably go now."

I nod. "OK," I say. "Thanks for talking to me."

In the elevator on the way down I think about Rachel, sitting at her desk late at night. Newspaper cuttings stuck on her wall. What was her project? What was she up to?

On the ground floor through the dirty windows, I see the rain is still battering at the glass. I pull my hood up, head home. I can't face it tonight. But I know what I need to do next. Where I need to go. To the club Jane mentioned. The X.

I know exactly where it is. I've been there plenty of times.

It's the club where Charlie works.

Helen

I AM SO HUGE now I can barely drive, but the vet's is too far to walk. The bump presses into the bottom of the steering wheel. I have to push the driver's seat right back on its sliders. It is icy now, but none of my coats fit. I've pulled on one of Daniel's sweaters instead, the sleeves bunching at my wrists.

As I start the engine, the radio blasts on automatically. I quickly turn the volume down. Monty is staring miserably out of his cage on the passenger's seat. When we drive over speed bumps, the baby presses down on my pelvis. I wince. Monty howls. I squeeze a tuna treat through the bars. It makes the car smell like fish. I feel a wave of nausea, press the button to open the window. The air is sharp and cold; it makes me gasp.

And then I hear something that makes me turn the radio back up.

"Police have today launched a murder inquiry following the disappearance of Rachel Wells. The twenty-five-year-old disappeared in Greenwich, southeast London, after attending a party a fortnight ago. Police have been appealing for any information about her disappearance, which they described as being out of character . . ."

I feel hot all over.

I flick on the turn signal, veer left, and pull over so I can listen properly, cutting off another car in the process. He honks loudly. Monty starts to howl. I shush him, shove another treat through the bars.

"Detective Chief Inspector Lauren Betsky said the force was keeping an open mind about her disappearance but had become increasingly concerned for her welfare. It is understood Miss Wells has not had any contact with her family or friends since the night of November fifth."

I can hear my own breathing. I can't seem to process the words.

Murder inquiry. They think she's dead. They think someone's killed her. So that's why they turned up yesterday. That's why the new detectives are involved. That's why they searched her room. Asked us everything, all over again.

"At a press conference earlier this morning, her family appealed for anyone with any information on her possible whereabouts to come forward."

I frown. Her family? She never mentioned any family. Except her mother, whom she said she was going to stay with.

"If anyone knows anything about where my daughter is," a gravelly male voice on the radio is saying now, "I would ask them to please, please—"

My phone rings. I jump, turn the radio down.

"Hello, Mrs. Thorpe? It's the Greenwich veterinary practice. Are you still coming in with Monty today?"

I take a deep breath. I apologize, tell them I'm on my way. I turn the radio off, start the engine. I can't take it in. I can't think about this now. I can't keep letting it go around and around in my head, blocking out everything else.

When the vet sees Monty, he smiles. "It's been a while, hasn't it, old boy?" I can tell he means it kindly, but a stab of guilt pierces my stomach.

With everything that had been going on, neither of us had really noticed how oddly Monty had been acting. But the morning after we got back from the police station, I saw that his food bowl had been left untouched again. I looked at him properly. Was he always so skinny? I'd placed my hands on either side of his body and his ribs had felt hard as curtain rings against the soft palms of my hands.

The vet holds Monty's abdomen in his hands, feels along his ribs, his spine. Listens to his heart, then places him on the scale. It beeps, and the vet frowns.

"Yes, he has lost a bit more weight than I'd like. Is there anything obvious that could account for his not eating? Anything going on at home?"

I hesitate, unsure whether to mention the police. I think again about the radio. A murder inquiry. My stomach twists.

The vet breaks my concentration. "I guess . . . there have been a few changes, in the house. Cats can be very sensitive to changes in their environment." He is looking down at my belly over the top of his glasses.

I force myself to smile, happy to let him attribute my silence to the pregnancy.

"Yes, how did you guess?" I say, trying to make my voice light. "Actually, we're having some fairly major building work, too."

"Aha."

"Yes. The whole downstairs is being done, plus a basement extension." I stroke Monty's back. "He hates it all. Especially since we laid the concrete—it's a new foundation. He won't go near the cellar anymore."

The vet nods sympathetically. "His food bowl—is it in that area, by any chance? By the cellar?"

I look up at him, feeling like an idiot.

"Try moving it somewhere quiet, where Monty feels a bit safer."

As he talks to me about a new diet, animal Prozac, microchip cat flaps, I notice that the vet is rubbing Monty between his ears, like Rachel used to do. He'd lie in her lap for ages, as if under some kind of spell. I think of the night we watched *Sliding Doors*, tucked up on the sofa together, Monty asleep on her legs. She'd had one hand on his ears, tapping away on that gold diamanté-clad phone with the other. That wolfish grin. *I love cats. They don't give a fuck, do they?*

I tell myself to stop thinking about her like that, as if remembering someone who is dead. I run my fingers through my hair. It feels greasy. When was the last time I washed it?

"Um, sorry, Mrs. Thorpe. Did you want to take any of these?"

I force myself to concentrate, focus on the vet's questions.

"Sorry. Yes, thanks. I'll take all that." I hand him my debit card.

"Have you got long to go?" he asks.

"Depends on the builders, really. But a few more months, at least, I'm afraid."

The vet looks confused.

"Oh, sorry, you meant the baby!" I force a laugh as I tap in my PIN. "Due any day now. I'm nearly forty weeks."

"Well, best of luck." He frowns. "Oh, that card seems to have been declined. Do you have another?"

I shake my head. "No, that one should be fine. Could you try it again?" But it is declined again. I tap my pockets, search my bag, but I know it's the only one I brought with me. I don't understand. There should be plenty in our joint account. I transferred a load from our savings the other day, in case we needed any more baby stuff, Daniel having obviously forgotten.

When I pull up back at home, I'm exhausted. I need to call the bank, try and sort things out with the vet, but all I want to do is sleep. I must call the builders about that crack as well. I must do that today. Before it gets worse. I'm just so tired. And I keep thinking about Rachel's father on the radio. Of what he must be going through.

It's such an effort to haul Monty out of the car and up the path that I barely notice the man with the patchy stubble, smoking outside the Plume of Feathers pub. It's only after he's in my front garden that I realize he was waiting for me. He is rubbing the hair at the back of his head, shifting his weight from one foot to another.

"Can I help you?"

The man locks eyes with me. Something about him is familiar. Something about the mouth.

"Are you Helen?"

I feel a prickle of anxiety on the back of my neck. Monty's carrier is weighing down my right side; I can't run, even if I wanted to. The man bounds up to me. Before I can say anything else, he grabs my arm, tight as a vise. I gasp. His face is close enough for me to smell alcohol on his breath, the staleness of his clothes. And then I figure out who he is.

"I want a word with you," he spits. "I want to know what happened to my daughter."

Katie

AS SOON AS I see the press conference, I can tell things are about to change, that Rachel is about to become big news. It's been a slow week, and now we have a murder inquiry: a young woman, missing after a party in one of London's most exclusive neighborhoods. A plea from a tearful father, begging for information. I can already tell it will be replayed again for the news at six, then at ten, and round the clock on Sky News.

A picture of Rachel is also doing the rounds, too. And it is a front-page picture, no doubt about it. It looks like a selfie she took at Helen's house, in the spare room. Someone must have found it on social media. She is wearing that red dress, that red lipstick she had on at Rory's birthday. You can even see Helen's shelves in the background, her mother's old glass vase. It is all too close to home. Far too close.

I steer well clear of it, volunteer to write a dull report about house prices I know will barely make the paper, so I don't have to concentrate. By the afternoon, though, I can't stand it anymore. I call Helen, but it goes straight to voice mail. I think about calling Charlie, but then I decide against it. I slip out of the newsroom. I know where I need to go.

I don't know what I am expecting to find. Maybe I am hoping to find nothing. Maybe Jane got it wrong. It is a popular club. Rachel could have just gone there sometimes.

The rain has lessened to a drizzle by the time I reach it, passing the scruffy wall outside with its blocky graffiti, bill poster upon bill poster. On Friday and Saturday nights, there's always a line along this wall, but today is Tuesday, and the club won't be open for hours. I push the door and am surprised to find it unlocked.

There is no one in the black-painted entrance, where the bouncers usually stand. The little window to the cloakroom is closed, the shutters pulled down. I walk down the steep steps, clinging on to the banister. How did I ever do this while drunk? I wonder. I haven't been here for a while. I know Charlie has started to get fed up with it. He's even been talking lately about getting a proper job. I'd told him it was about time.

There is a girl at the bottom of the steps, mopping the floor. She looks like she's barely a teenager. She is wearing a Goldfrapp T-shirt, cut off just below her breasts, exposing her navel. Her sneakers are metallic, her jeans ripped, her hair long on one side and shaved on the other. Her face looks familiar—I wonder if she was at the bonfire party.

The girl looks up at me with a bored expression. "We're closed."

"I know. Sorry. I'm . . . I'm a friend of Rachel's. Rachel Wells. She used to work here?"

The girl sighs, twisting the mop to squeeze the grayish water out of it.

"You a journalist as well?" She rolls her eyes, doesn't wait for my answer. "None of us know anything about Rachel," she says. She is chewing gum, transferring it from one side of her mouth to the other. "None of us have seen her in ages. The police came round already. You should speak to them."

She picks up her mop and bucket, turns away from me.

"You shouldn't really be here," she adds, speaking over the clatter of the metal bucket. "If you want Paul, the manager, he'll be back around nine." She pushes the double doors through to the bar with one hand, swings the mop and bucket through in front of her, then follows them.

I stand glued to the spot, unsure what to do. All right, just because Rachel worked here, it doesn't necessarily mean she knew Charlie, I tell myself. Maybe they never met each other. Maybe they worked here at different times. I'm sure there's an explanation. Because if he knew her, he would have said. Wouldn't he?

I turn to leave. I should just ask him, I think. It suddenly feels wrong, coming here behind his back.

I take one last look through the windows in the double doors, and a flash of color on the wall catches my eye. A bulletin board, behind the bar, covered in pictures.

When I am sure the girl is out of sight, I follow her through the double doors into the bar, holding on to them so they don't swing back and make a noise. The girl is nowhere to be seen—she must have taken the mop and bucket around the back. I slip the latch off the gate and sneak behind the bar to get a closer look.

The pictures have been stabbed to the board with red and yellow pins: clubbers with their tongues out, their faces pressed up to the camera; girls dancing on podiums, the bar on fire, cocktails pouring with dry ice. I flinch when I first see Charlie's face, but then I see he is in several of the pictures—his arms around different guys, and girls. One with his top off, neon paint on his face.

And then I see it. Right in the corner, in a section dated last year. Pin-sharp, unmistakable. Charlie, grinning away, his arm around a girl.

And the girl is Rachel.

Helen

I SET THE MUG down on the coffee table. "Please, have a seat," I tell Rachel's dad. But he does not sit, or smile.

I open the shutters, but the light is fading fast, and it still feels dark in the room. I lean over to switch on the lamps, my bump pressing awkwardly against the side of the sofa. The glow illuminates the swirls of dust in the air. I should really tidy up, I know. The place is such a mess. It smells of unwashed dishes, unwashed floors. My enthusiasm for cleaning has waned with my increasing exhaustion, my preoccupation with Rachel. And I'm tired. So tired.

I couldn't sleep last night. I was up watching TV until late. As I pass the armchair, I snatch up the packet of chocolate biscuits and the pair of ski socks wedged in the side of the armchair, where I left them. The nerves in my back protest at the effort of straining to reach.

Rachel's dad—John, he said his name was—is marching around the room, as if looking for clues, things to write down in a notebook he grips in one hand. A pencil is lodged behind his ear. He's not a tall man, and is slight, like her. Everything about him seems to be constantly in motion.

"I heard you on the radio this morning," I say. "I'm so sorry, I can't imagine what you must be going through." I pause. "I'm happy to tell you anything you want to know. I really don't know what else I can tell you, though. Except what I told the police."

At the mention of the police, his face contorts.

"I don't trust them," he says. "I've been after them for two weeks. I told them it's not right, that she wouldn't just disappear. I told them something must have happened to her. And they've done nothing."

"I . . . I think they are taking it seriously now. I mean, the press conference—"

"About time."

"I'm sure it will help," I say, trying to sound encouraging.

Now his bravado slips a little, his shoulders sloping. He finally slumps down into the sofa, gives a long sigh, like air escaping from a crumpled balloon.

"I dunno, Helen. I hope so. I hope it's not too late. I couldn't bear it if . . . I couldn't bear it." He drops his head, presses the balls of his hands into his eyes. I touch his shoulder, gently, but he flinches. I quickly pull my hand away.

I wish Daniel was here. He's said he wants to work late every night this week—that way we'll have more time together when the baby arrives. "It's not long now. I'm just getting ahead," he said. "It makes sense, doesn't it? Call me if you need me. Or if anything happens." I agreed at the time. But now I'm starting to regret it.

"You know, she didn't have that many friends," John says gruffly.

I sit down gingerly on my inflatable birthing ball. I try to sound breezy. "Oh, I'm sure she had—"

"No," he says bluntly, shaking his head, "she didn't." There is an expression of sadness on his face. "She had trouble with friends, our Rachel."

I am not sure how to react to this. John cracks his knuckles in his lap. It's too warm in here. The central heating's on too high. I stand up to open a window. Without me weighing it down, the ball drifts off and bounces gently against the wall.

"The police said that you reckoned Rachel was pregnant," he says. "Was she?"

I nod. "Didn't she tell you that?"

He shakes his head. "Why wouldn't she tell me?"

"I can't answer that."

"No, that's right," he says, the anger in his eyes flaring up again, like a gas light. "You're the same as them. No one will give me a straight answer, and no one seems to care."

I take a deep breath in and out. I press my hand into the side of the sofa, try to calm myself down.

"Listen," I say, trying to sound gentle. "That's just not true. I'm worried about Rachel, of course I am. But you have to remember, she sent me that—"

"I should have taken better care of her." He starts pacing around the room again. His boots are filthy. It is as if he's forgotten I'm here, as if he's talking to himself. "I was proud she was in London. That she was making something of herself. If I'd known how she was living . . . When she said Dalston, well. I didn't know it would be like that . . . that horrible apartment building, those two stuck-up girls always sneering at her. And now you tell me she was pregnant—"

"Hang on. Dalston? Like, you mean in east London? When was she living there?"

He stares at me. "Until she moved in with you."

"But that can't be right. She definitely lived around here, in Greenwich. At least by the time I met her in the summer."

John frowns and sits back down. I glance at the tea on the table. It must be cold by now. A gray semicircle is forming on the top.

"Definitely not," he says. "She never lived round here. This was miles away from her place."

"But I don't understand. She was always around here. She told me she lived on the other side of the park."

He shrugs.

"But . . . she was at the Greenwich prenatal classes."

"The what?"

"Prenatal classes. You go when you are pregnant," I gabble. "It's only for Greenwich residents. The whole point of the classes is that you go to your local . . . you meet local people."

I try to think. Did she really tell me she lived around here? Or did I just assume it? We never went to her place. Did she ever even tell me where it was? Did I ever ask?

"Sorry," I say. "It's just . . . it doesn't really make sense. There are prenatal classes all over London. If she lived in Hackney, and was pregnant, she would go to the classes there. She never mentioned Hackney, or Dalston. She never mentioned any roommates. I thought she lived alone."

"She'd have been better off," he says darkly. He stands up, starts pacing again. "Ask her roommates. If you can get a civil word out of them."

I sit on the ball again and rock back and forth, trying to massage the pain out of my hips. I feel like screaming. None of what he is saying makes sense. Why didn't she tell her dad she was pregnant? Why was she always here, if she lived miles away? What was she doing in Greenwich all those times? And if she lied about that—what else had she lied about?

I think of all the times I'd seen Rachel in Greenwich, after I met her. Had it really been a coincidence, bumping into her all those times? Or had it been deliberate? Had she been following me? The thought makes the hairs on my arms stand on end. But why would she do that? Why?

"John, Rachel told me she'd been signed off work with high blood pressure, because of her pregnancy. Do you know where she worked?"

"A bar, or a club, maybe," he says. "I don't remember the name. She never said anything to me about blood pressure. She just said she had something else she wanted to do. Some project. No point pressing her. She knows what she wants, Rachel. She does things her own way. Always has."

I grip the side of the sofa. The room feels as if it is tilting. I've told all this to the police. I think about what I said to them in that gray room that smelled of stale old papers. How I'd leaned into the tape recorder to make sure they got everything down. She was from somewhere in Greenwich, met the father through her work at a music venue. Heavily pregnant. Signed off with high blood pressure. And it was nonsense. All of it. They must think I am a complete idiot. Or worse. Maybe they think I am a liar.

John is still talking. "She wasn't easy, you know. As a teenager. And then . . . after what happened to her . . . Well, she changed then. You couldn't blame her. She was angry, very angry."

He says this as if I must know what he is talking about. I blink, say nothing. He looks up at me, eyes glistening.

"Didn't she tell you?" He drops his gaze, gives his head a little shake. "I expect she keeps it to herself," he mutters. "It's just that I thought you two were so close."

I clamp my mouth into a line. *We weren't close,* I feel like screaming. *We weren't even friends. It's nothing to do with me. She has nothing to do with me.* I realize I want this man out of my house as soon as possible. But he is still talking. It is like he can't stop.

"She'd been calling me every week, until the day of your party," he is saying. "That was the last time I heard from her. I could tell she was looking forward to it. Said there was someone who was going to be at the party. Someone important to her."

I feel the muscles in my shoulders tense. "Did she say who?"

He blows his nose on a hankie he has pulled from his cuff.

"No, she didn't. She said she'd call me soon. And then . . . nothing."

He is sobbing now, big, fat tears rolling down his cheeks. I go and fetch my hospital bag, sitting by the front door, and find the packet of tissues in the side pocket. He takes them gratefully.

I have no idea what to do. I am not used to seeing a grown man cry. I lean over awkwardly, placing a hand on his shoulder.

"Listen," I say. "Do you think it might be worth you talking to her mother, seeing as she said that's where she was going?" I pause. "I mean, I'm guessing you're estranged, but perhaps . . ."

John stares at me, his eyes narrowing.

"What do you mean?" he snaps. "She never said she was going to her mother's."

"She did. That's what she told me, the day after the party. That's what I was trying to say to you, before. She texted me, saying she was going to her mother's for a while. Didn't the police tell you that already?"

John stares at me as if I have gone mad. "She wouldn't have said that," he repeats. There is a new edge in his voice.

"She did. That's where she told me she was going. That was why I didn't worry."

John's hands have started trembling.

"Her mother's dead."

It is my turn to stare.

"I'm sorry?"

"Her mother's dead. She's been dead for near on fifteen years."

Stunned, I pick my phone up then, to show him the message.

"But she sent me this."

John snatches the phone, holds it in his hands, staring at it, his fingertips shaking. Then he drops it like a stone, as if he is too frightened to hold it any longer.

"Have the police seen this?"

"Of course."

He is agitated now. "Whoever sent that message, Helen," he says, with a tremor in his voice, "it wasn't Rachel."

40 WEEKS

Helen

I KNOW THEY SAY not to count the days, but what else is there? For months I've been repeating the date to people who ask me endlessly when I am due. The question always seems to me to mean, when are you going to stop taking up so much space? When are you going to get on with it?

I've had dates before, of course. Dates I've never reached. This one always felt different to me, though. When I went to see the doctor to tell him I was pregnant, he put his glasses on. Let me see, he said. I'll just calculate the date for you. There's no need, I told him. I've done it already. There were tools online.

The doctor looked disappointed. Oh, he said. Did I want him to have a look anyway? I got the feeling he liked doing it. That it was one of the few nice moments of his day, in between the rashes, the hypochondriacs, the dying.

So I said all right, and he retrieved a little tool from his desk drawer, two interlocking cardboard circles, and moved them so the first little window showed the date of my last period, and the bottom little window showed the due date: November 26. An unremarkable date. No clashes, no thirteens, no lucky or unlucky omens. This time, I thought. This time.

Now that the date is finally here, I should be excited. Something I have wanted for so long. It will happen, I tell myself, any moment now. I will have a baby. But it's no use. There's nothing. I feel as if I've been anesthetized. I can't seem to feel happy, or sad. I try to think of holding a little baby in my arms, dressing him in his first outfit, the one with little penguins on it, packed neatly in my hospital bag with its matching hat. But I just feel like I'm searching for answers in an empty room.

264   KATHERINE FAULKNER

I wish I hadn't agreed to Daniel working late this week. I know I'll need him most when I finally go into labor, when the baby is here. But the days are getting shorter and shorter, the nights longer and longer. Serena isn't returning my calls. And the police keep coming around, checking and rechecking our statements. I feel alone with the ghost of Rachel rattling around the empty house, half our furniture still covered in white dust sheets.

I watch the news endlessly, but they just keep going over the same few facts we all know already. There are no answers. Only questions. What happened to Rachel? Where is she? Where did she go?

Every hour now seems to stretch into the longest of my life. There are flurries of snow, the first of the year. The flakes whizz around, cart-wheeling, but not settling. Just a few of them catch in the gaps between the paving stones, on the bare branches of the hawthorns. The house is cold. With some effort, I make a fire, piling the last of the coal on top of some kindling, some scrunched-up balls of newspaper.

I sit in a comfy chair in the front room while it crackles at my feet, staring out of the window, over the front garden. I try to read, but really, my focus is pointed inward. I am waiting for a sign, the slightest shift, the slightest twinge.

I start to become desperate for it—for the drama of birth, the cata-clysm everyone talks about—the end of one part of your life, the begin-ning of another. Nothing will ever be the same, people say. And that's what I want, more than anything. To be transformed, to shed the skin of this dead time I am stuck in, with nothing to fill my time but thoughts of Rachel. Thoughts about where she might be, what might have happened to her. And others, that I try to push away. About what I might have done, by sending her away. What I might be responsible for.

Yesterday I went to the hospital for my full-term appointment. Daniel came with me. They said they were going to examine me. I held on to Daniel's hand, stared at the cheap ceiling tiles and tried to count them. Ten across, fifteen down.

"You're doing really well," Daniel said soothingly as I breathed in and out. His voice was flat, like something rehearsed. When I glanced over at him, he had his phone in his other hand and was checking his work emails.

"You're already one centimeter," the nurse said. "That's a really good sign. I'm sure it won't be long. Shall I give you a cervical sweep, try to get things moving?"

I nodded, pressed my chin to my chest, held on to the edge of the sheet with my fist. The pain was sharp as a knife, unbearable, as she inserted her finger through my cervical canal. I cried out, the sound of my voice echoing down the hospital corridor. My nails dug into Daniel's palm; I felt him flinch, sit up, stare at the midwife in horror. When it stopped, I was panting, staring at her, hot tears clouding my eyes.

"I didn't know it was going to be like that."

The midwife pulled her gloves off and laughed at us both. "You wait till the main event." Then she saw my face, and her smile fell away. "Sorry," she said. "Sometimes a sweep can be a bit more painful for some people. Don't worry. You'll be all right." She turned to her computer, started tapping up notes.

The sweep hasn't helped. Nothing happens. By four, the light is failing, the sun dipping below the hill, the spidery shadows of the bushes in the garden lengthen and darken. I take the blanket and pull it around myself. Most labors start at night, I tell myself. It could still happen tonight. I move to the sofa, face up, my gaze fixed on the ceiling rosettes, the swirls and cracks in the plaster as familiar to me as my own hands.

When nothing has happened for another hour, I throw the blanket to the side, stand up, set about rearranging another one of our drawers. But I soon get bored, put it back, make another cup of tea, sit at the kitchen table. I retrieve my book, but I can't get into it, my concentration drifting away at the end of each paragraph. I walk back into the sitting room, try to settle on the sofa. I close my eyes. I keep seeing her face.

The embers in the fire die to a weak red glow, then to a gray ash, light and delicate as the snowflakes outside. Finally I give up and go to bed early, but cannot fall asleep.

My phone rings at half past eight. It is Katie. I ask her about Rachel, whether she has heard anything, at work. She won't answer my questions.

"Can you meet me, Helen?"

"I'm already in bed, Katie. I'm exhausted."

"I know—you must be, I'm really sorry." I can hear the noise of chatter in the background. It sounds like she is in a pub. "Look, I'm at the end of your road," she says, lowering her voice. "In the Plume of Feathers. Please?" She pauses. "I wouldn't ask if it wasn't important."

"Why can't you come here?"

She doesn't answer.

"Please, Helen. Ten minutes."

I dress slowly and make my way there, the wintery wind stinging my fingers. Frost snaps in the air. I wish I'd thought to bring gloves. I walk slowly, unsteadily, fretting about the ice. The pavement isn't sanded, and the light from the streetlamps glints off the surface of the frozen puddles.

When I reach the pub, I throw the door open and feel the warmth on my face. I see Katie at a table on the far side, and she shoots me a relieved smile, rushes to help me sit down.

"I'm fine," I mutter. I wipe the melting snow off my trousers and sink into the green leather of a booth seat. I feel enormous, eclipsed by my baby. A man reaches to help me move the table back so I can fit into the seat.

"I'll just grab the drinks."

As I wait, I look around the pub, wondering how long it will be, after this, until I'm in a pub again. It is a nice pub, cozier than I remember. There is a fire crackling in the hearth, the chimney breast is covered in horseshoes, the wonky shelves squashed full of silver tankards and dusty old bottles with models of boats inside. There is a low hum of chatter, a smell of mulled wine and cider. There are decorations over the bar, in gaudy green, red, and gold. I guess it is nearly December. I haven't even thought about Christmas. It is as if the time has gone ahead without me. I'm stuck on the night she disappeared.

Katie returns with a soft drink for me and a large glass of red wine for herself. She places them down and hugs me, her arms barely reaching around me over the bump. "So close now, Helen," she says.

Katie looks worried; her shoulders are tense, her brow low over her eyes. She has already drunk one glass of wine; the empty glass sits between us next to the pieces of a cardboard beer mat that she has torn to shreds. Her hand keeps flitting to her right ear to tuck a strand of hair behind it.

"Thanks for coming," she says vaguely. "I've been here for ages—I hadn't noticed it had started snowing." She grimaces. "I hope you were OK getting here."

She glances at the door, takes a sip of her wine. She has shadows under her eyes.

I shift in my seat. "What is it? You said it was important."

Katie sighs.

My heart sinks as soon as I see the look on her face, and I know what the next words will be, even before she says them.

"It's about Rachel."

Helen

MY TRAIN PULLS IN and out of breeze-block tunnels through the alien city landscape, the huge ghostly towers of blue and green glass. The waters of the docklands are gray and flat. There are endless apartment buildings around the water, backing onto the railway line, outdoor furniture cramped onto tiny balconies. One has a plastic car and a child's tricycle. In the giant glass office buildings, the lights are still on, the glow of computer screens, people working, even late on a Friday night.

I hadn't planned to come here. I had planned to hear whatever Katie had to say then head home, have a long bath, get into my pajamas, see if Daniel wanted to order takeout when he finally got home. But I ended up staring at the photo, the one Katie had found in the club. And before I knew it, I was here. On my way to Charlie's. Texting Daniel to tell him not to wait up.

At South Quay the track starts to bend, taking my stomach with it. I haven't done this journey in a while. I can't say I enjoy it much. Reflected in the wobbly mirror panels of a skyscraper, the train looks like a toy in its primary colors. It shudders past the no-man's-lands of Mudchute, Westferry, Limehouse. There's a change at Shadwell, a steep flight of stairs. I can feel sweat under my arms.

On the Overground to Dalston, the landscape changes. Scrappy community gardens, low-rise housing projects with long brick balconies. Parks with playgrounds in garish colors, hooded youths lingering among the swings. Teenagers, BMX bikes, dangerous-looking dogs.

Finally, we reach Charlie's stop. There's no way I'll get a taxi here. I try Uber, but it says fourteen minutes. I might be able to find a bus, maybe, but I think better of it. The last time I did that, I went the wrong way, wheeling around and around the projects, one indistinguishable from another. I decide I'll have to walk. My feet are sore, my ankles swollen. I can feel the pressure at the bottom of my pelvis, hard now, sometimes like a shooting pain. Don't come now, I tell the baby silently. Not tonight.

I wonder if Charlie will have Ruby this evening. I find myself hoping he doesn't, and immediately feeling guilty at the thought. I think back to the last time I saw my little niece, in the spring, when Charlie came to see us in Greenwich. Charlie and I sat in the foyer of the Maritime Museum having an awkward coffee while she bounded around with the other children on the Great Map, her little spotty tights on, pink shoes going *slap slap slap* across the continents, her footsteps echoing around the high ceilings. She made her rabbit bounce from the Gulf of Mexico all the way to Nova Scotia.

She hadn't been that interested in the *Cutty Sark,* despite Charlie's attempts. He lifted her under her arms so she could steer the ship's wheel, pretended to throw her overboard, which made her giggle. But when I tried to show her the storybook of the legend she squirmed in my lap, asked if we could play zombie ships instead. I didn't know how to play zombie ships, or any of the other games she liked. I would never admit it to Daniel, but I dread the thought of having a child like Ruby—loud, boisterous, with the sort of confidence I have never had. I haven't the first idea what to do with her.

I walk past discarded McDonald's cups, their straws sticking out at angles, burst Happy Meal balloons. Cell phones behind glass cases, neon signs flashing: Mobile Phone Unlocking Repairs, Lycamobile, Call Home. The window of one shop is just mannequin heads. Western hairstyles, with a lacquered finish. Another shop window is filled with rolls and rolls of colorful fabric. Saris, block prints, Indian silk, piled up at the front of the windows, like a cross section of a riverbed. Next door the shops spill out onto the street with crates of vegetables I wouldn't know how to cook— yams, okra, plantains. Their names are written on neon cardboard stars. There is a smell of fried chicken. My pregnancy medical records are heavy in my bag. What am I doing? I think again. What am I doing here?

When Katie first told me, I could hardly take it in. Not only had she tracked down the address where Rachel was living in Hackney, she'd already been there and spoken to one of Rachel's roommates.

"What did she say?"

"She said that when she saw Rachel a few weeks ago, just before she moved in with you, she hadn't looked pregnant. She said she had looked basically the same as normal."

I shook my head. "No one would fake a pregnancy. Why would she want to? Why would she want to do a prenatal course?"

"I don't think it was the course," Katie said gently. "I think she wanted to get close to you. I think that was her plan all along."

I felt sick. "What? But why?"

"I don't know." Katie reached inside her bag and took out the photograph. "But I think this might have something to do with it." She slid it across the table.

Charlie and Rachel together, at the club. Charlie's hair long, the way it was last summer. Rachel's much shorter. Rachel's arms around Charlie's waist. A little slice of her midriff just visible between her belted black jeans and her tight top.

"But Charlie would have said something, if he'd known her from before," I stammered.

"That's what I thought." Katie stared at me. "What do you think we should do?"

I resented it then. Her putting this in my lap. "I can't deal with this now, Katie, I just can't." I felt close to tears. "This whole thing with Rachel—it's doing my head in."

"I know." Katie looked agonized. "I don't want to cause you any more stress. But . . . the police are asking me questions. And now I've found this. Charlie's your brother. I had to tell you, Helen. I don't know what to do." She paused. "You know, the night of your party, I saw Rachel going down into the cellar with someone. I don't know who—I just saw the back of her dress, and another hand, so I know she was following someone." She bit her lip. "I think it might have been Charlie. I saw him afterward, all covered in dust."

"Did you ask him?"

"Yeah. He says it wasn't him. But when I told him I was going to tell the police about it, he told me not to."

I became very aware of my breathing. The baby stirred inside me, my stomach pushed aside by his elbow.

"Katie, I have to go. I really . . . I just can't think about this now."

"But . . . Helen, wait. What should I say to the police? Are you going to talk to your brother?"

I was already pushing the door of the pub open, letting the icy air bite at my face. I saw Katie pull her coat on to follow me, but I shook her off.

"Please, Katie," I said. "Leave me alone."

But it was no good. Even as I got home, turned the key in the lock, I knew I would have to go to Hackney. I needed to know the truth. I needed to know who Rachel really was. And what she wanted from me.

Helen

WHEN I REACH CHARLIE'S place—a crumbling Victorian terraced house, broken up into apartments—I realize I don't remember which buzzer to press. I get the wrong one, but his neighbor buzzes me in anyway. There are wet footprints all the way up the communal staircase, a smell of frying onions. When I reach his door and knock on it, I'm breathless, irritable. I'm desperate for the bathroom, the baby weighing on my bladder. He might not even be in. I should have called, I think. This could all be a waste of time.

But then I see a pair of small purple wellingtons by the door. I hear Ruby's muffled voice, and the door opens. She is barefoot, in a T-shirt and leggings, a half-unraveled hair braid hanging down the center of her face.

"Auntie Helen!" Her face lights up into a gap-toothed grin, and she wraps herself around me. "Is the baby coming now?"

I laugh nervously. "Not yet. Where's your daddy?"

Ruby brings me in and starts jumping up and down on the sofa, giddy and excited. The ceilings are low and sloping—I'm worried she'll hit her head on the skylight. "Careful, Ruby," I say. I don't expect she'll do much damage to the sofa—it is already squashed and battered, covered in the same orange throw Charlie had in his teenage bedroom.

When I go through to the kitchen to find Charlie, he is nowhere to be seen. He must be in the bathroom. On the side are a chopping board and pans, two bowls of half-eaten spaghetti Bolognese on the side. There are onion skins and carrot peelings, an empty tin of tomatoes. I'm incredibly thirsty all of a sudden.

"Charlie, it's me, Helen," I call. "I'm just grabbing a glass of water."

When I open cupboards, looking for a tall glass, all I can find is children's cereals, cocoa, brown rice, peanut butter, pasta sauces.

Charlie emerges from the bathroom. He looks at me, puzzled. "All right," he says. "Everything OK?"

"Fine," I say, glancing back through at Ruby.

He pauses.

"Want a drink?"

"Just water, thanks."

He turns on the tap, lowers his voice.

"Are you here about—"

"I need to talk to you," I mutter. "When Ruby is in bed."

Ruby is still jumping up and down on the sofa when I walk back in, her hair braid following her up and down in the air, thumping against her gap-toothed grin. She is telling me about how she lost another tooth, and the tooth fairy came, and then it came again at Daddy's, because it must have gotten confused, and they are doing the Romans at school, and do I know what a charioteer is, and Nora isn't her friend anymore and can she stay up late? I tell her it's already quite late, and she'll have to ask her daddy, and that I need to go to the bathroom.

From the bathroom, I hear the muffled sound of Charlie telling Ruby it's bedtime, that she needs to brush her teeth or they won't have time for a story. As I wash my hands, I notice a pink pair of Disney pajamas warming on the radiator.

I make myself a cup of tea and stay in the kitchen, listening to Charlie reading *The Twits* to Ruby in her bedroom. Within a few minutes, I hear him creeping out, flicking the light off. The apartment feels still and quiet. I walk into the living room to see Charlie slumping down on his sofa, cracking open a beer. I sit down awkwardly next to him. His spider plant needs watering. The blinds on his window are broken.

"So. How are things?"

Charlie shrugs. "Fine. Same as always."

"Ruby seems happy."

"She *is* happy." There is a snap in his voice.

"You don't need to say it like that."

"Well, it's just so obvious what you're thinking, Helen. I don't know why you don't just come out with it."

I sniff, set my mug down on his coffee table. "I just . . . I don't know why you insist on living here. Not when you have all that money. You could live somewhere better. Somewhere with a garden. That roof terrace isn't even safe. It's like you live here on purpose, to prove something."

Charlie looks at me, and I recognize the anger in his face, from when we used to fight, when we were children. But it is a man's face, now. We are not children anymore.

"Anything else you want to tell me about parenting?"

The words sting me.

"I live here, because Ruby lives here," he says. "Her school is here. Maja and Bruce live here. My work is three streets away." He gestures into the air. "I don't know what you want, Helen. Normal children don't live in mansions in Greenwich Park with seventy-foot gardens. Normal families live like us."

He takes a deep swig of beer, puts the bottle down harder than he needs to.

"We take her to the playground. We take her to Brownies and football and forest school and karate. She loves her school. She has friends. She has hobbies. Occasionally she even eats fucking vegetables. She is happy. We are happy, Helen."

I look at my younger brother. I see that there is a sticky chocolate smudge on his jeans, bags under his eyes. I think about the homemade pasta sauce, the pajamas on the radiator. And I realize I don't know how to do this. Any of it. And my brother—my useless, naughty little brother—he is doing it already.

Charlie's face is so like Mummy. I think about when Ruby was born, how tiny she was, how perfect. The picture they sent of her with her little hands and feet, her rosebud lips. A picture I could barely look at. I think about all the times we said we'd go and visit, all the times I said I was going to do it, this time. That this time, I would get there. But then when we got to the car, I couldn't, I just couldn't. I think about Charlie's voice on the phone. "It's cool, Helen," he'd say. "We understand. I hope you're doing OK."

Then I think about when I'd gone to see Ruby with Katie, on her third birthday. How the present I'd got her was too babyish, and she didn't really like it. How she'd run to Katie, and not me. I think about later, all the times they came to Greenwich and I tried to take her to educational things, and she'd been bored, fussing at Charlie's feet, asking if she could go and splash in the fountains, or watch the busker and the bubble man at the park gates, or ride on the merry-go-round, or get an ice cream from the van. Why didn't I just say yes? Why was I always trying to be like Daddy?

"I'm sorry," I say. "It's just. Sometimes, you feel . . . so far away."

I see his face soften. His eyes. Mummy's eyes. And then he does something he hasn't done in years. He puts his arm around me. After a moment, I hug him back.

When I sit back into the orange sofa, Charlie rises and plucks an Action Man from the beanbag and throws it into the toy box, then sinks into it, so he is now opposite me.

"You didn't need to come all this way, Helen," he says eventually. "You must be worn out. I'd have come to see you, if you'd said. If you'd wanted to talk."

I nod. I say nothing.

"Why did you come?"

I pass him the photograph Katie took from the club. He looks at the picture, and I see his pupils dilate. He inhales sharply.

"Where did you get this?"

I don't answer the question.

"I need to know the truth, Charlie. About you and Rachel."

41 WEEKS

Helen

DANIEL AND I GET to Serena's exhibition late, and it is busy, glasses of wine clinking, the hum of chatter spiraling up into the high roof of the warehouse. The room is dark, except for the white beam of the light boxes that display her photographs. There are eight on each wall. The pictures cast blurry white reflections in the shiny floor, like a moon over water.

"What do you think?" I ask Daniel.

He shrugs. "We've only just got here."

I turn and look at him. "Daniel, is something wrong? You're being so short with me."

He looks at me, then at the floor. "I'm sorry," he mutters. "I'm just stressed about work. And I know you're cross with me about coming home late."

He looks so dejected, like a little boy.

"I don't mean to give you a hard time," I say. I take his hand. "I just need you at the moment, that's all. And this Rachel stuff doesn't help."

He sighs, pulls me to him. I'm so big he can barely hold me close.

"I know," he says. "I'm sorry. I promise I'll do better at being around, all right?"

I exhale, feeling tears gathering in my eyes. "Thank you," I murmur into his shoulder. When he pulls away, I blink the tears back, try to smile. He takes my hand.

Rory and Serena have been away in Italy. She has been posting pictures on Instagram of their vacation, a hotel painted in bright opal colors, a turquoise sea. In one of them she is sitting in a Jacuzzi, even though the books tell you not to during pregnancy. I couldn't see her bump in it. I'm looking forward to seeing her, seeing whether she is looking bigger now, like me. If her baby is early, it is not inconceivable that it could even come before mine.

While Daniel stares at the first photograph, I crane my neck around the room, but I can't see Serena. I grab a glass of orange juice from a passing waiter and follow Daniel around, trying to look like I'm deep in thought.

Eventually I get bored of going at Daniel's pace, so I skip a few pictures ahead. I need to find one photograph and think of something to say about it if I need to. Not this one—I can't actually quite see what it is supposed to be. It looks like something wet and bumpy, like the back of an avocado, or a snakeskin handbag. Something reptilian. Glancing to the side first, I cheat and look at the little card next to the light box. *Cobbles on the mews in rain*, it says. It doesn't give a price.

I try the next photograph. It is an image of a slender man, almost in silhouette, leaning against the wall of their upstairs balcony. Behind him the city is a mass of light, and his face is in darkness, a plume of smoke escaping from his lips. It takes me a moment to recognize the outline as Daniel's. He doesn't look like my Daniel. He looks strange, unknowable. The outline of his face seems no more human than the squiggle of the London skyline.

The picture gives me a strange feeling. When was it taken? I look at the card, but it says simply: *Untitled*. There is a little red dot next to it, to indicate that it has been sold. I turn to Daniel, to ask him when it was taken. Only then do I notice that he seems to have run off somewhere.

"Helen! So good to see you!" Serena is beside us all of a sudden, a column of silk and perfume. She is bigger now, her bump cocooned in the pale, shimmering fabric of her dress, round and perfect, like a huge pearl.

She kisses me, her soft cheek brushing against mine. "I can't believe you came—you must be so fed up. How long are they letting you go over?"

"Only until Sunday. Or it's the dreaded induction."

We grimace at each other.

"Poor you."

"Thanks," I say. "I hope he gets a move on soon. Did you have a good trip?"

"The best."

"I'm glad. You look great." I hesitate. Should I mention Rachel? I wonder whether the police have been to see her, or Rory. I decide not to bring it up. Instead, I gesture at the photographs. "This is all amazing—as usual. You're so talented."

Serena beams. "You're so sweet, Helen. Thank you."

I glance at the photograph next to us again, the one of Daniel. I'm about to ask her about it, but I see her expression flicker, as if there's something she's just remembered.

"Helen, do you want to get out of here? Come over for some tea or something? It'd be good to catch up. Properly."

"Now? What about your party? Won't people be surprised—"

"Oh no, it doesn't matter about all that," she says, dismissing the gallery guests with a wave of her hand. "Renata will get people's details if they're interested, and everyone knows I'm pregnant. Come on." She takes my arm. "It's so boring anyway. It's all just bankers and hedge fund managers. None of them have a clue."

"Well, all right, but I'd better tell Daniel—"

"He won't mind," she says quickly. I can't see where he has gone. "Come on, let's get out of here."

Outside, it is so cold it makes me gasp, my breath escaping in tiny clouds. I struggle to keep up with Serena as she strides up Maze Hill, the wind stinging my cheeks. It is a relief to step into the familiar glow of her home, the warmth of their front room. I perch at the seat in the bay window while Serena makes tea in the kitchen.

The photograph of Serena and her bridesmaids is in its usual place on the mantelpiece. It's an image I have looked at so many times that I could probably paint its likeness from memory, but still, I can't resist hauling myself up and picking it up for a closer look, feeling the heavy silver weight of it, the familiar mosslike softness of the fabric mounted on the back. I know from experience that my thumbs will leave marks on the edges of the frame that I will have to wipe carefully before Serena is back in the room.

When the photographs of Serena's wedding came back from their photographer, there was not a single one like this of her and me. There were lots of the bridesmaids. I suppose they were a photogenic bunch. And there was no reason for the photographer to know I was Rory's sister, and such a close friend of Serena. I didn't have a corsage, or a special dress in duck-egg blue. The photographer had also taken several of Serena in the morning, getting ready. The bridesmaids were all there, and Serena had given them all special pale pink dressing gowns. The pictures showed them clutching flutes of Buck's Fizz with elegantly manicured nails, helping Serena tie the line of pearl buttons at the back of her dress.

The thing about Serena is that she somehow seems to collect female friendships, effortlessly, like the bangles she wears on both wrists. I think of that awful bachelorette weekend in Cornwall again. There were friends from Serena's primary school, secondary school, university, work, "hockey"—I had lost count. How do some women amass such huge collections of people who love them, yet I can't even go to a prenatal class and make one nice, normal friend?

As I place the photograph back, I notice something on the mantelpiece that wasn't there before. A business card, the same one that sits on our mantelpiece at home: DCI Betsky, Homicide.

I sink down into one of Serena's sofas just as she returns. Serena places the tray onto the mango-wood coffee table. She pours fresh tea into the mugs and hands one to me. Then she drops two cubes of brown sugar into her own, wraps her slender fingers around it, then curls back into the sofa, looking as if she's taking her place in a painting.

She has changed from her silk dress into jeans and a white sweater that drapes off one shoulder. Her eyes are still painted the same shimmery silver as the dress she was wearing. She leans back into the sheepskin throw around the back of the sofa. It seems to enclose her in its soft fingertips. Her sleeves are rolled up and I can see her forearms are brown from her vacation. I feel pale and self-conscious in comparison. I pull my own cuffs over my knuckles, my cardigan around my middle. It won't go round the bump anymore.

"You're so lovely and tanned."

"Italy was heavenly," she says. She leans forward, places the mug down. "But then we got home to find two detectives on our doorstep." She shakes her head in disbelief. "Which was somewhat surreal."

Serena puts her hands on her knees as she stands. It's the first time I've really noticed her seeming to feel heavier. "I'll show you the card—"

"I saw it—the same woman came to see us, too. DCI Betsky. I'm so sorry you had to go through all that."

She turns to look at me, puzzled.

"It's not your fault, darling. Why are you sorry?"

My jaw tightens, my mouth feels dry. She is being kind. She knows exactly. I am responsible for all this, I think. Rachel was my doing. I brought her here.

Serena plucks the card from the mantelpiece, turns it over. "Rory said something about Charlie," she says. "Did you and he have some sort of argument?"

"He's not speaking to me," I confess. "Or at least, he's not returning my calls." I realize I've been fiddling with one of her Mongolian hair cushions, the strands knotted around my fingers.

"Why not?"

I sigh. I'm sure she'll find out sooner or later. "You won't believe this. But Charlie knew Rachel from before I met her."

Serena's eyes widen. "Charlie knew her?"

I bite my lip and nod. I tell her about the photo of Charlie and Rachel that Katie found at the club.

"Christ. Did you ask Charlie why he never told any of us that he knew her?"

"I did more than that. I made him go to the police."

As soon as Charlie admitted he'd known Rachel from before, I'd called Maja, asked her to pick up Ruby so Charlie and I could go to the police. Maja and Bruce arrived within twenty minutes. It was obvious they'd been out for dinner; Maja's hair was pinned up at the back of her neck, a woody perfume on her coat. Ruby's eyelids barely flickered as Bruce gently lifted her from her bed, carried her down to their car.

"Thanks," I said to Maja at the door. I hadn't seen Maja in years. She looked great, her clothes more grown-up looking, expensive. A few strands of gray in her hair. She's not the sort to dye it.

Maja stared at me coldly, as if I was an idiot. "She's my daughter, Helen," she said. Then she turned and followed Bruce down the steps, holding Ruby's bunny by the neck.

It was only when I got Charlie to the police station that it occurred to me we'd picked the worst possible time. The plastic chairs in the waiting room were packed with Friday-night drunks, blokes with cuts on their heads, skeleton-faced drug addicts. I had to shout to be heard by the woman on the other side of the glass case. I assumed they'd be able to pick up the details, that the case would be on file somewhere. It had been on the news. Surely they knew what I was talking about? Instead, we were met with blank faces, shaking heads, flickering computer screens that yielded no information. We were told to wait.

So we waited. I sat down next to a homeless man who kept falling asleep, a balled-up coat wedged between him and the radiator. Charlie stood, pacing round the room, his fists clenched, pretending to read the crime prevention posters and look out of the window. Anything rather than speak to me.

Finally, after what seemed like hours, someone turned up, a brisk young detective with shiny shoes, and showed Charlie into a room. He held the door open for him with one hand, pressing his tie flat to his chest with the other, his spine soldier-straight. I was asked to wait outside. The door was closed before I could object.

I felt in desperate need of sugar. I dug out a pound, keyed in the hot chocolate option at the drinks machine. It squirted a hot brown stream into a beige cup. I took the drink and slumped back into my chair. When I'd finished it, I massaged my bump, hoping to feel the reassuring shift of movement in response to the sugar, a kick or an elbow. Nothing. I stared at my shoes, tried not to make eye contact with the drunks.

When Charlie and the detective emerged they were laughing like best mates. He was told he could go home. The detective even shook his hand, glanced at me wryly, as if they were all boys together, and I'd caused a whole load of unnecessary fuss.

I called a cab, waited outside the station. Charlie stood with me, but refused to meet my eye.

"Just tell me, Charlie. Were you together?"

"Of course not! For fuck's sake, Helen. Why can you never just leave things alone?"

When the taxi pulled up, Charlie walked off. I haven't heard from him since. It's all such a mess.

When I finish telling Serena the story she sits down again and picks up her mug, takes another sip. It covers her face, so I can't see her expression.

"I can't believe he knew her," Serena murmurs. "Do you think it's possible that the baby is his?"

So the police haven't said anything to them about Rachel's pregnancy.

"Well, for one thing . . . it turns out she might not actually have been pregnant."

A vertical crease forms between the arches of Serena's eyebrows. "What? How?"

I put my tea down, tell her the whole story. Serena always makes mint tea. I have told her before that I like it, but I'm not sure I really do. It is making my stomach swim a little.

When I have finished, Serena exhales, shaking her head.

"Do you think . . . Rachel could have been murdered?" I ask. The question comes out in a whisper. My baby kicks square between the ribs.

Serena grimaces, pulls her spine straight, as if restoring normality. "I'm sure it's nothing like that," she says, her voice returning to its usual confidence. "The police will find her. Look, Helen, Rachel was . . . well, she was clearly a troubled person."

I nod, embarrassed. A troubled person whom I introduced into all our lives.

"I just think she's probably taken off somewhere," Serena adds. "Of her own choosing. She'll turn up."

"That's what I keep saying!" My voice sounds slightly hysterical. I take a deep breath, try to calm down.

"You look so tired, Helen," Serena says after a pause. She cocks her head to one side. "It sounds like you've been through a lot. I feel bad that we weren't around."

"Don't be silly."

"Still, I hope you're not letting all this Rachel stuff get to you. It's such an important time. You shouldn't let it play on your mind too much." She gives an almost involuntary flick of one hand, as if this can all be batted away, if we wish it to be so.

"The thing is, I still don't properly remember everything from the night she left."

"That is strange. You weren't drinking, were you?"

"Of course not."

"I didn't think so. But I mean, you remember our conversation, don't you? In the kitchen?"

As she says it, something stirs in my memory. Lights behind a curtain, flashing. Something caught in my hair. Her thumb, brushing against my forehead. I went outside. Was she in the garden with me? The images swim together in my mind. I can't make them out.

"You said you'd been outside—there was a bit of something in your hair," Serena says, seeing my confusion. "You told me you'd . . . maybe disturbed someone. At the bottom of the garden? You remember that?"

"Monty!" I cry with delight. I thought I'd seen Monty, near the fire. He'd gotten out somehow. I'd gone to get him, to try and chase him away from the flames, get him to come inside. *That's* why I'd been out there. I do remember that part. I do.

"Yes, the cat, you said you'd been chasing a cat." Serena is nodding encouragingly. "And then you saw a couple or something—at the end of the garden?" She hesitates. "You did say . . . that you'd had a bit of a fight with Rachel?"

My sense of relief evaporates. "That's the bit I don't really remember properly. I mean I remember getting angry with her. I know I shouted." I ball my fingers into fists. "It wouldn't matter if I could just know for sure she is all right, but—"

"Hey, don't get upset." Serena comes close, wraps her slender arms around me, like a necklace. I smell her perfume again, deep and sensuous. It makes me think of black flowers. "You're under such a lot of pressure," she says. "Pregnancy does strange things to you—it's stressful. Don't read anything into it. I forget things all the time."

I shake my head, feeling tears welling in my eyes. "This is different. People forget to turn the oven off, or take their keys with them when they go out. You don't forget whole chunks of time." I pause. "What if . . ." I lower my voice. "What if it was because of me? I should never have shouted at her, told her to get out. What if something happened to her, and it's my fault?"

Serena's eyes grow wide. "Helen, don't be ridiculous! None of this is your fault."

I wipe my face, sniffing into my cuff. "It's so strange, though. How can she have just disappeared? How can no one have seen her leave?"

Serena shrugs. "It was busy. People were drunk. Why would they notice a girl they didn't know leaving a party?" She stands up, places two hands on her lower back. Her belly looks so much bigger now. "If people aren't looking for things, they don't see them."

I watch her as she gazes out of her window, massaging the bottom of her spine with her fingertips.

"Serena," I say. "I need to tell you something. Something about Rachel. I should have told you ages ago."

Greenwich Park

THE RAIN SCATTERS EVERYONE, washes all the people from the streets. They do awkward crouching runs with makeshift umbrellas—magazines, newspapers folded in half. They cower in doorways, under the awnings of shops. They pull out their phones and call for rescue.

In this part of town, no one looks at anyone. I pass a pizza place, a job center. In the launderette, the machines spin around and around like rolling eyes. It is a place and yet it is nowhere. Pavement puddles hold up a gray mirror to the metal sky.

The telephone booth is under a huge billboard, a peeling election poster for the side that lost. He pulls down his hat as he reaches it. There is no CCTV here; they have checked. There is only concrete, the roar of traffic, the skid of potato chip bags across the pavements.

The phone booth stinks of piss, but the phone still works. He takes a coin from his jacket pocket with a gloved hand. As he dials the number, the pornographic eyes of girls stare blankly back at his.

Helen

KATIE AND I ARE sitting on her sofa, pizza boxes piled in front of us, an old rom-com on pause. Rain is beating at the windows, a dull drum roll over the sound of the wind in the trees in Dartmouth Park.

I couldn't be at home anymore. Daniel and I are under siege, reporters knocking all the time, asking about Rachel. It's the same for her roommates, too, apparently, and at Charlie's club. I texted Daniel, told him I was going to Katie's to get away from it all. He was worried, didn't want me going so far from Greenwich, with the baby due any moment. But I assured him I'd be OK. Even if I do go into labor, it'll be hours before I need to go to the hospital, I told him. *As you would know if you'd come to the prenatal classes,* I felt like adding.

It is cozy in Katie's flat. Of course it's silly to envy Katie her place—after all, it's barely the size of our living room—but I do sometimes wonder what it would be like to have a little space that is just mine, not Daniel's. Katie's cat, Socks, is curled up on the sofa between us. As we pull slices of pizza away from the box, coiling the stray strands of mozzarella with our fingers, I ask her if she'd seen Charlie since I took him to the police station.

Katie shakes her head. "He called me that night—late, it must have been when he got back from the station with you. He asked me what I was doing, taking that photograph, showing it to you, instead of talking to him first. He was angry, we fought." She looks down, fiddles with the blanket over her knees. "I haven't spoken to him since."

"I'm sorry."

"It's not your fault." She pauses. "Helen, what exactly did he say about how he knew Rachel? Did he just know her from the club? Or did something happen between the two of them?"

I glance at her uncertainly. She rolls her eyes. "Come on, I can take it," she says firmly.

I feel blood rush into my cheeks as I recall the conversation. "He was maddening, actually. He kept saying they were friends, and that he only kept the fact that they knew each other a secret because she asked him to. He claims he doesn't know about her pregnancy—or lack of it. Or why she wanted to keep it a secret that they knew each other. And that he didn't ask."

"That doesn't make sense."

"I know. But you know what he's like. He doesn't talk to me. He's probably told the police more than he's told me."

Katie finishes her slice, presses her fingers into her eyes.

"I don't know what to think," she says quietly.

The rain is picking up. It occurs to me how much safer I feel here in Katie's apartment than I do at home. Earlier, when I arrived, I pressed a set of spare keys to our house into her hand. "When the baby comes," I said, "would you mind—if I have to stay in the hospital with the baby— coming and feeding Monty, keeping the plants alive?" She looked at me. I knew what she was thinking. It was a long way to come to feed the cat. But for some reason, I felt strongly that I wanted her to have them. I wanted to entrust the house to her. In case something happened. I didn't think too much about what. She nodded, slipped the keys into her bag. Of course, she said.

"You know," I say, "before she left—before all this Charlie stuff—I was starting to think something was going on between Rachel and Rory."

"Rory? Jesus. Why?"

I tell her about the two notes I found, the first one in Rory and Serena's bathroom, then the other one in Rachel's suitcase.

Katie looks at me, one eyebrow raised. "You just found them, Helen?"

"All right," I mutter.

"What did they say, these notes?"

"Nothing really. I couldn't understand them. One said 'wear to show me.' I never read the other one—just saw the initial." I pause. "But you've got to admit it's weird. Finding them in his house and then in her suit-case."

"I guess so." Katie nods slowly, but I can see she is unconvinced.

"It's not just that that made me think it," I add. "Do you remember how Lisa thought she remembered Rachel?"

Katie furrows her brow. "Oh yeah. I thought that was odd."

"And the way Rory reacted, when he saw Rachel in his kitchen. Remember, when he dropped all that glass?"

"You don't know that was because of Rachel."

I sigh. She is right.

"You think I'm an idiot."

"No, Helen. I don't think that. You need to stop putting yourself down. But I mean—I just think it doesn't prove anything. And it certainly doesn't explain what was going on with her and Charlie—unless—hang on . . . If Charlie knew her from the club—could Rory have met Rachel through him?"

I consider this. "I suppose that would explain why Charlie was told to keep it secret that he knew her." I chew my lip. "Oh God, Katie. Do you really think Rory could have been having an affair with her? And hiding it all this time?"

"I don't know. None of it makes any sense." She shifts in her seat. "Where is Rory, anyway?"

"Home. They're back now, from Italy. I went to Serena's exhibition the other night."

I'd finally told Serena about the notes. It hadn't gone well. She just looked at me, her face white, then muttered some excuse about wanting to lie down. And I haven't heard from her since.

"Didn't that seem a bit odd to you?" Katie is saying, wiping her mouth with a napkin.

"Didn't what seem odd?"

"Rory and Serena. Going abroad, so soon before her baby is due. I'm surprised she was even allowed to fly."

"She got some private doctor to sign off on it, I think."

"But why would they want to go away? When the baby is due so soon?"

"I hadn't really thought."

The rain gets louder, and we both glance up at the skylight. The taste of the pizza is so comforting. The food of sleepovers, when Katie and I were teenagers and she'd come over, and we'd watch *Clueless* and *Scream* on repeat. After we've finished the pizza, Katie collects the boxes while I head to the kitchen to scoop ice cream into bowls.

"Anyway, I'm sick of thinking about it," I say when we are both back on the sofa. "Tell me what's going on with you. I saw your front page. That interview with the girl in the rape case, it was amazing. You must be really proud."

Katie smiles, looks away, but I can tell she is pleased. There's been a lot of talk about the interview, about how Katie persuaded the girl to waive her anonymity.

"Helen," she says, swallowing a mouthful of ice cream. "You know I asked you before about that other rape case years ago. When you were at Cambridge. The boathouse rape?"

I nod slowly.

"Did you really not remember it?"

I start fiddling with my spoon, avoiding Katie's eye. It's pointless trying to hide things from Katie when she is in this sort of mood.

"I mean, it was such big news at the time. And it all happened the summer you—"

"All right, all right."

Katie stops. I shift on the sofa, the baby digging under my ribs. I suppose it doesn't matter now.

"I'm sorry, Katie. I wasn't entirely honest with you."

Katie frowns. "What do you mean? Why not?"

"I suppose I knew you'd want to ask questions, and Daniel . . . he hates talking about it. We were interviewed about it, you see. By the police. The four of us. Daniel, Serena, Rory, and I."

Katie's eyes widen. "Why?"

I shrug. "They thought we might have been in the boathouse. That we might have seen something." I look her in the eye. "We *hadn't* seen anything, obviously. We'd been out punting all day. None of us had anything helpful to tell them." I sigh. "I wish we had. That poor girl."

Katie considers this. "So why does Daniel hate talking about it so much?"

"I just remember he was upset, when those horrible boys got off. Even though there was nothing he could have done." I smile sadly at Katie. "It's just what he's like. He cares about people."

On the table in front of us, Katie's phone rings. "Probably work," she says. "Sorry." I motion that I'm going to the bathroom anyway.

When I come back, she is sitting on the very edge of the sofa.

"Katie?"

"It wasn't work," she says quietly, looking up at me. "It was Daniel. He said he'd been trying to call you. Where's your phone?"

I frown. "In my bag, I think, or . . . maybe in your kitchen. Why—what's going on?"

She opens her mouth, closes it again.

"Katie?"

"He . . . he said you should come home straightaway. The police are searching the offices—"

"What, Daniel's office?"

"Yes . . . and . . . Helen, your brother's been arrested."

It can't be real, I think. It doesn't feel like real life.

"Charlie?"

Katie shakes her head. "That's just it. He said . . . he said they'd arrested Rory."

Serena

THE ROOM SMELLS OF bleach, of dust, of neglect. A single light hangs overhead. I take a seat in the gray plastic chair in front of a screen, a constellation of little holes drilled into the glass, like in a banking kiosk. A little gap underneath. I sit down, carefully, steadying myself on the glass, hugging my bump to my body. Things are getting more difficult now. I place my bag on the floor, twist to spread my coat across the back of the chair so it doesn't crease. I sit there, waiting, for what seems like a long time.

Finally, there is a buzzing noise, harsh, institutional. The sound of a heavy door opening. And there, on the other side of the smeared glass, is my husband. A day-old stubble on his cheeks, a haunted look in his eyes. A blue nylon bib on his chest as if he is off to play football in the park. Except he is not. He is in police custody, facing a charge of murder.

Rory's eyes widen when he sees me.

"Serena," he says. Then his expression collapses. He slumps into the chair, covers his face with his hands, like a child trying to hide. His forearms are brown, still, although the color has faded a little. Just a couple of weeks ago, we were still on vacation, sailing out to Capri. The sky had been overcast, but there had been a brightness behind the clouds that made you squint. The sort of day where you burn without realizing.

I lean toward my husband, try to reach my hand through the flap. "No touching," a voice snaps from the corner. I look up to see a guard standing in one corner. I hadn't even noticed him come in. I pull my hand away.

"It's all right," I tell him. "It's going to be all right." But the truth is, I don't know if it is going to be all right. I really don't.

When he has calmed down, I lean again into the little holes in the glass.

"Rory." He looks up. "I need to know what happened." I hold his gaze, to be sure he understands. "I need to know everything."

And so he tells me.

He tells me about the interview room. The female detective, her hair pulled back from her face. How she had watched him with her dark brown eyes as she spread out six photographs on the table.

Despite the blurry focus, the graininess of the half-light, there was no mistaking what they showed. The purple sign of the cheap hotel visible in the corner. A mane of dark hair, his hand buried in it. The florid milky pink of his face under the glare of the flash. His eyes red, like a rabid dog's, where the flash had gone off in his eyes.

Her voice was clear, devoid of emotion, like a recorded message.

"Do you recognize the individuals in these photographs, Mr. Haverstock?"

Yes, he did. It was him and his secretary, Lisa Palmer.

He'd known they would find the pictures as soon as he'd heard they were searching the offices. They'd ordered Daniel to hand over the code to the safe. Daniel had refused, said the safe was private. But they'd shown the warrant, threatened to charge him as an accessory. Terrified, he'd agreed.

The detective leaned forward, nudging the photographs closer toward him with her fingertips.

"How did these photographs come to be in your possession, Rory?"

He didn't know, he said. Lisa had put the envelope on his desk one day, saying someone dropped them off while she was out at lunch. She hadn't seen who. The detective nodded then. Told him that Lisa had confirmed the story, had told them she did not recall ever seeing the person who had dropped off the envelope, that she had no idea what the contents were. Luckily, though, the detective said, they had obtained fingerprints from the envelope. Fingerprints that were a match for an individual whose DNA profile was held on the database. That person was Rachel Wells.

DCI Betsky pulled out another piece of paper from the same folder, spun it around, and slapped it down in front of him.

"For the tape, the witness is being shown item KXG-09. An email you received from the email address RRH078147@gmail.com. Do you remember this email, Rory?"

He did. The address hadn't meant anything to him, except the first three letters, his initials. He had assumed someone was mocking him.

> Hope you enjoyed the photos. Looking forward to your
> birthday drinks. Hope no one causes a scene.
> PS—I'll be the one in red.

He still had no idea who it was, he told them. Not when he got the email, anyway. But then, that evening, when he'd walked into the kitchen, he had seen a girl, a stranger, in a red dress. Even without the dress, he thinks he would have known.

Lisa on her left. Serena on her right. Rachel was grinning. She had been laughing at him. Before he had known what was happening, there had been glass everywhere, blood dripping into golden pools of champagne. It had taken him a minute to realize the blood was even his.

DCI Betsky spun around another sheet of paper.

"For the tape, the witness is being shown item KXG-10," she said. "This is an email you received the day after your birthday dinner, at 8:37 a.m., from the same email address."

> Enjoyed your dinner. Sea bass was sublime. Nice house. No
> idea you were so rich! So price has just gone up. £100k, sooner
> rather than later. See you on Bonfire Night. Bring half. Unless
> you want to end up as the Guy.

The atmosphere in the room changed then. He felt his lawyer stiffen, push her glasses up her nose. The detective leaned in toward him.

"You were being blackmailed, weren't you, Rory? Rachel was threatening to ruin your marriage. She was threatening you physically. Wouldn't you agree? What did you do after you received this email?"

He hardly needed to reply. They pulled his bank records, of course. A withdrawal dated November 4, the day before Helen's bonfire party, for £50,000. From the company's account in the Cayman Islands. And CCTV photographs of the Greenwich Park branch of his private banking provider, showing him, Rory Richard Haverstock, organizing the Cayman withdrawal and leaving the offices with a large white padded envelope containing the cash.

So yes, he admitted that he had taken the money. And yes, he'd been planning to give her what she wanted. He had wanted it to go away. He hadn't wanted his wife to know.

Rory looks at me, his eyes pinched and raw.

"I'm sorry, darling," he says. "I'm so sorry."

For some reason, his tearfulness makes me angrier than ever. I shake my head. "Keep going," I tell him, my teeth gritted. "I mean it, Rory. You tell me everything. Or I swear to God I will walk out of here and never come back." He nods, still staring at the floor. Takes a breath.

DCI Betsky didn't flicker. "On the night of November 5," she continued, "did you give the money to Miss Wells?"

He hadn't, he insisted. He hadn't even spoken to her. He went to look for her, later in the night, but she must have left. He couldn't find her anywhere. He didn't know what to do.

"So what did you do?"

He did nothing. Just went home, hid the cash in his study.

"You didn't seek her out?" DCI Betsky's eyes narrowed. "This woman who was threatening to destroy your marriage? A woman you'd gone to the trouble of withdrawing £50,000 in cash for?"

He did seek her out, he insisted, sweat blooming on his forehead. He just couldn't find her.

"How interesting. You see, Rory, we have spoken to almost everyone who attended the party that night. Not one is able to vouch for your presence there after around 9 p.m. It seems you just . . . disappeared."

That wasn't true, he said. He was there.

Then the detective showed him a text message. The message had been sent from a number registered to Rachel Wells to his sister, Helen Thorpe. This message had been sent the day after the bonfire party.

Hey Helen. I'm really sorry about last night too. I'm going back to my mum's for a while. I hope that we are still friends. Good luck with the baby. See you soon xxx

"I'm sure you're aware, Rory," she said, "that telecommunications data allows us to pinpoint exactly where a cell phone is when a message is sent. Our mast triangulation data tells us that this particular message was sent from an area matching the vicinity of your home on Maze Hill in Greenwich." DCI Betsky cocked her head to one side. "Could Rachel Wells have been present at your home the day after the party at your sister's house, Rory?"

Of course she wasn't, he said. He was there with his wife. They would have told the police if Rachel had been there.

"Well, I suppose that makes sense," DCI Betsky said. "Given the fact that Miss Wells is very unlikely to have sent this message herself."

She used her index finger to trace the two lines on the paper in front of Rory, as if showing him a fascinating puzzle they were solving together. "You see, Rory, the grammatical nature of this message is a poor match for Rachel's usual, more colloquial messaging style. 'I'm really sorry about last night too'—Rachel didn't usually use full sentences of that kind in her messages. In addition to that, Rachel Wells's mother has been dead for the last fifteen years." She paused at this point, drumming her fingers gently on the table.

"If Rachel didn't send this message, Rory, it would seem that someone else did. Someone who was situated in or around your house the morning after Rachel went missing. Someone with access to her cell phone. And someone who would have a reason to impersonate her."

Rory did not say anything. He had nothing to say. DCI Betsky leaned forward, pushed the paper toward him.

"You sent this message, didn't you, Rory?"

He hadn't, he said. He swore he hadn't. His lawyer had come to life then—something Rory had interpreted as a bad sign. She wanted a break for her client, she said. "In a moment," DCI Betsky snapped.

"For the tape," she continued, "the witness is being shown item KMF-0019. Do you recognize this item, Mr. Haverstock?"

DCI Betsky picked up a package, slid it over to Rory. Through the thick polyethylene of the evidence bag, he could see the familiar fabric, the worn collar. This must be a dream, he thought. It must be. He had the sensation of being surrounded, of the walls and ceiling moving to enclose him. Yes, he said. That was his coat.

"A coat," DCI Betsky said, "that you were seen by several witnesses wearing on the night of November 5. A coat that my officers found hidden under a large pile of shoes, in a black plastic trash bag in the back of a forest-green Land Rover Discovery registered in your name, parked outside your home in Maze Hill, Greenwich."

She sat back in her chair.

"This item has undergone extensive forensic examination. A number of blood traces were found on the coat. This blood matched DNA samples held in the police database for Rachel Wells. The probability that the blood on this coat belonged to Rachel Wells is greater than 99.9 percent."

The silence in the room felt loud and close, like the noise of water when you are underneath it. Rory wanted to put his hands over his ears.

"You killed Rachel Wells, didn't you, Rory?"

No.

"You realized it wasn't going to stop with the money. It was never going to stop. You were never going to be free of her. You had no choice. You snapped."

No.

"And then, you panicked."

No. It was ridiculous, he said. He hadn't killed anyone, he said. He—

"You had her phone, didn't you, Rory? People were looking for her, weren't they, Rory? Her dad, ringing, leaving messages. And a message from your sister of all people, worried about her whereabouts. You needed to give yourself some breathing space, didn't you? You needed people to think she was still alive. To give you time."

Time to do what? he said. He didn't understand, he said. This was madness.

DCI Betsky slammed a hand to the desk. Both Rory and the lawyer jumped.

"Time to dispose of her body."

Rory found he could say nothing at all. He could feel the eyes of his lawyer searching for his, looking for some kind of sign, but he found himself unable to meet her gaze.

When DCI Betsky spoke again, her voice was softer. As if Rory were just a little boy, caught in a lie.

"Look," she said gently. "It's over now, Rory. It's time to start telling the truth. It will be so much better for you if you do. Tell us what you did with her, Rory. Tell us what you did with the body."

I stare at my husband through the glass. He can't tell me the rest. He is crying now, his head in his hands.

I place my shaking hands over my bump to steady them, to feel the warmth of my little baby. There is a lump in my throat. I can't speak. I wish I could. I want to ask him what went through his mind in that moment. Did he think of me? I want to ask. Did he think of his pregnant wife, of the baby in my belly? Or were there other things on his mind? Things he couldn't push away, however hard he tried? Like an image of a girl in a blue velvet dress. Her eyes wide, staring blank at the ceiling, her neck broken in two. A pool of blood, spreading out behind her, like a scarlet cape.

Katie

AS I PUSH AGAINST the glass of the revolving door, Charlie is waiting on the other side. I've never known him to come to my work before. I didn't think he even knew where it was.

"They let you out, then."

His face clouds over, his eyes full of anger.

"They had nothing to charge me with, Katie," he says furiously. "I didn't do anything."

I roll my eyes. "Come on. Before someone sees you. Your brother's face is all over the bloody news."

I pull my coat tightly around myself. The streetlamps are already on, the car headlights swishing at us as they turn the corner of the street. I take my scarf out of my bag.

I'd been dying to get out of the office. The Rachel case is now huge. Rory's arrest has propelled it to the top of the news list—the wealthy son of a famous architect, questioned over the disappearance, possible murder, of a pretty young single girl, who may or may not have been pregnant.

Her father's red-eyed press conference is still being endlessly replayed on Sky News, along with the new footage of Rory outside the Haverstock offices, being led into a police car, his eyes locked on the ground. All the other news—war in the Middle East, the latest Brexit crisis—has been reduced to a few lines on the news ticker at the bottom of the screen.

Of course, it had gotten back to Hugh that I knew her, that I'd been questioned. "I'm sorry," I'd told him. "I just can't get involved." Hugh had shaken his head, looked away. "Fine," he'd said. And handed me a pile of rewrites.

Normally I would have been gutted that he was disappointed in me, but now I was too preoccupied to care. I kept staring at the huge TV screens, the footage of Rory being shoved into the back of a police car, a police officer's hand clamped to the back of his head. Could it have been Rory I saw her going into the cellar with all this time, and not Charlie? Could Rory have done something to her?

"It's cold out here," Charlie says. "Can we go somewhere and talk?"

The bar has a red velvet curtain across the door—as we step beyond it, it is deliciously warm after the icy wind outside. We are shown across the diamond-patterned floor, and seated at a corner table, a low lamp between us, and handed two leather-backed menus. I order a glass of Malbec, and Charlie asks for a beer. The waiter brings him a glass. He ignores it, takes a sip from the bottle. In the mirrored walls, I see the waiter glance back at him disapprovingly.

"So you know about Rory being arrested, do you?" Charlie says, taking a swig.

"I work in a newsroom, Charlie, what do you think? It's been all over the TV all day. Sky must have got a van to his office before the cops did." I pick the menu up, stare at it, put it down again. "Helen is beside herself. She said she's had reporters knocking. Poor thing. Due to give birth any minute." I push the menu away. "I've told her about speaking to the media regulator. And I've told our lot to lay off. I don't know how much good it'll do."

Charlie sighs.

"So. Helen told me you found out about how I knew Rachel."

I nod. I find I can't even look at him. I'm too angry. Charlie tries to take my hand, but I pull it away, shake my head.

"I don't understand. Why did you lie to me? Why didn't you just say you knew her from the club?"

"It wasn't that simple. She told me not to. I know it sounds weird." He rubs his hand against the stubble on his chin. "I'm sorry, Katie. I did it because she asked me to." He searches for my eyes, smiling slightly. "You didn't need to go the full *Spotlight* on me, you know. Going to the club. Scouting out the bulletin board—"

"Don't patronize me, Charlie. Don't you fucking dare. And anyway, I obviously did have to. I obviously can't rely on you to tell me the truth.

The smile falls from his face. I look past him and stare into the mirror on the wall.

"So what. You were fucking her, is that it?"

He looks at me, then down. He doesn't reply. I look at the reflection of us together, sitting at the table. We're not young anymore, I think crossly. Why does he not understand that he needs to stop acting like a child?

"All right," he says eventually. "Yes. It was before me and you got back together. It wasn't serious. But yes. There'd . . . there had been a couple of times when . . ."

My heart sinks. Of course. "Oh, spare me the details, Charlie." I take a deep sip of wine.

"It's strange. She'd sort of disappeared from the club, too. She'd been working there a few months. Then we had this big night, the one Rory and Daniel came to, Serena, too. They brought some client with them. I remember she was there then. But not long after that, she quit, and no one really knew why."

He pauses, drops his gaze, runs his fingers through his hair. "Then suddenly she's at Rory's birthday dinner. Looks totally different, all dolled up and stuff. Somehow she has become mates with my sister. And obviously I could see by then that she looked . . . you know." He grimaces. "Pregnant."

I sense he is telling the truth. Still too angry to meet his eye, I scan the room for the waiter. I need another drink.

"The night of Rory's dinner," he continues, "they sat her next to me. So I asked her what she was doing there. She was really intense about it. She said she needed me to keep it a secret, that we knew each other from the club. I didn't really understand why, but she just kept saying it was important, that I needed to trust her." He raises his eyes again, looks at me. "She said there was something she needed to do, and she couldn't do it if people knew who she really was."

I stare at him, incredulous. "You went along with this? Knowing she was lying to your sister—moving herself into their house?"

"I didn't know she had moved in with Helen. She said she was just staying a night or two. I didn't think—that she was lying, exactly. Oh, I don't know—she was so intense about it. I just agreed because . . . well, it seemed a bit easier, for one thing."

I frown. "What do you mean?"

"Come on, Katie," he hisses. "Obviously I didn't want you to know about me and her. You'd given me another chance, I didn't want to fuck it up again. All right?"

I stare up to the ceiling, try to focus on the line of brass lights, the mahogany pillars, the mirrors bordered in green and gold. I try not to let the tears welling in my eyes spill down my face. This is not what's important, I tell myself. There is a girl who could be dead.

"So Rachel wasn't having an affair with Rory?"

Charlie's eyes widen. "With Rory? God, no. I mean—God, not as far as I know. What makes you say that?"

I ignore him.

"And the baby? If there was a baby?"

He drops his head, pulls at his hair again.

"As far as I know, she really was pregnant," he says miserably. "I asked her if it was mine. At Helen's party. When you saw us talking."

I nod grimly. At least I wasn't going mad. I knew it wasn't some casual chat. The look in her eyes. It was important.

"She told me it wasn't. That I shouldn't worry." He pauses. "But honestly?" He swallows, looks away. "The timing would . . . sort of fit. So . . . I don't know."

The waiter returns, takes Charlie's empty bottle. I order another glass.

We are silent for a long time after that. My wine arrives and I take a large gulp from the glass.

Charlie clears his throat. "Katie, I swear you and me weren't back together then, or I would never have—"

I cough my wine back into my glass, then slam it down, cheeks flaming. "Oh my God, Charlie. Are you fucking serious? This is so far from being about you and me. Jesus."

I fold my arms. I can't look at him. And when I finally do, I realize it is over between us. It has to be. And in that moment, I can see that he knows it, too.

"I don't know what to say," I say eventually. "I don't know what you want me to say."

"I want you to believe me." His eyes are wide. He grabs for my hand again, over the table. "Katie, I have no idea what happened to Rachel, OK? I had nothing to do with any of this. I was telling the truth about the cellar thing—whoever you saw her go down there with, it wasn't me. That time you saw us together, when we were talking—that was the last time I saw her. I swear. She told me the baby wasn't mine. We talked a bit. Then we parted as friends. That was it. Honestly."

We sit in silence for a while. I have another sip of wine. I can tell that Charlie is searching my face, trying to work out what I'm thinking.

"I still haven't told the police about the cellar thing," I say quietly. "I'm starting to wonder if I even saw it. Maybe I was just drunk. Maybe I was seeing things."

Charlie says nothing. I rub my hands over my face.

"This is a fucking mess, Charlie."

"I know."

I finish my wine. When the waiter arrives, asking if I want another, I nod without even thinking.

"How have you left things with the police?"

Charlie scowls, rubs his knuckles against the side of his head. "At first they didn't seem that bothered when I went in and made that statement," he says. "But now this new team has taken over, and they're all over me. Taken my phone, searched my apartment. It's because of the drug thing last year. They'll pin something on me if they can."

"So why has Rory been arrested?"

He shrugs. "No idea. If Rory knew Rachel, that's news to me." He pauses. "Can we go for a smoke?"

I wince. "It's so cold out there."

"Have my jacket."

So we sit on Kensington High Street, he smokes, and I cradle my glass of wine in both hands, his jacket around my shoulders. I look over at the blinking Christmas lights, the sparkling window displays. People are flagging cabs, gloved hands outstretched. Shiny black taxis purr up beside them, their wheels quiet in the slush.

"I know what people think," he says. "What the police think. You can see it all over their faces. They talk to me like I'm a drug dealer or something."

He looks so sad.

"Come on, Charlie. No one thinks you're a drug dealer."

"Not you. But them. Them and my fucking brother. You know after everything, he still expects me to bring him stuff, to his parties. It's the only reason the two of them want me around. Fucking hypocrites."

"What do you mean, the two of them?"

Charlie shakes his head. "Forget I said anything."

"Charlie, come on. What are you talking about? Does Serena ask you for stuff, too?"

He exhales a plume of smoke into the night air. "No. Well. Not coke, anyway."

I stare at him.

"What then?"

"It was only once recently she asked me for something. It pissed me off, that's all. I told her no way. Anyway, she wanted weird stuff—stuff I'd have no fucking idea how to get."

"What?"

"Some kind of benzo, something heavy duty. Xanax, maybe, or diazepam?"

I'm stunned. "Are we talking about the same Serena here?"

He gives a sad smile. "I know, I was surprised, too."

"What the hell did she want that for?"

Charlie shrugs, brings the cigarette to his lips again.

"Search me."

Helen

LAST NIGHT, DANIEL AND I watched it on the news together. I pulled the blanket up over my knees, held on to Daniel in horror. They replayed the footage of Rachel's tearful father, his voice shaking as he appealed for anyone, anyone who knew anything, to come forward. The more his voice cracked, and tears welled in his eyes, the more the cameras snapped and flashed, as if he was setting off a crackle of electricity. Then came the photograph of Rachel—her painted face, her dark red dress. Her crooked pirate smile. They showed a view of Rory and Daniel's office with a police offer standing guard outside, a bit of the promo film of the wharf project. Then, startlingly, there was a clip of Daddy at Haverstock in the eighties that I'd never even seen before. I gasped when he appeared on the screen, looking just as he did in our childhood photographs, with all his hair intact, grinning away as he unveiled plans for his famous redevelopment of Tobacco Docks, shaking hands with Margaret Thatcher. Then came the footage, pin-sharp by comparison, of Rory walking into the police station the other day, his face like thunder. He was wearing his smartest suit, one I've seen him wear a hundred times, his glamorous female lawyer trotting to keep pace with him. I could see in his eyes that he was scared. Tears had pricked my eyes then. Whatever he's done, he's still my big brother.

Daniel left before light this morning. I've never seen him so upset, so stressed. His face when the news showed footage of Haverstock. My heart is breaking for him. He has put so much into that company. I can't help but wonder if it will ever recover. I'm only glad Daddy didn't live long enough to see it happen.

Rory's arrest couldn't have come at a worse time—the client hasn't signed off on the next phase of the new development yet, and now they are talking about holding off until "things are more settled." The police have got the offices locked down—Daniel can't even get in.

He's been going to work in the library. He's told me to call the second I need anything, if there's any sign the baby is coming. He is only around the corner. I just nodded and turned the news back on. The police seem to tell the reporters more than they tell us. Rory still hasn't been let go. It's been nearly a whole day. What are they asking him? What is he saying?

I think about scenarios over and over. I do this all the time now. I imagine Rachel on a train somewhere, speeding north, Scotland perhaps. Or in a fast car, driving between tall fir trees, brake lights like rubies dazzling behind her, the forest opening its mouth and swallowing her up.

At night, I dream of her. I have nightmares where she is hit by cars, where she is dead in gutters, thrown out of windows, glass shattering. Sometimes, she is there even after she is dead, ghostlike, dressed in a long red cloak, the hood pulled down so there is only darkness where her face should be. In some of the dreams, I become Rachel. I am chased by a wolf through the trees in the park, a woodcutter, an axe swinging at his waist. Or I am drowning, and then I see myself from above and I am not myself, but her. It is her pale face bobbing in the shallows of a pebble beach, her black hair splayed in the gray-green surf.

I wake late, stumble downstairs, trying in vain to shake the dreams from my aching body. As I open the mail, I wonder whether she could have been in an accident by the river. She liked drinking in the Trafalgar Arms. I think about the low wall, the brown swell of the Thames. I wonder how long it would take for a body to wash up. Hours? Days? Months? An image comes to me, unbidden, of her body, facedown, rising and falling, her flesh pale, her joints bloated by river water, a blanket of maggots seething underneath. I close my eyes. Stop, I think. Stop.

I'm so lost in thought that it takes me a moment to register what the letter is saying. No, I think. This can't be right.

Within minutes, I'm on the phone to Brian, our financial adviser. My battery is low, and my only charger is upstairs. I clutch the letter in one hand, my phone in the other. I'm put on hold, given some Elvis Presley to listen to. It seems to go on forever; I'm worried the phone will go dead.

"Helen? Sorry about the wait. How are you? How can I help?"

The sound of Brian's voice, the normality of it, is calming, and I feel myself take a deep breath, my heart slowing slightly. I imagine him in his office on the parade, the little bowl of sweets in gold wrappers on his desk, the photograph of him skiing with his kids. The reassuring dullness of it all.

"I know this sounds mad, but bear with me," I tell him, trying to keep my voice light. "I've just had this letter addressed to me. It says something about the house being remortgaged. And obviously, um, we haven't remortgaged, have we? I mean, you arranged our last mortgage and there's still about five years to go on it till it's all paid off. That's right, isn't it?"

"Yes, that's what I thought," he says. "I certainly don't remember us arranging to remortgage."

"I'm sure one of us would remember," I say, trying to laugh.

"Quite," chuckles Brian. "Hang on, I'm just getting back to my desk. What does the letter say, exactly?"

I read the letter out to him.

"And this is the weird bit. It talks about a remortgage for home improvements?"

"That is strange. To what value?"

My heart rate creeps up again, the hand that's holding the letter shaking slightly.

"Um. It says here it's for 85 percent of the property value. It's . . . it's £3.6 million."

There is silence at the other end.

"I'm sorry. You've lost me," Brian says eventually. "Your previous mortgage was next to nothing, wasn't it?"

"That's what I thought."

"That's right—I've just pulled up your records here. It was less than £100,000. Just that chunk your parents had left at the time of their death. Yes, I remember now." I hear him click, closing a window on his screen. "Why would a lender think you wanted to take on a £3.6 million debt?"

I have no answer for him.

"All right, Helen, don't worry," he says. "I'm sure there's an innocent explanation for all this." But he doesn't sound sure at all. He sounds worried. I feel my pulse climbing, the palms of my hands starting to sweat. "Leave it with me, all right? I'll look into it for you. I'll call the lender. Who is it?"

I read him out the name, the number it says to call. "I've never even heard of them. Have you?"

He doesn't answer.

"Brian?"

"Um, OK, Helen, I don't want you to call that number. Don't do anything, all right? I'll look into this straightaway for you. Keep your phone on. I'll come back to you as soon as possible."

I nod, tears forming in my eyes. "Thanks, Brian," I croak before I hang up.

I try Daniel, but there is no answer. I tap out a message telling him to call me immediately. Then I slump down in the chair, my back aching, and stare out of the window. It is raining again, the street a gloomy watercolor, the sky and the puddles leaking into each other. My fingers find the wedding ring on my left hand and I turn it around and around and around.

As the sky darkens, I check my phone several times. Nothing from Daniel. The battery is dying; I'll have to go and get the charger. Serena hasn't returned any of my calls since I saw her. I want to let her know I'm here for her. I want to know how Rory is. But she's been so distant ever since I told her about the notes I found, my suspicions about Rory.

I head into the kitchen, take down the silver caddy where I keep the chamomile tea. I feel so tired, as if all the energy has drained out of my body. I just want to sleep. I think about curling up on the sofa, a pillow between my knees, another behind my back.

I hear a key turn in the front door. I turn around. There is the shadow of a figure, moving behind the cloudy glass.

Helen

"HELEN? ARE YOU THERE?"

I hadn't realized I was holding my breath. I lean on the sideboard, cursing myself for being so on edge.

"Helen, you want to see me."

"Yes, sorry. I'm so sorry. Come in."

It's just Vilmos, the builder. I'd completely forgotten I'd asked him to come and look at the cellar foundations, that he's still got his key. I usher him in.

I feel like telling him to go away. I'm desperate to lie down, get some rest. But he is here now. I tell him about the concrete, the crack that has spread across the new foundation. "I know Daniel said we wanted to pause the work for a while, but I was a bit worried about it. Can you check it for me?"

Vilmos looks at me, confused. "Helen, I not work for you anymore. Daniel told me. He is using other guys now."

"Who?"

Vilmos sniffs. "Some other guys. Here, take these." He hands me the spare set.

I close my fingers around the keys. There is an awkward silence. Why didn't Daniel tell me we'd changed our building company? I thought he'd worked with Vilmos for years.

"Helen, I don't like ask," he says, staring down at my belly. It is huge now—almost comedic. I feel ridiculous even walking down the street. "Your husband—I need money. For my guys. He needs to pay me for work we have done. I wait a long time for this."

I rub my forehead, embarrassed. "Vilmos, I'm really sorry. I didn't know we were behind. I thought Daniel was organizing it all. He's had a lot on his mind. I'm sure, I'm sure . . ." I hold the sideboard. The world is swimming again, the little twists of black and white crinkling on the sides of my vision, like candy wrappers.

"Please, Helen," he says. His face is etched with kindness. "Do not worry for the money now." He pauses. "You said in your message there is crack. You want I have a look?"

When he emerges from the cellar, his hair and clothes are dusted with grime. His expression seems to have clouded over slightly.

"What do you think?"

He shakes his head. "Could be too much water in concrete mix, wrong type of concrete. But . . . I don't know. It doesn't look like this." He scratches the side of his head. "Can I ask another guy, bring with me?"

"Of course," I say. "It's not urgent really."

He nods. "OK, I come back tomorrow. And you are OK now?"

I force a smile, look up at Vilmos. "Honestly, I'm fine." I get up, flick the kettle on. I will have that tea, try and sleep for a bit.

"OK, good," he says, smiling back uncertainly. "I see mark." He motions to his own forehead, then gestures at mine. "I worry you bang your head."

The kettle clicks off, the steam rising between me and Vilmos, clouding the windows. I stare at him.

"What are you talking about? What mark?"

"In here." Vilmos frowns at me. "Come, look."

And he beckons me toward the cellar door.

Katie

I'VE NEVER BEEN TO this part of Cambridge—it's a new housing project, the homes like little rabbit hutches, the lawns perfectly manicured. I pull up around a corner—I know what these places are like about parking. Even so, as I approach, I feel the pale shrouds of net curtains twitching at me.

An overcast sky bears down overhead, huge and flat as the fens. An icy wind blows, a spinning washing line creaking on one of the front lawns. All the houses look the same. It takes me a while to find the right one, toward the end of a cul-de-sac. I see a shaft of movement inside after I press the doorbell, its artificially jaunty tune jarring in the wintery quiet.

The door opens, and I'm faced with him, a beaten-looking man, small and slight, like a jockey. Rachel's dad, John, the man from the press conference.

"Thanks so much for agreeing to see me," I say. He just nods, steps aside so I can pass.

He leads me into a conservatory at the back of the house. It's chilly, the wind whistling loudly against its plasticky exterior. In the back garden is a rusty barbecue, halfheartedly coated in a rain cover. It looks like it hasn't been used in years. Next to it is one of those plastic poles with a ball on a string attached, two broken racquets leaning against a shed at the back.

I didn't tell Helen I was coming here—in truth, I hardly knew myself. I'd planned to go for a run on the heath, wander around Hampstead, find a new book, enjoy my day off. Instead, I'd found myself in my car again on the Archway Road, passing under the bridge and speeding out toward Cambridge, that same album playing over and over.

The other media had been warned off. Press conferences only, that was the deal. No door knocks. Family liaison officers were all over him. I broke the rules even by calling him on the phone. But I had to talk to him. He might know why Rachel was hanging around us, what she wanted. There must be a reason. He might know something that could help Charlie.

I tried not to think about the other possibility. That he will know something that will make Charlie look even guiltier than he already does.

John brings me a coffee and I sip it gratefully, even though it's milkier than I'd usually like, and the instant coffee grains haven't completely dissolved. They float on the surface, like little brown ants.

I gesture to a large silver frame, with the word Family engraved across the bottom. It shows John with a bottle-blond woman and two little blond girls.

"That's a lovely picture. Which one is Rachel?"

I realize after I've asked the question that neither looks particularly like her.

John looks embarrassed. "That's me and my missus, and our two girls," he says. He picks up the frame for a closer inspection, as if he hasn't really looked at it in a while. "My two youngest. Mine and Stacey's. That's Holly on the left, and on the right is Abby." He sighs, puts the picture back, winces a little. "Rachel had left home by then. She and Stacey . . . well, they didn't always see eye to eye."

I look around the room, at the other photographs on the wall. There are pictures of the two blond girls everywhere—in a vacation swimming pool, in their school uniforms, on a log flume in bright T-shirts and baseball caps, waves of water flying up either side of them. I can't see any of Rachel.

"So you and Rachel's mother separated, a long time ago?"

"She just left one day. Rachel was only six." He sniffs. "Liked a drink. You know. She died a few years after that."

I nod slowly. "So you were a widower. That must have been hard."

John shrugs, looks out into the garden. "I did my best," he says. "I always did my best for her."

"I'm sure."

"She wasn't easy."

The wind is picking up—one of the racquets leaning against the shed clatters over, onto the patio. The rain cover on the barbecue looks as if it might fly away.

"This man who's been arrested," John says. I see his fingers twist into fists. "Do you know him?"

I nod. "I do know him," I say.

John takes a deep breath. "Could he have done something to Rachel? Could he have hurt her?"

I think about Rory when he was a little boy, bullying Charlie, throwing firecrackers at Helen, even though he knew she was scared. But then I think about him at his wedding, when Serena walked down the aisle. How he couldn't resist turning around to look at her walking toward him. How his eyes had filled with tears when he saw her in her dress. I can think of times when I have disliked Rory intensely: the way he lords it at his parties, sneers at my job, belittles Charlie. But then I can think of moments when he has been kind to Helen, or when his love for his wife has been plain for all to see. I have known Rory most of my life. But do I know him, really?

"I don't think so," I say carefully. "But . . . I honestly don't know for sure."

John stands up, starts pacing up and down the conservatory. The wind rattles at the frame of it, as if determined to get in.

"John," I say. "Rachel didn't tell us the truth about who she was. Where she lived, what she wanted. She must have gone to some lengths. She told us she was pregnant, and she looked . . . So if she wasn't, she must have been wearing some sort of prosthetic . . ."

I trail off. He has heard this already from the police. He is screwing up his eyes, as if the words cause him physical pain. I lower my voice.

"I think Rachel must have had a good reason for doing all that. For coming to Greenwich. I think there was something she wanted from one of us. I can't work out what it is." I pause. "I think that if . . . if we figure out what that was, it might help us find out what has happened to her."

John looks at me, his eyes blank.

"Is there anything you can think of that might help me figure out what it was? Was there something she was angry about? Or someone? Something from her past, maybe?"

John doesn't say anything for a long time. He turns his back to me, stares out of his conservatory at his little square of lawn. After a few minutes, I see his shoulders start to shake, his fists opening and closing at his sides. Then without a word, he walks out of the room and up the stairs.

For a while I wonder if he is going to come down again. When he finally returns, he is holding a cardboard box.

"I saved it all," he said. "In case the police ever came back to it, you know? In case something turned up." There is a wobble in his voice. "I thought it might be useful to have it."

He sets the box down in front of me. I take the lid off. It is full of old newspaper cuttings. I take the pile from the top and start to read.

TEN YEARS EARLIER

Cambridge

THEY COULDN'T HAVE KNOWN *it would be something like that. They didn't know. Really, they didn't.*

She didn't touch him again after that. They had walked home, fast, instinctively. When they finally got back to college, he'd said, fuck fuck fuck. We need to tell the police.

She had looked at him then, as if he was mad. Don't be stupid, she'd said. People can't know we were there. What we were doing.

What? What are you talking about? He had stared at her. Didn't you see what I saw?

We don't know what that was, she'd said carefully, not meeting his eyes. Not for sure. We don't know that she hadn't . . . that she wasn't . . .

We do, he had said.

I mean, she was quite drunk, I could see it wasn't the best, but . . .

Wasn't the best?

We couldn't see what was going on. Her voice had snapped like a branch in the woods. And what are we going to tell people when they ask why we were there? Alone? Together?

He had shaken his head. No. No, come on. We need to go to the police.

But she said nothing. They said nothing.

And that was their first mistake.

41 WEEKS

Helen

I PUSH OPEN THE cellar door and flick the light on. It takes a moment before the bulb responds. There's a fizzing sound, then brightness, a pool of yellow light. The crack in the cement is longer now, inching toward the stairs like a lightning bolt.

The cellar smells of paint, glue, damp wood, and it is cold, really cold, as if I've stepped outside. On either side of the stairs are exposed copper pipes, piles of paint cans. The cat carrier from the other day is crammed into a gap on top of a pile of sandpaper and tubes of filler.

I clutch my belly as I inch onto a step. I never come down here—what if the wood is rotten? I am so enormous now. The step could give way any moment.

It's only when I get to the third step that I can see what Vilmos is talking about. A smudge of dark red, almost black, at forehead height, on one of the low beams over the stairs. It could be a blob of paint, I think at first. It could be dirt. But then I look closer.

Vilmos hears me gasp, topple forward. Sees me clutching at the rickety banister.

"Please, I help you." Two strong arms reach out, pull me back up gently, but firmly. My heart is pounding. My stomach is upside down. I feel faint.

Vilmos has pulled me up against his chest. He smells of tobacco, his sweater surprisingly soft. He leads me back into the kitchen.

"Please, Helen, come and sit." I do as he says. He fetches me a glass of water.

"I'm so sorry."

I take a sip of water. Vilmos stands in the kitchen, hands on his hips. I see him glance at the clock.

"Thanks, Vilmos," I say. "I'm better now." I force a laugh. "I just don't like to see blood. Makes me feel sick!" I pause. "I think it must have been Daniel who hit his head."

Vilmos nods. He looks awkward. "Anyway—I see you tomorrow, Helen. Ten o'clock OK for you?"

"Sure."

When I hear the door close behind him, I put out a hand to steady myself against the hallway wall. My heart is pounding. Surely not, I think. It can't be. It can't be. And then I think about what Katie said. About seeing Rachel go down into the cellar.

Katie

WHEN HE TURNS UP at the pub, DCI Carter is in another one of his golf sweaters. I try to suppress a smile at its purple and green diamond pattern. He still has his bag of clubs over one shoulder. He looks like he's gained a couple of pounds since I last saw him, the bags gone from his eyes.

"I got you a coffee," I say. "It might be a bit cold."

He sits down heavily in the leather booth, swinging his bag down next to him so the clubs clatter together.

"I wondered how long it would be before you dragged me out of my comfortable semiretirement for something or other," he mutters. "I thought I might at least get a whole round of golf in."

"Sorry." I laugh nervously. "I didn't know."

"Yep, I'm a part-timer these days." He grins, stretching his arms. "Friday is my golf day."

"Apologies. Isn't it a bit cold on the course today anyway?" I had forgotten how it gets in Cambridge, the icy wind from the fens threatening to blow you over. Even inside, I am sitting on my hands to warm them up. Every time the pub door opens, a blast of freezing air rushes in.

"Come on," he says. "Spit it out." He is looking at me with a mixture of annoyance and amusement, but his face changes when I begin.

"It's about Rachel Wells," I say. I unfold the old article and slide it across the table toward him. "I'm sure you remember her."

It had been her all along. The victim in the boathouse rape. Just fifteen years old. I'd traced my fingers over the cuttings. The summer Helen, Rory, and Daniel left. Then I thought again about what Helen had said. About Daniel not liking to talk about it. Even she had lied to me about it at first. It couldn't be just a coincidence. There must have been some connection, something that made Rachel seek them out. But what? What had she wanted from them, after all these years?

I'd stuffed the articles into my pocket, gone into the kitchen to find John. He had poured himself a whisky and was staring out at the garden. He hadn't even replied when I said goodbye, thanked him for his time.

I had called Carter as I started the car. The icy roads had been dead, flurries of snow starting. It hadn't taken me long to reach the pub.

DCI Carter looks at me, then the article, then to me again. "Look," he says. "You know I can't discuss who this is. Doesn't matter how long ago it was—it's a section 18. Lifetime anonymity." He lowers his voice. "Come on, Katie. What are you playing at? You could get me into serious trouble."

"Did you not know she's gone missing?"

I see the concern on his face instantly.

"I heard something on the radio—didn't catch the name—it's not—the same Rachel . . . ?"

"Same one."

DCI Carter puts his head in his hands.

"I didn't make the connection," he says quietly.

I take out the rest of the cuttings I took from John's box, unfold them, place them on the table in front of us.

"Look, I'm not asking you to disclose that she was the victim in this case—I know it was her already. Her dad told me, all right?"

He eyes me as if I am a dangerous animal that needs to be handled carefully.

"This is more important than that anyway. Homicide is on the case. They think she's been murdered." Anonymity isn't much good to her if she's dead, I feel like saying. But I stop myself. I sense I've said enough.

He takes a deep breath in, then out. Starts to massage his forehead.

"It's to do with what happened to her before, in Cambridge. I know it is," I say. "I just don't know how."

DCI Carter looks up.

"I need your help," I tell him. "Please."

"All right," he says eventually. He starts to pull his jacket off, one sleeve, then another. Sets it on the back of his chair. "But we're talking completely off the record here, Katie. Understood?"

I nod.

"OK," he says. "You start. Tell me what you know about how she went missing."

Helen

I NEED TO FIND my phone, to call the police. This could be important. Where is my phone? I used it to call Brian earlier. I rush over to the armchair, find it down the side of a cushion. I pick it up, dial DCI Betsky's number, but then I remember the battery. Before the call connects, the phone dies, and the screen goes black.

I haul myself upstairs, the nagging pain in my back sharpening into something more, starting to move around to my front, like a belt tightening. I hold my belly to stop it weighing on my hips. The charger is at the top of the house, but halfway up, I find I need to stop and catch my breath. I collapse into the chair in the spare room, the one we were supposed to have made into a nursery by now. I look down at my hands and see that they are still shaking.

A smudge of blood, a nick of something else. Maybe hair. Maybe skin. Every cell of my being is trying hard not to think about what it could mean. I don't want to think about it at all, in fact. I don't want to be involved in the thinking. The finding, the analyzing. I just want to hand it over, to give it to someone else. I can't bear it pressing down on me anymore.

I notice there is a charger plugged in by the door. It must be left over from when Rachel was here. As soon as the phone flashes back to life, I call Daniel. But it goes straight to voice mail. I hold my phone tight against my ear to stop the trembling. I wait for the beep.

"Daniel? It's me. Listen—you need to come home. I've found something, in the cellar—a mark. It looks . . . it looks like blood. I'm about to call the police. But please—come home." I feel a sob rising in my throat. "Please, I need you here. Be as quick as you can."

As soon as I hang up, I dial DCI Betsky's number again. It goes straight to voice mail, too. I try once more, but after a couple of rings, the phone dies again. The ache is coming harder now.

I stumble back to the chair, try to slow my breathing, calm my thoughts. I remember a meditation exercise I learned once, something about focusing on fixed points, objects in the room. I look from one to another. The chest of drawers, with the changing top. The blinds, the books. The glass vase on the shelf.

When my gaze moves to the vase, something shifts in my mind. I walk over to take it down. As my hands close around its thick glass rim, it is as if a fog is lifting. I remember holding this. I remember turning around. And there it all was. It wasn't just Daniel's laptop. There were other things, too—a note, money, boarding passes. Boarding passes—for who? And a passport. My passport, with my face cut out of it. But why?

But before I can even think about what it means, a new wave of pain drowns out the other sensations in my body. That's when I realize. This is different. These aren't just aches. The pains are radiating out, around from my belly and back and into the deepest parts of my abdomen. A tightening, squeezing pain. A pain that feels bright red. My bump is hardening. This is it, I know. It's starting.

Katie

I FILL DCI CARTER in as quickly as I can. He listens carefully, says nothing. He tips a little paper tube of sugar into the coffee I bought for him, then starts rolling up the packet very tightly with his thumbs and index fingers.

"I think she came to Greenwich because she was after somebody," I say. "One of my friends. I'm sure it was something to do with what happened to her back then."

I give him our names. Everybody. Me, Charlie, Rory and Serena, Daniel and Helen.

"Can you think of any reason she'd have had to seek us out?"

He leans forward a little. "The names of the defendants in the previous case are a matter of public record," he says carefully, pointing to the article I've unfolded from my pocket. "Thomas Villar and Hector Montjoy. They both went abroad. Their parents got them jobs; you know how it is with that sort. One of them went to Hong Kong, went into banking. The other one to America—can't remember what for. They managed to repair their so-called ruined lives, if you ask me."

DCI Carter shakes his head. I sense he is starting to soften.

"As for Rachel. I failed her, really. She was brave. Really brave." He stares out of the window. "She was drunk, of course. That was what did her in, in the eyes of the jury. But I never for one minute doubted she was telling the truth. She was completely consistent. Completely compelling. And her injuries . . . If we could have just found her witnesses, things would have been different."

He takes the little ball of paper he has made between his forefinger and thumb and taps it on the table three times.

"What do you mean? Were there witnesses?"

DCI Carter cringes, as if he regrets saying it. "Oh, I don't know, Katie," he says. "Maybe not. A lot of my colleagues just thought it was her getting mixed up—with other faces she'd seen before, or at the hospital that night. It's entirely possible there was no one there." He pauses. "But . . . yes, she thought there had been someone else there. Two people. A boy and a girl."

He takes a sip of his coffee, sets it down neatly on the coaster, then centers it with his thumbs.

"She gave us a detailed description. Said they'd seen her. She said they weren't part of it. She said for a moment she'd thought they were going to help her. And then they disappeared."

I think of Rachel, alone on the floor of the boathouse, looking up and seeing two faces, thinking she was going to be saved. How could anyone have done that? How could they have seen that, and done nothing? Said nothing? I shiver.

"Did you ever find them?"

Carter gives me a sad smile, shakes his head.

"I tried, believe me. We went through all the club members, anyone who might have been there working, or cleaning, or training. All the boats were signed in and out, in a book. We went through the lot. Not one of them fit the description. So then we looked at anyone who'd been seen on the river that day. Anyone who was even seen nearby. At one point, I thought I'd found them."

He pauses.

"A group of them who'd taken a boat without signing it out. They weren't supposed to. A girl and a boy admitted returning the boat. But they denied seeing anything. Said they'd been at the boathouse, but earlier in the day. That it had been empty when they got there, empty when they left. That they couldn't help." He looks up. "I thought they were lying. That they'd been up to something they shouldn't have. But I couldn't prove it, and you can't force people to testify. My boss wanted me to keep going, put more pressure on them. I didn't think we needed to. We've got the DNA evidence, I thought. Her internal injuries. What more do we need?"

He smiles sadly. "I was still a bit naive about sexual assault cases back then, only just made detective. My boss always said it wouldn't be enough. He was sorry to be proven right." He sighs. "It was a lesson for me. Juries can be . . . well. Rape cases. You know the challenges."

We sit in silence for a moment.

"Do you remember their names?"

He blinks at me.

"The boy and the girl," I prompt. "The ones you thought were lying. Do you remember their names?"

Carter wipes his mouth with the back of his hand. "It was a long time ago, Katie."

"Was one of them called Rory?"

DCI Carter looks me in the eye. He is giving nothing away.

"I'm not looking for a story here," I say, trying to control my voice, even though I feel like shouting, slamming my hands down on the table. "I'm trying to work out why a girl has gone missing. Maybe even been killed. I'm trying to work out what . . . what might have happened to her."

DCI Carter stares down at the table. "Katie, I appreciate your concern for Rachel but . . ." He scratches the back of his head. "We're talking here about stuff that might not even be in the case files."

"You'd have it, though. You'd have the names. In your notebooks. Wouldn't you?" I know I'm right. "You wouldn't close a file on a case like that. They'd be somewhere. You know they would."

DCI Carter shakes his head, holds his hands up. "Katie, I can't help you," he says. "I'm sorry. I've said too much already."

I stand up. I feel heat rising to my face. "Fine," I say.

"Where are you going?"

"I'm going back to Greenwich. If you're not going to tell me, then I'll just have to ask them myself."

"Katie, wait—"

I get in the car and start the engine. I pull my steering wheel around and speed out of the parking lot, snowflakes swirling on my windshield. Before I pull off, I picture him still at the table, turning his phone over and over in front of him.

Katie

THE SIDEWALKS ON MAZE Hill aren't sanded. The steps up to her house shine like icy mirrors. I bang the elegant knocker, then ring the bell. Nothing. The painted shutters in the bay window are closed, the lavender on the windowsills in gray-green hibernation. There are lumps of snow nestled on the soil inside the pot.

Irritated, I lean over and bash on the glass of the spotless bay window. The sound seems to echo around the cold, quiet street. There are no cars on the drive, no one on the pavements. Fuck, I think. Rory must still be at the police station. But where is Serena?

Then I remember—her studio. I've never actually been there, but I'm sure Helen said it was around here somewhere. I bet she's there. I call Helen, but her phone goes straight to voice mail. Fuck. I'll have to go around and ask her. She'll have the address.

As I get back to my car, my phone rings.

"Katie? It's Mark Carter."

I switch the phone between my elbow and my ear so I can rub my freezing hands together.

Carter is breathing rapidly. I hear a rustle of paper, the noise of the wind in the background—he has to lift his voice to speak over it. "I had a quick look. I haven't got access to everything. I don't have a record of the woman—not that I can get to easily," he says. "But I found the guy, all right?" He pauses. "The guy's name wasn't Rory. It was a Daniel. Daniel Thorpe. Is that the Daniel you mentioned?"

I stare across the road. You can see the park gates from here. Children in hats and scarves, people with bags of Christmas shopping.

"Look, between us, Katie—I've called homicide, spoke to the senior investigating officer. I've passed the information on. That's all I can do. But listen. If you think this Thorpe could be involved, Katie—do me a favor. Don't approach him."

I think about Helen. About the set of house keys she pressed into my hands. The look on her face, almost as if she knew that something bad was going to happen. I turn on the ignition. Her house is only five minutes from here. Less in the car.

"Are you listening to me, Katie? This Daniel Thorpe. I don't want you to approach him, OK? Katie? Katie?"

I hang up, throw my phone into the passenger footwell. Then I start to drive.

Helen

I LEAN AGAINST THE wall, rest my forehead on the back of my hands, and rock my hips from side to side, as if to move them out of the way of the pain. But it chases me, to and fro, stronger every time. And then I feel a wetness. I try to get to the bathroom but I'm forced to crawl. There is fluid on my legs.

When I get to the bathroom, I see the black-green marks. The waters should be clear. Not like this. I have read the books. I know this is a bad sign, a warning. I need to get to the hospital.

I stumble back into the spare room and pick up my phone. It's charged up a bit now, but there is nothing from Daniel. I call Katie once, then twice, but there's no answer from her, either. In desperation, I dial 999. The pain comes again, and I put the phone on speaker while I grip the sides of the chair, try to breathe through it. It rings and rings. Come on, I think. Come on.

I'm listening so hard for the operator to pick up that I don't hear the footsteps on the stairs, the floorboards on the landing creak. I don't hear anything at all until he is there, with me, in the room.

As soon as I see him, I'm flooded with relief.

"Oh, Daniel, thank God," I say. I feel a sob rising in my chest. "Thank God you came. I think we need to call the police and . . . and I think the baby is coming."

I'm already anticipating the familiar, woody smell of him, the smell of his pencil shavings and ink, the smell of books and clean sheets and safety. But then I see there is something strange about his face. The bags under his eyes are so deep now he almost looks like someone else. But it's not that. It's something in the eyes themselves. Something I have never seen before.

"I'm sorry, Helen," he says quietly.

"What?"

And only then do I notice that he is holding something in his hands. The vase.

There is a white flash of pain as it slams against my skull. And then everything goes black.

Katie

THERE'S NO ANSWER AT Helen's house. All the blinds are pulled down, the shutters closed. I call Helen's cell, but it goes straight to voice mail. Perhaps she has turned it off so she can sleep. I suppose she could have gone into labor. I wonder if I should walk away, give her a ring later. But something makes me stop. Their car is on the drive. It's too early for Daniel to be home. Something feels wrong. Something I can't put my finger on.

I kneel at the door and push open the brass flap to look inside. Helen's hospital bag is sitting by the door, neatly packed. Her maternity notes are sticking out of the top in their blue folder. I know Helen—she doesn't go anywhere without that bag. Not now. She dragged it all the way to Dartmouth Park with her the other night. No, Helen is here. She must be. I'll just check that she's all right.

I feel for the spare set of keys she gave me the other day. It takes me a few moments to work the unfamiliar lock, but with a final twist, the catch gives way. As I cross the threshold, the atmosphere changes, the silence inside feels heavy.

"Hello? Helen? Are you here?"

Daniel appears at the top of the stairs. He stares at me. He doesn't say anything.

"Oh, hi, Daniel," I say. "Is Helen here?"

Daniel's face changes. He smiles. "Katie!" He jogs lightly down the stairs. "Hello. I didn't know you had a key."

"Helen gave me one," I say as he leans forward to kiss me on the cheek. "Just to feed the cat and stuff, when you're in the hospital." I pause. "I guess Serena is nearer, but, um . . ."

Daniel seems to flinch at the mention of Serena's name. Did I imagine that? I wonder.

I look at his face. He looks exhausted, the bags under his eyes leaden. His cheeks are weirdly flushed, as if he's been working out. Sweat glistens on his brow. He is standing ever so slightly too close to me.

"Is she all right?" I ask.

"Who? Serena?"

I stare at Daniel. "No," I say, blinking. "Helen. Is she OK? Is she here?"

"Oh yeah, of course," he says distractedly. He pushes his glasses up his nose. "She's just sleeping. Upstairs."

"Oh, OK," I say.

I look over Daniel's shoulder but he moves forward. Blocks my view. "Is someone else here?"

Daniel clears his throat. He doesn't move. He speaks too quickly, too loudly.

"To be honest, Katie, it's not a great time." He wipes at the sweat on his brow. "Helen really needs quiet. She needs to have a bit of a rest. Can I get her to give you a ring later?"

As he speaks, the phone he is holding in his hand starts ringing. The words Brian Mortgage Adviser appear. The phone is in a case with a cutesy, flowery pattern. I don't think it is Daniel's phone. In fact, I am pretty sure it is Helen's.

Daniel looks at the screen. He hits cancel, smiles at me. But within seconds, the same number flashes again.

"Maybe you should get that," I say quietly. "Might be important."

"It's not. It's fine." He presses cancel again, shoves the phone into his back pocket.

The air in the house feels thick, the silence heavy.

"Daniel, are you sure everything's OK?"

He looks at me through his glasses.

"Of course. Why wouldn't it be?"

The phone rings again. I look at Daniel. He looks at me. And then I decide. Fuck you, Daniel. Fuck you.

I step past him as if I'm headed to their kitchen. He flips an arm out to stop me, and as he does, I run straight up the stairs.

"Katie?"

I can hear in his voice he is trying to stay calm.

"Just using the bathroom," I call. "That's OK, isn't it? I won't wake her."

The phone is still ringing. Daniel throws it on the floor. I hear it smash as it hits the stone tiles. The crack is like a starting gun. Daniel has begun to follow me up the stairs.

"Katie," he is saying. His voice is different now. "It's really not a good time. Really. Katie!" His voice is desperate now, his footsteps heavier.

I am on the first landing. I don't know what I'm doing. I don't know what I'm looking for. I am throwing doors open—a bathroom, a study. Then I push open the door to the spare bedroom, the one where Rachel was staying. And there is Helen, slumped on the floor, one arm outstretched, another around her belly. Her eyes are closed, and as I come closer, I see there is a cut on her head, blooming red. A smashed vase lies in jagged pieces around her.

I spin around, but he is too fast. His fist is in my hair. I feel a sharp wrench of pain at the back of my head, another arm around my waist. He is strong, too strong for me.

"Daniel, what the fuck have you done?"

"Be quiet, Katie," he mutters, dragging me backward.

"Daniel, call a fucking ambulance. That's your wife, your baby!"

"I said be quiet," he snaps.

I kick frantically, elbows flying, but nothing works. He is taking me upstairs. The pain at the back of my head is unbearable. I see a floating curtain, an open window. And then I am in fresh air, my body held over a steep drop.

I see roof tiles, a rotten gutter. The green of the gardens far below, divided up into neat little squares that from here look no bigger than community plots. The landscape wheels in front of my eyes, the dark outlines of trees against a pale sky, the wonky rooftops. The pain at the back of my head.

"Let me go, Daniel! Let me go!" But my voice is hoarse and I am screaming into thin air. I am screaming into nothing.

Daniel is panting, his voice hoarse. "This is your fault, Katie," he hisses. "I told you. I told you to go home. Didn't I? But you don't listen. You never listen."

He pulls my face closer to his, so I can see his eyes, the deep hollows underneath. And in that moment, I wonder if I have seen this before, this ugliness in my friend's husband. If I have detected this in him, before now. And deep down, I know the answer is yes. That I have seen it in the pencil lines of his face, in the blankness behind his eyes. And I did nothing. Because he seemed normal. And because you don't. Because it's awkward. And because how do you say? How can you?

And now this. Now this. Because of me.

And then he lets me go. My stomach collapses in on itself, my breath escapes my lungs. I close my eyes, wait for the slam as my body hits the ground. But it doesn't come, and instead I seem to swing, as if I'm caught. And I realize that before I knew my hands had even moved they have gripped tightly around something. The steel rings of the gutter. I am here, still here. But my hands are weak, and the metal is hard, and every muscle in my body says let go, I can't hold on. I can't, I can't.

Nothing about this moment feels real. The smell of the bricks, of the moss in the gutters. The cool silence of the air. And then he is back. I see his blank face, and his hand, a hammer in his hand. He is grimacing, as if in physical pain, as he holds the hammer up, just above my fingers, where they are gripped around the metal of the roof.

"Daniel," I cry. "Don't do this!"

Daniel's face is blank, as if he is looking straight through me. The hand holding the hammer is trembling. My fingers are holding tight, but I can feel the metal give way slightly, almost imperceptibly. It is over, I know that now. This will soon be over.

"You should have listened, Katie," Daniel says again. His expression hardens. He pulls his arm back, preparing to slam down the hammer. I grip tight, close my eyes.

There is a bang, a slam. But the impact I am braced for hasn't come. Shouts, voices. When I open my eyes, there is a voice I know.

"Katie? Katie?"

There are hands reaching out. More shouting. The voice is calling my name. I know I have to let go, to reach my hand up. But I am too afraid. My cheeks are wet. I feel the wind in my hair. It's so high, and I can't let go. I can't.

ONE YEAR LATER

Her Majesty's Prison Bowood

November 5, 2019

You used to talk about that day often, and we were all forced to listen. And I suppose it was perfect, to you. You just never knew the truth.

There really was something about it, a sort of golden quality. The light on the water dazzling, like diamonds. We'd all been so drunk, on the sun, our youth. Each other.

You didn't see us on the opposite bank, under the willows. You couldn't see past the leaves, under the surface. I wish I could say that was the first time. But it started long before that.

At the back of the theater, after a rehearsal one night. Everyone else had gone home. It had been building for weeks. She tormented me. I couldn't stop thinking about her, that Red Riding Hood cloak. When I was awake. When I was asleep. When I was fucking you, Helen. I am sorry to cause you pain. But that was how it was. I couldn't stop.

It was raining the night it happened. I was hanging around on purpose, hoping she'd be doing the same. I'd heard the scrape of a chair, footsteps, slipper soft. And she was there, at the back of the empty stage. Still in her costume, but her feet were bare. She'd pulled her hood down. Let her hair fall over one shoulder. Until then I hadn't known she felt that way. That first time. The sound of the rain, the smell of the stage paint. It felt like a revelation. I'm not trying to hurt you, Helen. I just want you to understand. I had never felt anything like it. And the more I had of Serena, the more I wanted. And that day, when I reached for her, under the water by the punt, she reached for me, too.

When she said she didn't mind taking the boat back, and she looked at me, I knew then what would happen.

We were on the floor, on a canvas sheet, when we heard them. I could see their stupid Ravens drinking society ties. I knew one of them. Rory's mate. There was no time. They were going to catch us, they'd tell Rory. They knew we had taken the boat.

Serena started going mad then. Saying, hide, I don't want them finding us here. We'll be expelled. I laughed. I was high, giddy with her. I told her not to be so stupid. We'd taken our exams, we'd paid the fees. They weren't going to expel us for taking a boat. But she insisted. Just stand the fuck back there. Stay in the shadows until they've gone. They won't see us.

It took a while before we could see what they were doing. But we did. We saw. And Serena was right, they didn't see us. The girl did, though. She looked right at me, her green eyes locked on mine, her lips parted, trying to say something. And I didn't do anything.

And she saw that, too.

Serena didn't touch me again that day. I knew what we'd just seen. What we'd witnessed. But Serena saw it differently. She wanted to stay out of it—said we didn't know the whole story. And anyway, she said, there would be questions. About why we hadn't helped. Why we had done nothing.

You insisted we all go out that night. You were so happy, Helen, and it was like it would make it all OK again, if we all went along with you. I remember in the line for the club, looking at your face, your innocence. You were so pure, so beautiful. I kissed you like you were my child, buried my cheek in your red hair. I'd wanted to be good again, like you. But all I could think of was the girl in the boathouse. How she'd cried. How she'd wriggled, struggled underneath the boy. How her glassy eyes had found mine, asking for help.

The next day, the police came around. You'll remember this part, of course. Someone they'd questioned had seen us on the river, noticed the college crest on the punt. Mentioned it to the cops. The cops figured we'd have had to go to the boathouse to take it back. They had no evidence. I think, though, they knew it was us.

The four of us were in your room when the officers came. I'm sure you remember how it went. Serena spoke first. Yes, Officer, we were at the boathouse, she said. My friend Daniel and I. But it must have been before, there was no one there when we took the boat back. Or when we left.

The police officer frowned. The victim knew she'd seen witnesses. One a girl. Blond. Another a bloke, with spectacles. The officer gave me a long stare and I felt like I was made of glass, that I was about to shatter into pieces. I felt if I could just keep every muscle firm, every tiny part of my body still, I'd be safe.

You're sure you didn't see anything, he asked again. And I said no. That I was sorry. That I wished I could help. And you squeezed my arm, Helen. Believing me. And I had felt like the worst person on earth. I remember the officer, as he left the room. He glanced back. First at me. Then at Serena.

I tried to ignore the coverage of the trial, but it was impossible. The jury took so long over the verdict. It was too late, of course, by then. I had been praying they'd have enough, without us. Of course they will, Serena said. Haven't you heard of DNA? But it wasn't enough. They didn't believe her.

I remember listening to it in the radio in the car, sitting outside my mum's house, a fly buzzing in the side mirror. Her knocking on the window, asking what I was doing. When it came back not guilty, I had opened the door and leaned over to be sick.

Years went by. I thought it had all gone away. Serena and I were never going to last—I loved you, Helen. And she loved Rory. I stopped thinking about the girl, about what we'd done. But then every time we lost a baby, a voice in my head would tell me that it was because of what I did. That I had brought it on us. That it was all my fault.

Did you ever suspect, Helen? There was a time when I wondered if you had caught us out. I found a photograph I didn't know existed, of the four of us, at that play, the one where it all started, me in my wolf suit, Serena in her red cape. You'd torn it, right down the middle, between Serena and me.

But I kept that picture, stuck it back together. As a reminder of what I'd nearly lost. You. And the four of us. We were something precious, weren't we? Despite everything. I know you felt that.

When you got pregnant again, and things finally seemed to be all right this time, I started to think maybe I'd had my punishment, that we were going to be left alone. Until that night, in Charlie's club.

It had been Rory's idea to take a new client there, a bloke who was always going on about places that "felt corporate" or "soulless" or "out of keeping with the community." I have to admit it was a masterstroke of his, taking him to Charlie's dodgy club in Hackney. He loved it, kept saying it was "real." Rory even made Serena come along, help to charm him. Rory had been lying through his teeth all night, making out like he went there all the time. I think Serena and I were both a bit fed up, to be honest. It was just by chance that we went to the bar together, to escape for a bit. And that's when she saw us.

She'd been working behind the bar, a glass in one hand, a cloth in the other. She'd recognized us straightaway. I hadn't known her face, but the truth of what she was saying registered immediately. My chest tightened, my palms were damp. I looked into her face and saw those green, watery eyes, the open mouth. Of course, by law, none of us had ever been allowed to know her name.

She wasn't making any sense. She was hysterical. She said she'd spent years looking for us, after it all happened. She knew we'd lied. She just kept asking us why, saying we'd ruined her life. She started demanding we go to the police. Changing our story, all these years later. It was insane.

Serena picked up her bag and walked away. But when I tried to follow, the girl grabbed my arm, her fingernails piercing my skin.

Don't, she said. Don't you dare. You fuck me around again, I'm warning you, you will regret it.

Then she turned up at our offices. She lied, gave the name of the client, the one we'd taken to the club that night—she must have gotten it from the guest list. Lisa let her in, was fussing around her, bringing her a coffee, thinking she was someone important. I wanted to run, to throw her out of the fucking window.

But I played along for Lisa, took her into my office. When Lisa was gone I asked her real name. She said I didn't need to know, that I had no right to know. I told her I was sorry, that I'd been a coward, that I remembered that night and I wish I'd said something. I told her I was trying to protect my girlfriend, now my wife. My pregnant wife.

That's why I'd lied to the police. I told her I was sorry, that I wished I could undo it. And then I asked her to keep quiet. I begged her. I offered her money. Anything to keep my secret.

As soon as I finished my speech, she gave this little smile, started tapping away on her phone. And that's when I saw how stupid I'd been. She'd recorded me. And before I could grab her phone, she'd sent herself the sound file. It was too late. There was nothing I could do.

She said I had three options. I could go to the police, tell them I lied, and risk getting arrested for perverting the course of justice. I could let her take the recording she'd made to the police. Same outcome, maybe worse. Or, I could give her money. It didn't feel like much of a choice. I didn't know then that money was never going to be enough.

At first, I just took money from the company account. By now you'll know, of course, that I'd moved the accounts offshore to make it harder for Rory to find out. Looking back, I can't believe how naive I was. I'd meet her in the new development, hand her the cash in envelopes. But of course, it was never enough. She kept coming back.

Even as I was giving her the stacks of fifties from the company safe, she was starting to worm her way into our life. Turning up at your prenatal class, making friends with you. I didn't even know her name, so it meant nothing to me, all this talk of Rachel, your new friend. She was laughing at us—she must have been.

I only found out later that she was blackmailing your brother, too.

It was when she said she wanted the money from the house that I really lost it. She deserved it, she said. Her baby deserved the sort of life that we had. She called it justice. I went too far that night, I admit that. I hadn't meant to grab her throat that hard. But it was like she wanted to destroy us.

I told her to forget it, to leave us alone, for good. She did the opposite. She turned up at our house, that very same night. Our anniversary. And you told me this was her—your new friend, Rachel. And that was when I saw that I couldn't scare her. She wasn't going anywhere.

Having her in the house was like being slowly suffocated. She wouldn't rest until she'd taken our home, or put me in prison, or both. I'm sorry, Helen. I am. But in the end, it felt like the only way. She had to be stopped. She left me with no choice.

You know the rest. Charlie had left the cellar, gone outside to find Katie. I took a coat from the pile in the hallway, so I could hide the brick *inside it. And then I found Rachel, wearing that velvet dress. I told her I'd made a decision, that I had worked out how to get her the money quickly. I pulled her down to the cellar, and I closed the door behind us. And then I did it.*

I thought I could make it look like an accident. But every time I tried to leave the cellar, I could hear people on the other side of the door. And there was so much blood. On my hands, on the brick, on the coat. Spreading out behind her head, like I'd knocked over a can of paint. And then when I looked closer, it wasn't just blood. Something white and clear. Something that told me there was no way back. In the end, I panicked. The concrete just seemed like the only way. I thought I could make it go away. For you, for us. I was wrong.

I'm so sorry about Rory, about what I put him through. I didn't know it was his coat I'd taken. I hadn't planned it like that. But when I realized—I suppose it just presented itself as an easy solution. I know how insane that sounds. I think I really did lose my mind, for a while.

I am sorry, Helen, about your beautiful house. I'm sorry about the dreams you must have now. I hope they are nothing like mine. I'm glad that, unlike me, you are still able to wake up from your nightmares.

My lawyer tells me that our son, our precious boy, is all right now, that you are both doing well. He told me the name you had chosen for him, Leo James. I say his name to myself, before I go to sleep. I am sorry I was never more interested in your lists of names. I am sorry I could never think of ideas, of any names of my own. I wish I had now. I wish a lot of things. I wish I had listened, that I had been a better husband to you, Helen. Leo James. I would never have thought of anything even half as beautiful.

I long to see him, Helen. I know I have no right to ask, but I am asking anyway. I would give anything to see my son. Even just a picture of his face. I dream of him. I dream of you both.

I am sorry, Helen. More sorry than you can ever know. Forgive me, Helen. Please, forgive me.

Daniel

Helen

I PUSH THE PLAYGROUND gate with one hand, the stroller with the other. Katie rushes to help me, while Charlie lifts Ruby out of the swing. "I'm fine," I insist. I am learning to manage things myself.

The trees are shedding again, the golden leaves dusting the playground like confetti. There is a cool, watery sunlight, a smell of burning leaves, bonfires. I can hardly believe it's been a year already.

Ruby wants to play with Leo, to push him on a swing. I haven't tried him on a swing yet. I wonder whether he is still too little for it—he is not sitting up fully yet, still toppling forward, a look of surprise in his huge blue eyes. He should be crawling by now, pulling himself up, starting to take his first steps. Every time I see him wobble over, it feels like a fish hook snagging at my heart.

Charlie says it doesn't matter. They all do everything eventually, he says. He shows me how to ball up a blanket from the stroller to wedge him into the swing, instructs Ruby to push him gently. Leo is stunned, an amazed smile lighting up his face. He giggles, kicks his legs for more. And in this moment, I try not to worry. About whether he is too hot or cold, whether he should be wearing a hat, or a thicker coat. Whether he is damaged forever. I try to just stand and smile. To see it as a gift. To be here, despite everything. Me and my son. My brother. My friend. My niece. In the park, in the sunshine.

Later there are thunderstorms. We walk back to the house. Katie and Charlie play with Leo. Ruby watches cartoons and I make her hot chocolate. When Charlie goes home, Katie follows him to the door. I think I hear him kiss her, but I can't be sure, and I don't look. It's none of my business.

Leo is rubbing at his eyes, pressing his forehead against my legs. I gather him up in my arms and take him upstairs. He settles in his crib, his arms thrown over his head, the way he always sleeps. I watch his eyelashes fluttering until they rest on his chubby cheeks. Until his breathing slows.

Downstairs, Katie is sitting at the kitchen table we share. We've been here nearly a year now. The decor isn't what I'd have chosen, the garden tiny, overgrown with ivy and cow parsley. But it's cozy and warm, and the landlord let me repaint Leo's room, put hooks in the ceiling for the elephant mobile Katie bought for him. New curtains, with a dandelion pattern. A soft carpet he can play on. It's home, for now.

Katie has put some thick socks on, made a pot of tea, arranged the remains of the misshapen cupcakes Ruby brought us on a plate. The thunder cracks overhead—I close the kitchen window, yanking it hard to stop it sticking. I check that the clothesline is empty.

"So," she says. "Are you going to show me this letter?"

I hesitate, unsure at first whether this is a good idea. Eventually, I reach behind the coffee pot, retrieve the envelope from the shelf. The paper is pale blue and cheap, flimsy in my fingers, the hand unmistakable. My husband. The murderer. Katie's eyes widen at the sight of it.

"How did he find your new address?"

I shrug. "No idea."

"I thought they checked their letters, made sure they weren't sending stuff like this. Especially when there's a court order."

"I know." I toss the letter at her. "I don't know how it got to me. Or what to make of it. Maybe you will."

Katie unfolds the letter and reads it. Every so often she makes an expression of incredulity.

"I picture you in your kitchen! As if you could have ever lived there again!"

I sigh. There are times when I long to go back. Some nights I dream I'm back there, in my lovely house on the park, everything back the way it was before. But then some nights I dream about other things. The buzz of the dehumidifier, the smell of smoke. A crack opening up underneath my feet. A body, hollowed out and rotting, underneath.

The cameras were all there by the time they found her body. Lights flashing, drones buzzing over the house, even a helicopter. It's all online, if you want to find it. I couldn't stop watching for a while. The drilling had taken several hours, I read. Then the money shot that they had all been waiting for. Four white-suited men, like astronauts, carrying the stretcher through my front door, so carefully, like something so fragile, so precious. It occurred to me that no one had ever been careful with Rachel before.

Katie is shaking now. Tears in her eyes.

"How dare he write these things? About Rachel, about the blood. How dare he haunt you with them? Oh, Helen, you ought to burn it. And for him to talk about Leo!" Her voice is cracking now, and I feel the stir of a lump in my own throat. "How can he think you'll let him see Leo, after what he did? After what you were put through?"

I try not to think too much about those early days. When I'd woken up in hospital, I'd tried to scream, but no sound had come out. I couldn't work my mouth, couldn't work my lungs. My head hurt, something pulling tight above my eye. When I'd put my hand to my head, there had been the sting of ripped flesh, raised contours, lumps of stitches. But then my hands had gone to my stomach. A hot, searing pain across my belly. And my baby was gone. And I was alone, all alone.

The nurse had come, then. Explained some things, avoided others. She explained I'd had a head injury, that the paramedics had found me unconscious. That they'd had to operate straightaway to save the baby.

He was small, much smaller than he should have been at full term, and floppy, refusing to feed. They didn't know why he'd stopped growing in the final month. Was I sure I hadn't taken any medications? Anything at all? Any benzodiazepines? I'd shaken my head. Of course not. I would never have taken pills. Never. The doctors had glanced at each other, but they hadn't asked again.

In the end, they said it might just be one of those things. They gave him oxygen, steroid injections to help his lungs to grow. But he was here, he was alive. And then later that day, they'd taken me in a wheelchair to see him. His little head, all squashed and puffy. His tiny hands. His perfect, sleeping face. He didn't know anything about what had happened. I had tried not to think about the two police officers, lurking outside the swing doors to the ward. Waiting to ask me questions. I just looked at Leo, and I felt I could hold on to that. He got me through, in the end. He got me through everything.

Katie has pulled her chair closer to me now, her hands on top of mine. "I don't know how you can be so calm."

I smile. Maybe it's lucky I'm so tired. Leo is difficult at night, always has been. He has nightmares, or at least I think that's what they are. I'll find him screaming, inconsolable, his little face contorted, even though he's not really awake. Sometimes, I have to hold him for a long time before he will go back to sleep.

"It was horrible when I first read it. But—I don't know. At least it explains some things."

"Does it? That's what I'm trying to work out."

I fold the letter back into its envelope. "What do you mean?"

"It's just . . . I know this explains *some* of it. Like why she pretended to be pregnant."

I can still hardly believe that part. The lengths she'd gone to. It came up in the trial, the device she had been wearing whenever she saw us, the website she had ordered it from. The papers had gone mad for that part of the story, of course.

"I suppose it also explains the money—why she always had so much cash," Katie goes on. "But it doesn't explain other things. Like, what about all the other stuff you told me about? The notes you found in Rory's house? What were they all about?"

I shake my head. "Oh, Katie, who knows what I thought I found? Some old scrap of paper from years ago—it could have been anything."

"I suppose," she says gently, "they could have been . . . from Lisa?"

It was Lisa, the secretary, who'd saved Rory in the end. She'd been having an affair with him for months, she admitted—and could give him an alibi for the night of the bonfire party when he'd left the house at 9 p.m., as well as most of the other gaps he'd disappeared for. Once

Daniel confessed to the whole thing—including that he'd been the one with Rory's coat—the case against Rory had fallen away.

Not that they didn't fight it. Daniel said he had acted alone. But DCI Betsky wouldn't have it. She just couldn't drop the idea that someone else was involved. According to Rory's lawyer, they dragged it on for far longer than they should have, talking endlessly about fibers on Rachel's body that they thought could have been from Rory's house, and about the phone triangulation data that placed her phone at Rory's the next day, when that text was sent.

Luckily, his lawyer had it all thrown out of court in the end. We found experts of our own; they said Daniel's and Rory's homes were too close for the cell signals to indicate with any real accuracy that Rory had had the phone at his house. But still, the police insisted. Even that detective, Carter, the one who saved Katie's life, wasn't entirely supportive. He kept asking awkward questions, making out like it couldn't have just been Daniel, that there must have been someone else involved.

Katie keeps going on at me, saying we should listen to him, and what if he's right. We have nearly fallen out over it once or twice. I don't know if Katie is still talking to him, even now. I hope she isn't. I wish she would just lay it to rest, that both of them would lay it to rest, like I have tried to.

Serena left Rory before it even came to trial. Neither she nor Rory came to see Daniel in court. Only me. Amazingly, Rory and Lisa are still together. They have moved west, somewhere near Bristol. I keep saying I'll go and see them, but it seems so far. And it is difficult, being on my own.

Serena, meanwhile, has moved abroad with her baby, Sienna. A little girl, the same age as Leo. My niece. I've never even seen a photograph. Rory doesn't like to talk about her. It must break his heart. But she has washed her hands of me, of Rory, of all of us. If I'm honest, I would have liked an explanation, about her and Daniel. I know it was years ago, but it still hurt. Then again, after everything that's happened, who could blame her for cutting ties, for moving far, far away?

"I don't know, though," Katie is musing, stirring her mug of tea.

"Could the note you found at Rory's really have been from Lisa? If Lisa was W, why would Rachel have had it? How would she have got hold of it? And why would Rory call Lisa W?"

"Oh, I don't know. Maybe they weren't even love notes. They were probably—I don't know . . . a figment of my imagination." Not to mention all the other weird stuff I thought I saw.

She looks at me, shakes her head. "Helen, I can't believe you are still letting him do this."

"What do you mean?"

"Daniel! He was always encouraging you to think you were stupid, or that you were losing it. You weren't. You lost your parents and had four miscarriages. You were very, very sad, as anyone would be. You were not *crazy*."

This is her latest theme—that I'm a victim, just like Rachel. Except Rachel is the one who was raped, robbed of justice, and who ended up dead. Not me.

"I'm just saying. If you saw those things, you saw them."

I sigh, put my hand on hers. The hand that was bandaged for months, after that day. Sometimes I struggle to believe it really all happened. To think about her, clinging to the drain hooks. To think about what might have been, if DCI Carter hadn't deduced that Katie would head to Daniel's house. If he hadn't gotten into his car, turned up there when he did. Gotten his police contacts to find him the address as he drove. Found Katie's car outside. Rung once, then again. Then smashed our door down.

"But the thing is, I really wasn't thinking straight back then. I see that now. I mean, I think I knew something was going on. But I didn't know what. So I came up with these mad theories."

"I still think there's stuff that doesn't add up. So does Mark. I know you won't hear a word against Serena. But he says there's no way that Daniel could have—"

"Oh, Katie, I know that DCI Carter means well. But please. Enough."

She sighs, folds her arms. I gaze past her, out of the window. The rain is easing, a cool sunlight reappearing behind the trees.

"Look," I say, giving her hand a squeeze. "It's all over now. Why dwell on the past?"

I step behind her and throw the doors open, let the smell of the rain pour in. I'll cut the garden back tomorrow, I think. Maybe I'll plant some flowers, water them with Leo, like Mummy and I used to do.

And then I take Daniel's letter, tear it up, and throw it into the recycling.

Serena

"CAREFUL, DARLING," I CALL to Sienna. She is striding straight into the water. Walking, at less than ten months. And utterly fearless. Just like me. Her nanny hovers next to her, in case she falls. I watch them both in the shallow turquoise water, the strands of light playing on the backs of their bare legs.

I lean back on my lounger, sip my White Russian. I should leave soon, really. Start making plans. But every time I think about it, I feel the fine pale sand between the creases of my toes, the stars overhead, the swaying palm trees. I can stay here a little longer, I think.

"Is this yours?"

I'd hardly noticed the man standing by my lounger, holding out a stuffed bear. Sienna must have dropped it on the sand.

"Thanks." He's older, but not bad. I think I've seen him before. Maybe in one of the harbor bars. There's a lot of his type around. Salt-and-pepper hair, twinkling blue eyes.

"No problem." He smiles. "Have I seen you before? In Bojangles, maybe? Or Coconut Shack?"

I make a face. "Bojangles, maybe," I reply. "*Not* Coconut Shack."

He laughs, looks away.

"Well. Maybe I'll see you there later."

"Maybe."

I watch as he walks away. When he is out of sight, I reach into my bag and pull out the thin pale blue paper. A copy, he said, word for word, of what he sent to Helen. I read it over and over, considering each part carefully. I imagine I'm Helen. How much would I believe?

What about the notes? I'd said to Daniel when we'd spoken the last time. Didn't he tell me that he'd found one of them one night, tucked into her book? Won't she wonder what they were all about? He said it didn't matter, that the notes didn't prove anything, that she wouldn't understand them. And I suppose he's right. After all, Helen has failed to understand rather a lot over the years.

I twist the cocktail stirrer in my glass until it knocks against the ice cubes. The sun disappears behind a cloud and the sand on the beach fades from brilliant white to gray. I thought I'd be gone by now. Hurricane season is coming. It's not proving as easy as I thought, though. The plan.

My tolerance is lower than I expected for these yacht-owning types, their potbellies, hairy backs. The look in their eyes, as if everything here is for sale, from the ceiling fans and the white-painted balconies to the rum cocktails and the woman drinking them.

I stare out at the sea, twisting my wedding ring between my fingers. Daniel hated my wedding ring, used to tear it off sometimes, with his teeth. That's what he meant in that stupid note in the bathroom cabinet, a silver necklace in the envelope. Wear to show me, he said. I knew what he meant. Fuck the ring. You're mine. So typical of Helen to see it, but fail to understand. She thought the charm on the end was a dog. It was a wolf. From my Wolf. And I was his Red Riding Hood.

All the mistakes were his, all the little slip-ups. I mean for God's sake—why use notes, which can be left lying around? Why give me a damn necklace? But of course, he is paying for it now.

A warm light rain starts to prickle across the surface of the water. People start closing the beach umbrellas, winding in the awnings of the cafes down the shore. Vivienne returns with Sienna, now wrapped in her rainbow-colored towel. Back at the house, as Vivienne puts Sienna in her high chair, I kiss the top of her head, then skip upstairs for a bath. As I lean back in the steaming water, I pour in a measure of the bath oil I brought from home, watch the little golden drops collect on the surface of the water. I close my eyes, breathe in the woody smell. Rosemary for memory, I read that somewhere once. The scent fills the room, transporting me back home. To Maze Hill. Our house on the park.

WHEN RORY and I moved there, it just became so easy to start it all again, Daniel and I. I think about the passage in that letter where he said he used to think about me even when he was fucking her. That can't have been for poor Helen's benefit. No, that part was just for me.

Of course, it was wrong. And of course, that was the appeal. It has always excited me, the way he craves me, the look in his eyes when I do things to him, things he never even dreamed about before me. And how I make him act in ways he never thought he would, or could. I suppose, in a sense, it's his innocence that excited me. Although it seems strange to say that. Now that he's the one behind bars.

Daniel felt guilty, made up his mind a thousand times to stop. But he's so weak. I could do anything, and he'd still keep coming back. It's tiresome, anyway, all that guilt. He should have married someone like Rory—someone who fucks around, too. It wasn't just Lisa. I'm sure he would have fucked Rachel, too, given half a chance. But in fairness to her, Rachel had bigger fish to fry. Women usually do.

It was Richard's idea all along to get Daniel into Haverstock. The old man had always known Rory didn't have the talent, or the application. Unfortunately, his mad wife drove him into a highway median at ninety miles an hour before he had a chance to properly sort out the succession planning. But once he was gone, I managed to convince Rory that Daniel being there would work to his advantage, that it would save him doing the grunt work of running the firm.

Rory had the family name, but the talent had skipped his generation. He always needed other people to prop him up, people whose ideas he could steal, whose work he could take credit for. That's where Daniel came in. I don't think he even cared that Rory was using him. He just wanted me close. He would have done whatever I said.

When I finish my soak and wrap myself in a towel, the house is silent. Sienna must be asleep. I pad downstairs to her nursery. Vivienne has left the window ajar, the sound of waves crashing outside. There is a smell of fresh linen, of island air. I pull the window open wider until the roar of the water fills my ears. I close my eyes, try to fill my senses with the sound, with the wildness of outside. Daniel liked fucking me in the studio, the heater glowing orange in the darkness, the red light from the darkroom. But I always preferred to be outside, in the wild, up against the earth, the damp walls. I never feel the cold. He loved my body, the wet taste of me, the smell of the woods in my hair. We thought we were smarter than other people, never using phones and email—too easy to trace. But then he started leaving those notes for me, in places he thought no one would look. Of course, he wasn't counting on Helen.

I pull the window closed, check Sienna's crib. Vivienne has changed the bedding, retied the edges of the bumpers into exactly even bows, dressed Sienna in a freshly laundered sleeper. I watch my daughter, fast asleep, flat on her back, arms out at her sides. She always sleeps in this star shape, as if she has been struck by lightning. I gently blow over her beautiful face, her nose, her cheeks, her perfect forehead. She stirs, her eyelashes flickering a little, her breathing whistling. I kiss her head, then leave her to sleep, closing the door behind me.

As it went on, I started to tire of Rory, for the first time. I knew that Daniel would never mess around, like Rory was doing with that bloody secretary. I knew Daniel would do anything for me. There is power in that. And when I found out I had his baby growing inside me, I felt more certain than ever. That we should leave them. Rory and Helen. Start again, with our child.

Daniel wanted to, but there were complications. We needed money, of course. He wasn't blind. He knew who I was. He knew it mattered to me, the life Rory and I had: he knew he had to give me those things. And he couldn't. Not without Helen. All his money was tied to her, to the house. He couldn't get at it. Not unless he got Helen to remortgage. She'd never agree to it. But there were ways around that.

It hadn't been hard to sort out the passport. You just had to find the right places. Places where you could meet people, get things done. I found a guy who knew a guy. We met him in the tunnel. Three months later it was done. Helen's details, my face.

There had to be some kind of building work, to give us some sort of cover. Daniel was able to get most of it started on a promise. People trusted the Haverstock name, had never known them not to come through. We'd never need to actually pay for it—that was the plan. Of course the lender we found was dodgy—who spends £3.6 million on renovation work? But they got their fee, and it seemed to be going through. As soon as the cash landed, we'd get it overseas, plus anything more we could get from Haverstock. Rory was too busy with Lisa to look at the accounts and see that his firm's cash was draining away, disappearing into thin Cayman air.

It was starting to come together. We just needed a bit more time. I hadn't even really worried when Helen announced she was pregnant again, not at first. They'd been through it all so many times. I knew she would lose the baby, just like she had lost all the others. They were doomed, the two of them.

Except that it was different this time. She kept getting bigger and bigger. I thought you said she couldn't, I kept saying to Daniel. It got so I couldn't bear it, that fat bump of hers, under my kitchen table, swinging around in my hammock. It was like she was taunting me with it.

There were moments when I was worried. Daniel told me he was all right, that he could do it, he could still leave her. But I saw him wavering once or twice. Helen told me about the scan, when the little arm flickered blue and black on the screen. How he'd sobbed when the nurse had told him the baby was waving at him. It had felt like a message, he admitted eventually. Like an arm reaching out to him, telling him not to leave. He was starting to love this baby, his son. I was losing control.

Then everything else started going wrong, too. The money for the building work got out of hand. Daniel was having to take more and more from the getaway fund. For fuck's sake, I kept telling him, we're not supposed to be actually doing this remodeling. Can't you just say it's stalled? But Helen was asking questions about why nothing ever seemed to progress. And I was impatient, too. I wanted to know when we'd have the three million, when we'd finally be able to leave. Take it out of the company if you need to, I'd said. Rory won't even notice. Even when he found out all the firm's cash had moved to the Cayman Islands, Daniel told him it was all just tax planning, and he seemed to accept it. But there was only so long you could do stuff like that before it was discovered. I knew the clock was ticking.

Things just went from bad to worse that night in the club, when Rachel came on the scene. We didn't know her name then. We just knew it was the girl from the boathouse floor. Daniel and I were only there because Rory had dragged us there to charm some sleazy client. It was the worst luck in the world.

All the blood had drained from Daniel's face. He looked terrified. I knew what I needed to do. I'm sorry, I said sweetly. You've got the wrong person. I've got no idea what you're talking about. Excuse me. But Daniel fucked it up. He engaged. And when you engage with someone like that, nine times out of ten, you'll lose.

I walk back to my bedroom, sit at my dressing table, start on my hair. I can hear Vivienne loading the washing machine, tidying up the bathroom. I take out my dark eyeshadow, my red lipstick. As I pull it across my bottom lip, I am startled by my reflection. By the thought of another pair of red lips and charcoal eyelids, with nothing behind them. I rub the lipstick off.

Daniel told me he'd taken care of it. But he hadn't, of course. Not even close. It was only when she came to my studio that day that I found out he'd lied to me, that she hadn't gone away. So I tried to talk to her. But she wouldn't listen. She wouldn't even tell me her name. She said I didn't need to know. You just need to know what I know. About you.

That was when I realized how serious it was. She'd been hanging around outside our houses. Mine and Daniel's. She'd been tracking all of our social media. That's how she found out I was booked into Helen's prenatal classes: Helen had tagged me in a post about it. And she'd followed us, Daniel and me, one night, in Greenwich Park. The pictures are a bit dark, she said. But let me play you a recording. Halfway through, I told her to switch it off. She knew everything.

All right, I said. How much do you want? But she just laughed. You're not listening, she said. Either of you. I don't care about the money, not really. Though it will come in useful. I want justice. I want you to tell the truth.

She sat down in my chair, her hand on that ridiculous bump of hers.

I get it now, she said. Why you never said anything. You didn't want people knowing you were fucking. Be a bit worse if it came out now, wouldn't it? That and the fact you'd been at it behind her back. I bet that baby's his, too, isn't it? I still wasn't that worried. But then she pulled the documents from her bag.

Even then, I had no idea that she and Rachel, this girl from the pre-natal class who had befriended Helen, were the same person. That she had been turning up at Helen's house, pretending to want to have lunch, or a chat, when in fact she was making excuses to snoop on what we were up to. She'd taken Daniel's laptop, worked out his pass-word by asking Helen his favorite football team. Men—they are so fucking stupid. And of course, once she had that, she'd found every-thing. She'd laid it all out for me, there and then, on my studio table. The mortgage. The money transfers. The tickets, the bank account de-tails. She knew everything. She knew where we were going. She knew the whole plan.

I told Daniel all this. He lost it then. Lost control. Grabbing her around the neck that time, in the tunnel, was a particularly stupid touch. I had to hand it to her, I didn't expect her to call his bluff like that. Turn-ing up at his house the same day he did it. Knowing that Helen would take her in.

Anyway, that was it. It was obvious to me then. She wasn't going to stop. That was when I knew we had to do two things. We had to get rid of her. And we had to make it look like someone else had done it.

The second part was easy enough. Daniel always took Rachel's cash out in Rory's name anyway, used Rory's security pass to get on and off the site where he would hand it over to her. Just a basic safety precau-tion, to distance us from questions about it.

I know all Rory's passwords—he's had the same ones since univer-sity, never changes them. I gave them to Daniel and let him get on with it. When we realized we needed a fall guy, Rory was the only real choice.

It already looked like he'd been taking out vast sums of cash from the company account and making secret trips to deserted sites to bring her the money. Now we just needed to give him a motive. And if we could make it look like Rachel had been blackmailing him over his affair that would be simple enough.

Actually, it was quite fun, waiting in the shadows until he and Lisa emerged from their seedy little hotel and snapping them in the parking lot. I sent the emails, too, of course, from an email account in Rachel's name. And I knew Rachel wouldn't be able to resist wearing that slutty red designer dress I left in her room. That was all she needed to do to scare the life out of Rory. Convince him she was the one behind the photos, the emails, the threats that she would tell me the truth about Lisa. I only wished I could have seen his face a bit better when he opened the envelope.

I have to admit, that was a masterstroke of mine. Sending them in the envelope Rachel had left on my desk at the studio. A ready-made envelope, with her fingerprints all over it. I'd handled it carefully, using a pair of plastic gloves from the darkroom. Meanwhile, I made sure my electronic traces showed up plenty of evidence that I, the wronged, innocent wife, suspected Rory was having an affair—moronic Google searches, browsing for private detectives and tracker devices.

The last email was the final piece, the demand that he hand over a load of cash at the bonfire party. Of course, he'd gone and gotten the cash. Got it ready for her. Taken it to the party, after telling me some stupid lie about why he had his gym bag with him. That would have been a laugh, seeing her face, when he presented her with the fifty grand—fifty grand she'd never asked for. But of course, she never got that far.

I decide on the long black dress with the deep neckline. I twist off my wedding and engagement rings, toss them into a silver dish on my dressing table. I leave my neck bare, and select the earrings Rory bought me for our first anniversary. "It's supposed to be paper," he'd murmured into my ear, "but I thought you'd prefer diamonds."

When Rory was arrested, I thought it would all be all right, that the plan had worked. There had been moments when I'd wondered. They had been so slow to unravel it all—Daniel had to travel to a telephone booth out of town, give them an anonymous tip-off, a bit of a helping hand. But once they searched the office, it was all there for them. The pictures, the withdrawals, the emails on his computer. And even if they weren't convinced by that, I knew that after they'd spoken to Rory, they'd know he was hiding something. I knew they'd think he was lying, I knew they'd think he was guilty. Because of course, that was the real beauty of it. He *was* lying. He *was* guilty.

Admittedly, not of the murder itself. I couldn't leave that to Daniel. He'd have never had the stomach for it. I told him to work out the concrete, keep Rory and Helen out of the way, and let me get on with it.

In the end, that part was easy enough. After Rachel had finished talking to Charlie, he went into the garden to smoke and mope after Katie, and I saw my chance. I told her we'd sorted things out for her, that we were going to go to the police, tell the truth about what happened to her. I said I just needed a quick chat first, suggested we go to the cellar, where there would be no one around. I wasn't sure she'd go for it. I made sure the coast was clear, in case I needed to shove her in. But she agreed, trotted happily down the steps, good as a little lamb. It was only when I shut the door that she looked like she'd realized, her red lips parting as she figured it out. But by then my hand was around her mouth, and the brick in my other hand. The force of the blow had slammed her against the rafter, her head cracking like a melon. And then she was at the bottom of the stairs, the angle of her neck all wrong. Her eyes wide open, as if she couldn't believe she was dead. And a bright pool of crimson, spreading out behind her, like a red riding cape.

Just as we planned, Daniel brought Rory down a few minutes later, telling him he wanted to show him how the work was coming on. The idea was that Daniel would pretend to be shocked and threaten to turn me in, and Rory would stop him to protect me. I don't think much pretending was necessary when he saw her.

I started gabbling about how there had been an accident, that she had attacked me, that I hadn't meant to push her back so hard, that she'd fallen. Daniel's big moment then. I had confidence he'd be convincing, that Rory would think he really planned to go to the police. I knew from experience Daniel had a good line in pretending to want to do the right thing. All that nonsense back in Cambridge, saying he wanted to mess everything up, just because some silly girl we didn't know had gate-crashed a party, drunk her body weight in vodka, and then changed her mind about having sex.

It was a gamble, but it paid off. As soon as Daniel started threatening me with the police, and I started shaking and crying and all that non-sense, I knew Rory would want to protect me, that he would think of the idea himself. The cement was already doing its bit, suggesting itself as the perfect solution. Parts of it were starting to subsume her—her arms were being pulled down into it.

"All right, Daniel," he said. "Let's just calm down, shall we? Let's just think about this." And of course, we both knew what Rory was thinking, the fifty grand heavy in his gym bag. He didn't want a police inquiry into what had happened to Rachel any more than we did. This solved his problem, too. Just a few more nudges into that deep, gray pool, and his blackmailer would be gone. Out of his life, out of all our lives, forever. After all, she wasn't coming back. There was no coming back from that.

So while the boys took care of the body, I took care of Helen. She'd told me about the drugs she used to be on for depression as a teenager, how she'd refused to take them anymore after they started giving her blackouts. In hindsight, it had been stupid to ask Charlie about them. Some drug dealer he turned out to be. He'd flatly refused—and that left me exposed. The most annoying thing was that when I looked in Helen's bathroom cabinet at her party that night, there were benzos every-where anyway—they must have been left over from her Sylvia Plath days. It made me laugh as I tipped the pills into my clutch bag—the idea that for once it was me looking through *her* cupboards. Katie was there when I came out of the bathroom. But she was far too drunk to notice anything.

I probably went a little bit overboard on the dose. A bit in her water, a bit in a soft drink. A lot in that last cup of tea. It worked perfectly. Her whole evening was wiped out. Everyone else at the party was smashed. Between the treatment I gave Helen and the bit I'd slipped into that sad-looking saucepan of mulled wine that only Katie was drinking from, I knew reliable witnesses would be pretty scarce.

The next day, Daniel had jogged over to our side of the park. I'd seen him at the window, walked down to the park gates. Helen was getting agitated, he said. So we'd sent the message from that phone in its hideous plastic case. It seemed to work. Why wouldn't Rachel go back to her mum's? Helen thought it was over. We thought it was over. The trip I booked was just a precaution, so I could keep myself out of the country if the police started asking questions. But Daniel seemed sure it was safe, that everything was leading in Rory's direction, as planned. That no one was looking for me. We decided it would be safe enough for me to come back for the birth. We could make our escape after that.

As soon as Helen found that mark, though, the game was up. I told Daniel to ignore her message—to meet me at the studio, bring the passports, my doctor's note lying about the due dates, whatever cash he could lay his hands on. We'd go abroad, get what we could out of the company, and take it from there. But instead, he let himself get drawn into a confrontation, messed everything up. Why couldn't he just have left her there, told her he was on his way to get help? I mean, what was she really going to do, in full-on labor? That's his problem, Daniel. No imagination.

Next thing, Katie appears, starts getting involved, too. What possessed him to take her up to the roof I'll never know. But of course, there was no getting out of that one, not for him. Not after her ridiculous detective turned up to save the day. It would have been crazy for my name to be drawn into it. Daniel didn't take much convincing about keeping me out of it. Love is a powerful thing. Plus the promise of all this—this beach, this life, all this money, when he's out.

We decided on our story, and we've stuck to it. Rory, too. By that point, he was happy to say anything if it meant he wasn't going to prison. He had worked out by then, of course, that he'd been played, in more ways than one. And of course he was angry. But what choice did he have?

The divorce went through quickly. Unsurprisingly, the terms were more than generous to me.

Before I leave, I pick up Daniel's letter to Helen again. So what was this, in the end, I wonder. An attempt to shore up his story, make himself feel better, make Helen feel better about him? I'm not sure. I think there's a part of him that believes the last part, that he loves his son. I hope she does let him see her son one day. He won't be seeing his daughter.

I'll be long gone by the time he realizes the truth. As long as he believes I'm waiting, he'll stay quiet. But it's not that much, what we got in the end. The fraud squad stopped the remortgage—that hopeless Brian called them in at the last second. Helen held on to the house.

So now it's just what we siphoned out of the company—not even a million, in addition to my divorce settlement from Rory, and the bits of cash I squirreled away from my own job in those last few months. Not enough, Daniel, not enough. That sort of money won't last forever. Sienna and I have got bigger plans.

I hover on the landing, pulling on one stiletto, then the other. In the kitchen, Vivienne is microwaving her dinner, preparing for a night in with *The Bachelorette*.

"Have a lovely evening, Miss Serena." She smiles, wiping her hands on the tablecloth. I smile back.

"You are an angel," I say. "Help yourself to everything. And don't wait up for me."

The tropical evening air is as warm as a kiss. I head down to the Bojangles, on the beachfront. A line of palm trees, a sweeping drive. The fans circle overhead, the scented candles on the tables glint. The polished bar is the color of a shell.

I approach the bar, lean against it. I catch sight of myself in the mirror. I've done a good job. I glance around. I know what I'm looking for. It is the details that give it away. The type of boat shoes, the logo on the car key. Mostly they are unbearable. But I only need one.

And then I spot him, the pale gray hair, cut short, the strong line of his shoulders. It's the man from the beach. As he turns around, I see he's obviously been playing golf. A green-and-purple-patterned sweater. I'll have to sort the clothes out. But still.

"Hello, you."

"Hello again." He smiles. He opens his wallet. Slides out a police badge.

"It's Serena, isn't it?"

Acknowledgments

I OWE A HUGE debt of gratitude to the novelist Sarah May, my tutor at the Faber Academy, for giving me permission to call myself a writer and helping me grow *Greenwich Park* from a half-formed idea into a real-life book. To my talented Faber peers—especially Gill, Martin, Susie, Suzy, Nicky, and Melissa: thank you for your unrelenting support and encouragement, and for reading more drafts of this book than I can bear to think about!

Thank you so much to my brilliant editor, Alison Hennessey, and the extraordinarily talented team at Raven. I could not have imagined a more perfect home for *Greenwich Park*; thank you so much for your commitment to it and for your boundless energy and enthusiasm. I feel so privileged to be working with you all. Thanks, too, to the wonderful Jackie Cantor and Nita Pronovost at Gallery, for having such an exciting vision for *Greenwich Park*.

I am so grateful to my brilliant agent, Madeleine Milburn—truly the agent of dreams—for believing in *Greenwich Park* and being its most tireless champion, and to everyone at the Madeleine Milburn Literary, TV & Film Agency for all their help, guidance, and patience.

I'm extremely grateful to Colin Sutton for his expert advice on police procedure; any remaining errors are undoubtedly my own.

Those who remember that first prenatal class in the Drapers Arms will know how grateful I was (in the end) for the experience. Thanks Ali, Bonnie, and Beth for getting me through it, and for navigating the strange twilight world of new motherhood with me.

Thank you, Mum and Dad, who have been encouraging me to write my stories for as long as I can remember. Thank you to my sister, Jo, for always being my greatest supporter, as I am yours. Extra thanks to Mum, Jo, Lara, Kirsty, Sue, and Brendan, and anyone else who was roped into looking after my children for me while I escaped to libraries and cafes to write.

A special thanks must go to Kate and Hannah, for first encouraging me in my mad scheme to write a book during what I'll always think of as "our" maternity leave. Thank you both—and Jen, Ellie, Portia, Emma, Olivia, and Lizzy—for being the kind of friends Helen could only dream of.

To my daughters, Emma and Maddie. Thank you both for sleeping (occasionally).

And my final thanks go to Pete, without whose unfailing love and support this book would never have been written, and to whom it is dedicated.

About the Author

KATHERINE FAULKNER, an award-winning journalist, studied history at the University of Cambridge, then completed a postgraduate diploma in newspaper journalism. She has worked as an investigative reporter and an editor and was formerly the joint head of news at the London-based *Times*. She lives in London, where she grew up, with her husband and two daughters. *Greenwich Park* is her first novel.